Katie Flynn

writing as
JUDITH SAXTON

Sophie

arrow books

Published by Arrow Books, 2014

2 4 6 8 10 9 7 5 3 1

First published in Great Britain in 1985 by Sphere Books Ltd

Arrow Books
The Random House Group Limited
20 Vauxhall Bridge Road, London, SW1V 2SA

A Penguin Random House Company

www.randomhousebooks.co.uk

Addresses for companies within The Random House Group Limited can
be found at: www.randomhouse.co.uk/offices.htm

The Random House Group Limited Reg. No. 954009

A CIP catalogue record for this book
is available from the British Library

ISBN 9780099598732

Printed and bound in Great Britain by Clays Ltd, St Ives plc

For Toby Roxburgh, whose original
idea grew into this book.

Acknowledgements

My thanks to Gwyn Erfwl of Harlech Television in Mold, who not only read the manuscript for me in order to point out any errors regarding studio and location procedure, but who also came up with alternative suggestions (which I used) when my own ideas had proved impracticable. Equally helpful was Mr Erfwl's assistant, Lesley Drury, who checked on the role of the production assistants when making television films.

Trevor and Olwen Williams of Penrhyn Bay Farm, on the island of Anglesey, will doubtless recognise their delightful caravan site; along with a good few other people. I know of no better place to have a holiday, or for that matter, to write a book, since a good bit of this one was written on the island.

I am also, as always, grateful to the staff of the Wrexham Branch Library, particularly Marina Thomas, who must surely get asked some of the oddest questions ever when I'm researching, but who always manages to find the right answers.

Chapter One

'Oh, Sophie, not one? Not even home economics? It isn't just cooking, I know that, there's a lot of . . . but I had hoped . . . you seemed to be working so hard!' Devina Markham, trailing draperies of Indian muslin, got up from the kitchen table and drifted over to where her daughter stood, at bay, by the back door. 'I'm not *reproaching* you, darling, because I'm sure you did your best, but what on earth are we to do now?'

Sophie had pressed herself against the door jamb until she could feel it almost touching her backbone despite the intervening layers of fat. She had gone down to school quite early that morning to find out about the A levels, but had not felt the slightest urge to rush home and tell everyone. Not with three ungraded results. She had hung about until tea-time and then hunger and habit had brought her back to Glydon Grove. Now she hung her head and wished she could conjure up a few tears, but the delicious smell of Devina's cooking brought only saliva to the mouth and not salt water to the eye. Besides, she had known all along that she would fail, so had her teachers and her sisters and so, presumably, had her mother. It was foolish of Devina to pretend that her third daughter might actually have done something right for once!

'It doesn't matter, Mum, we'll work something out,' she muttered now. Her mother tried to envelope her in her arms, which was like a tiny, vivid spider trying to get a bumble bee into its embrace. Sophie lurched to one side, Devina hugged space, and then the two of them, mutually embarrassed by the size of the other, turned with one accord and stared across at the oven. Sophie sniffed.

'Is that apple cake in there? It smells delicious.'

Devina gave a little cry and hurried across the kitchen, tugging the oven door wide open.

'Thank goodness, it's not overcooked. Yes, it's apple cake. Would you like a piece?'

1

There was the slightest of slight hesitations before the offer; Sophie had the grace to feel a trifle ashamed. Only yesterday she had started a new diet and when she was dieting she was not above snarling that her weight problem was entirely due to her mother's cooking. That meant, of course, that she had to refuse food which she wanted and would later take and would, later still, deny touching. A vicious circle, another skirmish in the mean, sniping, mother-daughter war which the two of them so frequently fought. Now, looking down into her mother's kohl-rimmed eyes, at the slight tremble of her over-painted lips, Sophie tried not to remember that this was the woman who had been at the root of her weight problem, not by her cooking or her own example, but by marriage to a man whose own mother, Sophie's grandma, had died at fifty weighing twenty-five stone, whose sister Mabel was five foot tall and five foot wide, and who himself suffered embarrassing problems with his uniform, for fat postmen are few. But the apple cake smelt delicious, and besides, if she refused some now, her mother would put it down to surliness, and the result would be additional coldness and acidity over the wretched examinations.

'Just a small piece, please, Mum.'

Devina turned the apple cake onto the wire tray she had placed in readiness. It came out cleanly, as perfect as all her cooking, the shiny, sugar encrusted top settling onto the wire grid with a crisp little crunch and a faint sigh of steam. Sophie swallowed. The bag of chips and the Mars Bar seemed a life-time ago; she could have eaten the whole cake without pausing for breath.

The knife sank in, and Sophie watched as two pieces were cut, one noticeably larger than the other. Devina picked up the tray and took it over to the open window, where the cool, rain-drizzled August air would help to firm the cake. Casually, Sophie leaned over and took one of the slices. It was warm and moist in her hand. Comforting. Devina was making a pot of tea, talking about someone she had met in town that day. Sophie bit. The sweetness of the cake blended exquisitely with the sharpness of cooking apples. Devina, returning to the table with two cups of tea, took the remaining slice and tasted it. She made no comment on its size, probably never even realised that Sophie, quite without meaning to, had taken the larger piece.

2

They were eating in companionable silence when the back door opened. Sophie immediately tried to hide her slice of cake, then picked up her cup, relaxing against the wooden chair back once more. It was only her father. He would have finished work, picking up parcels from the small post offices and emptying letter boxes, would have left his little red van at the depot and walked home slowly, because his feet hurt him. Now, flushed and rain-spotted, he came across the kitchen, giving his wife a perfunctory peck on the brow and testing the teapot with one hand.

'One for me in there? Well, you two celebrating, are you?'

Sophie felt her face grow hot. Trust Dad! He must have known that she would fail, no one who had hated school as much as she had could possibly have done well there – she had told him that once, and he had sympathised, said it didn't matter, that she would shine in other spheres. Knowing that, why must he pretend as well? She mumbled her reply through the last of her cake.

'Didn't get any of 'em.'

Benjamin Markham turned from pouring his tea. He looked surprised, a little red around the gills.

'Of course, you took 'em as well, course you did. I was thinking of Lavinia, actually – got all three, she said. I rang the corner shop earlier and . . .' His wife's glare finally penetrated. He let his voice trail away and brought his mug of tea over to the table. His small eyes shifted uneasily from one face to the other as he hooked out a chair and sat on it sideways, sipping the tea and grimacing at the heat of it.

'Oh well, never mind, gal, I don't suppose you expected . . .' Devina's voice overrode his and he subsided, gulping his tea too quickly, perspiration beading his brow and upper lip.

'You're early, Ben! I was planning quiche and a salad tonight, with a hot pudding to follow, but it's a dreadful, rainy day; I daresay I could manage something more substantial if you'd prefer it.'

'Me? No, quiche and salad will be fine. Unless you feel that Lavvy's results call for a bit of a celeb . . .' Devina kicked his ankle and he scowled at her, baffled. 'Damn it, Devina, I'm bloody pleased the girl's done well, and Soph didn't expect to pass, she said so enough times. I'm damned if I see why we've all got to pretend!'

3

Sophie got up, pushing her chair back with a horribly loud squeal on the polished tiles. She headed for the door. Over her shoulder, casually, she made them a present of guiltlessness.

'Of course I knew I'd fail; don't worry about it, either of you. Lavvy always was the clever one, I've never envied her *that*.' Only her slender figure, her pretty face, her ease with the opposite sex, that was all she envied Lavinia. She left the kitchen, shutting the door firmly behind her. She was still wearing her light jacket and in its pocket a chocolate wrapper and two crisp packets rubbed shoulders noisily. She took them out and stuffed them behind the hallstand, then began to mount the stairs. Her legs ached; she had walked a lot today, because it was easier to walk than to come home. Something inside her ached too, though she could not have said what it was. Her heart? Or was it merely her tummy, objecting to the doughy, indigestible apple cake?

At the top of the stairs she paused, wondering whether it was safe to go into her bedroom, or whether she would find Poppy up there, playing with friends. At twelve, Poppy led an active and varied social life amongst a group stigmatised by her elder sisters as nasty brats. But, even as she hesitated, Sophie heard Poppy's voice downstairs, raised in shrill altercation. So that was all right, then. She went into her bedroom and locked the door, then flung herself heavily onto the bed. She was still wearing her jacket, but didn't bother to remove it; instead, she made herself comfortable, lying on her back and contemplating the cracked and stained ceiling above her. For the first time, it struck her that she had left the school system for good, finally and at last. She had taken three years to fail those A levels; at nineteen, no one would expect or even allow her to remain at school.

Was this freedom? She experimented with the thought of an adult Sophia Markham, rolled it round her tongue so to speak, tried to imagine herself in adult situations. It proved difficult, not to say impossible. The trouble was, she had no point of reference, it was not as if she had ever had a Saturday job or gone baby-sitting or any of the other things that teenagers seemed to take for granted. She had tried, half-heartedly, to get a job in Tesco, but the manager had lied and told her that the position was filled the moment he saw her standing beside one of the cash points, dwarfing it with her bulk. His eyes had flickered from the till, with the swivel chair impossibly close, to the narrow doorway, and he had lied. She knew he had lied because two days later a girl in her class had applied for the same job, and got it.

She hated the place now, with its stupid, embarrassing turnstiles which were so difficult to squeeze through on the way in, and its narrow cash points, almost worse, which you had to pass to go out. She had vowed never to go in there again and she never had – well, only to buy chocolate and crisps, anyway. When she was rich, she would go to the independent shops, like Drapers, and give huge orders and make Tesco sorry. That would teach them!

Not that she was wild about Drapers, come to think of it. The girls who worked there were right little bitches, nudging each other and giggling if she bought chocolate – who were they to assume that the sweets were for herself, they might have been for some poor, elderly person who could not get out to do her own shopping. Sophie's eyes almost filled with tears at the thought of those girls being so wrong, so needlessly cruel. But of course, she did not shop for an old age pensioner, though she did pop in from time to time with a list of her mother's cooking requirements. It annoyed Devina that her daughter would no longer shop at Tesco, but Sophie did not intend to tell her why. Let her think what she would!

Remembering her mother's shopping made her recall that she had another grudge against Drapers. The Christmas raisins had been bought there. That had been a nasty business, and who had got the blame for it? Sophie, of course, just because she was fat, just because when her mother had stormed back to the shop complaining that she had been given short weight the girl behind the counter, the one with eyes like needles and a beehive hairstyle, had said she had watched the small Sophie going up the road, eating raisins through a hole she had made in the bottom of the packet.

Horrible, trouble-making woman! A confused memory of tears, protestations, her mother's shame, jostled for top place in Sophie's mind. It was not fair, she had only been *ten*, a child of ten could scarcely be blamed if there was a hole in the wretched packet through which the raisins had fallen. Indeed, it was the shop's fault, bad packaging, every bit as blameworthy as short weight.

A thundering on the stairs, as Poppy and some friend rushed up them, caused Sophie to tense, then she relaxed again as the footsteps thundered straight past. Recently, because Dad had suggested it, Poppy had been moved from Sophie's room to Lavinia's, so that Sophie could get some peace and quiet. Until then, it had been Lavinia who needed peace and quiet to study in. Sophie had been studying too, of course, but it was fair enough, she had been allowed a bedroom to herself for the first year at sixth-form coll. And if she was honest, she had not done much studying in her room, anyway. So she had not minded all that much when Poppy had been moved in – but it was rather nice, now, to have the room to herself again.

Through the thin wall, Poppy's shrill tones came to her sister's ears.

'So I said right, Alison, but now you know I know, and I'm surprised you can still look me in the eye, and she said it wasn't knowing that mattered, it was what you know, and so I said, look, I've already broken friends with Paula because of it, and if you really were my friend, the way you say you are, you'd have broken friends with her too, so she said . . .'

The interminable wrangling of twelve-year-olds! Sophie felt all the weight of her nineteen years. Such childish squabbling, yet it seemed so important to Poppy that she had to relate every single word which had passed between her and the unfortunate Alison.

Sophie slid open the door of her small bedside cabinet. Had she eaten the last of the extra-strong peppermints? She only bought them because she didn't much like the things, so they lasted longer. Her groping fingers found two more mints, a little dusty from their protracted stay in the cupboard, but perfectly edible.

She popped the first one into her mouth, then reached for her book. She opened it, and was immediately lost in the words she read. *His hand moved from her shoulder to the front of her shirt, hesitated, then the warmth of it was on her trembling breast*, she read. Good, she must be getting near the sexy bit which this particular author always inserted about halfway through her books. She just hoped that the peppermints would last out, she could not enjoy the sexy bits as they should be enjoyed if her mouth was empty. Sucking as slowly as she could, Sophie read on.

Perhaps because it had been such a miserable August, September was specially fine and dry. Lavinia was to start at the local teacher training college in October, but Sophie, who was doing a secretarial course at the tech, was back in class already, resenting the loss of freedom and the dullness of her lessons. Now, she was lying on her bed, pretending to study shorthand outlines but really reading a romance, though the shorthand book was laid out on the bed, ready for her attention should it ever be removed from the page before her.

'Sophie?'

'Lavinia's head, with its short, curly fair hair which never looked untidy, appeared round the edge of the door. She smiled at her sister, but perfunctorily. She wanted something, Sophie could tell. Lavinia always used that particular smile when she intended to ask a favour or wanted to borrow something. Not that she borrowed much from Sophie, due to the size difference. Sophie had shoved her romance out of sight the moment her sister spoke, but now she lifted her eyes from her absent-minded perusal of the shorthand outlines and raised her brows.

'What?'

'I'm writing out the invitations for my eighteenth. I've asked all the usual crowd, I just wondered if there was anyone special you'd like to invite.'

'What, from the tech?' Sophie thought of her class, which seemed to consist largely of sixteen-year-old morons. Pretty, slim morons, what was worse. 'No fear. Unless . . .'

'Unless what? Surely there are some nice boys at the tech?'

Sophie snorted and pretended to return to studying her shorthand. She had thought that being at the tech would at least give her imagination a chance, allow her to pretend a bit about boys, tell Lavinia mysteriously that there was a certain someone . . . But that was denied her because Devina taught weaving there two mornings a week, and home economics three afternoons. If Sophie made mysterious remarks, Devina would get all excited and start to check up, and there was nothing worse than being made out a liar.

7

'Come on, old darling, are there or aren't there?' Lavinia could be nice when she wanted to be. Now, she came across the room and sat on the end of the bed, peering at Sophie's book. 'Gracious, how you can understand all those squiggles is beyond me. Look, I saw you with a fellow the other morning, walking down from the bus stop. Who was he?'

With a good deal of effort, Sophie managed to remember his name. He had slowed down as he drew level with her and asked her whose class she was in; she could not remember his exact words. He had walked about six yards with her and then he had seen a friend in front and hurried off. He was a striking chap though, she knew that much, not at all the sort of boy to notice someone like her.

'Oh, you mean Peter Brewer. He's nice, isn't he?'

'Yes, if you mean handsome. Does he like you?'

'Oh, really, Lavvy, how on earth should I know? He isn't in my class, lads don't do shorthand and typing. What makes you ask, anyway?'

'My dear woman, because he had no *need* to walk to school with you if he didn't like you. Just ask him if he'd like to come to a party; you'd be surprised, he'll probably jump at it.'

'We-ell . . . I suppose there's no harm in asking.'

It had occurred to her that if she brought a boy to Lavvy's eighteenth, it would be an absolute triumph. She had stayed down at school and had been forced to mingle with Lavvy's class in order to take her A levels, and it had been worse, some-how, more humiliating, to be left out and ignored by girls and boys a year younger than she, than it had been to be left out and ignored by her contemporaries. And now, as if to show her that she had not yet plumbed the depths, she found herself in a class of children younger still. She was so bad at it all, too, dreaming in the shorthand classes and forgetting to do her learning home-work, typing slower than anyone else in the class and making more errors because the wretched chair was at the wrong dis-tance from the typewriter when her bulk was in it and her arms, which were probably the normal length but which could not compete with the jut of her stomach, never quite allowed her to hit the keys in comfort.

'It's sensible to ask. If you don't ask you never get.' Lavinia's voice was smug and for a second Sophie was puzzled, then

8

dismissed it as irrelevant. It had been very kind of Lavvy to suggest that she brought a friend, and it really would do no harm to ask Peter Brewer. No one need know if she was turned down flat, and if they found out, she could always say loftily that it had been her sister's invitation, really.

'Okay, Lavvy, I'll ask him first thing on Monday morning.' Sophie waited for her sister to leave the room, then got ponderously off the bed and went over to her dressing-table. She peered at her reflection in the mirror. Was it possible that Peter whatsisname really *did* like her? Could it be true, as Lavinia had implied, that he had only spoken to her because he wanted to get to know her better? Lavvy seemed to think it was so, and she was so much more experienced than Sophie that she might well be right. At eighteen, Lavvy had had a score of boyfriends; not like Sophie, nineteen and never been . . .

Sophie picked up her book again but, for once, the words on the page could not hold her attention. Peter Brewer. A nice name! Suppose, just suppose . . .

To think is to act, Sophie said firmly to herself on Monday morning, as she walked up the gravel drive towards the tech buildings. To think is to act. Only it was not so easy – she could scarcely walk up to a total stranger, or an almost total stranger, and ask him to her sister's eighteenth birthday party! It would look more than odd, it would look desperate, as though she had no friends in the world, and that was the last thing she wanted him to think. It was only the recollection that she had never had a boyfriend, that unless she asked him she would walk into the party as she usually did, alone, that gave her the courage even to consider it.

She was so immersed in her thoughts that she did not hear his footsteps crunching on the gravel beside her, until his voice said in her ear, 'Good morning, Sophia!' and then she was so startled that she jumped visibly before turning towards him. Her heart was thumping so loudly that she was sure he could hear it, and she knew she was unbecomingly flushed. Beet rather than rose, she thought despairingly. But she could not just stare at him, scarlet and tongue-tied.

'Oh! H-Hello!'

'Do you come here often?'

Peter Brewer was walking beside her. He had come up to her without her having to say a word. And he was joking with her as naturally as though he had known her for years. Sophie tried to pull herself together and answer naturally, the way Lavvy would have done had she been present.

'Yes, much too often. And you?'

'Only in the mating season!' He laughed, and she realised she should have said that, but it didn't matter. He was still walking beside her, smiling down at her, assured, handsome, the sort of boy who absolutely never took the slightest notice of her!

'Oh . . . Isn't it a n-nice day?'

'It 'ud be better if I didn't have physics first period. You're on a course here, but I don't know what you do.'

'Shorthand and t . . . I mean, I'm doing a secretarial course.'

His smile was genuinely amused.

'Go on, shame the devil, say shorthand and typing if you want to. Or isn't that grand enough for one of the Markham sisters?'

She was gratified to think that he had taken the trouble to find out about her, and it was nice to hear herself described as one of the Markham sisters, instead of being somehow singled out as the odd sister, the fat one, the unsuccessful one. It made it easier to reply.

'I don't mind what it's called, I hate it anyway. But Miss Edwards gets very uptight if you say it's just shorthand and typing. *Her* pupils are supposed to be above that sort of thing, we do French and bookkeeping as well!'

'I see. There's more to it than one would think.'

They reached the front hall and Sophie hesitated, not knowing what she should do. Should she move away without saying anything more, just smile and go, or should she say goodbye, or pretend to see a friend, mention a class, faint . . . the alternatives were suddenly endless.

Peter Brewer solved the dilemma.

'Got to rush, must get a decent bench, but look, are you doing anything at lunch time?'

Dazed, she shook her head.

'Right. Meet me here, at half twelve, and we'll get ourselves some lunch.'

With a lift of the hand he was gone, without waiting for her reply, taking it for granted that she would meet him. How right he was! She stood just where he had left her, dizzy with an accomplishment which had cost her nothing, not even effort. He must like her!

She got through the morning somehow. Happiness was a physical thing, so that when she made mistakes and got told off, she could afford to smile gently. Poor Miss Ryder, struggling to teach typing, shouting at Sophie from behind her eye-shrinking glasses – she did not know what happiness was. When half past twelve came she was almost afraid to go down into the front hall in case it had all been her imagination or his idea of a joke, in case she waited and waited and he did not come and she lost even the consolation of her lunch.

He came. He was in a hurry, taking her arm and steering her out of the building and across the road to a small milk bar where the older students congregated. He ordered two pizzas and two glasses of milk without consulting her; she thought such masterfulness was wonderful and sat meekly at a table with a shiny blue plastic top agreeing with everything he said. At that moment, had he suggested that they make a pact to climb the Eiger, Sophie would have agreed unhesitatingly, and she had no head for heights. When he leaned over the table in the course of their conversation and touched her hand, she thought it quite possible that she might die of love, for what she felt must be love! Her heart beat suffocatingly in her throat, she saw him ringed with a halo of light, she was so amazed by her own good fortune that she almost forgot to ask him to the party.

But she remembered. Just as they were entering the front hall once more, it came to her.

'Oh, Peter.' He had been turning away from her, but at her words he turned back, one eyebrow raised. Her heart did a huge hop and her stomach churned with slow, excruciating pleasure.

'Yes, lovely?'

'I suppose . . . it's my sister's eighteenth birthday party in three days, and she said I could invite . . . I suppose you wouldn't like to come?'

'Great, thanks very much. Is this a formal invitation, or do I have to give you my address and wait for the postman to call?'

11

'I-It's formal, but I'll send an invitation if you like.'

He grinned at her. He was looking extraordinarily pleased.

'Tell you what, bring it to school tomorrow, save postage. I'll meet you here, same time.'

Sophie walked into her class still on cloud seven. She smiled when Annabel Roxy, who was pert and pretty and popular, muttered 'Silly cow' because she had knocked her shorthand notebook off the desk. Picking it up, she said 'Sorry, Annabel' with real conviction, and Annabel had the grace to look a little ashamed.

Sitting down in her own place, she just could not prevent herself from smiling. Life was wonderful, and he was coming to the party. How on earth was she to get through the next three days?

'Sophie dear, just put the individual trifles, very carefully, onto the trays, would you? Then Daddy and Uncle Cyril will take them over to the hall. And do slip on an overall, we don't want to see your pretty dress ruined.'

Devina's cheeks were flushed from long hours of baking, her voice was high with excitement. A party for a hundred guests is no sinecure and she had been busy for days, but now at last the night had arrived, the cake with its burden of marzipan and pink and white icing, its eighteen candles, its bouquet of miniature roses, was at the hall, on the top table. All that now remained was to take over the various sweets that she had concocted, the trifles, the orange and lemon soufflés, the gâteaux, the meringues and the delectable, gleaming jellies.

Sophie was dressed and ready. After deep consultation with Devina, who seemed for once to understand perfectly what an important occasion this was, though Sophie had not mentioned Peter Brewer's name to her, they had bought a blue dress. She had wanted to wear white, but had finally been persuaded into the blue. With its deeply scooped neckline and waistless, flowing lines, it was certainly pretty, and far more expensive than any other garment she possessed. She was a little doubtful about it, dreading that she might look either pregnant or like Hattie Jacques, but it was useless to deny that her figure was difficult, and at least the dress was plenty big enough, and swirled in a satisfying fashion when she turned. Perhaps it had

12

been a mistake to let Lavvy do her make-up, for heavy make-up was fashionable with Lavvy's set and, though thick mascara, a sprinkling of gold tinsel on the cheekbones and lipstick paler than health demanded might suit some people, Sophie felt that it did not suit her. Furtively, she scrubbed the lipstick off whilst arranging the trifles, and felt a little better. Peter, after all, was the one who mattered, and he knew she had nice eyes and long, dark lashes of her own. Now he would discover that she was light on her feet and could dance just as well as Lavvy. He might even notice she was thinner – she had eaten nothing for three days, because she wanted so badly to look her best.

But at last they were at the hall, all of them, standing in a sort of reception line. Poppy looked sweet in a scarlet mini-skirt with a brightly embroidered, peasant-style blouse, Lavinia was in white with a sequined bodice and the two older girls, Elsa in brown and Janine in emerald green, looked elegant. Sophie, squeezed between Elsa's husband, John, and Poppy, could hardly drag her eyes away from the guests. Soon he would be here, and everyone would know that she, Sophie, was just like the other Markham sisters – she, too, could find a boyfriend!

When she spotted Peter, in the line wending its way towards them, her heart skipped a beat, then gave a couple of quick extra ones by way of making up. He looked marvellous, he was easily the best looking man present, and he was wearing a dark blue velvet jacket. He looked like the heroes of all Sophie's favourite romances rolled into one – and he was her date for the evening, he liked her best.

He smiled down at Lavvy with easy assurance, indicated Sophie, laughed, then bent and kissed her hand. Lavvy was actually blushing – Lavvy, the sophisticated, the one who knew it all. She was actually going red over something that Sophie's friend had said! Sophie shifted impatiently and nudged Poppy.

'Here he comes, Poppy, the guy I asked to the party – my Peter!'

He was in front of her, staring in open admiration, smiling at little Poppy, then transferring his attention back to Sophie.

'I *say*! You look lovely, Lovely!'

They laughed together over his small joke. *He calls me Lovely*, Sophie heard herself telling her classmates next day. *Just a nickname, he doesn't mean anything by it, but it's rather nice, don't you think?*

Together, they strolled across the dance floor, to where small tables and groups of chairs had been set out.

'Shall we make it a family party?' Peter was saying, his hand warm and possessive on her bare elbow. 'Sit with your sisters and their fellows, I mean?'

'That would be lovely,' Sophie breathed. Everything he said was lovely, *he* was lovely. To sit with her sisters, knowing that she was with the best looking man in the room – that would be loveliest of all.

An hour later, she had run away. With her eyes tear-filled, biting her lip to try to prevent its trembling, she ran across the little park which separated Glydon Grove from the hall where the party was being held. She was rolling uncomfortably in her high heels, and when she caught her dress on a rose bush she never even noticed. A toe stubbed on uneven paving, a wrist banged against an unseen wall, a garden bed mown down by her heedless, heavy feet, all went unregarded. A man, skulking in the shadows, saw her and called out but she ignored him. What was the use? It had all been a cruel joke and now, back in the hall, Peter Brewer and Lavvy were dancing together with eyes for no one but each other, not caring if she were dead.

She reached the house, and of course it was all locked up. Front and back. There was a low, sloping roof to the utility room; the other girls had been known to climb in and out of their rooms by that path when they didn't want their parents to know they were out.

Sophie couldn't do it, couldn't heave her weight from the ground as they did, with their strong young muscles. She hung for a moment by her hands, struggling fruitlessly, then collapsed against the wall and wished she were dead.

When Peter Brewer came round the corner she could scarcely believe it. He looked at her in embarrassment, and she knew that he had never really seen her as a person. All that charm, all that gentle teasing, had been for one purpose and one purpose only; to meet Lavvy.

Now, pressed against the brick wall, she felt absolutely desperate. She knew she must look a sight, knew her face was still tear-blubbered, and, glancing down at her dress, she saw the rip, saw her lovely shoes mud-caked, her tights dirt-splattered.

14

But she could see no repugnance in his face, only embarrassment. For a moment hope bloomed. Could she have misunderstood the words she had overheard? Could she have made a dreadful mistake?

'Your mother sent me with the key, she thinks you've just come back for a few minutes to . . . to do something or other.' Hope died. 'Look, I'm awfully sorry . . . you heard, I suppose?'

She nodded, teeth clenched to control the shudders which threatened to overwhelm her.

'Don't think too badly of me, Sophie, I really *do* like you, you're a gr . . . ' He looked down at her, swallowed, and changed it to 'a wonderful girl. But I caught a glimpse of Lavvy trotting along beside you, looking . . . oh, I don't know, I just felt I'd got to meet her. Then someone said she was your sister and . . . well, it went on from there.'

'I see.' She held out her hand for the key, but he shook his head.

'No. You're still upset, I can see. I'll come in and make you a cup of tea.' He unlocked the door, stepped inside and put the light on. Sophie passed him and crossed the kitchen to the sink, taking the kettle off the draining board and holding it under the gushing tap. When she turned to take it to the cooker, Peter had lit the gas for her. She smiled at him.

'Look, it doesn't matter, Peter. Just let's forget it, shall we?'

'It matters, but if we can both forget it . . . ' He held out a hand. 'Can we still be friends?'

She tried to smile. Of all the fatuous remarks! But he wasn't to know how much store she had set by his friendship.

He took her hand, then bent over, lightly kissing her cheek. She winced, unable to ignore the look in his eye. It reminded her of a line from a television programme. *To bravely go where no man has gone before*; it would be funny, if only it wasn't so sad.

'All right, Peter, we've both said our say, now you might as well go back to the others. I'll watch telly for a bit and then go to bed. I'm tired, we've all worked very hard to get this party off the ground, I could do with an early night.'

'You won't come back?' He stared at her doubtfully; she could see he was half relieved at the idea of her absence. 'But what will people think? They haven't even started eating, yet.'

15

'Tell them I'm feeling bilious.' She wished she could have thought of an ailment which at least had some dignity, but nothing sprang to mind. 'Tell them I just want to be left alone.'

'All right, if that's what you want.' He waited, but she said nothing more. He sighed. She had her back to him, she was watching the kettle as it began to hiss, but she heard him open the back door, slip throught it, shut it behind him. He had gone.

At once, the need to behave without decorum or dignity seized her. She gave a sob and headed for the stairs. She flung the door of her room open violently, then slumped on the bed. Even in her deep unhappiness her observer self was seeing her, rather romantically, as The Spurned Woman, but a glance in the mirror killed all that. She sat up on the bed and stared, mouth dropping open. She looked plain bloody terrible! Her make-up had run, mascara streaked her plump pink cheeks, and her hair looked as though birds habitually nested in it. There was dirt on her chin and her lipstick was badly smudged. She gazed bitterly at her reflection. How loathsome she was! Even with her heart broken clean in two her cheeks were pink. She turned away from the mirror, then got up and dragged the once admired dress over her head, dropping it on the floor, kicking off the mud-caked shoes and dirty tights. She saw then that her legs were mud-streaked too. Very well, she would have a bath, then get herself something to eat and go to bed. The worst of it was, she was sharing with Lavvy tonight because both the older girls were home, so she could not even guarantee how long she could be miserable in peace, but a glance at her watch showed that it was barely ten o'clock. It would be more like one or two in the morning before they had said goodbye to all their guests and cleaned up the hall, she was safe for a while, at any rate.

She had run the bath and was shedding her final garments when she heard a noise downstairs. She wrapped herself in a bath towel, and was half-way down again when she remembered what it must be. The kettle! She arrived at a flurried gallop just in time to stop the bottom burning out of it and then, since she was downstairs anyway, she decided to get her snack now, even if she ate it after her bath.

The fridge yielded cold turkey, some tomatoes, a bowl of

leftover filling for the salmon vol-au-vents, a plastic pot of cream and some raspberries. The pantry provided a thick slice of chocolate cake, a stick of celery and a pile of cheese straws. On the cold slab she found an individual trifle and a lemon mousse, and when she had piled everything onto her tray she realised that she needed a drink – everyone at the party would be having a drink soon. She made her way into the dining room and picked up the almost full bottle of brandy with which her father and her brother-in-law had been giving themselves Dutch courage earlier in the evening. She hated the stuff, but took a good swig, then put the bottle on the tray. It wasn't that bad, it warmed her stomach and made her feel less helpless.

She carried her provender rather unsteadily upstairs and climbed into the bath. The water was gloriously hot and she lay there a long time, eating steadily. She also had several more pulls from the brandy bottle. It was horrible, of course, but it did make things easier to bear.

At length even the brandy could not cloud her mind to the fact that the water was getting steadily colder and that her hands and feet were beginning to take on an ancient, wrinkled look, like white crêpe paper. She got out, wrapped herself in the biggest towel she could find, and returned to her bedroom. Lavvy's little radio was already beside the spare bed and she switched it on as she passed it, though it wasn't easy with the brandy bottle in one hand and the remains of her feast in the other. Music jarred, made her wince a bit, but she needed it to enhance her image of a with-it teenager. She looked at her naked body in the mirror, and hastily took another swig of brandy; yes, now her white and whale-like figure definitely looked less repulsive. She lay down on her stomach on the bed, the with-it teenager again, only it was so terribly uncomfortable when you had a stomach like hers. She seemed to balance on it, like a rocking horse, with her legs up in the air one end and her head up in the air the other, and all her weight on her huge, curved belly. She held the pose for an uncomfortable thirty seconds then, with a sigh, rolled onto her back. That was better.

She lay on the bed for what seemed like a long time, eating the rest of her supplies and drinking steadily. Dimly, she saw that Peter had been her one chance and, somehow, she had

17

failed to take it. She had let Peter slip through her fingers. The fact that he had never been her Peter, that hers had not been the fingers he had been caught by, seemed immaterial. When all the food had been eaten and all the brandy drunk, she turned on her side and went to sleep.

She awoke, much later, to pitch darkness. She felt terribly, unbelievably awful. Her head was splitting and she had such a thirst that her mouth felt like a desert. She sat up and found that she was cold, ill, trembling. She could remember nothing of what had gone before, save that she must be quiet, because Lavinia was in the other bed, and that she must have a drink or die.

There was water in the bathroom, but water was not what she needed. A cup of tea! That was it, lovely hot, strong tea. She swung her feet onto the floor, groped for her slippers, failed to find them and so padded to the door barefoot. She noticed a faint glow coming from Lavvy's radio and fainter music, and thoughtfully turned it off. The daft cow must have forgotten it and gone to sleep with it on.

The journey to the kitchen was not difficult. Across the moonlit quiet of the upper landing, down the stairs, avoiding the one which creaked, up the hall and over to the kitchen door. She knew the way so well that she could have done it blindfold and certainly did not need to turn on any lights. Ever since she could remember she had walked this way by night, wooed by cakes or biscuits, by a night-time memory of a dish of jelly in the fridge, by the sticky sweetness of a honeycomb, or a dish of succulent strawberries, or that last, solitary ham and pickle sandwich, left on the plate because none of the girls would take it and risk being an old maid.

She opened the kitchen door and stood for a moment, framed against the darkness of the hall, caught and dazzled by the brilliance of the light as a night-time moth is dazzled.

The room was crowded! Vaguely, she saw her parents, her sisters, their friends. And Peter. All silent, all staring. She sensed conversations cut off, jokes untold, because of her sudden appearance. She was rubbing her eyes, opening her mouth to speak, when Lavvy began to shout at her. Lavvy's voice was strident, her cheeks scarlet. But . . . but wasn't Lavvy upstairs,

18

asleep in bed? Was this all some horrible nightmare?

'Mum, Dad, It's disgusting, it's horrible . . . in front of my friends . . . she's done it on purpose . . .'

It had no meaning, the sudden tirade, but she knew that she must reach the sink. A great bubble of something hot and acid and beastly was rising up in her throat. She was ill, they must realise she was . . .

She got half-way across the room when Lavvy stepped forward to bar her path – and it was too late, by then, for anything but a gasped apology as she vomited violently onto Lavvy's white dress. She was weeping, still trying to blunder her way to the sink, when she felt her mother's thin little arms go round her waist, felt Devina start to guide her to the door. The silence was broken, she could hear voices, an uncle saying it happened to all of us, her father's voice, deep as the buzz of a bee, comforting Lavinia.

Then she was in the bathroom, leaning over the sink whilst her mother got her a drink of water, listening to Devina's reproaches without understanding them, until she felt the coldness of the handbasin pressing against her skin and looked down at herself.

Streaked with vomit, shuddering with cold, she was mother-naked.

She did not remember how she stumbled back to bed, but only that she was there, staring at the ceiling, sick with self-contempt. She waited for Lavinia to come to bed, but her sister must have decided to sleep in the living room on the couch rather than share a room with the drunken party-pooper.

She left whilst the stars were still bright, tiptoeing down the stairs and pausing in the hall only long enough to ascertain that all the lights were off. She glided into the kitchen, sure that no one, no matter how desperate for a bed, would be kipping down on the wooden table or on the upright, wheel-backed chairs. Also, on the mantelpiece there was a tin where Devina kept spare cash.

She fumbled for it and discovered, quite by accident, that the mantelpiece had been used by Elsa to keep her return ticket to London Euston safe. Thus are great decisions made. Sophie fled to London because she had a ticket to get there, not because she particularly fancied the city. She had three pounds in her pocket, half a loaf of bread and some cheese in her handbag, and a great, aching void where her heart should have been. But it never occurred to her for one moment to stay. She could not stay in the place where all her friends – and enemies – would soon be talking about her abandoned behaviour. She could not face Lavinia's scorn and derision. Pretty Lavinia. Peter-owning Lavinia. She told herself, as she trudged to the station, that, at nineteen, it was high time she left home and found some independence. She never even considered that she had nowhere to stay in London, or that she knew no one in that city. Nothing mattered but her escape from an intolerable situation.

Chapter Two

'I think it possible that madam could take a slightly larger size.'
The shop assistant was elderly, mauve-haired, enviably skinny.
To Sophie's relief, she also seemed quite understanding. 'A
twenty is quite big enough in most clothes, of course, but this
designer has always been a bit mean with material, though his
dresses are excellent value. For a fuller figure, however, you'd
probably find that the skirts hang better in a larger size.'

Sophie, facing herself in the mirrored cubicle, saw herself
looking mountainous in her white slip and nodded uncertainly.
No use arguing with the woman, she told herself as the assistant
left her, though no way did she need a larger size, especially in
the dress that she had just tried on, which had looked awful,
strained across her breasts, the skirt dipping in front and lifting
at the back. Anyway, now that she came to think of it, she
didn't even like the dress particularly. Heavens, why had she
agreed so meekly to the suggestion? Panic-stricken at the
thought of being over-persuaded by an experienced sales-
woman, Sophie reached stealthily for her saggy brown jumper
and the elderly tweed skirt that had shrunk and could only be
worn on a chain of extending safety pins. If she could just get
herself dressed before the woman returned . . .

'Here we are madam, try these. The blue's very nice, but the
honey is what I'd recommend. It's a generous cut, and . . .'
The assistant appeared not to notice that Sophie was half into
her skirt. I'll take another look along the racks whilst you try
these on.'

She disappeared and Sophie took the latest offering off the
hanger and eyed it suspiciously. When the woman said it was a
generous cut, did that mean that it was a size larger? She sighed,
then began to scramble out of her skirt again. The little room
smelt of someone else's scent and of the sweat of fear which
always attacked her when she was buying clothes. Nothing was

ever quite right, yet the dress of her dreams must exist some-where. She looked at the honey-coloured dress. It wasn't the sort of thing she usually tried, but she was getting desperate and it did look quite nice.

She slid the soft wool over her head, ready to drag it off at once with some excuse if it felt tight but, astonishingly, it really did seem to be the right size. It had long, full sleeves caught in at the wrist by neat bands, and a V neck which minimised her large breasts. It was long enough, too. Sophie, who took up a good deal of material width-wise, often found that, inexplic-ably almost, hems were above the knee which should have been below. She turned towards the biggest mirror, and the skirt swirled. She felt a tiny smile starting. It was really nice! Of course she didn't look slim, but she looked just right to start a new job with a new boss, even though it was only a temporary position just while a secretary was on holiday.

'I wondered if madam mi . . . ' The assistant's voice broke off short. She came right into the changing cubicle, eyes darting approvingly over Sophie and the honey-coloured dress. 'Well now, that really does look good!'

'Yes, I like it.' Sophie swirled again, considering her reflection carefully. If she could just get hold of some dark brown shoes, high-heeled ones, she might make quite a good impression on Monday morning, might even look the part of Stephen Bland's new secretary.

'You'll take it? Or would you like to try the blue first?'

It would be tempting providence to try the blue. If it looked nice then she would want them both, which was impossible with the money she had available, if it looked horrid then she would lose the warm and lovely glow that the honey-coloured dress was giving her. She shook her head, her eyes still on her reflection.

'No, I won't bother with the blue, thank you, this is so nice. How much did you say it was?'

The dresses she had chosen had all been in the special offer range; now it occurred to her, belatedly, that the assistant had brought the honey-coloured one in, presumably off a different rack. But it couldn't be *that* expensive.

'It's a Suzette original, madam.' The assistant named a stag-gering price. Sophie's heart, which had been sky-high, sank into her scuffed walking shoes. She began to unbutton the dress, being extra careful. To spoil such a thing – it must have been sewn with pure gold thread!

'I'm afraid that's too much. Perhaps I'd better try the blue after all.'

'I'm afraid it *is* one of the better dresses,' the assistant admitted. 'Isn't it always the way though, just when we find . . . ' She darted forward as Sophie laid the dress sadly on the little velvet chair in the corner of the cubicle. 'Well I never, that dress has a fault! See, madam, under the arm there? A seam's been sewn quite badly crooked – it'll have to be reduced, I couldn't let that go as perfect. I'd be prepared to make quite a substantial reduction for a quick sale, if . . . '

Sophie, petticoated, stared at the dress, then at her reflection. Mont Blanc had been transformed by that dress into something almost beautiful!

'How much?' she asked bluntly.

The assistant, who had probably looked forward to a little genteel haggling, looked disappointed, but named a sum. Sophie swallowed. It would mean no canteen lunches for a fortnight, certainly no brown court shoes, and possibly she would have to walk to the office. But she did have some black shoes which wouldn't look too bad, and walking was good for one. Lunches would just have to be foregone.

'I'll take it.'

She struggled into her skirt and jumper again, not sure whether to be absurdly pleased or a little downcast. No lunches for two whole weeks, and only a snack for elevenses, and a new boss to face! But she knew she had done the right thing. If she had been forced to walk into the television centre on Monday in her old school skirt and blouse which had been doing yeoman service ever since she first got the job in the typing pool, she would have died of shame. Her flatmates, Penny Wintle-Smy and Anya Evans, had impressed upon her how difficult Stephen Bland could be, as well as how gorgeous.

'The youngest producer in the company, and the most promising,' Penny had said, when Sophie had first returned to the flat with the news that she was to work for Mr Bland whilst his secretary was away. 'Aren't you the lucky one, Sofa?'

Penny was a smooth blonde with one of those wide-eyed,

innocent faces which frequently hide a personality which is quite otherwise. She was, in fact, sharp-tongued and impatient and, although she could have had her pick of young men, she was addicted to tousle-headed, drug-taking, arty types. Or at least, they looked as though they took drugs when they slouched into the flat to pick Penny up, or lounged in a chair drinking coffee and grunting after an evening out.

Anya, on the other hand, was dark and dramatic, with very white skin and really black hair. She was extremely intelligent and could be cutting, but she had more patience than her friend and was inclined to gloss over shortcomings which Penny pounced on. The two of them had been friends for years and Sophie knew she was the outsider, the one who had come in just so that the other two could stay solvent, but they tolerated her most of the time, especially Anya, and Sophie was content with the flat and with their offhand companionship.

When Sophie had told them about Mr Bland they had been preparing their evening meal, and after Penny's remark, Anya had turned and surveyed her with a bright, considering gaze.

'He's gorgeous all right, but he's got a fearful temper and he's a stickler for getting things just right. He won't appreciate your schoolgirl freshness either, Sofa, or not the rig-out, anyway. *Do* get yourself something decent to wear. I know the job's only for a week, but it might lead to another. It's very rare for someone of your age to get into a secretarial situation even for five minutes.'

'I know, Miss Murray told me how lucky I was. I'm going to get paid extra for the week or two weeks or whatever, so I could splash out, I suppose.'

Anya frowned down at the salad she was arranging in a bowl.

'Mm. I know you don't pull down the sort of salary that Pen and I get, but you aren't that badly paid in the pool. You've bought nothing to wear since you've moved in, and though I know the rent's quite heavy . . . '

Unsaid, the criticism was nevertheless there. The big lunches in the canteen; when most of the girls were having soup and salad Sophie worked her way through the three most substantial courses on the menu. The machines in the corridor which dispensed hot soup and snacks – she was their most constant customer. And the frittering of any money that was left on chips, hot pies, doughnuts.

'Yes, I know,' Sophie said quickly. 'The fact is, I-I've been saving up to get myself a decent outfit. I'll go down to the shops tomorrow and get something really nice.'

Now, in the small changing cubicle, she put on her navy school macintosh, which would no longer button up, picked up her shoulder bag and made her way to the counter where the mauve-haired assistant was folding the dress in tissue paper and placing it reverently in a carrier bag with the shop's name on the outside. Sophie took out her cheque book and card and reflected that it was a good thing her bank manager couldn't see her now, this cheque would bounce all the way to the bank and would only turn respectable on Thursday, when her next salary was paid in. As she was turning away from the counter, the shop assistant came over to her, faded lips pursed into a hiss.

'Psst! If you go down to the big Dolcis shop on the corner, dear, there are some lovely imitation crocodile shoes going cheap – they'd look a treat with that dress.'

'Thanks, I'll go down there right away,' Sophie said, beaming. How kind people were – the poor woman wasn't to know that if she bought shoes now it would mean borrowing money for next week's rent from one of the girls, and she could never do that.

'I hate to ask you, Anya, but I seem to have overspent – it's only for a few days; until Thursday, in fact.'

It was Sunday afternoon and Sophie was tackling Anya whilst she could. Penny had disappeared on Saturday night with her latest scruff and had not yet reappeared, so Sophie had let Anya sleep until noon and then she had taken her a nice hot cup of tea. One look at Anya's white, crumpled face had sent her flying for the aspirin bottle but now, at nearly three o'clock, Anya had got up, slung on her dressing-gown and come saggingly into the kitchen for another drink. And when Anya neither threw up nor went back to bed she thought it the right moment to broach her question. Anya, wincing at the brightness of the light, seemed quite amenable.

'For the rent, is it? Well, you won't be the first one to spend her rent money, but don't make a habit of it, there's a dear. I'll put it in with my cheque, and you give me your money. Will that do?'

'Marvellous!' Sophie looked wistfully at the packet of ginger-nuts which Anya had brought out of the pantry, but refrained from helping herself to one. She was empty, so empty that she felt sure she could be beaten like a drum. Because on a Sunday the girls provided their own meals. Normally, she would have gone down to the Indian shop on the corner and bought bits and pieces to keep body and soul together or, if she had been in the money, she would have gone to the Chinese take-away and come home with sweet and sour chicken, noodles and piles and piles of savoury rice. But today, due to a financial emptiness which rivalled her stomach's, she intended to exist on cups of tea and the odd slice of bread and butter.

'That's all right. Well, what did you spend your substance on?'

It was gratifying to have something to show Anya, instead of the other way around. Sophie went to her room, put on the honey-coloured dress and the brown imitation crocodile-skin shoes and came back, pushing the door open with a hesitancy which was not unbecoming.

'It cost a lot. What do you think?'

'Too good for the office,' Anya said at once, her experienced eye recognising the quality of the dress. Then, seeing Sophie's face fall, she relented. 'It's really nice, Sofa, it suits you, and provided you don't go covering it with food stains, it'll do very well. How much was it?'

Sophie told her. She waited for Anya to shriek at her extravagance, but Anya merely nodded.

'That's reasonable, for a dress like that. It's easily the nicest thing I've seen you wearing – they wouldn't recognise you if you went back to the caff!'

When Sophie had first come to London she had worked as chief cook and bottlewasher at a tiny workmen's caff off Finsbury Circus. Anya and Penny were intrigued, but she never told them much about it, for one thing because there was not much to tell and for another because she had been rather happy there, which they would find kinky and unbelievable. The proprietor, who looked such a villain with his hooked nose and flashy, mediterranean smile had been unexpectedly kind to

26

her. When she had stopped working late shifts so that she could go to evening classes in shorthand and typing he had been pleased for her, boasting to his very mixed clientele about 'our Sophie', and when she had landed the job in the typing pool at the television centre he had put an extra fiver in her wage packet, and thrown in a big catering pack of tomato soup, because he knew she had a passion for it.

The girls assumed that it had been life at the caff which had forced Sophie to take evening classes, but it had been nothing of the sort. It had been the hostel. Shut in every night and on her days off by her lack of friends and lack of money, living in a tiny cubicle six foot square, she had almost considered giving up, going home. But that would only have shown the girls in the hostel that they had been right to dislike Sophie, simply for being herself. They had made her life a misery with their barbed remarks, meant to be overheard, their cruel, unfunny jokes and a constant barrage of unwanted advice – eat less, wear something decent for once, haven't you heard that washing's good for spots – so that her main object in life became to leave the hostel.

But to leave, she had to earn considerably more than Joey and the caff could provide. What was more, she wanted to leave in a blaze of glory, so that all her tormentors would envy her, wish they had been nicer whilst they had the chance.

Perhaps it had been her unhappiness at the hostel which had made her evening classes not only bearable, but enjoyable. The very subjects that had seemed dull as ditchwater and horribly hard at home soon became interesting, a challenge. And one, moreover, which she could conquer. Her shorthand was neat, readable, soon incredibly fast, and her typing followed suit. Even bookkeeping – not her favourite subject – proved less formidable than she had expected, and when the end of term examinations were held she excelled herself, not only passing out head of her group but getting her Pitman's certificates for 150 words per minute in shorthand and the equivalent in typing.

As if she had suddenly found a magic formula for success, she was sent for by Mr Matthews, head of the Business Studies Department.

'I've arranged for you to have an interview at the Television

Centre, they want someone with really first class shorthand and error-free typing, which is why I put your name forward,' he said. 'Go up to the centre tomorrow, at 10.30, and don't let me down, Miss Markham.'

She got the job, and within three days of starting there, saw an advertisement on the staff board in the cloakroom. *'Wanted, third person to share flat in Gloucester Terrace. All expenses shared. Apply Anya Evans or Penny Wintle-Smy,'* it read.

She had never met the girls in question, but found out from others in the pool that they were important people, secretaries. It seemed impossible that they would agree to let her share with them, yet they did. They wanted someone quiet, someone willing to share the work of the flat and the expenses, someone who would not object to anything they might wish to do, provided, of course, that it did not jeopardise their lease.

Hoping that no one would expect her to take part in gang-bangs, whatever they might be, or drug parties or similar orgies, Sophie agreed to everything. She did not kid herself that she was a good judge of character, but she thought shrewdly that Anya and Penny probably were. If they thought she would fit in, she probably would. And in the month they had lived in the flat together, no one had seriously annoyed the others. Sophie, who had plenty of horse sense, would have accepted the situation without comment if either of the other two wanted to bring men home for the night, but this did not arise.

'Penny's father is subsidising the flat,' Anya explained the first time they were alone in the kitchen, dreaming up a meal. 'He made it plain that he wouldn't stand for anything like that. And the couple who own the house keep an eye on us for him in a fairly unobtrusive way, thank heaven. That's why we chose you to share with us, you didn't look the type to start flogging it all round the neighbourhood, nor to object if we spent the odd night away from the flat.'

'Flogging what?'

Anya giggled. 'Your tail, of course! My God, Sofa, where were you drug up?'

Now, posturing before Anya in her new dress, Sophie put the sixty-four thousand dollar question.

'Do I look the part? Like Mr Bland's secretary, I mean?'

28

'You do. In fact, if your shorthand and typing is on the same level as your appearance, he won't ever want to lose you!'

It was Monday, and Sophie was walking to work. It had been raining heavily when she woke, but fortunately the clouds had cleared and now it was a lovely morning, with frail sunshine brightening the April buds on the sooty plane trees and with the puddles reflecting a blue, springlike sky. Sophie wore her sensible lace-ups and her elderly mac, but she revelled in the knowledge that beneath the mac was the honey-coloured dress and, in her zip bag, nesting beside a supply of dark chocolate biscuits, the crocodile-skin shoes waited. In the agreement which she had signed so cheerfully it had been clearly stated that the girls should pay for their own lunches but that the evening meal and anything that followed it, such as biscuits and hot drinks, should be provided out of communal expenses. However, with no money to buy lunch, she had been forced to take the biscuits. She just hoped she could last out until she got home, when they always had a hot meal. Usually Penny, who was in first, had got it well under way by the time Sophie slogged up the stairs. Penny was having a sort-of affair with her boss, and one of the perks was that he let her leave work at four, when he did, instead of continuing to pound the typewriter until five-thirty, like Anya and Sophie.

The affair was only sort-of because, according to Penny, it was unconsummated and likely to remain so.

'He's very dynamic and with-it, Gio is,' she explained casually to Sophie, who had shown a certain amount of curiosity over their relationship. 'He's Italian, of course, and they're very hot-blooded. He thinks he *ought* to be having it off with his secretary, especially as I'm of good family, but he's got a rich and very beautiful wife and two lovely kiddies, so he doesn't intend to jeopardise all that just for a bit on the side.'

'Then why pretend to be your lover?' Sophie asked, fascinated. 'Why not just admit to being a dull, old, happily married man?'

'Sofa, what a dumb question. Gio's got his reputation to think about! What would everyone at the centre say if they knew he wasn't laying the best looking bird there, especially when you consider his opportunities. His wife knows it's just a *canard*, but everyone else thinks we spend all our spare time knocking.'

'What's a canard?'

'A duck,' Penny said unhelpfully. 'Didn't you do French at school?'

'Oh.' Sophie thought, but it still didn't make sense. She asked her next question. 'Then what about your reputation, Penny? Surely you don't want people to think you're Gio's woman when you're not?'

'They can think what they like,' Penny said grandly. She was ironing as they talked, and now she held out a nightie, black as night, fine as a cobweb, waving it before Sophie's admiring eyes. 'Gio brought me that last time he was in Paris, and a matching set of undies. I couldn't afford that lot on my salary.'

'Yes, but what are undies compared with your reputation?' Sophie persisted obstinately. Surely all the values she had been taught could not be so lightly tossed aside. Penny seemed to be selling her birthright, not for pottage, but for a few pairs of knickers!

'Look, everyone sleeps around these days,' Penny said succinctly, throwing the nightie over the back of a chair and picking up a pink mohair sweater. 'I'm not thinking of settling down yet, and men only mind if you sleep around when they're contemplating marriage. Besides, I don't want to settle down, and I like variety, and the sort of man I go for takes it for granted that I sleep with Gio.' She pressed the iron onto the pink mohair and screamed as it snatched at the light, dandelion-clock fluff. 'God, this bloody iron's too hot!'

'Yes, but suppose something happened.'

'Like what? This, my little canard, is the day of the pill.' Penny sang the last few words to the tune of the British Rail advertisement and, attracted by the aptness of it, repeated it several times, finishing off with a high note that many a diesel might have envied. 'Now, any more questions? I love educating the ignorant.'

'Yes. What do your parents think?'

Penny was bending down and unplugging the iron and, for a moment, she went still. But only for a moment. Then she was upright again, wrapping the lead round the iron, folding the board, leaning it against the wall until she had time to take it through to the kitchen.

'My parents only know what I choose to tell them. But if I had to take a bet, I'd put money on the fact that my Mama thinks I spend most of my time at the television centre screwing Gio into the ground. She probably thinks I only hold down my job because I'm such a good lay. So what? She's my mother and he's my father, sure, but they're only people.'

'You'll say it's my upbringing, but if I thought my parents . . .'

'Oh, Sofa, what is it this time? Surely the pill and freedom for women have reached the wilds of North Wales by now?'

'Of course. It's just that . . . oh, Penny, he's *married*!'

'So what? I'm not going to get preggers and shame anyone, or land Gio with a little bastard. I mean I wouldn't, if we were sleeping together. I just don't see why a married man's any different from a single one, these days.'

'You wouldn't, unless he happened to be your married man,' Anya observed. She had been sitting on the couch taking no part in the conversation but concentrating, with beady-eyed severity, on a tiny piece of knitting. She was dressing a doll for one of her nieces and the task, begun lightheartedly enough, had become an obsession. Sophie quite envied the doll its huge wardrobe of lovingly made little clothes and sometimes wondered if Anya would ever actually bring herself to hand it to a heedless child.

'No one owns anyone else.' Penny said. For some reason she gave Sophie a quick, hard glance. 'Do they, Sofa?'

'Well, no, but if you've made those vows . . .'

'Vows that you're forced to make by convention don't count. Anyway, it ought to be *cleaving only unto him so long as I can stand him*,' Penny announced. 'People make mistakes; you might find you hate working for Stephen Bland, Sofa. But that doesn't mean you have to stick to the job, just because you said you'd take it and signed a contract and things. Besides, I haven't made any vows, it's Gio you ought to be lecturing.'

Sophie was sure that there was something badly wrong with the argument, but she also sensed that Penny did not want to continue it. Perhaps, underneath, she was ashamed of her behaviour? There was no reason to suppose this but Sophie, with a sigh, changed the subject.

And now, walking down King Street towards her new job, she thought that there was one good thing about being fat.

31

Mrs Stephen Bland would not have one single thing to worry about once she saw her husband's replacement secretary.

She found the thought so annoying that it quite spoiled her sense of achievement over walking to the office.

By the time Sophie reached the corner of Gloucester Terrace that evening she was worn out and her stomach was actually rumbling with hunger – a state seldom achieved by Sophie, who normally ate little but extremely often. The thought of the hot meal which should, by now, be almost ready gave fresh impetus to her step, so that when she reached the foot of the nine steps which led up to the front door of No. 7 she viewed them with less distaste than usual. After all, she was late, it was dark, and there was hardly anyone about to watch her laborious ascent – and besides, food, like first prize, waited at the top!

Having climbed all nine, she stood still for a moment, fumbling for her key, and got her breath back. What a day it had been! Frightening, messy, disorganised and yet, in retrospect, she knew she had enjoyed it. She had revelled in the responsibility, and Mr Bland's work was far more interesting than that dealt with in the anonymity of the pool.

She had been frightened, at first, by the sheer efficiency of the office she was to use. Three telephones on the desk, walls lined with filing cabinets, a huge electronic typewriter the like of which she had never been allowed to lay a finger on before. On the credit side there had been the electric percolator which bubbled away all day, providing Mr Bland, his visitors and herself with a seemingly endless supply of excellent coffee. Even Mr Bland's ill-concealed annoyance over the absence of fresh milk, which had worried her at first, soon seemed trivial. How could she have known that his secretary, Cynthia, usually bought two pints of fresh milk each day from the corner shop? Anyway, she knew now and had been given money from the petty cash to buy a supply for the rest of the week.

Inside the front door, she plodded grimly up the stairs, thinking that if this was hunger, though it might make the next meal more welcome, it was not an enjoyable sensation. Biscuits were all very well, but they could not sustain one in the course of a day such as that which she had just lived through.

She unlocked the front door of the flat, hung up her mac and went straight through into the kitchen, but to her disappointment no smell of cooking assailed her nostrils. Instead, Penny and Anya seemed to be quarrelling.

'Look, I'm accusing you of nothing, I'm just saying that someone's been in, and we'll have to do something about it. I don't like the thought that . . . ' Anya swung round as Sophie came right into the room. 'Oh, Sofa, I suppose you didn't come home at lunchtime, did you?'

'No.' Sophie glanced hopefully at the cooker. Nothing simmered. The oven light was off. Whatever had happened? 'I'm awfully sorry I'm late, but Mr Bland doesn't seem to know about leaving-off time, he just went on and on working and so did I, and then at about six, when I was really feeling desperate, he came through my room and said "Why the devil haven't you left?" I felt ever such a fool.'

'We're all late,' Penny said. 'When I got back I went straight to the pantry to get the makings of a meal, and I helped myself to a chocolate biscuit, one of Anya's. I'd just started breaking eggs into a basin – I decided to do cheese omelettes because I'm going out later – when Anya came in, and she said Freddy was coming round. So I said her biscuits were a bit low and hadn't she better buy some more, and . . . '

'Oh, it's a fuss about nothing, probably,' Anya said. 'The thing is, Sophie, that there are only two biscuits left, and just before I went to work this morning I checked the packet, so I'd know if I needed to buy any more, and I noticed particularly that there were only two missing. Yet now there's only one left. So I said I thought we'd had a sneak-thief.'

Sophie felt her cheeks go hot and her new dress suddenly felt too tight round the collar.

'Why on earth? I might have had one yesterday, when I was making tea.'

'No, you probably had one from the old packet. I had two last night just before I went to bed, and that was all that was missing this morning. And I was last to leave, so Penny needn't glare like that, I'm not accusing either of you.'

Sophie's face was on fire. She should tell – but she could not! She said awkwardly, 'Are you sure it was almost full, Anya? I'm awfully sorry, I might easily . . . '

33

'Bless you, it isn't the biscuits I grudge, it's the mystery.' Anya seized the box of eggs from the table, opened it, and began to break eggs into the waiting basin. 'Look, Pen, it's daft getting upset, I know damned well that you don't even *like* the sodding biscuits! I daresay I made a mistake, it was darkish in the pantry and I was in a hurry, as usual. Let's forget it and get on with our meal or the guys will be here before we're ready for them.'

The three of them bustled around getting the meal and very soon, seated around the table eating their omelettes, Anya remembered to ask Sophie how her first day had gone.

'Quite well, I think. Mr Bland came in late and dictated some letters, and there was some copy typing, too. The rest of the time I was answering the phones and making coffee and trying to sort out the filing system.'

'What about lunch? I didn't see you in the canteen.' Penny's voice had a suspicious ring to it, and it brought the scarlet flooding back into Sophie's cheeks. Suppose Penny put two and two together?

'I didn't have time, not today. The telephone never seems to stop ringing. Tomorrow I'm going to buy a ham bap or something from the corner shop. And I can drink coffee until it comes out of my ears, of course.'

'Yes, I remember Dotty saying that Stephen drank a lot of coffee when she was doing the job last year. It was odd that they brought you in, when you'd think that Dotty was handy – but I did hear that Stephen didn't think much of her work, and she's an awful gossip, her own office is always full of people talking about other people. Did you meet Dotty?'

'Do you mean Dorothy Saunders? I met her.'

'That's right, that's Dotty. What did you think of her?'

'I only saw her for a minute,' Sophie said guardedly. In fact, she thought Dotty quite the nastiest person she had met. Dotty had been talking to someone in the corridor outside Sophie's office and she had said, in ringing tones, 'Have you *seen* Stephen's latest? She's *huge*, she quite dwarfs the desk. I know rumour has it that he wanted someone less glamorous than poor Cynthia, but I didn't know he wanted a *freak*.'

After that, when Dotty came in, all smiles, to ask if Sophie would like to go to the canteen with her, it was easy to say no thank you, that she was too busy now and would rather go later. And when Mr Bland came in with some stuff to be filed and had advised her to get Dotty to come round and explain the system, she had told herself that she would rather die than ask that woman for help. Instead, she had simply stuffed the files into her desk drawer and later, when the telephone stopped ringing for a moment, she had examined them, to see if they looked important..

They did not, so they could stay in her drawer for a week and at the end of it, when Cynthia came back, she could sort them out. No way would Sophie apply to Dotty for help!

'What did you think of Stephen?'

Sophie considered. He had been a bit of a disappointment at first. She had expected him to be tall, dark and handsome but, instead, he had fine, light brown hair which flopped over his forehead and was constantly being pushed out of his eyes, a roman nose, and a chin which had far too determined a look to it to appeal to a secretary! He was tall though, and so far as she could judge, broad shouldered, though since he had worn a navy-blue shetland wool sweater all day, he might have been thin as a lathe beneath it.

'Just a man, a boss. But if I stick it for the whole week he'll represent a new mac,' Sophie said truthfully. 'And he said something about Cynthia being away a bit longer than he'd thought, so if it runs to two weeks, I'll get a decent skirt as well.'

'If you then go back to the pool though, you won't want to bother with a new skirt,' Penny said rather waspishly. It never failed to amaze her that Sophie could be so indifferent to what she wore. Penny was the sort who would have dressed up to go to the guillotine. 'Anyway, what did you think of *him*, not of his job.'

'I thought he'd be better looking, actually, more like a film star or something. He's quite ordinary, really. Very nice, though, I'm sure.'

Anya raised her eyes to heaven.

'Very nice! Whatever Stephen may be, it is *not* very nice. He's fiendishly attractive, sexy, eligible, he has a formidable intelligence, and Sophie dismisses him as "very nice"!'

'Well, you asked me what I thought, and I told you,' Sophie said defensively. 'I haven't seen much of him, honestly, he dictated the letters onto a tape, and he only came through two or three times, on his way somewhere else. His voice is . . .' she stopped short, biting off 'very nice', and changed it to 'interesting'.

'That's better. I wonder why you didn't spot his charm, though.'

Sophie said nothing but she accepted, without even thinking about it, that Stephen Bland would never notice her as a person, so why should she notice him? He would be judged solely on his ability as a boss, and she hoped that he would judge her solely on her ability as a secretary. If he did, and she managed to pass inspection, she hoped that he might be persuaded to give her a good reference for the next secretarial job that came up.

Anya had been watching her. Now, suddenly, she smiled. Anya's smile was three-cornered, enchanting. Sophie smiled back. Anya had an uncanny knack of guessing what one was thinking, and it seemed that, on the whole, she approved of Sophie's attitude to Stephen Bland.

'Oh, Sofa, you're a rum 'un! Look, how about me bringing sandwiches up to your new pad tomorrow lunchtime, and you providing the coffee? Then, if there's anything that puzzles you, you can ask me about it. It's a bit tough, if you ask me, to throw you into Cynthia's job when there's only Dotty to give you a hand. And I wouldn't be surprised if Dotty was so annoyed because Stephen hasn't asked for her to help out that she's sulking.'

'Oh, Anya, that would be marvellous, especially if you could explain how the filing system works,' Sophie said eagerly. 'I can't make head or tail of it, and I won't ask Dotty.'

'Why not?' Penny cut herself another slice of bread, then sighed and pushed it away. Without waiting for Sophie to answer, she added: 'I'd better not eat too much; knowing Jeremy he'll suggest pie and chips after the film, he can't go for long without food. I take it that I'm not included in this cosy little sandwich cum filing party?'

Penny and Anya sometimes met in the canteen for lunch, but it was by no means a regular thing. Anya looked a little surprised and raised her thin, black brows at her friend.

'Come by all means, Pen, you know as much about filing as I do, possibly even more.'

But it appeared that Penny had been joking. She shook her head and got up from the table.

'No, you may do your good deed in solitary splendour.'

Sophie winced. An act of friendship was one thing; being someone else's good deed quite another. Besides, she still thought that Penny, although she had no idea how Sophie had performed the conjuring trick, knew it had been done, knew who had crunched down the best part of a packet of dark chocolate biscuits. It would make her uncomfortable company, until the matter faded from her mind. If I'd come clean and told them what I'd done, it wouldn't have brought the biscuits back, Sophie told herself as Penny left the room. Worse than that. though, telling would have broken her cover, given the girls the secret of a useful little idea. If you told people how to do your conjuring tricks, they were tricks no longer, that was the trouble, although this one was so simple that a child could have thought of it. A child *had* thought of it. Sophie had been nicking biscuits by the identical method since she was about four.

You waited until the packet of biscuits was open and the top one eaten. Then you abstracted as many as you wanted from the middle of the pack, and replaced one, delicately balancing it near the top. Anya had thought she saw an almost full packet of biscuits; Penny had absent-mindedly taken one from what she, also, assumed to be a nearly full packet. A simple conjuring trick — annoying that it had so nearly gone very wrong.

Oh, well. She would not do that again and, once Thursday came with the extra money she had been promised, she should be able to afford sandwiches, if not a full canteen meal.

Both girls went out and Sophie had a quiet evening, reading a romance which Deidre in the top flat had lent her and at last, from sheer necessity, eating a plateful of bread and jam with her night-time drink. She had been in bed and asleep for a long time when the door of her room suddenly opened. A figure, framed in the light from the hall, said sharply, 'Sofa! Wake up, I want to talk to you!'

Groggily, Sophie sat up, leaning on her elbow, unable to make out who was talking.

'Whadder you want?'

'Don't take what doesn't belong to you, and don't borrow money, or there'll be trouble.'

37

Sophie rubbed her eyes and stared harder. It was Penny, swaying in the doorway. There was a man with her, his shaggy head close to her smooth yellow hair.

'Sorry? What do you mean? Oh, the rent! Anya didn't mind, she said she . . .'

'I mind. No borrowing. Nor taking. Is that clear?'

Penny's voice was blurred, though the words came out loudly. Sophie was sure that she was drunk. Or perhaps she had been smoking pot. She was on some sort of a high, anyway. It would be pointless to argue with her tonight, she would wait until the morning and say something then.

'All right, Penny. Sorry.'

Penny and her man continued to stand in the doorway for a moment, then they lurched off towards the kitchen, leaving the door open and the light still on. Sophie waited a moment, then got out of bed. She padded across the floor, horribly conscious of a pyjama jacket which could no longer button across her bulges and trousers which did not come up nearly far enough. But no one was about. She reached the door, closed it softly, and returned to her bed. For a little while she lay there, wondering why Penny had been so cross over the loan, and then her mind went to the new job and the glorious possibility that she might get another one like it, with her own little office, her own bank of telephones and no skinny, pretty young girls around to nudge each other every time they heard a toffee paper being unwrapped or a biscuit being crunched.

It would be worth working very hard indeed to attain such a nirvana.

Chapter Three

From the moment that Anya had explained the complexities of the filing system to her, Sophie had enjoyed every moment of her new job. After ten days she knew it would break her heart to leave her dear little office, her wonderfully efficient coffee percolator, her electronic typewriter that scarcely seemed to need more than thoughts to control it. So when Mr Bland called her through into the inner office one morning at ten o'clock, after he had been closeted with Miss Ridge from Staff Appointments, she went with a heavy heart. She knew that Cynthia was not expected back just yet and guessed that he had arranged for someone else to do the job until her return – she had tried so hard to be what he wanted, it just wasn't fair.

'Sit down, Miss Markham.'

She sat down, heavy with dread. Her eyes noticed almost without her volition that he had several files on the desk before him and that he would soon be wanting another cup of coffee, for his present cup was nearly empty. A tape lay in his 'out' tray, waiting for her to take it for typing.

'Miss Ridge tells me that you were told you were only here on a temporary basis.'

He waited for a reply, but disappointment kept her dumb. She nodded, her eyes on her hands, lying in her lap. If only she was glamorous, efficiency just was not enough.

'But I know what the grapevine's like, so I expect you knew that Cynthia wouldn't be coming back – and why.'

Surprised, she met his eyes.

'No, honestly! No one's said a word about her, to tell you the truth.'

He grinned. The best thing about him, if you were looking for a hero-figure, was his white, even teeth.

'That just proves you aren't a gossip, like . . . like some. That's a good thing, an advantage in a secretary. Well, now, let me fill

39

you in. Cyn ran off with an actor who'd been working on one of my programmes. The chap got an offer from the States and they both upped and offed, Cyn without a word, mind you. I wouldn't have her back even if she wanted to come, which is unlikely. Though how long . . .' He broke off, looking slightly self-conscious. Sophie wondered what he had been about to say. 'Well, as you can imagine, I can't have someone working for me who'll let me down like that.'

He paused again, so Sophie murmured agreement. She now realised why she had been thrown in at the deep end, why there had been no one to explain things to her.

'So perhaps you can guess why I've called you through.'

'Yes, I think so. You've engaged a permanent secretary and you'd like me to show her the ropes before I go back to the pool.' She gathered all her courage and stared appealingly across at him. Her voice trembled with the force of her desire. 'I'll do my best, sir, but . . . could you possibly give me a reference for the next secretarial job that comes up? I've e-enjoyed working for you very much, and I'd like a secretarial job one day. I'm s-sure I could do it.'

He looked very surprised, she saw, but smug, too, as though he knew something that she did not.

'It won't be necessary. I'm offering you the job permanently, Miss Markham. And if you decide to take it, you'll be Sophie and I'll be Stephen; we aren't a formal lot, here at the Centre.'

Sophie couldn't speak, but she could smile. A beam spread from ear to ear. She knew she ought to say something sophisticated yet grateful, but she could think of nothing suitable. It would be lovely to have that little room for her own, to continue with the delightful salary that went with the job. It would be nice to continue to work for Mr Bland – Stephen – though she still could not think of him as a vulnerable, ordinary man, but only as someone who dictated very fast but very accurately, who knew exactly what he wanted but usually wanted it yesterday, and who sometimes blew his top and shouted and raged and had to be humoured and calmed down with coffee. Not that he had ever shouted or raged at her, or not yet, at any rate. It was usually the studio staff that got his goat, or some unfortunate actor or actress.

40

'Well, Miss Markham? Is it to be Sophie?'
'Oh yes *please*, Mr Bl . . . Stephen!'

When she had left him, Stephen sat and stared down at his blotter without seeing it, wondering whether he had done the right thing. Miss Ridge had been doubtful, because of the girl's youth and also, frankly, because of her size.

'Won't you feel awkward down in the studio when she's trying to follow you round to take notes?' she had asked him, fixing him with her piercing, light grey eyes. 'And what about location work – you often took Cynthia out with you, I know.'

'Yes, but frankly, Ridgie, the girl's incredibly efficient. She's been with me ten days, she's worked like a black, and she's not made one serious mistake. Not many little ones, either. After the tortures of Dotty, it was sheer bliss to have someone I could trust – she's a good deal better than Cyn was. The volume of work she gets through is unbelievable and she's quite willing to work late, or work straight through her lunch hour. I do know what you mean about location shots, but we'll cross that bridge when we come to it. For the time being, I'll see that she's kept in the background on the studio floor.'

But now, having got his own way, having burned his boats by telling Sophie that the job was hers, he was having doubts. She was very young, far more naive than he had thought it possible for a girl to be, and very self-conscious.

It was her weight, of course. She was terribly overweight and it was criminal, when you looked at her lovely face with those great big greeny-grey eyes and her soft, red-lipped mouth. He hated allowing his eyes to travel lower, to the bulging obesity of her body, the great legs like trunks ending in tiny, neat feet. Criminal! He had made sure that she was physically fit, checking her medical record with the company, though he had been certain that any sort of glandular abnormality would have meant that they would not have taken her on, even in the pool. He knew that she ate constantly, and all the wrong things, too; she probably thought he didn't notice, but he did. Her mouth was rarely empty, her wastepaper basket frequently contained sweet and chocolate wrappers, biscuit papers, empty sandwich packages. He knew she seldom lunched in the canteen but when he got back after his own meal the room usually smelt of food – of soup, cooked up in the percolator no doubt, of salami sandwiches, of cakes and chocolate.

He wondered how she would feel, down on the studio floor where all the women were either actresses or efficient and shapely career girls. He knew that the other girls on this floor, who had been Cynthia's buddies, would not mix with Sophie. Perhaps they would, of course, once they knew she was permanent, but more likely they would not. He knew that girls often hunt in pairs, though they would have indignantly denied it, and supposed that no one wanted to pair up with a girl who would make them look ridiculous.

He thought of her, stretching up to reach a high file. She was huge, terribly overweight, of course she was, yet she was still shapely, so that if you used your imagination you could see how different she could be if she could only bring herself to lose a few stone.

What would it take to bring her to her senses? Perhaps it would help to have a good job, some money to spend on clothes, and the eyes of the studio staff upon her? He did not know, he could only hope.

Sophie returned to the flat that night walking on air, hardly able to wait to share her great news with someone, to find her flatmates congratulatory but absent-minded. They were going out, not with Freddy and Jeremy, but with two new men who had come in to the television centre on business and had suggested to Penny that she and a friend might like to dine with them.

'Mine's gorgeous,' Penny enthused, as the three of them snatched a snack in the kitchen. 'Black, curly hair, white teeth, melting dark eyes . . . gosh, wait till you see him!'

It was taken for granted by both girls that Penny, having done the fishing, should have her pick of the catch. It was taken equally for granted that one did not do the dirty on a new male acquaintance by taking along anything but one's most beautiful friend to a rendezvous. Indeed, it never crossed Sophie's mind that Penny could have suggested she go along, and if Penny had done so, she would have died before agreeing. The sort of treatment meted out to an unwanted blind date could be too clearly imagined.

'Black hair, white teeth and melting dark eyes sounds like a spaniel,' Anya said practically. 'Still, it takes all sorts. What's mine like?'

'Quite nice looking. Handsome, almost. Well, he's chunkier,' Penny admitted. 'A year or two older than mine, but you'll go a bundle on him.'

'You mean he's fat, bald, and pitiful,' Anya said resignedly. 'Oh well, so long as he can afford me.'

'If he's fat and bald, why are you going to wear your flame chiffon?' Sophie asked curiously. Her flatmates' actions were sometimes completely beyond her. Surely one wore one's best clothes for important people, not just for ugly strangers?

'Oh, Sofa, you're so dumb!' Penny groaned, but Anya was kinder.

'I'm wearing it in the hope that they'll take us somewhere smart and expensive, the sort of nightclub that we can grace with our presence,' she said. 'Why don't you go up and tell John and Deidre about the job, Soph? They'll be ever so pleased for you.'

John and Deidre were the couple who lived on the top floor. Sophie didn't know if they were married or if they just lived together, but she supposed it didn't matter. They were very friendly and amusing, and Deidre was pregnant so she was home for most of the day and loved a bit of a chat. Sometimes Sophie thought they must be married because Deidre was pregnant and sometimes she thought that it didn't follow. At home, it would have mattered a lot, but here in London you could get away with anything.

As soon as the girls left and the washing up was done, she hurried up to the top floor, arriving, breathless, to find that John and Deidre were getting ready to go out. John was in the shower but Deidre, who had showered first, was unwinding her curlers and about to brush out her limp, mouse-coloured hair, and she invited Sophie in to watch and talk whilst she finished her hair and did her face.

Sophie was only too delighted to tell Deidre all about the job, and how excited she was at the prospect of visiting the studio when Stephen was working down there, and of going on location with the cast. Deidre listened and nodded appreciatively, then picked up her best maternity dress, a blue thing with innumerable tiny pleats which hung from the shoulders, took off her stained skirt and smock and pulled the blue pleats over her head.

43

'That's marvellous, Sophie. You must be the baby's godmother, like Anya. I'm sure you'll be famous one day, you'll be Discovered or something, and then think how proud my baby will be.'

'I don't think secretaries get discovered much,' Sophie said, with a giggle. 'But I'd be honoured to be a godmother, only hadn't you better see what John says first?'

'Why? What makes you think it's his baby?' Deidre's face, emerging from the pleats, was grinning wickedly at the expression on Sophie's. 'It's all right, you goose, I was only teasing. I asked John what he thought about having you ages ago actually, before fame came your way, and he agreed, so that's all right. What are you going to do to celebrate? Like to come to the flicks with us?'

'No, thanks all the same. I'm going to ring home and tell my folks, then I'll have a really hot, luxurious bath since both the girls are out, and then : . . I say, if you and John are out, I suppose I couldn't watch your telly for an hour or so? There's a programme I'd love to see.'

'You certainly could. Hang about, I've had another idea. If you aren't in a hurry for your little bed, stay until we come back from the cinema, which should be around half ten, and we'll have a drink to wish you luck in the new job. And we'll stop off at the chippie and buy a fish supper for three. How's that?'

'Lovely, except that I don't eat chips. But just this once . . .'

Deidre cast critical eyes over Sophie's expanse.

'I wish you really would try, love, because if you did you'd find your whole life would . . . Oh dear, you'll think I do nothing but find fault.'

'No I shan't, but I *am* dieting, honestly. It just doesn't seem to come off me the way it does off other people. You ask the girls, I hardly ever have lunch now and I don't eat puddings after the evening meal, or chips, and I don't buy cream cakes, I get fruit instead.'

Conveniently forgotten the caches of biscuits in her room, the feasts between meals at the office when Stephen was out, the forays into the pantry when everyone else was asleep for those last few cold potatoes or that piece of pie that someone had left.

'Right. Keep on trying, love. Ah, here's John, we're off, then. See you at ten-thirty.'

'Thanks Deidre.' Sophie grinned at John, a sweet-tempered, chunky young man with a face like a bull terrier's. 'Don't hurry home for me, I'll be quite happy sitting in front of your telly.'

Once back in her own flat, Sophie contemplated her evening. She would ring home from the pay telephone in the hall, then have her bath and then go up to the top flat. She had bought the biggest box of chocolates she could find on her way home, and to sit in solitary splendour in front of Deidre's television, watching an old smoochy movie and eating with no one to watch or criticise, struck her as the perfect way to celebrate. She took a handful of salted peanuts out of her bedside cabinet, in case it took her a while to get through to her home, and went down to the hall. She was lucky, the telephone only rang twice and then it was Devina who answered.

'Sophie, darling, how lovely to hear your voice.' She had written to her mother within two days of arriving in London, and phoned now and then, though she resolutely refused to give them an address or a telephone number through which they could contact her. Now, however, with the job and the flat behind her, there was no reason why they should not know where she worked and lived.

'Hello, Mum. I rang to tell you I've moved out of the hostel into a super new flat, and I've got a wonderful job. I'm personal secretary to a television producer. He's a marvellous person, and he thinks I'm pretty good, so I hope this will last for a while yet.' Her tone implied that if it ended, it would be because she had found something better.

'That sounds lovely – does it mean you might come home for a little holiday? We're longing to see you again, we miss you terribly.'

I bet you do, Sophie thought crudely, like you miss Atilla the Hun, or chicken-pox. But she did not say so aloud. It was kindness which made her mother lie, and it was kindness not to burst the bubble.

'Can't take on a new job and a new flat and then come running home,' Sophie said briskly. 'I need every penny I can lay hands on at the moment; I've borrowed a few quid off one of my friends to buy bits and pieces for the new place.' She had no intention of returning home until she was rich and successful – and glamorous, of course. Anyway, Lavvy's temporary infatuation with

45

Peter Brewer had proved far more permanent than anyone had supposed. Devina, who had never known why her third daughter had fled the party that dreadful night, frequently mentioned 'The nice boy who came to Lavvy's party – I don't suppose you noticed him, dear.' If she returned home, he would be produced for her admiration, and she didn't want to see him or any of them again until she was . . . transformed.

Just how the transformation was to be performed she had only the vaguest of notions, but an essential part of it would be a young man of her own, whom she could flourish even more triumphantly than Lavvy could flourish Peter Brewer.

'That *is* a pity, it seems so long since you were here.' Devina's voice was genuinely disappointed. 'Elsa did say she might come up to London and have a day with you, when the weather is warmer. If it wasn't such a long way . . . *What* did you say your new job was, darling?'

'I'm personal secretary to Stephen Bland, he's a television producer.' Sophie's voice rose alarmingly above the crackle caused by 200 miles of telephone wires. 'I get a marvellous salary, and I work with him, I take notes for him on the studio floor and I go on location with him when he's working on something that needs location shots. Did you get that, Mum?' It was essential that Devina not only got it, but passed it on. Success had eluded Sophie totally for the first nineteen years of her life; she had not even won the yearly bonny baby competition run by the local Women's Institute the way her sisters had, due to being short on hair at the critical time. She raised her voice to a positive scream. 'Mum! Did – you – get – that?'

'Yes, darling, you're personal secretary to a television producer.' Devina sounded satisfyingly amazed. 'I always knew you had it in you to do something wonderful – all my children are talented.'

At this point the last of Sophie's tens disappeared with a click, and they only had time for hasty goodbyes before the pips took over. Sophie replaced the receiver with a sigh of satisfaction, returned to the flat and ran her bath as hot as she could. Wonderful, to know that even now Devina was telling everyone that Sophie was as talented as the rest of her children – possibly she was sighing, saying how her daughter had changed, but that was on the credit side. A change might not be a transformation, but it was a start!

Once in the water she lay there for a long time, half-mesmerised by the heat and by the sweet, heady scent of Penny's luxury bath salts which had been lent for the occasion. Just to make everything perfect she had made herself a plateful of honey sandwiches which she ate slowly, getting maximum enjoyment out of her hedonistic pastime. She felt wonderful, like Cleopatra in her asses milk or whatever it was that the Egyptian beauty had bathed in.

A glance at her watch, however, balanced on the cork-topped bathroom stool, told her that she would have to get herself dried and dressed soon or she would miss the beginning of her film. She struggled upright and as she did so, felt a horrible, unfamiliar drag on her hips. She stopped moving. Strange! She tugged, then tried to turn on her side, and realised what had happened. She was wedged firmly in the narrow end of the old-fashioned bath. Panicking, she lashed wildly from side to side, sending waves of water out onto the floor. But she remained trapped.

After five minutes of futile and tearful tugging, she sat still to consider the situation. The bath had probably been put in when the house was first built, a hundred years ago. It was sturdy, battered, but it could not possibly have broken the way she had been imagining. No, what she felt was not the awful grip of a crack in the enamelled metal, but merely suction. And suction could be broken, if she just used her common sense. If she did not, if she continued to tug and panic, she would find herself being rescued by the girls, or by their men friends, and that would be a humiliation far worse than drowning!

In the end she was visited by inspiration. She tweaked the plug out with her big toe and, once she was high and dry, she found it quite easy to get to her knees and then to climb out of the tub.

She was shaking all over though, and she sat for a long while on the bathroom stool, wrapped in a towel, trembling and feeling sick. She had missed her smoochy film and her bottom was black and blue, but more than that, she knew she should see this as a warning. Today the bath, tomorrow the lift at work! She must make an effort to lose weight.

But I am trying, she kept telling herself. I do eat very much less. Deep inside, a nagging little voice mocked her. Liar, liar, it said, you aren't eating less, you're just eating more secretively. But she would not listen to the little voice. It was a liar itself, how could one eat secretively, for goodness sake? She would heed this warning, though, she would begin to eat less. She would start tomorrow.

She glanced again at her watch, Nine-thirty. In an hour Deidre and John would be back, she must get herself dressed and up to their flat or they would suspect that something was wrong. Half-way up the stairs, she remembered the box of chocolates. She hesitated. She should not eat them, of course, but on the other hand they were bought, someone had to eat them, and she *was* celebrating the job. She turned back. She would just have a few, the rest she would give to Deidre. Poor Deidre would appreciate a few chocolates, shut up by herself in the flat all day.

She was eating the second layer and telling herself that she should stop any minute when she realised that, if she did as she had planned, Deidre would know that she had not been entirely truthful over her dieting. With a sigh, she pulled the box onto her lap once more; fingers, already sticky, selected the next chocolate. This would be a final blow-out before she cut sweet things right out altogether. Tomorrow.

Just after Easter, Anya and Penny decided to have a party.

'Nothing too noisy or crowded, since we don't want anyone to grumble. Just some drinks and a buffet supper. We could ask a couple of extra girls and a couple of extra men. Anyone you'd like to ask, Sofa?'

'Well, what about John and Deidre?' Sophie said, but Penny snorted.

'No fear, it isn't a married sort of party! Why don't you ask Stephen?'

Sophie's mind registered that John and Deidre were married and that Stephen was not, the last with some surprise. They were getting on very well at work, but she still knew almost nothing about her boss. She bought red roses on his behalf sometimes, and tickets for shows or for the ballet, and had thought it quite likely that he was either married or, at least, engaged to some glamorous actress or other.

'I couldn't ask Stephen, we're not on those sort of terms,' Sophie said, having thought the matter over. 'Are you sure he isn't married, Penny? Or engaged, or something?'

'Sophie, you're without normal human curiosity! Didn't it

occur to you to ask anyone if he was married?'

Anya was smiling, but Sophie was a little stung, nevertheless. She smiled back rather stiffly.

'No, I never think about it. I just assumed that he was taking a wife or a girlfriend or something to the theatre and things, when he asked me to book tickets.'

'He probably takes a different girl to everything,' Penny said. 'He likes women, does Stephen. You can ask him without feeling bad about it, you know; he's quite different away from the centre.'

'No I couldn't. It wouldn't do at all. Look, shall I go out for the evening? I could, easily. For that matter, I could stay out all night if it's going to be a late party.'

Penny began to speak, possibly to say that it was a good idea, but Anya cut across her impatiently.

'Really, Sofa, anyone would think you still felt an outsider in this flat, and I'm sure I've done my best to make you feel at home. Of course you must stay. I'll invite some nice young man who'll suit you down to the ground.'

'Thanks, but no thanks,' Sophie said quickly, with hideous visions of Peter Brewer crowding into her mind. 'If that was what I wanted, I'd go out and look round for myself. Thanks.'

'Yes, but that's no guarantee that you'd find.' That was Penny, sharp as ever. 'Look, we'll make it three extra girls and four extra men, that'll make everyone comfortable.'

'Except me.' Sophie glared at Penny. 'If you think it's amusing to watch four men manoeuvring so that they don't get landed with the fat girl, I don't think much of your sense of humour. I said no and I meant no!'

Anya who usually took Sophie's side, scowled at her.

'Blimey, Sofa, what do you think we are, for God's sake? This is a civilised get-together, not a mass screwing session or a gang-bang! We aren't going to pair off for anything other than conversation.'

Abashed, Sophie mumbled an apology and promised to buy herself a new dress especially. It annoyed both Anya and Penny that, despite her large salary, she still bought very few clothes, apart from what they called 'sensible stuff' to wear to the office. This, as she had guessed it would, calmed them both down, and they were able to discuss the party without any more acrimony.

Next day, during her lunch hour, Sophie hurried along to C & A and bought a black lace dress with tiny thin shoulder straps and a plunging décolletage. Privately, she thought she looked like a sorrowing Spanish widow in it, but the girls thought otherwise.

'It'll do fine. Look, you must wear a bright scarf tucked into the belt and a pair of gaudy earrings,' Penny said. 'That way, you'll catch eyes without drawing attention to your size. Are you going to give us a hand with the catering?'

This was tongue in cheek, and Sophie laughed obligingly. She was the only one of the three who was capable of anything but the most basic cookery, and the other two were loud in their praise when she decided to try out a new recipe. Furthermore, she was the only one who actively enjoyed cooking, so it was only fair that it should be her main contribution to the party.

'I'll do it all, how's that? Then I'll be so busy listening to the praise of my cooking that I shan't waste time wondering whether I'm making a good impression.'

That was a dig at Penny, who had said in a moment of rage that Sophie spent far too much time wondering what other people thought of her instead of doing something about it. The truth in the remark had stung, but, as yet, Sophie had still not acted on what Penny had said. As yet, the diet was in the mind but not off the stomach. Being stuck in the bath had given her an awful fright, but it had not made her eat less. Instead, she shut herself in the bathroom, ran a bath and knelt in it, having inadequate sponge-downs. She excused herself on the grounds that it was only a temporary thing and that any day now she would lose the few extra pounds which had caused her humiliation.

The party, which had not given her much pleasure when they first talked about it, began to seem exciting as the day drew near. It was to be somewhat smaller than Penny had suggested, since now it would consist of the three girls themselves and Tara, a young actress who Penny knew vaguely. The men would be Freddy (Anya's) and Jeremy (Penny's), and two others, Garth and Phil.

'Garth isn't a name, it's an old cartoon' Sophie had objected, but Anya assured her that Garth was a nice young man, very respectable, who worked in a bank.

The evening, and the guests, arrived. Tara was not the total stranger that Sophie had expected; she remembered seeing her, vaguely, in crowd scenes in one of Stephen's productions. She was very pretty, very catty, and very loud; her asides were delivered in such ringing tones that Sophie was sure they could be heard down at the television centre, and since the first of those asides dealt with her own weight, she hated Tara accordingly.

'It's Stephen's new secretary, isn't it?' Tara had said to Penny, in a clearly audible hiss. 'Darling, I'm sure she's just as efficient as they say – there's so much of her that if she hadn't been efficient she'd have been extinct, like the good old brontosaurus.'

It had not helped that Penny had sniggered, nor that Garth, talking to Anya, had passed a hand across his mouth.

Furthermore, it soon became clear that the best laid plans were about to take a nose-dive. Garth, a friend of Anya's, had been intended, in the nicest possible way, as a spare man who could talk to Sophie so that she did not feel out of it. But Jeremy had supplied his friend Phil for Tara, and Tara and Phil loathed each other on sight.

'What *is* it, darling, a walking haystack?' Tara had hissed. And Phil, eyeing her dyed black hair with little beads threaded into it, her see-through muslin blouse which revealed her small, droopy breasts, and the stage make-up which adorned a fairly unprepossessing countenance, had been equally unenthusiastic.

Garth, on the other hand, thought that Tara was fascinating. He laughed at her catty remarks, asked questions about her 'work' as though she was a budding Glenda Jackson, and when at last they went into the kitchen to help themselves to the buffet supper, was so firmly attached to her side that they looked as though they had been glued at the elbow.

Sophie, ruefully piling her plate, prepared to be haystacked all evening. He could, she thought resentfully, have cut a small hole in the front of all that hair, so that she could see whether he was looking at her or not. He should have got on so *well* with Tara, too! He, like she, had beads sewn into his thatch at intervals, what looked like a well-gnawed finger on a leather thong round his neck, and though he had drawn the line at a see-through blouse and voluminous skirt and wore perfectly ordinary jeans and a grubby sweater, both he and Tara were clad in those awful leather sandals which are held on by laces knotted, like varicose veins, around the calves.

Although Anya had waxed so indignant at the thought that

they might pair off, that was exactly what happened. Sophie, hoping that Phil might prove to have an interesting mind, failed to find it beneath all that hair. Trying to ignore the increasingly amorous behaviour of everyone else in the room, she asked him some questions and found him to be a man of few words, and those that he did utter were in such a broad, if unidentifiable, accent that she was quite glad when he did not embark on any lengthy sentences.

'Did you try some of the prawn fondue? It was nice, wasn't it?' she essayed, as they sat down and began to eat.

'Yump,' came the reply from somewhere under the hair. Sophie, watching closely, saw that he had a large mouth and a lot of very sharp teeth and presently discerned a pointed, longish nose reminiscent of a weasel's. Occasionally small, beady eyes could be seen as he turned his head the better to tackle his supper. But since these glimpses merely served to confirm her impression of an animal at bay, it did little to ease the conversational desert they seemed to be wading through.

'Umm . . . do you know Jeremy very well? I suppose you work together. What do you do, Phil?'

The chewing stopped. She could tell because his heard ceased to waggle up and down.

'I don't. I'monnerdole.'

'Oh.' She was only saved from saying, brightly, 'That sounds interesting,' by the sudden realisation that he had said he was on the dole. Quickly, her heart thudding at her near faux pas, she said, 'Well, I expect something will turn up. Have you tried the barbecued chicken?'

The haystack swung from side to side; he had *not* tried the barbecued chicken. He appeared to be intimating that he would like to do so, however, so Sophie offered a piece of her own, holding it out rather fearfully towards where she imagined his mouth was.

He laughed. It was an odd laugh for one so large and hairy; it was squeaky, almost feminine.

'Iwon' bycher!'

'No, I'm sure you won't, but I'd better get you a piece of your own.'

She hurried into the kitchen and leaned against the sink, feeling quite dizzy with the effort of acting naturally. She was trying very hard not to notice Tara behaving in an uninhibited fashion on the floor with Garth, or Penny and Jeremy, who seemed, at first glance, to be inhabiting the same loose white shirt. Even the reliable Anya was lying on the cushions with Freddy's head pillowed on her crotch. How long can I stand it, Sophie agonised. Phil had to be the weirdest; she could not face the thought of an entire evening spent making conversation with someone who did not even speak English!

She returned to the living room and her companion, but soon it became obvious that some people had drunk a lot more than they should have done. Penny was squirming across Jeremy's lap, making movements which Sophie normally associated with randy dogs. She noticed and quickly moved so that her back was to the couple, which gave her a first-class view of Garth and Tanya; Tanya's skirt was rucked up and her blouse was gaping. Pained, Sophie turned round a bit more, and discovered that Anya and Freddy had actually left the room. Gracious!

After that, the pattern of the evening was set, though Sophie did not realise it. Another twenty minutes of monosyllables from Phil and strained, self-conscious small-talk from her, and Penny and Jeremy also got up and staggered out. Sophie knew that they were going to Penny's bedroom, and though she told herself she was not shocked, she did feel a little uneasy.

With reason, as it turned out. Five minutes later, Tara whined in her peculiarly resonant stage voice, 'Why haven't they gone, then? Bugger it, this is supposed to be a party! I'm not performing with them sitting there like the audience at the Lyric, Garth darling!'

Sophie glanced uneasily at the haystack. Suppose he realised that her bedroom was unoccupied, suppose he was waiting for her to suggest . . . She shuddered. If he had nurtured any such ideas, why hadn't he even attempted to hold her hand? It was extremely insulting, really, except that he was such a turd that even he must know it.

'Comeonen.'

He was standing up, holding out a hand to her. She noticed that in his other hand he was grasping the neck of a bottle of gin; he had been taking swigs out of it all evening.

Feeling every sort of fool, Sophie surged to her feet. She had better go with him, and then she would tell him that she had to go up to the top flat to see her friends, and would suggest, nicely of course, that it was about time he went home. He took her hand and pulled; he was surprisingly strong, really; she found herself close to him without any clear idea of how she had crossed the intervening space. Together, they went out into the hall.

'Whichizit?'

'If you mean my room, it's that one, but . . .'

He pushed open her bedroom door, towed her inside, and shut the door behind her. Rather to her surprise Sophie felt a tingle, only partly of apprehension, run up her spine. She decided, on the spur of the moment, to be a good sport. After all, everyone else had been carrying on this evening, and if it was expected of her . . .

He pushed her onto the bed and grabbed her. His kiss was forceful and his mouth was wet, dribbly almost. What was more, his beard was prickly and uncomfortable and he definitely smelt. Of gin, yes, but of something else, something very much nastier. A strong, male, ammoniacal whiff which made her eyes water. He was kissing her again, pushing his tongue between her lips, *tasting* her in a very odd fashion which, despite her murmur of protest, was exciting in a horrible sort of way. Then he pulled and pushed her, as if she was made of some sort of malleable dough, until she was resting against the pillows, and his hand slid across the top of her dress, hesitated, then pushed inside.

She stiffened, her breathing quickening, for his hand, with its long, strong fingers, had the authority that his mouth lacked. He lifted her breast from the cup of her bra, not without difficulty, for her breasts were large and the dress fitted snugly across them- and began to squeeze and caress her nipple.

Somehow, she did not know how, he managed to free both her breasts from her dress. In the dim moonlight coming through the window he gazed at them, or she supposed he did. He certainly sat very still for a moment, with his head slightly bent, as if he was gazing at them. Then he supported one of them up to his mouth.

It was then that she knew what it was that made Penny move her body against Jeremy's, why Anya and Freddy had left the party to be alone. She groaned his name, moving so that he might reach her more easily, and her hands went to his hair, sliding down the sides of his face, feeling the jawbone beneath the beard, the movements of his mouth as he began to suck.

When he pushed her away, she thought that it must be so that they could move on to some other phase of love-making. She lay, bare-breasted, looking up at him, consenting. But he was turning away, shuffling towards the door.

'Gorrergo,' he mumbled. 'Fanks.'

'Oh, but Phil . . .'

The closing door shut off her words, killed the plea in her throat. She rolled onto her stomach, the desire which he had roused in her still strong, so that she could not believe it was not the same for him, could not believe he would not, presently, come back. Had he gone to have a pee, perhaps? Or for something else to eat?

He had not. She heard the outer door of the flat close, heard his footsteps fumbling downstairs. She felt as though he had slapped her in the face – God, but she had been shameless, she had been prepared to let him do what he would, and for why? Lust? Had her big, overblown body lusted for a man without her even knowing it? She shuddered and wished she could blame the drinks she had drunk, but she knew it was not that.

Presently, she rolled off the bed and turned on her radio. She felt awful, degraded not by Phil the haystack, but by herself. The disc jockey had just put on one of her favourite records, perhaps she would feel better when she had heard it. She sat on the edge of the bed, willing herself to concentrate on Simon and Garfunkel and the sweet, schmaltzy music. She loved this one, she knew it well, it had comforted her often as she worked around the flat.

And then, suddenly, she was really listening to it, as though she had never heard it before, and the unconsidered words were being sung to her, were sharp as a knife, twisting in her bowels:

> *Asking only workman's wages*
> *I come looking for a job*
> *But I get no offers,*
> *Just a come-on from the whores*
> *On Seventh Avenue.*
> *I do declare,*
> *There were times when I was so lonesome*
> *I took some comfort there.*

By the time it ended she was in a crumpled heap on the floor, sobbing, biting the back of her hand, almost out of her mind with the pain of it. No comfort! A man could find comfort of a sort with a whore and she had tried to find comfort with Phil, for that was all it would have been, the comfort of acceptance. But all she had known was the bitter taste of rejection, for Phil had not wanted her. What was it Tara had called her? A brontosaurus, someone so huge that they should be extinct. Tears, hot and blinding, channelled down her cheeks. She ached with misery; it was a physical pain so acute that she hugged herself, cradling her body in her arms, trying to give herself the comfort that Phil had refused her.

She could not have said how long she crouched there, nor how dark were the thoughts that festered in her mind. She knew that she had reached a watershed in her life, that after tonight nothing could ever hurt her quite so much again. She knew, too, that there had been a moment when there had seemed to be only one course open to her. A quotation, half-remembered from school, had floated in the shadows of her mind: *Finish, good lady, the bright day is done, and we are for the dark*. Finish, good lady.

She knew, then, that she could not go on like this, getting worse and worse, caring less and less. She might not end it now, but one day, when she had lost even more pride, when she had sunk lower, she would choose the dark.

She sat up, tear-blubbered, and made a vow. This must *never* happen again. She was young and healthy, she had will-power and determination. It was up to her to see that the life that had been given to her was not wasted, thrown away, because if she did not care, no one else would.

Chapter Four

At first, no one even noticed that Sophie was dieting, let alone losing weight. This was largely due to her own behaviour in the past, she knew, but being only human she was disappointed in Anya and Penny. Surely they should notice that she was eating very much less? After all, they frequently ate together.

But Anya and Penny, had they been asked about Sophie's appetite, would merely have said that Sophie never did eat much, not at meal-times. It was in between meals, when no one was watching, that Sophie stoked up. So now when she eschewed potatoes, when she ignored bread and butter or cake, when she carefully disinterred the meat from a steak and kidney pie so that she could leave the soggy, delicious pastry on the side of her plate, neither Anya nor Penny took it seriously. Made cynical by previous experience, they assumed that Sophie would hide the pastry and polish it off later, gobble bread and butter behind the pantry door and carry slice after slice of cake off to her own room.

In fact, her own aptitude at taking food from under the very noses of her flatmates now led them to believe that she had grown even more expert at the art, and when you weighed as much as Sophie did, you had to lose an awful lot of poundage before anyone would easily notice.

And then, when Sophie was still soldiering on alone, losing steadily but unnoticed, Anya and Penny had a first-class row.

Oddly enough it started, as had Sophie's diet, after a party, but this was not a quiet little get-together but a very large affair indeed, one of the parties which Anya stigmatised as a 'debby do' and usually avoided like the plague, though Penny adored them.

On this particular occasion, however, Anya's boss, Derek Eade, had been engaged on a programme which dealt with debutantes at play, so he wangled himself and a couple of cameramen invitations and more or less insisted that Anya went along as well. And so she actually witnessed Penny's behaviour, which otherwise might have remained a dark secret from her friends.

'Though she was bloody lucky I did go, and that I managed to persuade Derek to destroy the film,' she said furiously to Sophie, afterwards. 'But does she thank me? Not her! Just says tha she had no idea they'd be filming or she'd never have touched the champagne. It was due to that, of course. She's got no head for quantities of the stuff, I've told her so a thousand times, but she's wilful and stupid and . . .'

'What did she *do*?' Sophie begged, burning with curiosity. Penny was so complacent as a rule that it was hard to imagine her regretting any action, but clearly the affair had shaken her. She voiced these feelings aloud to Anya as they worked companionably on a salad and cheese omelettes for the evening meal but Anya, slicing cucumber, shook her head.

'You think it shook Penny? No, it wasn't what she did that shook her, it was her narrow escape from becoming the star of a blue movie. If you knew how I had to beg Derek to destroy the footage . . . well, I told him I'd leave right then and there if he didn't burn it. He did it because it's very hard to find production assistants like me, so I told Pen it was all right. But I admit I bet every senior exec had a private viewing first, even if they left poor Gio out.'

'What the devil did she do?' Sophie wailed, her voice rising to a squeak. 'It isn't fair to hint and hint – just tell me what she did, for God's sake!'

'I can't, she'd kill me if I told anyone.' Anya arranged her sliced cucumber artistically across the lettuce, viewed her work with her head tilted to one side and then began to slice tomatoes. 'Be a dear and sling some spring onions into the sink, Sofa. We're neither of us going out this evening so we might as well reek a bit.'

A lifetime of being left out had never inured Sophie to the experience. She said nothing, however, but proceeded with the omelette making, only glancing hopefully at Anya as she moved about the kitchen. Penny, she knew, had been edgy and bad-tempered ever since the party, and she quite understood Anya's desire to keep out of trouble, but on the other hand, she,

Sophie, would never show by word or look that she knew. Presently, as she turned the first omelette out of the pan onto its plate, she ventured to remark that since five hundred guests, two cameramen and Derek Eade were all privy to Penny's exploit, it could scarcely be termed a secret. Anya sighed, laughed, and then agreed.

'You're right, and it wasn't so terrible, I suppose. What annoyed me was the stupidity of it. So typical of that crowd and Penny says she despises them, yet . . .' The second omelette was laid carefully on its plate and Anya sat down, pulled her plate towards her, dished out salad and then pushed the bowl over to Sophie. 'Hell, I shall tell you – why not? It all happened because Penny got drunk, as you may have gathered.'

Sophie, who had been woken by the din on the stairs as two young men manhandled Penny up them, and who had gone out wrapped in her old school mac (now just about buttoning across the front) in time to see Penny vomit on the stairs, the landing, and all over the bathroom, agreed, faintly, that she had gathered as much.

'Yes. Well, you see Penny got a bit despondent because the guy she was with went off, or so she says. I think he got talking with some other fellows and just stopped paying enough attention to Penny, and if there's one thing that girl craves it's attention. So she decides to do a strip. Right in the middle of that huge ballroom, with everyone staring, she starts ripping her clothes off. Actually, it was the black lace thing, and she tore it, and I was going to wear it next,' Anya added rather sorrowfully. She and Penny frequently went shares on their more exotically priced dresses. 'She said afterwards that she was hot,' she added fairly, 'but I don't think it was that, I think it was attention seeking. You know what Penny's like, she does rather want all the men to look at her.'

Sophie, who had had no idea that Penny was like that, murmured agreement. She was so keen to get to the crux of the matter and find out just what it was that Penny had done that she would have murmured agreement to almost anything. To her, stripping in the middle of a dance floor seemed bad enough for anyone, but it was clear there was more to come.

'And . . .? Did someone stop her taking her . . . your . . . the dress off?'

'No, but she got entangled and some young men came forward and took her off. One of them pulled her skirt down and her top up, if you understand me, until she was respectable, and the oldest of them said they'd sober her up in the supper room. I was a fool because I didn't follow her, I stayed with Derek, expecting her to appear sobered up, but when she didn't, I went into the supper room. And Derek followed me, I suppose.'

'And . . .?' Sophie said again, trying not to sound too eager. 'What then?'

'There was quite a crowd, almost all men, and they were gathered round Penny, who was naked as the day she was born, drenched to the skin – it was champagne – and giggling and talking far too loudly. She had a huge bowl of whipped cream and she'd got one of those gun things, like an icing gun, from somewhere, and she was . . . well, decorating herself with it. She'd put a couple of thick whorls of cream round each nipple, another on her belly-button, and she'd made a sort of bikini on the rest of her. When we came in she was making bracelets or bangles of cream up her forearms and then she started on her ankles, only one of the fellows – he was drunk if you like – kept throwing glasses of champers at her and washing off her cream. She was getting angry – her language was pretty choice, I can tell you. And then, whilst I was trying to fight my way through to her – the men wouldn't budge, the buggers – she finished herself off with a crown on top of her head and invited them, if you please, to lick her clean! She said, "You all like champers, and you all like Penny, this way you can have both at once." '

'Did they?' Sophie's voice was awed. 'How dreadful!'

'Yes, a mixture of cream, champagne and sweat,' Anya said, wrinkling her nose. 'There was a concerted rush and Penny all but disappeared in a sea of debs' delights, baying like hounds and shouting hunting calls and emerging from the scrimmage with cream all over their faces. And the cameramen – you couldn't blame them – absolutely enthralled and recording every soggy second on film.'

'Poor Penny, she must have been stoned out of her mind,' Sophie said. She remembered that dreadful evening when she had left home and burned for Penny. 'No wonder she's been bad-tempered, she must be so humiliated!'

60

Anya snorted. 'Don't waste your sympathy, Penny was not at *all* displeased with herself; she rather enjoyed it in a drunken, devil-may-care sort of way. The only part she regrets was being filmed, because she could lose her job or her parents might make things difficult for her. I wouldn't be surprised to learn that she does something similar every time she goes debbing.'

'You can't be serious! No one would do something like that more than once! The embarrassment . . .'

'Do get it into your thick head, Sofa, that Penny wasn't embarrassed or humiliated. She's got a beautiful body which she loves showing off. We quarrelled because I told her that it was only numbers which stopped her from being raped and she sneered at me.'

'Then you think it was pretty bad, for all you tell it so coolly,' Sophie said triumphantly, reaching for more salad. 'I try terribly hard not to be narrow-minded, but you wouldn't do anything like that, would you?'

'Not me, I've got more self-respect and I'm not an exhibitionist,' Anya agreed readily. 'If Penny wants to spread it around once in a while I'm not silly enough to think I can stop her, but to put herself at risk like that – and then to turn round and blame me!'

'She didn't!'

'She did. She said I should have destroyed the film myself, or smashed the cameras when I saw they were filming. She can be rather unreasonable,' Anya said with considerable understatement. 'And then, when I told her the film had been destroyed, she rang Derek up and threatened him with a lawsuit if he reported the incident. Threatening him, when he'd held her in the palm of his hand and let her go, because I begged and pleaded with him! When he told me he was livid, of course. I could see he blamed me for getting him to destroy it, because with the film still in his possession she would never have dared to speak to him as she did.'

'You know, I think Penny probably really was ashamed of herself and embarrassed,' Sophie said rather shyly. 'Some people try to hide their feelings by becoming aggressive, I believe. If she really didn't care at all then there would be no reason for her to keep snapping at you and me.'

Anya finished her food, pushed back her chair, and smiled at Sophie.

'You can be sweet sometimes, Sofa – when I think of the way Penny treats you it's kind of you to defend her. What's more, you could be right. The more in the wrong she is, the more Penny swears she's right.' She pushed back her chair and walked across to the kitchen window. 'It's a marvellous evening, shall we take some fruit and a flask of coffee and sit in the square garden for a bit? It will be cooler down there than up here.'

It had been a hot day and was warm still, so Sophie agreed readily. They put the flask and some apples and oranges in a carrier bag and set off. Despite the fact that it was evening the June sun still shone, and they unlocked the gate and went into the garden, sure of privacy since few of the occupants of Gloucester Gardens bothered with the square. Only cross-grained old Miss Marshall from No. 17 used it, and she was unlikely to be there at this time of day.

The girls had always made good use of the place, so now Sophie and Anya went through the thick and concealing shrubbery and sat down on the small, circular lawn, white with daisies, in the full sun. There was shade, afforded by a laburnum tree which still dripped its gold over a fair-sized stretch of grass, but for now they were content with the warmth of the sun.

'This is nice,' Anya said. She lay back, crushing a thousand daisies, and closed her eyes. 'I'm a country girl at heart, I believe.'

'You can hardly hear the traffic,' Sophie said contentedly. She lay back too, crushing two thousand daisies. 'You can forget you're in London on an evening like this.'

'True.' Anya slitted a dark eye and looked across at Sophie. 'That reminds me, rumour has it that you've ventured down onto the studio floor at last. What do you think of it?'

'I love it; everyone's very kind,' Sophie said. In fact she was crediting actors, actresses, cameramen and production staff with a charity which they did not possess, since most of them were far too self-absorbed to be kind or unkind to a mere secretary. But Sophie was quiet, good at her job and neither tried to monopolise Stephen nor to give her own opinions. In short,

62

most of the studio staff scarcely noticed her. Even her size, after a first startled stare, became a matter of course. Stephen's fat secretary was just Stephen's secretary, and if she was considered at all it was because she had managed to keep her boss better-tempered than any of her predecessors had done.

'Kind, eh?' Anya chuckled. 'What about Stephen? Is he kind?'

Sophie was silent for a moment, thinking. No, Stephen was not kind, he was much more than that, and he did not treat her in any way as the rest of the studio staff did. To him, she was a valued employee; even, at times, a close friend. But at the moment he was in the grip of an obsession, and that made a difference. He was wild about Sumatra Jones and she was in his latest film and, since she would have seen any tantrums he cared to throw – not that he throws tantrums in front of me, Sophie reminded herself, but she had heard of his moods – he had to be on his best behaviour. Though Sumatra was not above throwing the odd tantrum herself from time to time, Sophie knew instinctively that she would not have been pleased had Stephen done the same.

Ever since the night of the party, when Phil the haystack had treated her so strangely, Sophie's interest in Stephen's love life had been slightly livelier. Taking notice, now, when she bought roses, booked theatre seats and arranged anonymous weekends at the coast, she realised the truth of Penny's remark that Stephen liked women. She thought he also liked change, since he had had three different girlfriends since March, with Sumatra as the latest.

Sumatra was different, though. She was all woman, exotically blooming, fascinating all males whether on the set, in the offices or simply sitting on a tube train. Sophie had once sat near her when Sumatra was homeward bound after a day at the studio, and she had watched with awe as male head after male head moved so that they could watch her, either in the flesh or through the window-pane reflection. Sumatra was beautiful, all right, but she was a mass of contraditions, with her lilting South Wales accent and her coffee-coloured skin, for Sumatra was the outcome of a brief union between a black seaman and a girl from the valleys who had spent a short time working in Cardiff, down by the docks. She had a deep, sexy voice, yet she could giggle up high, like a girl in her teens, or swear with a vocabulary apparently culled straight from the father she had never met. She could dance half the night – and then fall asleep in the unlikeliest places, like the canteen, or sitting on a hard little chair in the studio, waiting to be cued.

'Well, go on, dreamy; tell me what Stephen's like to you.'

Anya's voice was indulgent, not sharp, as Penny's would have been. Sophie sat up on one elbow, the better to explain.

'He's like a friend, sometimes. He really does appreciate my work, which is what I'm there for, and he appreciates the way I handle his social life, too. He thanks me when I do little things for him, he tells me if a show was good or a meal was nice. It was silly, perhaps, to say that the studio staff are kind, perhaps they just think I'm part of the furniture, but Stephen's much more. I like him very much and I think he likes me.'

'That's great; how I feel about Derek, I suppose. And Sumatra? What do you think of her? And she of you, come to that.'

'I think she's gorgeous and a darling, but she doesn't think about me at all. Why should she? I'm only Stephen's secretary.'

'Perhaps. I'm glad you're happy in your work – you *are* happy, aren't you?'

Again, Sophie took her time to answer, and when she did so, it was with quiet conviction.

'Yes. I think I'm happier than I've ever been before in my whole life. I feel I'm achieving something, that I'm someone, even if it's only Stephen's secretary.'

A week after their conversation in the square gardens, Stephen went to pass Sophie, who was stretching up to replace an old file on the very top shelf where the 'dead' files were kept. As he passed her he put his hands, very lightly, on her waist, and squeezed. Sophie squeaked and nearly dropped her file, which made him laugh. He continued on his way to the door which led into his own room and then, in the doorway, paused and looked back. He was smiling.

'Well done, Sophie – that skirt will have to be taken in a good two inches. You're trying hard, aren't you? And it's working.'

Overcome to find that someone had noticed at last, Sophie felt near tears, but she smiled as brightly as she could, knowing that she was pink-cheeked with the pleasure of it but not minding that Stephen should see her emotion.

'Yes, it's working. I've lost very nearly three stone.'

He whistled, his eyes travelling reflectively over her.

'That's marvellous. I wondered whether taking you into the studio would work and it obviously has. Keep it up.'

It would have been churlish to say that the studio had nothing whatsoever to do with her diet, and anyway, what did it matter? All that mattered was the fact that she was dieting, and that it really was working. For the first time ever she was consistently eating less and getting real pleasure from watching the result on the bathroom scales.

She realised, as she began to walk home that night, that Stephen's remark had made her day, her week, possibly even her year. For anyone to have noticed would have been marvellous, but for it to be Stephen, her boss, a man who had Sumatra Jones to look at, well, that was more than marvellous, it was epoch-making. She wondred if now Anya and Penny would also see the difference, but even if they did not she could not say anything to them. She could not even intimate that she was dieting because she had said it so often before, had cried wolf all over the place, only to be forced onto the defensive when it became painfully obvious that though she might claim to be on a diet, though she might appear to be on a diet, her weight continued to increase.

She wondered whether she could just hint at the change by sitting at the kitchen table tonight and altering her skirt, or by talking about buying something new, but acknowledged to herself that she would not do so. This time it was for real, and when something is for real then you can afford to wait, patiently, for someone to shout, 'You're thinner!' Well, perhaps not patiently, but at any rate you can wait.

In the event the wait was not destined to be a long one. That very evening, as the three girls washed up, wiped and cleared away after their evening meal, Anya glanced at Sophie, standing at the sink, began to speak, and then came to attention, very much as a setter does when confronted by a passing pheasant.

'Sophie, you've lost weight. From the back I can see a waist!'

Though not the most complimentary way of putting it, Sophie still felt a surge of gratification rush through her. Two people had now commented.

'I thought you'd never notice. I've been starving for a month and this is the first time you've said a word. Stephen remarked on it this morning, too.'

'He did? In the midst of his infatuation for Sumatra? Crikey! What did he say?'

Sophie repeated Stephen's words, her voice shaking a little from sheer pleasure. She felt like Miss World.

'How much have you lost, Sofa? I *can* see it, now that Anya's drawn my attention.'

That was Penny, as usual the first with the sixty-four thousand dollar question. Sophie told her that she had lost nearly three stone and waited.

'Three stone? What do you weigh now, then?'

Silence. Sophie had no intention of telling anyone, ever, what she weighed.

'You don't want to tell?' Penny shrugged. 'Okay, be like that. What made you start? If you've been at it for a month it must have been Stephen taking you down to the studios with him, I suppose.' She grinned. 'All those glamorous skinnies, enough to give anyone an inferiority feeling.'

Sophie was not sure even now, exactly what had triggered off her change of heart. The hideous spectre of her own girth increasing until she had no one, nothing, until she would kill herself rather than continue to live, was not one which she ever wanted to contemplate. Had it been that? Or had it been the fact that even the despised haystack had not been able to face more than a brief fumble? She glanced at Anya, wishing she could confide in her, knowing she could not.

'What started me off? I'm not sure, I think I just decided I'd have a go. It's quite easy at work now, because as you say I'm with Stephen much more and I can't keep eating when I'm with him. But it's hard when I come home from work and have to pass the shops. And here, in the evenings, if I'm by myself it can be a struggle. But I think the strangest thing is that I'm getting quite proud of myself, whereas before I just used to make excuses when I couldn't keep it up, and feel sorry for myself.'

'Just imagine what your parents will say,' Anya remarked, tidying the kitchen floor with the brush and a cracked and elderly dustpan. 'Poor Soph, struggling away and neither of us noticing. I bet it's been hard work sometimes, hasn't it?'

'Yes. It's been hell.'

Sophie thought of the moments of dark despair when she had starved and still the wretched scales showed only the most miniscule loss. Awful when you were really trying to cut down and yet for some reason – the time of the month, the fact that the weather was hot and so you drank a lot – those pounds would not come off the way you felt they should. Yet could anything be as bad as the week when you regressed, not in a big, delicious, worth-it sort of way, but in lots of tiny ways which you could not help feeling should not count? It was so unfair when you stuck to the diet at meal-times and did without chips, baked beans, fatty meat and stodgy puddings and merely cheated a bit by having a bag of salted peanuts instead of a salad, a healthy round of bread and cheese instead of plain yoghurt and an apple, and a teeny weeny half pound bar of fruit and nut instead of a grudging half-grapefruit. Then the mean, spiteful scales refused to show even the tiniest loss, shamed you by showing exactly the same weight as that of a week earlier, refusing to take notice of the fact that you were wearing your thinnest skirt, no knickers and a blouse which, due to its lack of buttons, simply had to weigh several ounces less than a more conventional garment.

But could anyone else possibly understand? Sophie eyed Anya's small bones, Penny's delectable slimness, and knew that though they might sympathise they could never really know the pains and torments that she, Sophie, had undergone to lose that weight. The times she had gone to bed, her stomach playing a Lament for Lost Lunches loud enough to keep her awake, and when she had slept at last, had dreamed of food as a starving castaway dreams, to wake and weep for its absence, to sit up, drink water until she felt bloated, and to sleep again, only to dream, as before, of crisp Yorkshire pudding floating in gravy and flanked by slices of beef pink as English roses; of treacle pudding hot from the oven and garlanded with melting double cream; of fruit cake, heavy with raisins, fragrant with rum and oozing butter. In such moments she knew that, given a choice between having Michael Caine, Dennis Waterman and Clint Eastwood in her bed or her will with that fruit cake, there would be no choice. The cake would win, hands down.

But there was no way of explaining to someone slim, someone

who had never known what it meant to yearn for food with all your soul, how very hard it was.

Penny finished her share of the work and left the kitchen, but Anya continued to help Sophie to clear the dishes and clean down the surfaces. The flat could sometimes look as if a bomb had hit it, but on a Friday – and this was a Friday – the place was always immaculate because their landlady, Mrs Fletcher, came up for the rent and for a little chat, and her needle-like eyes were everywhere. Penny's parents would get a report, and the girls were determined that it should be a good one, since none of them could have afforded the flat without the parental help given by the Wintle-Smys.

'And will you keep it up, Soph? Are you really hell-bent on getting thin – or thinner, I should say?'

Sophie allowed, for one mouthwatering moment, a picture to form in her mind. A huge honey sandwich, large enough to have kept a million bees busy for a year, swam dreamily across her inner vision, and beside it was an enormous mug of drinking chocolate, made with milk. And a slab of fudge for afters.

But another picture followed that one – in its way, a better, more satisfying picture. A girl was crossing the street, heading for a well-remembered house in Glydon Grove. As she put her hand on the gate the front door opened and the family came out – father, Devina and the girls. They all stared as the stranger entered the garden. She was so slim, so elegant! Taller than Sophie, her hair a richer and more glorious chestnut, her eyes a deeper shade, her mouth pouting with promise, yet undoubtedly it was Sophie. Sophie transformed, Sophie desirable, a Sophie, in fact, so beautiful that even before she recognises her, Lavinia's fingers have tightened possessively on Peter Brewer's arm. And Peter, eyes starting from his head in amazement, does not even remember her – only wants, desperately, to hold her in his arms.

'Sofa, don't dream! Are you hell-bent on getting thinner?'

Sophie jumped and dragged her mind from the dream, which was beginning to seem almost possible, back to the present.

'Thinner? Oh, yes, Anya. I wouldn't go through all that agony just to give up and get fat again. Not that I'm slim yet – but I shall be.'

Anya wiped down the draining board, dusted her hands together, and turned to Sophie, giving her the benefit of her sweet, three-cornered smile.

'I believe you, I really do. And from now on, I'll give you all the encouragement and help that I can. But Soph, I'd love to know what started you off.'

Sophie returned the smile. She knew she could not tell. Not anyone. Not ever.

Sophie had wondered whether it might be harder to continue to diet once Anya and Penny knew, but to her delight it became easier. To take a large helping of salad and to eat in company with people who were as thrilled by her weight loss as she was made the salad seem all the sweeter. Low calorie drinks no longer tasted quite as foul as they had done at first, when she knew that Anya and Penny hated them too and admired her persistence in drinking them. What was even better, Stephen's enthusiasm as her figure began to emerge from its cocoon of fat was heady stuff to someone who had never heard a word of praise before.

Even at the office things changed. People who had never bothered with her at all made a point of congratulating her and asked her how she had done it. Actresses talked health food and skin care to her when they weren't on the set, and Sumatra the beautiful actually came in to Sophie's room one afternoon, perched on her desk, and discussed weight.

'Too fat I am myself, girl,' she said ruefully, slapping one smooth, silk-clad hip. 'But there's difficult it is to lose when you're working hard and liking your food.'

'I don't think you're too fat,' Sophie said timidly. 'If I had a figure like yours . . .' A sigh finished the sentence for her.

Sumatra laughed and slapped her hip again.

'No, overweight it is; but the men like it. Just get cuddly, girl, and they'll be round you like bees round a honeypot. Met our Rex yet, have you?'

Sophie had met Rex and rather resented the fact that Sumatra was obviously attracted by him. Rex was a tall, drawling American actor with a charm to which, it seemed, Sophie was immune. Not so Sumatra. She liked him, he made her laugh, and Sophie had heard more than one technician remarking that Stephen would not take kindly to being two-timed, by which she deduced that Sumatra was seeing Rex outside the studio. If it had not been for Stephen, Sophie would have cheered Sumatra on, but as it was she resented Rex. Stephen was so good to her, so pleased about her weight loss, so proud of it, even, yet Sumatra seemed perfectly willing to cause him pain.

Now she tried not to let her feelings show, though her voice cooled a trifle.

'Rex? Yes, I've met him. He seems quite nice.'

Sumatra laughed. 'He's more than nice, love, he's a dish! But the point is, see, he said on the set the other day, "Where's that pretty secretary-bird of Stephen's? She'll run over to make-up and tell them to send over some No. 7." What do you think of *that*, eh?'

'He couldn't have meant me, he must have mant Mary, Stephen's P.A.,' Sophie protested. 'But one day, Sumatra, if only I can keep it up, someone will say something like that about me and mean it!'

'Anya's father's a bishop, but you'd like him. You'll meet him one day, I expect.'

Penny was getting ready to go out for the evening and, rather to Sophie's surprise, had invited the younger girl to see her trying out some new make-up. Sophie had entered the hitherto forbidden territory of Penny's room to find it unexpectedly tidy, though the array of bottles, jars and pots on the dressing table might have led one to expect the occupant to be a raddled old woman instead of a particularly pretty girl.

'A bishop? I didn't know that, but I'd like to meet him. Does he come up to London much?'

'No, but one of these days Anya will drag you down to Canterbury to meet him, and her mother, of course.'

Penny smeared an eyelid carefully with gold and then surveyed herself in the glass with a degree of critical attention which Sophie found almost funny. If I looked like Penny, she caught herself thinking, I'd be quite content with my dear little face! But then, if looking like Penny meant being like Penny, she would prefer to stick to Sophie Markham.

The thought was so strange, so unexpected, that she found

70

she was just standing there, savouring it. She would rather be Sophie Markham than Penny Wintle-Smy, for all her beauty and glamour and her string of boyfriends. The latest was one of those deb's delights that Anya thought so pathetic. His name was Aubrey and he was a self-satisfied young man who seemed to have outgrown his strength at some early stage, so that now he reminded Sophie of a weed which had been treated with Evergreen and raced remorselessly upwards, getting thinner and weedier as it went, until it simply keeled over sideways and died, leaving your lawn the prettier for its loss. However, despite this disadvantage and a nose the size and shape of a Viking longship, he remained a good catch, being fabulously rich and the son of a peer of the realm.

'Well? You haven't said anything about meeting Anya's parents. I expected you to say, "Oh, I couldn't possibly, they wouldn't want to meet *me*",' Penny said rather spitefully. 'Don't say you're getting some opinion of yourself at last!'

'If Anya felt she'd like me to meet her parents I'd go like a shot,' Sophie said equably. 'She's been a good friend to me and I'd like to see her home.'

Penny sniffed.

'I've seen it. It isn't much to write home about. They aren't terribly well-off, but they act as if they were. The family goes back yonks, if that matters to you; they either came over with William the Conqueror or were in the welcoming party, I'm not sure which. I think that's why Anya gets on so well with all sorts of people- she's got generations of gracious hostesses in her blood.'

'You make her sound like a Bride of Dracula.' Sophie picked up Penny's palette of eye colours and touched the pale blue with a wistful finger. 'Can I try some of this?'

'Why? Going out? Got a feller at last?'

If only Penny did not always sound so sharp, Sophie thought, hastily replacing the palette on the dressing table.

'No. It doesn't matter.'

'I didn't mean you couldn't. It was only a simple question, for Christ's sake.' Penny was putting a copper-coloured lipstick on her mouth and the words came out less aggessively for that reason, perhaps. The lipstick should have looked horrible, but in fact it looked marvellous. Lucky Penny. 'Go ahead, try it.'

71

'Er . . . thanks.' Sophie, glancing cautiously at the back of Penny's smooth, blonde head, picked up the palette and rubbed a little of the pale blue shadow on her eyelids. It looked nicer than she had expected it to look, yet not quite right, somehow. She rubbed it off again and slid the palette back onto the dressing table.

'Thanks, Penny. One of these days I'm going to get some decent make-up of my own.' She turned to leave the room, but was stopped in her tracks by Penny's voice.

'Sofa! What do you weigh now?'

Sophie moved back to stand behind Penny, watching her face through the mirror. What was up now?

'A lot less than I did. Why?'

'Because you're beginning to look quite presentable, quite shapely. From the back you look like someone else.'

'Thanks very much,' Sophie said resignedly. 'With friends like you . . .'

'Was that rude?' Penny sounded uncharacteristically surprised. 'I'm sorry, I only meant I can see you're slimmer. You'll be needing new clothes soon.'

'I'm saving.' Sophie said briefly. Not for worlds would she have admitted to Penny how she haunted the shops now in her lunch hour, gazing at clothes which she might actually be able to wear one day if she continued to lose weight. Jeans, tight sweaters, pencil skirts, even bathing costumes and tennis clothes had an allure impossible to describe to someone like Penny, who had never known what it was like not to look marvellously fashionable.

'Right. When you're thin enough and rich enough I'll come with you to choose, if you like. I know Anya will, but she isn't as clever with clothes as me, you know. I'll know exactly what will suit you best.'

Sophie murmured her thanks and an excuse about letters to write and left the room. She was shrewd enough to know why Penny was suddenly being almost friendly; Penny felt left out. Anya and she had been friends for years, from childhood almost, but lately Anya had been less willing to accept Penny's many faults and selfishnesses. In the early months of Sophie's flat-sharing, Anya had leaned towards Penny all the time, it had always been two against one even though Anya occasionally

72

sympathised with Sophie, but now Anya was balanced between the other two, sometimes leaning one way, sometimes the other. And ever since the champagne and cream episode, she had leaned to Sophie more often than she had leaned to Penny. It was probably because she felt she had been unfairly criticised on that occasion, but even so it was wonderful to Sophie that someone as beautiful and intelligent as Anya could enjoy her company.

Sophie had never had a real friend of her own, those fleeting friendships she had formed at school being the result of finding someone as unlovable and friendless as she herself. She had 'borrowed' friends from her sisters, but it had never been the same, she had guessed that. And now she knew that Penny was jealous of her, envied her Anya's companionship, and she knew, too, that she would do anything to keep Anya's friendship. She would even agree to Penny's accompanying them on their clothes shopping trip when it happened, though she dreaded Penny's satirical remarks and cringed already at the thought of the barrage of criticism which would greet her timid approval of any particular garment.

Later, writing letters at the window table and thinking about clothes, it struck her that she must be one of the few women in London who would be dressing herself *for* herself and not for some man. She would be thinking, not what will please him, but what will please me? She wondered, briefly, what it must be like, to want to please a man, to choose tight jeans because he admired them, or mini skirts because he liked to see her legs.

Later still, when she was getting ready for bed, she comforted herself with the thought that, though she would not be choosing dresses for a boyfriend, she would most certainly choose some of her clothes with a view to pleasing Stephen. He had been so marvellous about her weight loss, so encouraging about her diet, so boastful to others about Sophie's will-power, that she wanted to please him almost as much as she wanted to please herself.

She went to sleep on that thought.

'Where's Sumatra?'

They were doing stills for the film and Sumatra, who had been told when to arrive on the set with the rest of the cast, had not yet put in an appearance. Sophie glanced rather apprehensively at Stephen when he asked his question. Had he noticed how

73

Sumatra's interest in the film had waned as it progressed? And did he realise that her sudden lack of dedication was due, not to boredom with the part, but to the tug of a new attraction? She was in full cry now, after Rex, and Rex was flattered as well as keen. Stephen, with his flair, his kindness and his beautiful, dark brown voice, seemed much the more attractive of the two to Sophie, but she knew her viewpoint was quite different. Stephen was her good friend, she could never visualise him as a prospective lover, and this more than anything else made her see him through rosier spectacles than any she could possibly bring to bear on Rex.

Now, Seeing him anxious, script in hand, glancing round the studio, her heart hurt a little for him. He had been wearing a shaggy sweater, but the heat down here under the arc lights had forced him to take it off and now it lay over the arm of his chair, whilst Stephen darted about the set in jeans and a navy T-shirt with the slogan on the front so faded that one could scarcely read, any longer, the name of the lager that he – or the manufacturers perhaps – favoured. He looked more vulnerable, somehow, in that old shirt than when armoured in his sweater, and Sophie let her eyes follow him as he passed and repassed her. His hair had lightened with the advent of the brilliant weather; now it was toffee-coloured, overlaid with gold. And he was slightly tanned too, a nice, goldy sort of tan. Seeing him as a stranger for a moment, Sophie could see why the girls thought him so attractive, though for her, he was just the boss. Reliable, sensible, someone who trusted her and who she, in her turn, trusted. They had a good relationship. Not exciting, perhaps, but then excitement, from what she'd seen, generally brought a good deal of unhappiness in its wake. No, it was better to be Sophie the secretary-bird, genuinely fond of her boss in working hours, indifferent to him out of them, than some bit-part actress who would hold his interest for a few weeks or a few months and would then suffer the heartache of losing him.

'Sophie, love, could you run to make-up and see if Sumatra's there? She knows it's the stills today, because I reminded her yesterday afternoon.' Stephen turned to the rest of the cast. 'Look, we'll do some whilst we wait, Sophie won't be long.'

He had an extraordinarily sweet smile; when he used it, you

wanted to please him. Sophie ran all the way to make-up, then on to costume, and then, as a final resort, she paged Sumatra. It then became clear that wherever Sumatra was, it was not in the Centre. She must have forgotten all about the stills.

Sophie hurried back to the studio to find the photographer already busy. He was a freelance chap apparently, quite brilliant Stephen had said, and would not be best pleased that the star of the show could not be bothered to put in an appearance to do the stills. He was taking a group shot now and Stephen raised his brows at Sophie, then shrugged as she shook her head and beckoned her over.

'Find her a stand-in, Sophie, there's a good girl. Her part isn't all that important- if we can get someone of about her height to stand on the stage with Daniel, then we can get a good shot of him and perhaps a three-quarter back view of her . . . could you do that?'

Sophie nodded and was turning away when a voice spoke. It was the photographer, beyond the circle of the lights, half-hidden by his huge camera.

'She'll do – Sophie, is that your name? You'll do fine. Just step up on the stage, love. Stephen will show you how to stand.'

Stephen shot a quick, startled look at Sophie, then at the photographer, then he grinned.

'By God, he's got a point; I hadn't realised how much . . . Come here, Sophie, I'll show you just what I want.'

The words *Oh, I couldn't possibly*, rose to Sophie's lips and were sternly repressed. Poor Stephen, he had trouble enough with Sumatra playing up. It would cost her nothing to stand on the stage for a few moments whilst the photographs were taken, it was not as if she would actually be in the pictures.

She was right. Knowing that she was not the object of the camera's glassy eye saved her from full embarrassment, though she still felt a bit silly, knowing that the studio staff were glancing towards her. But it did not last long. Ten minutes, about ten different ways of standing, and then there was a commotion at the back and Sumatra appeared, charmingly breathless and apologetic. Her taxi had been caught in a traffic jam, she had baled out and run for it in the end, she did hope that no one had been inconvenienced because of her – should she get up on the stage right away, for her stills?

Perhaps only Sophie saw the fleeting coldness in Stephen's eyes as he told Sumatra that he quite understood, and that he would not trouble her with the stills now, since he had found a stand-in for her. Sophie was sorry in a way, yet glad for Stephen, because she could see that his eyes had been opened and that he would not regret losing Sumatra, and she knew that Sumatra intended to end the relationship. It was only very much later that she began to wonder whether Sumatra had done it deliberately. After all, if you had been having an affair with an up-and-coming young producer, it might well be wiser to end it with a whimper, which would mean that their working relationship could continue pleasantly, than with a bang which would reverberate round the Centre and make it impossible for them to so much as walk onto the same set.

She asked Mary Enderby, Stephen's production assistant, what she thought, and Mary was in complete agreement with her theory.

'She's nice, Sumatra,' Mary said. 'But so far as Stephen was concerned it was only a physical attraction. He likes cuddly women, but his affairs with actresses are always short and sharpish. He prefers more stable relationships.'

'And Sumatra? What about her?'

'Oh, she's a laugh! But she'd let him down lightly, same's you thought, so that they can work together in future with no hard feelings. Stephen won't bear a grudge, he's not that sort. Now it's look out for the next, eh, Sophie?'

Sophie laughed and nodded.

'That's right. More theatre tickets and more weekend bookings in Hastings. I've quite missed them whilst he's been with Sumatra – she didn't care for the theatre unless she was on stage and she had other plans for her weekends!'

'Seen him casting his eye round at anyone in particular? It's nice for us working girls to see who's next on the list.'

Sophie laughed but shook her head. She liked Mary, who was a stocky, plain girl in her mid-twenties with considerable intelligence and a great sense of humour, but she felt a little guilty at discussing Stephen with her even so. He was too special to be discussed like any normal, fallible man.

Chapter Five

'This will be your first experience of location filming, so let's hope all goes well. Of course, weather's tremendously important, but the forecast is good and we've got a couple of days, so you should enjoy it, I think. I'm taking you more for the experience than anything, but there will still be plenty you can do – taking notes, timing, running any errands that Mary can't find time for.'

Stephen was handing Sophie into his car in the early hours of Friday morning and Sophie, shivering with a mixture of excitement and night-chill, smiled and settled herself into the passenger seat.

'I'm looking forward to it. I've got my notebook and a copy of the script and everything, so now all we need is sunshine.'

Stephen fastened his seat-belt, checked hers, and then started the engine and the long, silver-grey car purred out into the main road. He looked cool and relaxed and Sophie, still befuddled from being woken out of a light and restless doze, could only envy his calm competence. After all, two in the morning is two in the morning, no matter who or what you are!

'Mary's organising a rowing boat, and someone's given me very good directions to find the spot. Of course, we shan't need to use the boat, but I want it drawn in close to the bank so that Glyn can fiddle with it whilst he's saying his lines. I don't know how it'll strike me when I see the spot, but at the moment that's the way I see it. I don't visualise either of them actually getting into the thing.'

Sophie murmured ambiguously, knowing that Stephen was really thinking aloud, trying out ideas on her and neither expecting nor wanting a reply. It was so pleasant, she thought contentedly, to be used as a sounding board from which Stephen could bounce his ideas. So comfortable to know that there could be silence between them which neither would feel guilty or ill-at-ease about. There is a skill in silence between friends which should never be underestimated.

The car was threading through quiet, narrow streets now, with never a soul in sight, unless you counted cats. But presently they reached the suburbs and here, occasionally, a light was on in a house or a figure slunk along the pavement. They passed a hospital and Sophie saw an ambulance unloading a figure on a stretcher, men in uniform carrying it, an air of urgency making itself felt even across the distance which separated them. She pointed it out to Stephen, who glanced sideways, then concentrated on the road ahead once more.

'Yes. Someone ill, perhaps, or about to give birth to a baby. It never fails to fascinate me, a glimpse into someone else's life.'

'That's what your plays and films are like,' Sophie said. 'A bit like a living room curtain being lifted just for a moment, so that you can see the life that goes on inside the house.'

'Yes, I suppose all plays are a bit like that. Did you get much sleep?'

'Not a lot. I rested though. I went to bed at five and stayed there until midnight.'

'Well, you could try to get some sleep now, or wait until we're on the motorway; it's so dull that I have to keep myself awake with the radio, but that might just lull you off for forty winks.'

'I'm not tired yet, but later I might sleep.'

The miles thundered by with the car rushing on through the darkness, and because it was a mild night the windows were down so that the air was noisy and immediate around them. Sophie, looking up at the brilliance of the stars in the velvet of the sky-arch, thought that, but for the wind's rushing she might have heard them singing. Certainly she could see them sparkling – tiny, frosty pinpricks in the cobalt sky, eternally glittering. It was a night she would remember always, because it was her first night drive sitting alone in a fast car beside a man she liked. She could not sleep, had not the slightest desire to sleep, and just at that moment, with her mind in tune with the darkness and the starshine and that mysterious feeling that comes with approaching dawn, she knew herself blessed, fortunate beyond belief. This was a beginning, though of what, she could not have said.

Time passed, and the car ate up the miles. Sophie thought she could see a faint lightening of the sky in the east, though it could be just wishful thinking. Then she forgot it as the car turned off the motorway and entered a huge car park area. Stephen braked and turned to smile down at her.

'All night service station. Fancy a coffee and bun? Or a visit to the loos?'

'Both,' Sophie said promptly. 'I'm not hungry, but I'd love a coffee, and I've never been inside a service station.'

They got out of the car and Stephen locked up, then came round and put a guiding hand under Sophie's elbow. Sophie felt her tummy lurch, and thought severely that she must not let starlight turn her head. This was the first time she and Stephen had been together in any social sense, that was why she felt so excited she supposed, but in fact this was as much work for both of them as it was when one dictated and the other took notes.

'Come on then. I feel quite honoured, being your introduction to a service station. I didn't know there was anyone in the country who'd never braved their portals before. This way.'

Sophie was enchanted by the service station. Right in the middle of flat fields and roadways there it was, glittering, loud, noisy, with its slot-machines, its amusement arcades. its souvenir shop and the huge cafeteria. The loos, when she reached them, were every bit as good, with plenty of hot water and liquid soap, warm air machines to dry one and huge mirrors with clean formica surfaces and even some chairs so that you could apply your make-up in comfort. She spent a good five minutes just admiring everything before using a toilet, and then she washed her hands twice, put a fifty-pence piece in a vending machine and received a very tiny phial of toilet water in exchange, before sitting down in one of the chairs to comb her hair and tidy herself.

When she had finished tidying she stood up, checked that her white shirt was tucked trimly into the waistband of her full navy and scarlet cotton skirt, and then surveyed herself carefully from top to toe. She had a very large navy shoulder bag, which contained all that she should need today, and her hair was held back with two unobtrusive clips. She thought proudly that she looked both efficient and neat. Neatness, so impossible at her former weight when nothing ever fitted, buttoned properly, or could be allowed time off to get over the rigours of being strained at every seam, was a new pleasure. With four stone gone now, she could afford what she would call "ordinary" clothes, clothes which could be bought from chain stores at reasonable prices. So much nicer, as well as so much cheaper, than the huge, tent-like garments that her figure had forced her to buy before.

She left the toilets a little timidly, supposing that Stephen would have got tired of waiting for her long since and made his way to the cafeteria but there he was, lounging before a space invader machine, watching the never-ceasing moves of the tiny, brightly coloured figures, forming and re-forming like contestants in some huge carnival of dance. He looked up as she approached.

'Ah, now we'll go and grab that coffee. And I'll let you have a bun if you're a bit peckish.'

The cafeteria was not crowded but there were people eating, a man and a woman making their way along the service counter and girls waiting to serve customers and looking quite pleasant about it, considering it was not yet four in the morning. Stephen ordered two bumper mugs of coffee and then, after a glance at her, went past the scones, doughnuts and cream cakes, each one hygenically packaged in clingfilm on its own germ-free plate. Sophie noted the price and thought that surely the plates must be bone china and might be taken home with the customers, otherwise such daylight robbery could not be tolerated!

'How about a salad? There are open sandwiches too, but you could throw the bread down in the car park, for indigenous sparrows, if you felt like it.'

Sophie shook her head. The salads and open sandwiches were priced at more than she could bear to contemplate.

'No, honestly Stephen, I'm not used to eating in the middle of the night, I'd better not start.'

Even as the words left her lips she remembered the midnight snacks, the quiet trips across the kitchen in search of the rest of the joint, or the bowl of cold custard. She felt a blush start and hastily burst into speech.

'Do you use these places much? They're amazing, like the star ship *Enterprise*; I love this one.'

Stephen, carrying the coffee across to a window table overlooking a park for sleeping lorries, shook his head at her.

'I don't visit any motorway services if I can help it, they're too plastic and loud; I'd rather leave the main roads and hunt down a country pub. It's convenient now, because we're in a hurry and it's the middle of the night, but they're pretty grotty by daylight you'll find.'

'They're expensive,' Sophie admitted. 'But very glamorous.'

'Glamorous? Awake and lively, when everyone else is asleep, perhaps.' Stephen took his seat opposite her. 'If you'd accepted my offer of a meal, though, you'd have known why I prefer to eat at a pub. Tell you what, if we finish in time this evening I'll take you to a place I know in Bath. It won't shatter the diet, they do good steaks and delectable salads.'

'Tonight? Oh! Don't we go home if we film a good sunrise, then? I thought we'd come back tomorrow, if we muffed it.'

'Sophie, that would be madness! The others are down there already, snoring their heads off no doubt, as you and I would have been if I hadn't had to meet that Danish chap and show him round the Centre. No, we'll plug away today and do as much as we can, and if we haven't finished we'll get ourselves a bed for the night and start again at dawn tomorrow.'

'Oh, I see. Well, if we aren't finished, I'll ring the girls and warn them I won't be back. Can you let me know around six o'clock?'

'Sure.' Stephen drained his coffee mug and glanced interrogatively across at her. 'Done? Shall we make tracks, then?'

Sophie basked in the indulgent glance he gave her as she got to her feet; it made her feel cherished, as did the guiding hand he put on her elbow, as they left the gleaming chrome of the cafeteria and headed out across the tarmac once more to where Stephen had left the car.

Back in her seat, Sophie could see that it had not been her imagination – dawn was on its way and the stars were paling. She settled herself comfortably, fastened her seat-belt, and glanced out as the motorway began to flash past once more. Stephen turned to her.

'Not long now and we'll be driving through country lanes. I enjoy that better than motorway travel. Ever thought of learning?'

'Not in London. We've a car at home but it's terribly old, and Dad's never suggested teaching any of us.'

In the faint light Stephen glanced across at her, one eye brow rising.

'Oh, so you do have a family, you weren't just hatched? You've never mentioned a family to me, so I've supposed you were an only child.'

'Far from it.' Sophie smiled. 'I'm one of five girls.'

'My God! Older than you, or younger?'

'Both. I'm the third, so there are two older than me and two younger.'

'Then you're the middle one. What are your sisters called?'

Sophie told him, conscientiously added their ages and then asked him, rather shyly, whether he had brothers or sisters.

'I've one brother, Paul. He's ten years older than I and the middle partner in a family firm of accountants. But we scarcely know each other, since Paul went with my father when my parents' marriage broke up and I stayed with Mother.'

'Oh? What does your father do, then? Is he an accountant?'

'No. He lives in the States most of the time and he's in our business, films and television. He's just married for the third time, but I haven't met her.'

'Oh. My father's a postman and my mother teaches at the local technical college. You make us seem rather dull, I'm afraid.'

'Nonsense, there's nothing exciting about broken marriages, these days. What does your mother teach?'

Sophie told him and then, foreseeing questions about her sisters which she had no desire to answer, said, with feigned regret, that she was terribly tired and would just close her eyes for a few moments. She had only meant to change the subject but oddly enough, when she opened her eyes after what she thought was about five minutes, the car was slowing down to negotiate a gateway and it was full daylight, though a pearly grey morning. The sun, it seemed, had still not risen.

Stephen drew the car to a halt under a clump of trees and turned to smile down at her.

'Hello, had a good sleep? We've arrived first, but only by a cat's whisker. Here comes Glyn and the rest of them are just behind in the vans and lorries, poor devils.'

Sophie, feeling crumpled and fat, got out of the car praying to God that she had not snored, or talked in her sleep, and that her body had not indulged in any of the uninhibited behaviour that bodies do indulge in when they're off duty. She went scarlet at the thought of what she might have done in her sleep – but Stephen was striding ahead, calling out to the crew as they clambered down from their various vehicles.

Sophie licked her dry lips and rubbed her eyes, hoping that she did not look as unsavoury as she felt and that no one would take any notice of her anyway. In the last wish, at least, she was to be fortunate. With the actors being made up and dressed for their parts, Stephen was able to concentrate on getting the camera crew to take establishing shots of the river, the bank and the general locality. Someone had set up a group of chairs, but Sophie felt she had been sitting down for quite long enough and so she stood in the background with her notebook in one hand and a checklist and a pile of dope-sheets in the other, ready for when Mary needed them. An observer still, not needed, she dreamed over the scene before her.

So quiet it was, with the river overhung with a white mist out of which the sallows lining the bank reared, mysteriously rootless, appearing to swim on the milky, moving vapour. The water itself, unseen, was no more than a background noise, a liquid chuckling, and as the light got stronger she could see the boat, nosing into the flag irises which grew along the bank here. It was a ghost-boat, an outline of reality rather than reality itself, and it focused attention because it was here presently, that Maeve and Glyn would begin their scene.

But over and above the quiet magic of early morning, the crews made their presence felt. Voices of cameramen calling the strange directions beloved of the media – crab, pan, tilt, track – whilst Stephen and Mary talked of angles, continuity and cutaways above the muttered voice of a wardrobe woman, mouth full of pins, who was trying to fix Maeve's gauzy scarf so that it looked as if it was about to fall off without actually doing so. No doubt the subdued murmur from the make-up people was of an equally technical nature, and the rattling and scraping of men at work came from the big covered lorry too, where something was being done, or undone, or started, or finished.

Sophie, listening loved it, though she loved almost as much

the quiet river sounds, the tinkle and slap of water as it sloshed against the bank when someone caught the mooring rope and pulled the boat nearer, the mutter of sleepy water birds and the shriller cries of blackbirds, thrushes and blue tits, disturbed by such unprecedented human clamour at this early hour.

'You timing us, Sophie love?'

·That was Stephen, speaking to her without turning away from his perusal of the script. Sophie, guiltily glancing at her watch, answered that she was.

'Right. Give us a nod for total quiet a full minute before the sun rises, will you? Then count us in, good and clear. Right, everyone, I want you all in your places and ready to start when Sopie says. Mary, if you'll . . .'

His conversation became technical once more and Sophie ceased to listen to him. A moorhen shot across the river and into the reeds, uttering a plaintive peep-peep and the nearest cameraman swung his lens round and took a shot and then, when it was a mere two minutes before sunrise, when everyone was talking, jostling, when cameras were being swung round to catch different views of the couple on the bank, Sophie saw the heron. It was standing further upstream, on a tiny island which looked as though it had been made out of flotsam and jetsam rather than out of solid earth, and as the mist lifted the whole bird came clearly into view. It looked huge, with that air of poised and strained attention that told Sophie it had had enough of them and was about to take to the air.

She moved forward and jerked at the jacket of the nearest cameraman. It was Leo, a blond and earnest young man with a face like a Greek god and the voice of a cockney barrow-boy. He stared at her, his expression impatient but Sophie, intent on something other than the impression she was making, had no time for subtlety. She nodded towards the heron and then, when he did not respond, caught his ear and turned his head round so that he, too, could see the heraldic bird.

'It's going to take off, Leo. If you can . . .'

Her whisper was so low that only Leo could have heard and just as Stephen began to muster his actors the heron rose ponderously, so slowly that every lovely action was clear to the last detail. The great, grey, trailing legs were brought up like an aeroplane's undercarriage, the long neck was curved into an 'S'

84

so that the crested head was tucked well back into the shoulders. For a moment the heron was huge between them and the thin, sucked-lolly scarlet of the rising sun. Beautiful beyond belief. Heart-catching. Totally memorable.

But not recorded. Leo's camera and attention was still fixed on Maeve and Glyn and, to Sophie's horror, she heard his voice begin the countdown which she should have been doing. Faintly, she heard Stephen hiss her name in a whisper which boded ill for later, and then the countdown finished and the scene before her sprang into life. Everyone was doing what they should be doing; Maeve's beauty glowed, Glyn's hand moved, tugging on the mooring rope.

Sophie's heady exhilaration oozed away. What on earth had she very nearly done? She must have been mad, to try and get Leo to film the heron at such an important moment, and she had gone and mucked up her only tiny contribution – the only bit of work which Stephen had allotted to her. But an apprehensive glance at Stephen showed him absorbed, the scene obviously working. She moved quietly out of the way, well back from the bank, and presently she heard Stephen call 'Cut!' and say something to Glyn, uttering a crack of laughter as he did so. Then he glanced round, saw her, and jerked his head. She hurried forward, book and pencil at the ready.

'Yes, Stephen?'

'Find this scene in the script. I want to add a bit.'

She obeyed, read it aloud to him, added the extra words, then retraced her steps. He had scarcely glanced at her, but she knew that this was not a sign of annoyance, since he found his work totally absorbing and had probably forgotten, for the time being, about her failure with the count. He would be unlikely to need her now, for his entire attention would remain on what was happening in camera range.

Released from duty, she watched the acting. In this scene Glyn had most of the dialogue and whilst he was talking he drew the boat towards him, let it drift to the full extent of the mooring rope, drew it in again. Absently, naturally, so that if she had not known that every one of his actions had been carefully scripted by Stephen, she could never have guessed it. Things were going Stephen's way, with Maeve never trying to out-act Glyn and a family of ducks appearing, quacking, just at the right moment, to give the scene that special touch which Stephen sometimes had to work so hard to achieve.

So totally absorbed was she that, when people began to appear and Stephen called a halt so that they could gather round a van dispensing tea and sandwiches, Sophie was taken aback. She glanced at her watch and saw that it was ten o'clock; the time had flown and the morning was just what they needed – a clear blue sky, sunshine, and only the gentlest of breezes.

'Not bad,' Stephen said presently, coming over to her and marking the script. 'We'll carry on filming now, we'll need a lot of cutaways; we can do them and the other river bank scenes and then we'll go over to the Blewitt's place and take some window-shots. It'll mean we might well get finished today, if we keep our minds on our work. We'll skip lunch.'

There was a groan, but not a very serious one. The team knew the value, in England, of seizing good weather with both hands and working right through break periods if they were lucky enough to find themselves filming in sunshine.

It was eight o'clock that evening before they finished work and then Stephen came over to Sophie, pushing his hands through his thick hair. He looked tired but nevertheless rather pleased with himself.

'What happened to make you miss the sunrise? If Leo hadn't helped you out you'd have been in dead trouble, I can tell you.'

'I'm sorry, but there was this heron . . .'

Sophie's stammered explanation was cut short by Leo, who had obviously guessed that explanations would be called for.

'Shot in a million it would've been, Steve, but the bloody bird chose its moment wrong. The gal tried to get your attention but you was busy, so I took over the count. All's well that ends well, eh?'

'Yes, but another time, Sophie, I want *all* your attention, not just most of it. And if you can't catch my eye, don't *ever* distract a cameraman; got it?'

Sophie glowed. He had said another time, so heinous though her crime might have been, it had plainly not been sufficiently bad to get her thrown out of location filming.

Having spoken quietly to her, Stephen then raised his voice to include the rest of the team.

'Right, everyone, we've done well today, we can sleep with clear consciences tonight. Get yourselves a meal and then you can go back to town in your own time.'

He walked over to where Mary was frowning over her notes, rumpling his hair with both hands, looking tired now that enthusiasm had been allowed to cool.

Sophie, with leisure at last to look round, realised for the first time what they had done to the river bank. She stared, saddened, at the crushed grass, the bent and mangled irises, the towpath churned into dust. But it would mend: give it forty-eight hours, another quiet, starlit night and another dawn with the sun rising, dispelling the mist, and it would begin to recover. The ducks would quack ashore and clean up the bits of food, the moorhens would guide their flotilla of young across the quiet water. Perhaps even the heron would return, to fish from his tiny island in the grey dawn.

Stephen had ordered a meal in a room at a nearby pub and the crew sat around, eating and drinking. The stars, Glyn and Maeve, had made their own arrangements but everyone else was here, relaxed, laughing, light-hearted now that the job was satisfactorily completed.

The meal was half over before Sophie realised that Leo, normally quiet to the point of taciturnity, had addressed her several times in an increasingly friendly fashion. Could it be the beer he had consumed, Sophie wondered? He had never taken the slightest notice of her before.

It was not, however, until he suggested that she might like to travel back to London with him in his M.G., that she realised he was trying to get closer to her. She felt a flood of crimson wash across her face and wondered whether she should explain that he had made a mistake, she was not at all the sort of girl who had attention paid to her by handsome young men. She had no wish to offend him, but before she had done more than begin to mumble uncertainly, Stephen had rescued her. Glancing across at Leo, he said rather thickly, through a mouthful of food, 'I'm taking Sophie home, Leo, since I brought her down here.'

Leo's face rivalled Sophie's in its scarlet splendour and Sophie realised, for the first time, that a hardened cameraman, if cursed with fair skin, could blush just as beetroot as a fat teenager. Poor Leo, Stephen had been rather abrupt!

'Sorry, Steve, I just thought that Sophie an' me might do the town together, later. The night's young, yet.'

'Quite. But Sophie's still working, I'm afraid, old lad. She's got a portable typewriter in the back of the car and she's going to get the script alterations typed out whilst they're still fresh in my mind. I can think round it in the car going back and then we'll get the work down in her notebook.' He smiled rather wolfishly at Sophie. 'And she can spend the rest of the evening and all day tomorrow translating her shorthand into nice, neat typescript.'

'That seems a bit hard.' Mary's voice was sympathetic, but was there something more behind the words? Sophie saw a quick glance exchanged between Mary and Leo, but then they began talking quite ordinarily and she supposed she must have imagined the whole thing. Anyway, working with Stephen was probably far more fun than an evening out with Leo would have been, what with her shyness and his. She smiled at him. Nice of him to offer though: later, when she was in bed, she would take the proposal out, examine it, savour it, and possibly, tomorrow morning, boast about it. Except . . . Well, she was different now, so hell-bent on losing weight that she could still see she was outside the ordinary boy-girl relationships. Before, she had boasted when there had been nothing to boast about; now she would not do so, because she could see herself so much more clearly and see, too, that she could be like all the others – would be like all the others!

And when it came down to it, she could never be sure that Leo had not asked her to go out of pity. Horrible and cringe-making though the thought was, it still had to be faced. In fact, when she thought how fat she still was, he must either be sorry for her or be less fanciable than he appeared. He had to have some secret but enormous flaw, she reasoned, otherwise why should he ask the fat girl out?

After dinner goodbyes were said all round and then Stephen and Sophie got into the car. Sophie leaned back in her seat with a sigh of total satisfaction. It had been a wonderful day and, even in the midst of her enjoyment, she had been sensible, refusing sandwiches and biscuits and drinking lots of coffee.

She had just enjoyed a small steak and a large and varied salad, and had rounded her meal off with a peach compote and more coffee. And though Stephen had been cross at first about the heron, once it had been explained he had understood. Now, she smiled across at him as he spoke.

'Well, Sophie? What did you think of that?'

'Wonderful. I'll never forget it.'

'Good. Look, there's a little pub near here where I'm going to take you, it's quiet and pleasant and they'll let us work in one of the rooms until we've sorted the script out, but you won't be back in town until tomorrow morning. Is that all right? You can telephone your flatmates from the pub.'

'Yes, I'm sure it will be all right,' Sophie said. It was nearly eleven o'clock and she was tired out, but if Stephen wanted to work, then work she would. She knew that in the ordinary course of events, a producer, even one of Stephen's calibre, would merit a P.A., but not a secretary. It was only because Stephen wrote plays and scripts and did so much editorial work on those manuscripts written by other people that he was allowed a full-time private secretary, and that meant that when he wanted to change a script or get an idea for a film down on paper, then she must be willing to work late, or early, or possibly over a weekend. She also knew that he wanted her to be able to do production assistant work, so that when Mary was on holiday or away sick Sophie would be able to step into the breach. All this, therefore, was part of her job.

They drove through the town and out into the velvet darkness of the countryside once more. Out here, darkness came into its own again, only it was a deep blue darkness, filled with stars and moonshine, lacking the velvety black of a lamplit London night. The breeze which came in through the car window was scented with lilac and laburnum, with the fragrance of grass, dried beneath the hot sun, and with the rich perfume of late-flowering May blossom. Sophie sniffed ecstatically. Could there be a more wonderful night? She doubted it.

It was a nice pub. The gardens, or what Sophie could see of them, sloped down to an unseen river and were romantically dotted with apple trees and with cottage flower-beds. Stephen booked them in, whilst Sophie rang the flat and explained to

Anya that she would not be returning until the next day, and then Stephen led her through to a small sitting room, shut the door, and got out the script. Side by side, they sat on the comfortable couch and Stephen began to dictate, sitting sideways so that he could watch her pencil as it raced across the page. From time to time he asked her to read a few lines back, or consulted her over the script. Yet she had the feeling that he was not really concentrating on what he was doing, but was watching her. Blushing, she struggled to ignore the feeling, which was clearly idiotic. Stephen had never watched her with any sort of interest apart from a natural interest in the speed of her shorthand. Of course, she was tired, her hand was not as sure as usual, her outlines were occasionally fumbled. He was concerned, no doubt, to see that she did not make mistakes; that was why his gaze seemed less abstracted than usual. She really must not let her imagination run away with her -- first she had thought Leo found her attractive, now she was actually daring to get ideas about Stephen. Pull yourself together Sophie and work! she demanded. Yet she went on feeling that he was watching her.

Stephen sat sideways, his head tilted a little, so that he could watch her. He found himself continually astonished at how much her weight loss had improved her. Her skin, always creamy, was fresher now, less stained with rose, and the shape of her face was beginning to show through, so that you could see the small, pointed chin and the clean bones at her jawline. He enjoyed just looking at her arms, which were dimpled at the elbows, small-wristed, and her hands were nice too, now that the fingers were no longer padded out with fat into small, tight-skinned sausages.

She had always had beautiful eyes, unusual, greeny-grey and fringed with lovely long, curly lashes. But now you could see how big they were, how clear, whereas before the curve of her plump pink cheeks had diminished their beauty.

As he watched, he saw the tide of soft colour rise in her face and he smiled affectionately. She blushed so easily – he liked that. He liked a woman to be shy, to wait for him to make the first move. Sitting close to her now, seeing her lit by the soft glow of a rose-shaded light, he was reminded of a bowl of cream or perhaps a very delicious, light sponge-cake.

His own comparisons made him smile. Odd, that he could only think of Sophie in terms of food, yet both analogies were complimentary. She was becoming beautiful with a creamy, dimpled sweetness which would rouse any man's appetite. He had always liked women with good bones and plenty of shapely, yielding flesh and Sophie had something else as well, a quality of innocence, of unawareness of her own attraction, which he had found increasingly delightful. His infatuation for Sumatra had been brought about because of Sumatra's warm, tropical curves and richly textured flesh. Perhaps he had set out to capture Sumatra because she reminded him of what Sophie might have been – only now Sophie was as she should be.

Leo's invitation to her had taken him aback, caught him wrong-footed, so to speak. He had known, suddenly, that he did not want Leo to be the man who awoke Sophie to her potentialities. He had told himself that she was too good for a mere cameraman, that in any case he did not want anyone to rush her, to sweep her off her feet while she was still finding them, testing her own resolve, her strengths. The truth was, he acknowledged now, that he wanted to get to know her much better himself. He wanted to be the man she turned to as she gradually gained confidence and self-respect.

So he had brought her here, to this quiet little pub, hoping to gradually get her to see him not as her boss but as a human being, someone who could take her out, laugh with her, kiss and cuddle her.

Not even to himself did he say that he wanted to sleep with her, but that was what he meant.

Chapter Six

'Is that the lot, then?'

Sophie put down her notebook and yawned behind her hand, still uneasily aware of his eyes on her and now beginning to be even more aware of the lateness of the hour. Here it was, well past midnight, and they were alone together in a small sitting room and about to go up to bed! It was enough to make anyone feel a bit silly.

'Yes, we're through.' Stephen consulted his wristwatch. 'Well, Cinders, can I tempt you to a nightcap? Whisky? Or rum? Or a coffee?'

'What I'd really like would be a hot chocolate,' Sophie said longingly. 'Not made with milk, of course, just half and half, but it would be so nice; it's what I always have at the flat. Though I'm so terribly tired that I daresay I'll fall asleep the moment my head touches the pillow.'

She thought Stephen gave her a rather enigmatic look at that and supposed he thought it strange that a girl of her age should not be used to late nights. Well, it was strange, but even if she had been used to it, she could scarcely be expected to feel fresh considering that she had not had more than a couple of hours sleep the previous night.

However, apart from the look, Stephen made no comment, but went through into reception and then came back whilst Sophie was still collecting her papers and announced that a cup of hot chocolate would be delivered to her room in about ten minutes.

'Lovely. Just time for a shower,' Sophie said, as she stumbled up the stairs beside him. She was quite dizzy with tiredness by now and could scarcely wait to collapse into bed. They reached her door and she unlocked it, then turned in the doorway. 'Goodnight, Stephen. See you in the morning.'

'Goodnight, love. Sweet dreams.'

He turned away and was gone into his own room before she had closed the door on herself.

The shower was brisk and colder than she had intended to have it; probably the boiler was allowed to cool off at this time of night, but whatever the reason, instead of preparing Sophie for bed the shower woke her up. She took her time under the water, keeping her head clear of the spray since she had no shower-cap, and then towelling herself briskly dry on the hotel's nice, fluffy white towel. It was only as she crossed the bedroom again, in response to a tap on her door, that she realised she had no night-things with her, and that she was clad only in the towel, which suddenly seemed to shrink.

However, all she had to do was open the door a crack, take the hot drink, and scuttle back to bed with it. She would pick up her shirt and the rest of her clothes and hang them up so that they did not look too bad tomorrow, and then simply get into bed and sleep and sleep.

According to plan, she opened the door a crack – and Stephen entered the room with a tray in his hands. There were two cups on it, and a plate of biscuits, and Stephen was wearing a green silk dressing-gown and, beneath it, cream-coloured pyjamas. He smiled at her, put the tray down on the bedside table, and then sat down on her bed. He did not look even slightly surprised to see his secretary wearing nothing but a diminutive white towel.

'Here's that hot chocolate, and I ordered one for myself as well, so we'll share the biscuits.' He smiled as Sophie, scarlet-faced, hung back. 'Of course, you didn't realise we'd be over-nighting – would you like to borrow half a pair of pyjamas, to spare your blushes? You can have the trousers or the jacket, I'm easy.'

He was obviously as fresh from the shower as she, his face glowing, his wet hair slicked back. She saw that his feet were bare, which gave her some slight satisfaction – at least he had not thought to bring slippers! She picked up her drink, still standing uneasily beside the bed, but shook her head when he proferred the biscuits. It was no use having little lapses because with her, at any rate, little lapses turned into big ones, and then into huge ones, and the thought of reburying her emerging waist and chin afresh was too distressing to contemplate. She sipped at the hot chocolate, though, eyeing Stephen distrustfully as she did so. Airy offers of pyjama halves were all very well, but whichever end she accepted would probably result in a blush-making situation.

'No biscuits? Well, perhaps you're wise. Have I ever told you how clever you are, my love, to starve yourself into such a delectable shape?'

Sophie wriggled. She knew she was still too fat, there was no need for him to say things like that!

'I'm still too fat, I know that. I want to lose lots more yet.'

He eyed her in a manner which made her suddenly suspect that the towel was not as well draped as she had assumed. She glanced down at herself, but she appeared to be respectably covered.

'Well, perhaps you should lose a little more, but you'll do it. You're a girl of character, do you know that?'

Sophie, who had no idea what he meant by a girl of character, muttered a bashful disclaimer and gulped her hot chocolate. Then she sat down on the hard little chair and waited for Stephen to go. Nice though he was, good friends though they were, she was finding this whole situation horribly embarrassing. She tried to tell herself to think of Penny and Anya and to do as they would, but it did not help much. They would both float round, towel-clad, making witty conversation and gobbling biscuits until they wanted Stephen to leave and then they would tell him to go. Well, Anya would, Penny would either shout 'bugger off' or worse. That was unless she decided she fancied him, in which case he would be dragged into bed and divested of those cissy silk pyjamas before you could say Jack Robinson.

The thought made her smile and Stephen, finishing his drink, smiled too.

'What's funny? Have you decided which half of my pyjamas to accept?'

Sophie giggled nervously and shook her head.

'No, nothing like that, my mind wandered, that's all. It's just . . . well, you and I . . . we don't usually sit around with you in peejays and me in a towel!'

'True. So why not make the most of the opportunity? Come and sit by me, lovely, it's a lot comfier, and what's more, that's a basket chair you're sitting on, you'll have the weave imprinted all over your pretty bottom, and I wouldn't want that to happen.'

Sophie had no high opinion of herself, had never been desired, could not even imagine what the victim of a heavy pass must feel like, but alarm bells clanged loudly in her head. Who was it had once called her Lovely? That swine Peter Brewer, that's who it was, and here was Stephen, who seemed so nice, doing exactly the same thing. She felt her spine begin to stiffen. He would charm her, woo her, perhaps even bring himself to make love to her, but he would only do it for a reason. Perhaps he had seen Anya or Penny and wanted to make their closer acquaintance. What better way to do it than to be introduced to the flat as Sophie's fellow, the fat one's bloke? It would then be perfectly natural and easy for him to transfer his affections to one of the others – and no more than she should bloody well expect. No one, particularly not the youngest and most promising producer at the centre, would want *her!*

'Well? Don't glare at me, puss, come and sit beside me.'

'No! Go away!'

The words burst from Sophie with all the force of deadly fear. To lose her friendship with Stephen, perhaps even her lovely job, just so that she could say, 'He kissed me, once,' would be a loss greater than she could bear.

He did not go away. He smiled at her, stood up and came over to her, lifting her out of her chair with apparent ease. Sophie, resisting, saw his face redden slightly and knew a malicious satisfaction that, whatever he might pretend, he was finding her weight an obstacle.

'What's the matter? Scared? Damn it, woman, haven't you ever been kissed goodnight before?'

He sat down on the bed again with Sophie sprawled across his lap and managed to get her more or less into his arms. Sophie pushed and squiggled, and then realised that a struggle would end in her humiliation and would make her look more of a fool than she looked already. Far better to be dignified, far better merely to freeze him off with feigned indifference. And not all that feigned, when she thought of the consequences of letting Stephen make love to her. He would, she believed, have to see her naked and he would find out, according to popular fiction, that she had never made love to another man in the whole of her life, and he would despise her on both counts. Except . . . perhaps he really did mean to do nothing other than kiss her goodnight? She wished, *how* she wished, that she knew more about men!

Accordingly, and with a very ill grace, she gave a deep sigh, turned her eyes ceilingwards, and then closed them and relaxed against the arms that were imprisoning her.

'I think you're being very stupid,' she muttered. 'I think . . .'

His mouth stopped her words, and she knew what it was like to be kissed by Stephen Bland.

It was wonderful. His lips were warm and gentle at first, then he moved his tongue against her mouth and, as if her mouth knew exactly what to do even if she did not, her lips parted, allowed his tongue access to its secrets, and when he touched her tongue with his and then moved it inside her mouth she knew a rush of desire which startled her with its intensity.

Vaguely, she remembered the haystack's kiss, how odd and foreign his mouth had felt on hers. This was different, for where the haystack had rudely thrust and shoved, Stephen delicately explored. His arms were hard but there was comfort in them. Suddenly, she no longer thought that he wanted to make love to her for some ulterior motive. She no longer thought at all. Her mind swooned on a sea of being wanted, accepted, desired, she could not have said which; she only knew that, for the first time in her life, she was right at the centre of someone else's attention. She, who had hovered so long on the outskirts, was at the core, experiencing and being experienced. Loving and being loved? She neither knew nor cared, she simply enjoyed what was happening to her.

She could not have said how long the embrace lasted, she only knew that it was wonderful, and when it ended, when Stephen held her gently away from him, she felt bereft, like a kitten torn suddenly from the warmth of the mother cat. And then she saw that Stephen had removed his dressing gown and was taking off his pyjama jacket.

Odd. Was he *that* hot? Or was he about to offer her the use of his jacket, as he had suggested earlier? Then he smiled lovingly at her, and tried to tweak her towel away.

Immediately, all her self-doubts came rushing back. She clasped the towel defensively.

'Stop it, Stephen!'

Stephen stopped reaching for her towel, though he put his arm round her and held her close, kissing the side of her face in a way which melted her bones.

'Why stop it, dearest Sophie? You like it as much as I do.'

'Yes, kissing's one thing . . .'

'All right, we'll stick to kissing.' He rolled her onto her back with an expertness which denoted a misspent past, and pressed her gently but firmly into the softness of the pillows and mattress. His kissing became more peripatetic now though, his mouth travelling around, waking pulses that Sophie had not realised were sleeping, rousing little devils of desire that she had never guessed she possessed. She moaned, wriggling, all her instincts wanting to respond, to encourage him in his delightful pastime. And then, damn it, his fingers were working at the top of her towel again and for a moment she felt the back of his hand slide down her breast, closely followed by his mouth, travelling across the soft skin which led down to her peaking nipple.

Desire was mingled now with a sort of horror, a feeling of sickness. She could not help remembering Phil the haystack yet, even afraid, disgusted with herself, she knew that her body wanted the experience he was offering, longed for it, even. She pushed at his shoulders, then grabbed his head and heaved him off her breast; he came with a breathless, sucking pop which brought laughter bubbling up, though she knew, shame-facedly, that she had only just conquered that other, lustful, sly Sophie who could be brought to life by a touch.

This time, she could see, he would not be stopped so easily. She dragged the towel up over her breasts again and shoved him with all her strength, then fell, with an appalling crash, off the far side of the bed. For a second she simply lay there, winded, horrified by what she had done, and then he was bending over her, pulling her into a sitting position. He looked rueful but not at all ashamed. And, glancing at his pyjama trousers and quickly away again, she realised that he was not only feeling rueful. The word randy, frequently used by Penny, took on a new meaning. An old proverb she had heard being sniggered

97

over at school came into her head: *A standing cock hath no conscience*. She clutched her towel tighter and glared at Stephen with something closely akin to hatred. If that proverb meant what she thought it did, then the sooner Stephen realised she would fight him every inch of the way, and that if he succeeded it would be rape, the better.

But apparently, despite appearances and proverbs, Stephen was still in command. He sat down on the bed again and began to put on his pyjama jacket. Then he stood up to don his dressing-gown. He looked at her sorrowfully, but without anger.

'I said only kissing, poppet, and that's what I meant. Did I frighten you?'

Sophie scrambled to her feet. She knew what she looked like, a vast, quaking white blancmange, and that was in the towel. If he had got it off he would have been horrified, totally repulsed. Thank God she had acted in time! No one, she knew, could continue to like her after they had seen her in the nude. Look at the way Lavvy had reacted at the birthday party, and her parents and relatives. They had been disgusted and shocked and no wonder. Stephen was not going to join their number, not if she could help it.

'It's all right, it doesn't matter. I'm very tired. Would you go now, please?'

'If you were to get into bed, we could . . .'

'No!' She stared appealingly at him. 'Stephen, I can't, I'm very sorry, I really can't.'

Tears began then, tears of exhaustion and misery at having to reject him when she would so much have preferred to please him, to say, 'Yes, carry on, we'll both enjoy it.' But it was a risk she dared not take. She knew herself to be unlovable, a hideous mound of flesh despite her weight loss. She could not risk seeing his face change, seeing perhaps kindness and pity alone forcing him to continue with his love-making whilst her hateful, disgusting body would probably let her down and show its pleasure at his touch, writhing with a desire which he, having seen her naked, could no longer match. The tears welled over.

She knew then that she had won, if winning it was. Remorse brought him over to her, but the arms round her now were brotherly, tender. She sobbed and rested her face against the silk of his robe, letting her tears soak into the soft material which smelt so beautifully of Stephen.

'I'm very sorry. I'm s-so sorry!'

'Dearest Soph, it's me who should be saying sorry to you, it doesn't matter at all. I promise it won't spoil things between us, so don't get fussed. I'm a fool, rushing you, never asking you if you were all right for tonight. I should have guessed why you didn't want to.' He kissed her lightly on both wet eyelids. 'Look, I'll go now, but there'll be a time when you're all right and then we'll continue with this . . . this conversation.'

After he had gone she put on her bra and pants and climbed into bed, her whole body aching as though she had been steam-rollered, and thought over what he had said. After a few moments, light dawned. He thought she was suffering from the curse – what a lucky break! And as for continuing with this 'conversation' when she was all right, she would simply have to be careful next time they filmed on location. Not that he would try again; he must have had too much to drink, that was it. Anyway, she was getting slimmer. Until she had reached the proper proportions she would make sure that she did not stay in hotels with young men. She would stick closer to Mary next time than any sticking plaster.

On this resolute thought she should have been able to go happily off to sleep, but in fact she could not. She continued to go over and over the episode in her head with less and less pleasure in her own behaviour, so that it was dawn before sheer weariness at last dragged her down into an exhausted slumber.

'Well, how did it go last weekend?'

It was a week after Sophie's location trip and Anya, who had gone home for a break whilst Derek did some filming in Scotland, had just got back from the station. She came into the kitchen, flung her light coat down on the table, and gazed hopefully at the pan which Sophie was stirring.

'Anything edible in there which could stretch to a third?'

'It's chicken soup. Penny's making a salad and I've prepared a mound of prawns in seafood sauce. We guessed you'd be back, so we did plenty. Had a good time yourself?'

Anya nodded and got a biscuit out of the pantry, then glanced round the room.

'Nice, thanks. Quiet. Where's Penny though? Surely she isn't doing a salad in her bedroom?'

Sophie chuckled.

'No, I forgot. She's gone up to make sure Dee's all right. She and John went down to visit John's parents for a week and in the course of it his father fell and broke his ankle. John's stayed down for a further week to drive the van for him – he's got a shop.'

'Mm hmm, I know. Right, now.' Anya finished the biscuit, brushed her hands lightly together, and delved into the fridge, emerging with a chunk of cheese. 'Tell about your weekend. I rang on Tuesday and Penny said you'd stayed overnight with Stephen at a pub.'

'Yes, because he wanted to rewrite a chunk of the script,' Sophie said. 'The filming went very well, I absolutely *love* location work, Anya, and then afterwards . . .'

Penny bounced back into the kitchen, hugged Anya and slumped down at the table.

'Bring on the soup. Dee's having a meal with the Fletchers tonight,' she said sharply. 'Come *on* , Sofa, I'm starving, and I've got a date later.'

'All right, I'm just going to pour it.' Sophie suited action to her words and then joined the other two at the table. 'I've done some batter for pancakes, so don't think I'm trying to get you both to lose weight as well.'

'You've lost yet more,' Anya said, tucking into her soup. 'Go on, Soph, you were just starting to tell me about the weekend.'

'Oh, was she?' There was a gleam in Penny's eyes which warned Sophie to watch her words. 'All I've got out of her has been that it was very nice.' She snorted. 'If I got Stephen Bland to myself for a night I wouldn't describe it in such feeble terms.'

Sophie had no intention of telling anyone that Stephen had made a pass at her for several reasons. For a start, they probably would not believe her – she could hardly believe it herself. And anyway, it had probably been a one-off, for next day he had picked up their friendly relationship just where it had left off, without a trace of that rather fullsome and loverish attitude which she had found so embarrassing. It had also occurred to her that Stephen might merely have wanted to kiss her because of the lack of any other kissable material. That this might be a

100

subtle insult to Stephen, insinuating that he was so sex-crazed that he would rather kiss anything than nothing, passed Sophie by. She simply assumed that a virile young man, finding himself in a bedroom, had to kiss something, and that kissing led by a natural progression to other things.

This led her to the conclusion that someone like Stephen, who could have any woman he wanted, had been passing the time. Yet she was fairly sure that he had enjoyed kissing her, whatever his reasons for doing so, and this fact cheered her considerably. After all, if he had enjoyed it at her present bulging poundage, then perhaps, if she really tried, kept losing weight . . . She could not expect to land someone like Stephen, of course, but perhaps Leo, or John's bachelor friend Paul . . . Perhaps, in short, there would be someone for Sophie.

'Sophie!' Penny's voice had that edge of irritability which her flatmates heard so often and her boyfriends not at all. 'Stop dreaming and gazing at the loaf and TELL US WHAT HAPPENED BETWEEN YOU AND STEPHEN!'

Sophie dropped her soup spoon, splattering her dress with soup, swore, and picked up her spoon once more. She drank her soup for a moment, then answered in the most annoying way she could dream up at short notice.

'Nothing happened, Penny, but your concern is most flattering. I'll tell Stephen how interested you are in his welfare and mine.'

Anya giggled.

'You're coming out of your shell at last, girl! By the way, has Penny said anything to you about the date?'

'No. What date?'

'Ours, if you'll agree.'

Sophie fluttered her lashes at Anya and put on a coy face.

'Gee honey, I never knew you cared! What *are* you talking about?'

'I rang Derek on Thursday, just to see that everything was all right, and he told me that he's entertaining a chap from the States to dinner next week. He's nice, Sam is, I've met him, and Derek asked me to find a friend and bring her along to make up a fourth.'

Sophie, bright pink, gawped.

'And . . . ?'

'And so when I rang Penny, I said what did she think about you being the fourth, and she said it was a good idea. It would be a sort of dress-rehearsal for other dates, the important sort. After all, at the rate you're going, you'll have reached your target weight quite soon and then you're going to get all social. You promised you would. What do you say?'

'I'd love to say no,' Sophie said honestly. 'That is, a part of me would. Are you sure? I wouldn't let you down?'

'Don't denigrate yourself, girl. Anyway, it isn't a date in the usual sense of the word, since Sam Schuck probably has a dozen ex-wives and girlfriends back home. Well? Going to be brave and come with us?'

'Yes, and I'll do my damnedest to look nice. I'll have to buy something to wear though. What should I get?'

'Tell you what, we'll go shopping on Monday, at lunchtime.' Anya turned to Penny, now dishing out prawns onto the three plates. 'What about you, Pen? You're our fashion expert, are you free?'

'To see that Sophie gets the right stuff, I'm always free,' Penny assured them. 'What does your clothes fund stand at, Sofa? Enough to get something really special?'

'Yes! And make-up? And shoes?'

Penny laughed and pulled her plate towards her.

'Gently, girl, one thing at a time. We'll make you look so good you'll have that Sam Schuck crosseyed!'

Stephen had gone off to Devon to visit his grandmother on the Tuesday following the location filming, so Sophie had scarcely seen him. He had, however, left her a pile of work and, on the day that Sophie purchased her dress, a pair of tights so fine that she doubted she would have the courage to wear them and some wickedly un-Sophie-like undies, he telephoned. Having briskly asked about his work, got her to check some details with Mary and told her that he would return on the Thursday, he then told her to keep her lunchtime free on that day.

'I'll buy you a salad and we'll catch up on each other's news,' he said before ringing off.

Sophie, dreaming round the shops at lunchtime, wondered if that could count as a date and decided, regretfully, that it could not. Never mind, Thursday was the day that she was going out with Anya and Derek and the American, so she would be justified in meeting Stephen for lunch in the new dress. And the new make-up. And perhaps even the new shoes, if she could persuade her ankles to remain rigid and to stop trying to imitate spaghetti and tip her sideways.

Tomorrow was the great day, so she had decided to take this afternoon off in order to practise beautifying herself and now, walking round Boots, she had selected a bottle of hair conditioner, a spray of much-advertised deodorant and a face pack, scarcely influenced at all by the fact that it was called a strawberry and cream one. She was actually heading for the tills when her eye was caught by another aid to beauty.

Leg Wax. Removes hair painlessly and your legs will remain fuzz-free for weeks. Sophie picked up the packet and gazed thoughtfully at the instructions. Warm the wax, spread evenly, remove with firm, even pull. Do not use on the underarms. Her flesh crept at the thought – was there anyone in the world silly enough to do such a thing?

The new tights were like cobwebs, so it might be as well. She picked up the leg wax, then a tube of depilatory cream for her underarms, which she usually shaved when the fancy took her. She had always been grateful that she was not hairy, but now, what with the wax and the depilatory, it seemed she was about to become very smooth indeed, if not downright bald. The price of the articles in her basket was a bit breathcatching, but then Penny and Anya spent more than that most days on make-up and bits and pieces. She paid up and carried her booty triumphantly back to Gloucester Terrace.

It was strange to be in the flat on a weekday afternoon, and alone, what was more. Outside, a fine rain was falling and it was quite chilly, but Sophie lit the gas fire and prepared to enjoy herself. First, she thought, she would defuzz, as they so charmingly put it, her underarms.

She took the depilatory into the bathroom, read the instructions through twice and then, with some trepidation, applied the stuff thickly to her armpits with the little wooden scoop thing provided.

The result was immediate and horrifying. A nasty tingling, burning sensation, a strong stench of chemicals, and, when she hastily scraped the stuff off again, a slight diminution in the number of hairs, though she counted four left in one armpit and seven in the other, apparently still quite firmly rooted. And, naturally, a red and angry rash.

'Sod the stupid stuff,' Sophie muttered, washing her armpits in soothing soap and water scattering talcum with a prodigal hand. She opened the window and the rain blew in, but at least the smell began to diminish. Ghastly odour – no wonder Anya and Penny preferred the perils of a razor! She then applied the face pack, which was soothing in that it neither hurt nor smelt, and puzzling in that it set as hard as concrete, making her fearful that it might never come off and entomb her for ever. But both Anya and Penny used face packs, and they always emerged whole, so she left it on for the required time and, when she started to chip it off, found, quite by accident, another method of hair removal. But her eyebrows did need plucking, actually, so that was not too bad.

She washed the rest of the pack off and was thrilled by the clean, fresh complexion beneath. This was a trick she would employ again! After an enjoyable bath, she returned to the kitchen, and the leg wax. She stared at the innocent little cake of stuff rather doubtfully, after her recent experiences. Was she being stupid? Suppose she could not get it off? But Anya, cursed with very dark hairs on her slim and shapely legs, went and had her legs waxed at the hairdressers of all places once a month, and she had once said that when she was home she did her own. She had said, moreover, that it was 'fiddly', but neither dangerous nor painful. The trick, it seemed, according to the instructions, was to get the wax off before it became too hard, but when it was hard enough.

Finally, she decided to give it a try simply on the grounds that it had cost five quid. At first she did a tiny bit of her leg though, about the size of a ten pence piece, just to make sure it was not agony. She spread the warm wax with the spatula, waited until it began to look opaque, and then pulled it off with the firmness advised by the instructions.

Eyes watering, for though not precisely painful it was by no means enjoyable, she did this a few more times and then decided she had the trick of it well enough to do a whole strip. Accordingly she melted the wax and spread like fury until she had a length of calf twelve inches long and about two inches wide thickly covered.

Then the doorbell rang. Sophie glanced at the clock, then hitched herself resignedly off her stool. It would not take her a moment to answer the door, and by the time she got back the wax would be hard enough to pull. She padded, barefoot, across the kitchen and into the hall.

'Thank God you're here, Sophie!' Deidre stood on the lino outside the door, pale and wild-eyed, clutching the enormous mound of her stomach. 'Is Anya here too? Or Penny?'

'No, just me. Is it the baby? Has it started?' Sophie's own stomach lurched. 'Where's John? Have you rung him? What about getting the doctor?'

'I think it's started. John's with his parents still, so I couldn't . . . Oh God, here it comes again!'

She went rigid and then, as if suddenly remembering a half-forgotten lesson, began, ostentatiously, to breathe deeply.

'Is it bad? Shall I ring John's mother? Or an ambulance – I'll ring for an ambulance,' Sophie gabbled. 'Don't you dare have it yet, Dee!'

'I'll do my best,' Deidre said as the tension drained from her bulging figure. 'The pa . . . contractions are quite far apart still, so that's a good thing, but I got a bit scared up there alone – can I sit in your kitchen for a bit?'

'Yes, of course, but . . .'

'It's all right, nothing's going to happen yet,' Deidre said, passing Sophie and sinking onto a kitchen chair. 'Sorry if I worried you, but I did feel lonely. They told me at the clinic not to ring until the contractions were coming every ten minutes and it's more like twenty at the moment, so there's tons of time. But I got the wind up when I found Mrs Fletcher was out and the hall phone wasn't working.'

Sophie, who had perched on the stool, leapt to her feet.

'The phone's not working? Dee, I must ring for the doctor! What's his number?'

'Oh not yet, don't leave me, I hate the thought of being alone in the house,' Deidre said forlornly. 'In a few moments Penny will probably be back and she can go to the phone.'

So-hie eyed the other girl distrustfully, as if she thought

Deidre might presently give birth just to spite her.

'But Dee, suppose it suddenly appears? I wouldn't have a clue what to do, except I believe you boil water. By the way, would you like some tea?'

'I would. Aah, is this another pain coming?' Deidre stiffened, frowned, then relaxed. 'False alarm. Put the kettle on, Soph.'

'Right, and then can I ring? Please, Dee?'

'Well, when we've drunk the tea then,' Deidre said reluctantly. 'Anyway, the phone down the road's usually bust, so what will you do then?'

'I'll go to a neightbour, or to the Indian shop on the corner. They've got a phone and they're ever so friendly, they'd let me use theirs, I'm sure.'

'Well, so long as you don't try Miss Marshall.' Both girls grinned. Miss Marshall hated young girls and the occupants of No. 7 in particular. She would take great pleasure in not allowing them to use her phone and would probably try to charge them for mounting her front steps. Hers was one of the few houses in Gloucester Gardens not converted into flats and she detested all the newcomers with a fanatical hatred.

'I won't, I'll go to the Indian shop if the box is out of order. As soon as we've drunk our tea.'

Whilst the tea was being made and drunk Sophie managed to ignore her impatience and her lively dread of becoming a godparent and a midwife all at one fell swoop, but once the cups were empty she could contain herself no longer.

'Dee, I'm going. I swear if it looks like taking me longer than fifteen minutes I'll buzz straight back here and get someone else to telephone. How does that sound?'

'I suppose you'd better, I've just had another contraction,' Deidre admitted. 'But do try to hurry! Why on earth isn't Penny back? It feels like hours since I arrived at your door.'

'Thank you for that – you've been here forty minutes, actually. As for Penny, heaven knows what's kept her, you can never tell; but Anya will be back around six or sooner. Look, let me write down the details so I don't get them wrong.'

Deidre's fears about the telephone down the road were upheld as soon as Sophie got inside the box; the receiver was on the floor, its connecting wires cut and someone had scrawled *Wogs go ome* in purple lipstick across the mirror and something worse across the glassed-in district code numbers. Sophie moaned, then dashed across to the corner shop where, after a brief explanation, she was willingly dragged round the counter and turned loose on the Rhaspani's own telephone.

'No need to pay,' the proprietor said, grinning all over his monkeylike visage. 'Miz Flowers, she be good customer when baby come.' He indicated the piles of disposable nappies, the tins of cheap talc and the jars of babyfood which took up a healthy share of the shelves.

Naturally, the doctor was out, but the receptionist who took the call seemed a sensible woman.

'It's all right, dear, I've got a note of the name and address now, so though Dr Crewe probably won't be able to see your friend, our Dr Mandable will do so. Her has a phone in his car so I can get in touch with him immediately and no doubt he'll ring for an ambulance, so if that reaches you first, perhaps you could ring me back and I'll tell him where the patient is. We run a delivery service, you see,' she added chattily, sounding as if bread and not babies were the topic. 'If mother prefers, her own doctor can deliver baby, and I see Mrs Flowers has opted for our service.'

'That's nice,' Sophie said with false enthusiasm. 'I'd better be getting back, but when do you think the doctor will arrive?'

'In about fifteen minutes. Don't worry, a first baby's more often late than early,' the receptionist said cheerfully. 'Good afternoon.'

Back in the flat Deidre was pacing the floor. She was obviously relieved to see Sophie.

'Is he coming? Did you get an ambulance? Oh, hell, not Dr Mandable? Miserable old soak, I just hope he can get up the stairs!'

'Well, the receptionist said the doctor would ring for an ambulance, so they may get here first,' Sophie comforted. 'How do you feel now? How are the pa . . . contractions, I mean?'

'Closer.' Deidre's face was shiny with sweat and her eyes were frightened. 'I'm not bothered by *them*, I know what to do and what to expect, it's just Johnny not being here and that fool Mandable coming. Oh, Sophie, when I've gone could you ring my mother-in-law and tell her that I've gone in and ask her to

107

make sure John doesn't come rushing back, trying to be in time for the birth, and get killed or something?' She gave a wan little smile. 'I want him badly, but all in one piece, not scattered over the motorway.'

'I'll see to that.'

Now that the phone call had been made and help was at hand, Sophie felt capable of dealing with any emergency. When, presently, Penny breezed into the flat and showed a tendency to panic when informed of the state of affairs, Sophie told her quite sharply to calm down and not to worry Dee.

'Everything's organised,' she hissed, with a hand on the kitchen door knob. 'The doctor will be here soon, and the ambulance, so don't let Dee see you're worried.'

And indeed, Penny showed herself in rather a good light once they entered the kitchen.

'Hi, Dee, cheating on John and bringing home the bacon two whole weeks early and with him away? Good for you! Shall I make you a cup of tea?'

Deidre was lying back in the wicker chair padded with soft cushions. She was panting, hands on ribs, eyes closed, but she opened them when she came to the end of her current contraction and smiled at Penny.

'Hello, Pen. No more tea, thanks, or I'll burst. What's that?'

Footsteps on the stairs sent Sophie and Penny rushing out onto the landing, but it was only Anya, lugging a heavy shopping bag up the stairs. She was almost as shattered by the news as Penny had been.

'Being born? In our flat? Mercy, send for a brace of doctors and midwives! I don't want to be a heroine, I just want my tea.'

'We have; Sophie rang ages ago,' Penny said complacently. 'Come in and have a cheery word with Dee, and don't worry her.'

But when they returned to the kitchen such sensible reactions were thrown to the four winds. Deidre was hunched up in her chair, scarlet-faced, and . . .

'Dee, you're pushing! For God's sake stop!' Sophie's voice was full soprano, the next best thing to a shriek. 'Dee, don't you go having that baby on the kitchen floor, take hold of yourself, girl!' She bent over Deidre, trying, without much success, to uncurl her. 'Where's that bloody doctor?'

'Not here,' Anya said unnecessarily. 'Penny, nip down and ring, see if you can hurry the ambulance up. Sophie, give me a hand, we'll have to get her through to my bedroom, it's nearest.'

'She can't be having it, though,' Sophie panted, as they struggled through to the bedroom with their shared burden stumbling between them. 'I've read her books when I've been up there sometimes, and she said she was still in the first stage of labour. You've got to be in the second – or is it the third? – before you start pushing.'

'No one told the baby, that's the snag,' Anya said as they dropped Deidre untidily onto Anya's bed. She shook a reproving finger at the recumbent figure. 'Don't just lie there, stop having that baby at once!'

'Bugger you both, do you think I *like* doing this?' Deidre muttered, giggling. 'Oh, oh, why the hell am I laughing? It hurts, it bloody hurts.' She hoisted herself into a crouching position, regardless of cries from her companions who urged her simultaneously to take deep breaths, to pant, and to bloody stop it, and she began to push. Scarlet-faced and making the most fearsome noise, she dragged on their arms, urging them to help her get it out.

'Get her knickers off!' Sophie shouted. 'Dee wiggle out of them, you can't give birth through cotton interlock.'

'I can if I bloody want to,' Deidre said through gritted teeth. 'I want to get it out! Anyway, I thought you didn't want me to bear it in your flat?'

'That's right,' Anya said, dragging Deidre's voluminous knickers off over her unresponsive kneecaps. 'Come on, don't be coy. I'm not taking them off so you can sully my virgin bed with that baby, I'm merely helping the hospital staff. It'll be one less garment to remove when you get there.'

The knickers came off and were tossed aside just as Deidre, purple-faced, gave an enormous grunt and a sudden, startled shriek and deluged the bed with what afterwards proved to be her waters, but which Anya, in the heat of the moment, thought to be something far more prosaic.

'My bed! Oh, Dee, all over my bed! Why didn't you tell us you wanted to wee, we could have brought you something. Oh, my poor bed!'

'Sod your bed,' Deidre shrieked. 'I've got to . . . I'm going to . . .'

'Don't, oh don't!' Sophie cried, unnerved to see Deidre suddenly straddling her legs and grunting with such abandon. 'Hold back Dee, there's a darling, hold back!'

Grrrunt! Three quick, gasping breaths. A roar, stifled. *Grrrrunt!*

'Don't! Dee, do stop it! Not on my bed! I forbid you to have that baby on my bed!'

Penny, entering the room as the two-way chorus broke out, stopped short, her mouth dropping open.

'My God, I wondered what the row was – what's happening?' She did not wait for a reply but turned and called over her shoulder to some invisible companion.

Sophie, glancing up, was surprised to see what at first glance she took to be a bus driver entering the room and pushing past Penny. She realised then that it must be the ambulance man and felt a wave of relief swamp her. Thank God! Something sinister and purple kept appearing and disappearing between Deidre's thighs – could it possibly be the baby's head? Or its bum? If it was its head, it seemed that Deidre was about to produce an absolute monster!

'Mind the way, love.' The man pushed the girls aside, cast a professional glance at Deidre's nether regions, and then gripped both her hands. 'Here we go then, my darling, just you push for all you're worth and it'll be over in two shakes.'

Deidre recognised the note of authority in the man's voice. She clutched his hands fervently and actually managed a tight little grin.

'Oh, thank God! I've got to . . . got to . . .'

'That's right, my darling, and just you give a few yells if it helps, don't listen to these silly cows,' the man said briskly, giving Penny, Anya and Sophie a quelling glance. 'Hoff with you, young ladies, if you don't want . . .'

He got no further. Ignorance might be bliss, but Sophie, Penny and Anya were destined to be in at the birth. Deidre gave a grunt even more obscene and charged with effort than her previous grunts. She rocked forward so that she was actually crouching for a moment on her toes and then she gave a huge, gusty sigh.

And Graham John Flowers was born.

110

Chapter Seven

That night, lying in bed, Sophie replayed her day since the moment that Deidre had come knocking on her door. It had certainly been an experience, and one which none of them would forget in a hurry. Indeed, by the time Deidre and her child had been taken off to hospital and Anya had lugged all her bedding down to the launderette, the three of them were almost too tired to talk.

But by seven o'clock they were recovering, sitting at the kitchen table eating toasted cheese, and were at last able to discuss what had happened with a certain detachment.

Penny started it, as she so often did.

'If that's childbirth, I'm not having any part in it,' she declared. 'Thank God for the pill. If I thought there was a chance of ending up like that, I'd foreswear nooky for ever.'

'It was off-putting,' Anya agreed. 'What was more, I thought new-born babies were supposed to be sweet; that one was just like a poor little skinned monkey – except for its hairy arms.'

'Dee thought it was beautiful,' Sophie reminded them. 'And I rather liked it. I touched its skin and it was so soft, impossibly soft, softer than silk. And I don't think that stuff on its arms was hair, it was more like fluff. Oo-ooh!'

'What's the matter?' Penny asked, crunching toast.

Sophie indicated her leg. Penny bent to look closer.

'What on earth have you done, Sofa, your leg's all shiny and . . . my God, it's wax! You fool, how long has that been on?'

'Hours,' Sophie said hollowly. 'I clean forgot I was waxing my legs when Dee came rushing in with her news. Oh blast, now I suppose it will be awfully hard to get off.'

She was right. In the end, having tried in vain to soften the wax with a flannel dipped in hot water, Anya advised her to sit down, stiffen her sinews, and submit to having it ripped off.

'Think of me as a surgeon and this as a minor operation,' she

111

advised, gripping the top of the wax. 'Here we go!'

Sophie's scream, Penny said afterwards, rivalled anything that Dee had produced, and it certainly had unexpected results. Anya must have left the front door ajar after her visit to the laundrette, for the kitchen door suddenly burst open and a man shambled into the room, heading straight for Sophie. The three girls got a confused impression of a dark suit, a lot of wildly untidy, white hair and a strong smell of whisky, and then he was bending solicitously over Sophie.

'It's all right, my dear, I'm here now, you'll be ri's rain in a moment,' the man said, patting Sophie's shoulder with a shaking hand and almost anaesthetising her with a gust of stale whisky. 'I'll ring for 'nambulance, soon have you safe on th'ward.'

There was a moment of startled silence before the three of them started to laugh, though Sophie, nursing her sore calf, wished that it had not been she who was mistaken for an expectant mother. Poor Dr Mandable, for it was he, gazed blearily from face to face but seemed to take very little in, until Anya told him that mother and child were already in hospital and offered to get him a drink to wet the baby's head.

This galvanised him into joining in their laughter with a squeaky little *hee hee* of his own and then, bloodshot eyes twinkling, he accepted a large brandy before setting out for his next unfortunate patient.

'I suppose if he drives into a lamppost or kills someone we'll be responsible,' Anya said as they returned to their coffee. 'I'll finish the waxing off for you Sofa, it won't hurt, I'm a dab hand at it.'

Sophie could not help feeling a bit apprehensive, but Anya managed to finish the waxing comparatively painlessly and she also made a remark which pleased Sophie.

'Poor old Mandable – do you realise, Sophie, that if he'd made that mistake two months ago you'd have burst into tears and stopped speaking to anyone for a week? You're getting more sensible every day.'

'Thanks,' Sophie said, as the three of them made their night time drinks. 'Do you know, I've done more living lately than I ever thought I'd do in my whole life?'

'I know what you mean,' Anya agreed. 'And tomorrow we're dining and dancing, so we'd best go to bed now and get what sleep we can.'

Having reached the end of her replay, Sophie wound the film back to the moment of birth. She felt she ought to go over it again so that it would never be lost. But it had been an exhausting day; the replay went slower and slower until it was lost in dreams.

'I'm going out tonight. Well, actually,' Sophie said, coming clean, 'Anya and I are being taken to dinner by Mr Eade and a client.'

She and Stephen were sitting in Flavell's having the promised salad. They had talked a lot and laughed a lot, and Sophie had related the story of the birth of Dee's baby with relish. Indeed, she might never have mentioned her date had not Stephen remarked on her new make-up.

'Going out with some chap Eade's dug up?' Stephen sounded quite offended. 'And he merits all that stuff on your face?'

'That stuff' was a dark lipstick and browny-gold eyeshadow, and Sophie felt the colour rush to her cheeks at his words.

'Is it horrid?' she asked anxiously. 'We thought – Anya and I, that is – that it made me look older and more sophisticated.'

Stephen made a derisive noise.

'Older! What on earth makes you want to look older?' He leaned across the table and pinched her cheek gently. 'I like you just as you are, without any make-up. Why not have a good wash and come out with me instead?'

Sophie laughed a trifle unsteadily. Stephen had asked her out – but only because he must know as well as she did that it was impossible. She had agreed to go with Anya and go she must.

'Sorry, I've got a previous engagement.'

They left the place soon after that and returned to the centre, and Sophie thought, regretfully, that she had probably heard the last of that invitation. But during the course of the afternoon Stephen had cause to come in and search for a file, and whilst he was searching he turned to her and demanded to know whether the new lipstick was kissproof.

Sophie, her heart fluttering, said she was not sure, whereupon he pulled her, quite roughly, out of her chair and into his arms.

'We'd better put it to the test then, hadn't we?'

Sophie felt quite an old hand at kissing, now. She leaned against him, responding like billy-o, letting her tongue flutter against his in what, had she but known it, was a very provocative

113

fashion. He groaned something against her mouth and then the door opened behind him and someone cleared their throat.

Sophie would have moved away but Stephen continued to hold her, though he swung round so that they were both half-facing the intruder. It was Dottie, looking sillier than usual with her mouth at half-cock and a cigarette apparently glued to her lower lip. She started to speak and the cigarette saved her blushes by falling to the floor, so that she had to bend down and pick it up.

'Yes, Dottie? Was it me or Sophie you wanted?'

Stephen sounded not only cool, but also sarcastic. He doesn't like Dottie either, Sophie thought joyfully. And won't she be furious that he was kissing me!

'It was Sophie, actually; I wanted to ask her if she'd got any milk to spare,' Dottie said. Her face was blotched with red and her little eyes darted from one to the other with greedy curiosity. Sophie was about to say yes, she had plenty of milk, but Stephen's arms tightened around her, keeping her silent.

'No. Sorry, Dottie. And now, if you wouldn't mind, we're rather busy . . . '

Without more ado he proceeded to kiss Sophie again with even more enthusiasm.

The closing of the door behind Dottie allowed Sophie to give a little giggle, leaning against Stephen's chest whilst he rocked her gently back and forth, smiling down at her, looking extremely pleased with himself.

'Dottie vanquished! She'll tell everyone how things stand, what's more, so you've got to give Eade's pal the go-by. Come on, I'll take you wherever you want to go, though I won't let you spoil yourself by eating foolishly. What about it?'

Sophie sighed and gazed adoringly up into the face above her own.

'It's so tempting, Stephen, but you know I can't. I couldn't let them down, having said I'd go.'

She must have sounded wistful, but she could not help it. She would have loved to dine with Stephen – but there were other nights. If he was as keen as the pretended . . .

'I accept that. Tomorrow night, then? We'll go down to a little place I know near the Thames, how about that?'

Sophie sighed blissfully.

114

'Oh, Stephen, that would be so nice. Thank you for asking, and I'll come.'

'Well, hello, there! We thought you'd be tucked up in bed by now.'

Sophie and Anya had been delivered home by Mr Eade and Sam Schuck in a taxi and, in view of the fact that it was two in the morning, had taken off their shoes and stolen up the stairs so as not to disturb Penny. But, entering the kitchen, who should they find there but Penny, swaying a little as she stood by the fridge, drinking milk straight from the bottle. She saluted them with it, then put it down.

'Hello yourselves. Had a good time?'

'Very nice, thanks,' Sophie said primly. She sank down on one of the kitchen stools and stretched out her legs in their fine tights, wriggling her toes, freed now from the grip of her new shoes. 'Gosh, but I'm glad to get those shoes off!'

'What was Schuck like?'

'Kind, amusing, you know. We had a delicious dinner too, didn't we, Anya? Clear soup, chicken, asparagus, and then strawberries with kirsch poured over them. Lovely.'

She beamed at them both. Truth to tell, the evening had been very run of the mill; what was so marvellous was to be one of them, in the kitchen at two in the morning post-morteming an evening out, instead of tucked up in bed in unbuttoned, seam-cracking, four-year-old pyjamas.

'We danced,' Anya said. 'In a very posh nightclub. And drank champagne. Sophie did very well – Sam said she was his idea of an English rose and she scarcely winced. What about your evening, Pen?'

'I had a ball. Aubrey took me to this gha-astly dive, down by the river at Islington, but then he got terribly drunk and went to sleep on someone's sofa and there was this beautiful man, with a dark brown voice and broad chest. He carted me off and we made beautiful music together in a tiny cabin on a tiny house-boat which he thought was mine and I thought was his.' She giggled. 'Someone's in for a surprise tomorrow morning; we felt hungry afterwards and ate pounds of bacon and a whole box of eggs!'

'Does that mean you've forgotten Graham being born?'

Sophie asked suspiciously. 'Poor Aubrey – who was the fellow?'

Penny shrugged.

'I'm on the pill, so I've persuaded myself that daft Dee probably wanted that baby and probably wasn't bothering to pop pills. Anyway, if you don't have fun, what's the point of living?'

'Now don't start any buts, Sophie,' Anya said quite sharply, for her. 'If you do we'll be here all night. I'm off to bed.'

She left the room and Penny, after giving a cavernous yawn, remarked, 'And what did you think of her Derek?'

'He's . . . ' Sophie broke off. 'What do you mean, her Derek?'

'He's her boss, isn't he? I probably call Stephen your Stephen sometimes.'

'Oh. Well, he's quite nice though rather sensible and serious. I can't imagine him kicking over the traces ever, though I suppose he may have done, when he was younger. He kept telling us about his wife, Ruth, and their Yorkshire terriers.' She took a deep breath. 'I hope Stephen doesn't carry on like that when we have dinner tomorrow evening.'

Penny, who had been half-way out of the kitchen door, stopped short, a slow grin creeping over her face.

'Really? Stephen Bland? Well, I'm damned! Anya said you were coming out of your shell!'

'Who was it?'

Sophie, who had run down to answer the phone and run up again, was still a bit breathless, but she was pleased with herself. Even a month ago she would have thought twice about running up and down the stairs but now it was nothing. She beamed at Penny, who was washing her hair in the bathroom and addressing her upside down, blinking the water out of her eyes.

'It was for me. Stephen's got a dinner in Tunbridge Wells on Saturday evening. It's an all-male do, but he wants me to stay over with him and have a day there on Sunday. I said I would.'

Penny grunted. Stephen was a frequent visitor to the flat now and it was clear that, though they never actually said so, Stephen and Sophie were more than just friends. But Penny doubted that they were lovers. She thought now, eyeing Sophie through the water running down her face, that she would have been able to tell if the younger girl had taken such a step.

116

'That'll be fun, I should think. Stephen's awfully good company. Is he calling for you here?'

'Yes. I'm just going to make omelettes for Anya and me – shall I do you one as well? We've got cheese, mushrooms and bacon, so I'll do plain omelettes and then stuff them with the other ingredients I think.'

'You and Anya make me sick, you seem to like living on slimming food.' Penny's voice was plaintive. 'I feel like chips and pies sometimes, you know. You're a good shape now, Sofa, don't go overdoing it.'

'I shan't.' Sophie began to break eggs into a basin. 'I'm going to buy some jeans on Saturday now that I don't bulge too badly. And I'll do you an omelette, shall I?'

'Oh, all right.' Penny emerged from the bathroom, shaking her wet hair, and wandered into the kitchen. 'Better get yourself a new nightie, too, if you're spending the night with the lad.'

'I'm not; Stephen isn't like that. Will you come with me to buy the jeans, Pen? Don't forget, you're my chief fashion adviser.'

Penny nodded.

'Right. I wonder what you'll look like in jeans?'

Sophie turned round and squinted down at her bottom. For a moment, doubts warred. It was small compared with what it had been, but was it small enough? Would she look like two ferrets fighting in a sack? Her waist was considerably smaller and her thighs were better too, but . . . oh, damn Penny!

'Damn you, Penny, why must you make me wonder if I'm doing the right thing? I'll buy the jeans if you and Anya approve, does that satisfy you?'

'I was satisfied before,' Penny said mildly, crouching down on the floor to plug the hairdryer into the socket. 'I only wondered what you'd look like because I've never seen you in trousers. Damn it, I said you were a good shape not five minutes ago!'

'So you did. Sorry, it's just that I have personal doubts. Is that Anya's clatter?'

Penny listened, then nodded.

'Yup. Are you two playing tennis this evening?'

'We are. It's terribly good for me, and Anya's keen, so we thought we'd hire a court. Why? Want to join us?'

'Not I! But I can't help wondering whether all this exercise is good for Anya, she's looking so pale and ill lately. One day she eats everything she can lay hands on, the next she starves. But anyway, it's her business. She's got some holiday to come, perhaps she can go home and rest up and forget whatever's bugging her.'

At that point the drier began to roar and presently Anya came into the kitchen, effectively putting a stop to any attempt to discuss her.

Whilst they ate, Sophie asked Anya when she was taking her holiday, and Anya promptly replied in kind.

'What about you, Sophie? When are you going home? Your mother wants to see the New You ever so badly, you know she does.'

It was a sore point. Sophie begged the question and changed the subject, but in her own room after the meal, changing into her tennis things, she returned to it. She knew she should go home really, she knew she was being very unfair to her parents, but she was loath to do so. She felt, weirdly, that if she returned home she would find herself becoming the old Sophie again. Not just fat but ill-at-ease, diffident, unsure.

When she thought about it, she realised that she had shed, not only her excess weight, but nearly all her shyness and awkwardness. It was as though she no longer needed to hide behind a wall of defensiveness, or shelter behind shyness. She could not only show the new, slimmer Sophie, but she could show the bolder person beneath, the girl who had always been there, only no one had cared enough to try to dig her out. That person had been revealed and had proved herself to be capable of friendship, generosity, perhaps even a degree of charm.

Yet, if she went home, would they immediately take the old, patronising tone with her, the 'poor old Sophie' tone? If so, it seemed possible that they might resurrect the old Sophie with it, the one who lied and boasted and stole just to give herself some armour against the cruel world. It was not worth the risk, for she had found she disliked and despised yesterday's Sophie as much as everyone else had seemed to. If I met the me of a year ago now, I'd treat her just like everyone else did, she realised with astonishment. Because, though I'm sorry for her, sorry for all the anguish she lived through, I know she brought almost all of it on herself. She could have stopped guzzling years ago, for all she said she could not. She could have made life easier and pleasanter for everyone, particularly herself.

'Well, Sophie? Shall we have a bargain? I'll go home when you do!'

Anya's tone was teasing, but Sophie would only shake her head. She had no idea why Anya did not want to go home but she understood her own reasons only too well, and knew that she was not yet strong enough to face up to Glydon Grove. Not quite yet.

In the middle of their game of tennis, during a particularly hard-won rally, Anya fainted. She put a hand to her head, dropped her racquet, and keeled sideways.

Fortunately it was a grass court and by the time Sophie had got round the net and knelt beside her, Anya was coming round. She raised her head, frowned, tried to get up – and burst into tears. This was so totally unlike her friend that Sophie was really frightened. She lugged Anya over to the green garden seat and sat her down, then called a boy over from where he had been playing in the park outside. He was about fourteen, but listened intelligently enough when Sophie said that she would give him a quid to fetch her a taxi and to get the driver to give her a hand with her friend, who had fainted.

Anya, however, was having none of it.

'Don't be daft, it was only the heat, and leaping around,' she said, trying to struggle to her feet. 'Let's get on with the game.'

'No. You're ill; we'll just nip round to Casualty and get you checked over,' Sophie said firmly. 'Honestly, Anya, you gave me one hell of a scare just now!'

'Me too,' Anya admitted. 'But it's nothing, really. I'm not going to casualty, so there!'

'Are you having a bad period?' Sophie asked, then shook her head at her own question. 'No, that's daft, you'd been leaping and bounding like a spring chicken two minutes earlier. Anya, you must have a check-up.'

'Damn you, Sophie! I've had one.'

'Ha! When, may I ask?'

'A month ago.' Anya sank her voice to a whisper. 'Since you're being so bloody nosy and difficult, I'll tell you. I'm in the club.'

Afterwards, Sophie maintained that it was not so silly to assume that Anya was still talking of tennis, but it certainly made for some ambiguous conversation until Anya made herself clearer.

'I've got a bun in the oven, Sofa, I'm up the creek, I'm increasing . . . damn it girl, I'm PREGNANT!'

'Oh!' Sophie bit back the words, 'but you aren't married', and changed it to: 'Well, that explains it.' She then helped Anya into the taxi, since the boy had so obligingly fetched both it and its driver, and they drove back to the flat in lordly silence. Indoors once more, however, Sophie felt that she could not leave the subject there.

'Anya, I'm sorry to pester, but what are you going to do about it? Who's the father? It's ages since you and Freddie . . . '

Anya snorted with amusement and put the kettle on the stove. She had gone very pale when she fainted but now her colour was coming back and she looked much better.

'I'm going to get rid of it, that's why I didn't say anything. In fact, in a fortnight there would be nothing to tell, because it will all be over.'

'Oh. And you haven't told Penny?'

'No, I haven't told anyone. It was a shock, because I've always been fastidious I suppose you could say, so I've taken the pill when I needed to do so, and when I'm not on the pill, I use the old contraceptive method of slowly shaking the head from side to side.' She smiled lovingly at Sophie. 'It's the method you've found rather effective, I know. Only I went out with a chap and for once I was foolish, and I found I was in trouble. I'm not the maternal type, I don't think, though I did go through a phase of wondering whether to go through with it, keep the baby and damn 'em all. But I love my job, Sophie, and it would break my parents' heart to have a bastard grandchild. As for the father – well, he's less than nothing to me, I doubt I'll ever see him again. So you see, being aborted isn't going to be a soul-searing experience. I'm too selfish to want a baby to hand over to someone else, and much too selfish to give up the rest of my life to a brat. So a fortnight on Friday I'm for the chop.'

'How on earth did you find out about abortions? Did you ring that number that's plastered all over the underground?' Sophie asked, trying to sound blase and sophisticated.

'I asked someone at the centre who's had one,' Anya admitted. 'She told me the name and address of a reputable clinic and I rang up and booked myself in. I saw a doctor, of course. It's expensive, but all mistakes have to be paid for, and I'd rather pay in money than my life's blood, which is how I look on being a Mum – especially after seeing Dee go through it.'

'Crumbs; you must have known then,' Sophie said, doing lightning calculations.

'I did. I hadn't made up my mind, then, but I decided soon after. Look, don't say anything to Penny, there's a dear. I don't think I could bear the things she'd say.'

'But she'd agree with you completely,' Sophie said, astonished. 'Penny's all for women running their own lives and abortions and so on. She won't have any doubt at all that you're doing the right thing.'

'Precisely.' Anya's voice was quiet. 'I don't want to be praised and encouraged to do something which a part of me believes is wrong. In fact, if she started telling me how clever I was and how right, I might just change my mind and decide to go through with it.'

'Would that be so wrong, Anya? If you're having doubts . . .'

'Blast you, girl, of course I'm having doubts, I wouldn't be human if I didn't. But I keep telling myself that in a mere two weeks now the decision will have been taken, the die will have been cast, and I'll be my own woman again, and that keeps me sane. So not a word to Penny.'

'Right. And why are you waiting two weeks, if you're certain that you're doing the best thing?'

'Money. Do you know what it costs to have an abortion?' Anya named a sum which made Sophie whistle expressively. 'I know I'm well paid, but I still needed a bit of time to lay my hands on that much!'

'And the father doesn't know? Anya, if you just told him, he might well pay half – it's half his fault, no matter how you rationalise.'

'He doesn't know and he isn't going to. A fortnight isn't long, it'll soon pass.'

'Right, I understand you don't want to tell him, or you can't, if he isn't around. But would you *please* accept a loan from my clothes hoard? I was reading in a magazine the other day that the later you leave abortion the more dangerous it is for the mother. Please, Anya? Heaven knows, I've borrowed off you, why shouldn't you borrow off me?'

'Thanks, Sophie, but it isn't just money, as it happens. I want

121

to have the operation on that particular day because the follow
ing week my boss goes off for a week himself, so I can safely take
some holiday without fear of jeopardising my job.'

'And you won't change your mind, bring it forward?'

Decidedly, Anya shook her head.

'No. The doctor said I wouldn't be at the clinic for more than a
total of about four hours and then I can get a taxi back to the flat
So you see, there's nothing to it and I'll probably be in to work the
following Monday. But just in case . . .' For the first time her
self-confidence showed a tiny crack. 'Can you be around
Sophie, when I go in and come out? On Friday fortnight?'

'Yes, I'll be around,' Sophie said. She had already decided to
take a few hours off herself so that she could go to the clinic with
Anya. Damn it, she said fiercely to herself, no one should have to
walk into a place like that without a friend to hold her hand. She
wondered, briefly, who the father was, but since Anya had
implied he had been chance-met, to put it no stronger, there
seemed little point in pursuing that angle.

'Thanks.' Anya got up and poured them both a cup of tea, since
the pot had been brewing throughout their conversation. 'I'm
glad it didn't occur to either you or Penny why I suddenly began
to take hot baths, to drink gin and to race up and down the stair
and round and round the tennis court.'

'I didn't notice, but then I'm stupid about things like that,'
Sophie said apologetically. 'It's odd that Penny didn't, though.'

'Penny is almost totally single-minded, and suffers from tun
nel vision into the bargain,' Anya said, sipping her tea. 'If you
have a problem she's never faced herself then it doesn't exist. In a
way, it's rather comforting to have a friend like that; she never
worries about anything, you know. And anyway, give me
another couple of weeks and my problem, too, will cease to exist
It will melt away like frost in June.' She sipped her tea again
then grimaced. 'Glory, this is so strong it could stand by itself
Where are the bickies? Chuck 'em over.'

Chapter Eight

On Saturday morning the three girls went shopping for jeans. Sophie was still very self-conscious in shops and far too easily persuaded by sales assistants, her friends thought, but in the shop of their choice, with music blaring, changing rooms like small stalls with a mere half door between you and the world, and the shop assitants all gum-chewing teenagers, interference from the staff was not likely to be an obstacle. In fact, since they were treated with total indifference, it was Penny who selected jeans which might do from the piles of seemingly identical garments on the shelves.

'Here, try these,' Penny advised, her voice rising by several decibels as she tried to outdo the music. 'They're all your size, but some are snugger than others.'

There was no room in the cubicle for more than one person at a time so Sophie had to struggle alone. She gave up on the first pair when they refused to go past her calves and on the second pair when they baulked at her thighs, but the third pair, like Goldilocks with her porridge, went on after some struggling. Indeed, she managed to do the zip up without holding her breath, and they looked very nice on her. The only trouble was that she seemed to be in danger of being sawn in two by the things.

She came, stiff-legged, out of the cubicle, sidling diffidently between the teeny-boppers who were waiting for their friends. She raised her brows at Penny, who had been cast into convulsions by her gait.

'Well? What's so damned funny? Are they all right or aren't they?'

'They're fine,' Anya said, too obviously trying not to laugh. 'Why are you walking like that?'

'Because they're clutching me in peculiar places,' Sophie hissed. 'Seriously, do they have to be this tight? A larger size . . .'

123

She was dissuaded from taking the coward's way out, the jeans were paid for and they left the shop.

'If you think I look so funny why did you tell me to buy them?' Sophie snapped five minutes later, when Penny's giggles showed no sign of abating. 'Christ, I'm not kidding, these jeans are reaching the parts other beers cannot reach! Can you look me in the eyes and tell me that girls willingly go round being sawn in twain by blue denim? Surely you can't all be so daft!'

'That's why there ain't no virgins left in Bloomsburee,' Penny chanted between giggles. 'It isn't the fellers, it's the denim jeans – rape by blue cotton!'

Sophie, still feeling like the bacon on a bacon slicer, managed a small giggle of her own.

'I admire you all, then. But glory, aren't they uncomfortable? I just hope I can get back to the flat without splitting them.'

But by the time they got back to the flat she was a little consoled, for before they bought the jeans Penny had persuaded her to buy some mini-briefs – tiny, cheeky affairs with slogans on them, the sort of thing which just never gets made in a size twenty. And afterwards they bought a nightie, a dream of a garment in double nylon, pale primrose coloured, and a strawberry pink T-shirt and a sort of string vest in white cotton. She knew she had never been so fashionable before and it did much to console her for the discomfort of the jeans.

'It isn't fashion, so much, it's being just like everyone else,' Anya said when Sophie stood before them at last, clad in her new garments and beaming from ear to ear. 'You look very sweet, poppet, and I like your hair in a pony-tail in that get-up, but don't go wearing it like that with ordinary clothes, it's a waste of the colour and the curls.'

'My hair is brown and hardly curls at all,' Sophie said, surprised.

'Your hair is chestnut and curls very nicely,' Anya corrected. She had been lounging against the living room mantelpiece, but now she straightened and made for the door. 'Coffee time, I think.'

'Jeans, eh? I like a pair of well-filled jeans. I thought we'd go straight to the hotel so that I can change for this dinner and get

124

it over with, and then we'll have the rest of the evening to browse round the town. Suit you?'

Sophie, in her jeans and pink shirt with a soft weekend bag slung over one shoulder, climbed into the car, settled herself in the seat with the safety belt fastened, and then nodded as he climbed into his own seat.

'Yes, it sounds great. Isn't it a lovely evening?'

The journey was enlivened for them both by gossip, though it was Stephen who did most of the talking. He was producing a play at the moment and suffering because the woman who played the lead, though popular with viewers, was a poor actress and temperamental into the bargain, and the writer was also an actor who had insisted on taking the male lead, despite the fact that he was patently unsuited to the part.

'I just wish Simon would realise that he's ruining an excellent production of a far from contemptible play,' Stephen groaned now, as the car speeded up to greet the countryside. 'I'll swing for him if he continues to show off like fury when he's supposed to be taking a back seat for once.'

Sophie, murmuring sympathy, remembered a remark she had overheard from a cameraman working on the new production.

'Enfant terrible meets enfant terrible,' he had muttered to his opposite number. 'They're two of a kind, so look out for fireworks.'

He had been more right than he knew, she thought wryly. Simon Waite admitted that Stephen was the best director he had ever worked for; Stephen admitted that Simon was quite possibly a genius – yet they could not get on.

'Perhaps you shouldn't have taken it on,' Sophie said, now. 'You've never worked well with Elena. But it must be nearly finished, isn't it? And they're talking about a big series, aren't they, with lots of kudos? I bet you're offered it.'

He sighed, then turned to her.

'That reminds me, I was just going to tell you to book a good photographer for the stills, and that brought it to mind. Remember standing in for Sumatra once, a good while back? When they were doing stills?'

'Yes, vaguely. Why?'

'The chap took some photos of you; he gave them to me a day or so back and asked me to pass them on. I wasn't keen on the way he did it, I think he was trying to get closer to you, so I just said I was having a weekend with you and I'd hand them over then. Know him, do you?'

'No. My God, I wish he hadn't photographed me then!' Sophie felt her cheeks begin to burn. 'It was kind of him to bring them round, but I was . . . well, I wish he hadn't.'

'I know what you're thinking, it was before the diet really got going,' Stephen said with considerable acumen. 'Yes, you were plump and of course they show it, though they're not bad – well, the fellow's highly regarded, that was why Sumatra wanted him to do the stills. Do you want to see them, or shall I get rid of them for you?'

'I'd better see them, I suppose,' Sophie said with a sigh. 'Did you bring them down with you?'

'I did. Right, you can take a look tomorrow morning, if you've a mind.'

Soon after that they arrived at their hotel. It was quite a small place but it was comfortable and near to the Pantiles, where most of the night-life of the town, such as it was, would centre on, according to Stephen.

'There are morris dancers performing later, and of course you can walk down to the pump room and have a swig of the waters if you like,' Stephen said, as he unlocked her door for her. 'I've booked you a quiet corner table in the dining room for seven o'clock, so you haven't got too much time, but after you've eaten, you can have a look round. I'll try to get away by nine.' He kissed her briefly, then pushed her into her room with a slap on the tightly-filled jeans. 'Be good!'

At first, everything went swimmingly. Sophie had a delicious and not too fattening dinner of hot shrimps on buttered toast, a medium rare steak with a side salad and then a fresh peach and several cups of coffee. Sated, she returned to her room where she watched television, feeling rather decadent since they only had a black and white set at home and none at all at the flat and Devina, she knew, thought that to have a television set in a bedroom was the first step on the slippery slope to hell.

She watched for forty minutes or so and then resolutely turned it off and made her way into the bathroom. Stephen would be back about nine, so she would have a hot bath, use her new talcum and toilet water, put on the smoochy black dress with the bodice that did such exciting things for her bust, and wait for Stephen.

That was Sophie's plan.

In the event, she ran the bath, took off her shirt, bra and socks, and then began to tug at her jeans. She tried pulling them off from the waistband, which meant heaving them down inside out, but they stuck on her hips, so she tried pulling them from the ankles, which meant contortions scarcely possible for one encased in skin-tight jeans.

Nothing worked. For all the good she did, she might just as well have been glued into the things from thigh to knee. Not an inch could she budge them by.

At a quarter to nine, tearful and panic-stricken, she gave up the unequal struggle. She pulled them up again, zipped them, then had a quick wash, brushed her hair and applied cold water to her swollen eyelids. Then she got out a blue and white striped shirt and a scarlet neckerchief and put them on, checked herself in the mirror and waited for Stephen's knock.

He was not late; at ten past nine he came in looking pleased with himself since the food had been good and his after-dinner speech a resounding success. He made no comment on her attire of course, but said he was going to change out of his dinner jacket and presently tapped on her door again, this time in silver-grey cords and a matching jacket, and suggested that the night was young enough for a stroll before bed.

'There's a good little pub at the other end of town, you'll love it,' he said, taking her arm. 'And then we'll walk along Million-aires' Row, though that isn't its proper name. You'll like that, all right, it's fantastic, like something left over from the last century. Very romantic, too, with gas lighting and trees meeting overhead.'

Sophie, clinging to his arm, knew that if he said she would like it he would be right. She was so lucky, he always knew what was best for her and what she would most enjoy. What was more, though he made it plain enough that he wanted to go to bed with her, he had made it equally plain that it was her choice, that she might call the tune. So now she cuddled up close to him and he put his arm right round her and smiled down at her with the proprietorial air which she so adored, and led her out into the fading light of evening.

The walk up to the top of the town was slow and romantic and, during the course of it and whilst they were in the pub, Sophie was able to put the jeans out of her mind. But walking along Millionaires' Row, where the Victorian street lamps gleamed through the dappling gold-green tree shadows like something out of a nursery rhyme, their tightness began to make itself felt once more. Women in the days of the crusades, Sophie recalled, had worn chastity belts. Well, the 1984 female had only to buy herself a fashionably tight pair of jeans and she would be every bit as safe from rape and pillage. Now that it was too late and she was wedged into the things, Sophie remembered the many times that either Anya or Penny had wailed for help to get their jeans off, when the jeans were new and stiff. But of course, when it was her, she had to be alone with Stephen in an hotel and probably at this time of night there would not even be a chambermaid on duty. If she rang down, some horrible, horny-handed old porter would be sent up to help her. She doubted that there was a soul awake save for themselves in the whole of Tunbridge Wells. It was the sort of town, she reflected bitterly, where people went to bed at ten. If they wore tight jeans they probably lived somewhere else.

'You're very quiet, pet. Tired?'

Sophie nodded and rubbed her face against Stephen's sleeve. Suppose he brought a hot drink to her room as he had that other time, and found her still fully dressed? He would think she did not trust him. On the other hand, she could throw herself into his arms with an abandoned cry and if he was as keen as he pretended, then it would be his task to winkle her out of her clothing!

A little giggle bubbled and broke as a purr of laughter on Sophie's lips. She could just imagine it – Stephen, all ardent, being foiled by these bloody jeans!

'What's funny, love?'

Sophie sighed. She could not possibly tell him. Why did every predicament into which she fell always turn into farce, though? Some people managed to go through life being dignified if nothing else, but with her it had to be one long fumble. Here she was, possibly about to lose her virginity, and the event looked like being as comic as anything Muir and Norden could dream up.

'Nothing's funny, really, I'm just so happy!'

They made their way back to the hotel foyer where Stephen ordered hot chocolate and biscuits for two to be brought to his room in twenty minutes. Sophie thought, wildly, that she could say she was no longer thirsty, bar him out, but she knew it was not possible. She could not hurt Stephen like that, when he had gone to such lengths to prove to her that though he wanted her, he would be content with whatever she chose to give. They had a comfortable routine of love-making when he took her out which consisted of kissing, cuddling and some pleasant though innocuous petting and she just knew that he would not go beyond that, even in a hotel bedroom. She would get the jeans off, she vowed grimly, even if it meant taking a layer of skin with them.

Alone in her room, she started at once to try to remove them. Tugging, swearing, sweating, she simply got nowhere. She could get them almost off her hips but not quite, by rolling them inside out, or she could drag them down over her heels by straightforward pulling. But remove them altogether she could not.

Stephen's knock caught her struggling back into them again, and she pulled up the zip and fastened the top button with her hand actually on the door. She was almost in tears and this time made no attempt to hide the fact and Stephen took one look at her face and then stood the tray down on her bedside table and came and took her in his arms.

'What's the matter, pet? You aren't scared of me, for God's sake? You know very well that I'm letting you set the pace, and . . . Sophie?'

'I can't get these bloody jeans off!' Sophie wailed. 'I've tugged and tugged, I've tried inside out and straight pulls, and I can't budge the buggers. And I'm sick, bloody sick, of being a laughing stock. It's always *me*, Stephen, the fat, stupid one who gets stuck in doorways and in baths, and I've t-tried and tried. I've starved myself to get into a pair of jeans, I felt I'd *achieved* something when I got them on, and now . . .' She stopped to stare furiously up into Stephen's face. 'If you laugh I'll never speak to you again and you can get right out of here! If you tell anyone, if you dare . . .'

He was not laughing. He kissed her wet cheeks, then held her back from him. Did his mouth twitch? But his eyes were serious.

'My poor love, everyone has a job to get out of tight jeans; it takes time and lots of tugging. You're stuck out of fright, pet, not because you're any fatter than anyone else. Just sit down on the bed, stick your legs out, and relax. Or are you going to forbid me to help in case the sight of bare legs gives me terrible ideas?'

Sophie sat down and stretched out her legs; she even managed a watery smile.

'The sight of my legs wouldn't give anyone ideas – except perhaps a hippo. Tug away.'

'Right. I'll start at the ankles and just pull smoothly until they're below your knees and then you'll be able to manage.' The rooms were en suite and he jerked his head at the bathroom door, both hands already busy with their task. 'You can go in there and change.'

'Right. And you'd better drink your chocolate before it gets cold,' Sophie said, as her jeans descended. She stood up and pulled the garment off with considerable relief. 'Thanks, Stephen.' She straightened and made for the bathroom, picking up her nightie en route. 'I'll go and change into this, shan't be a tick.'

The nightie would, she thought, be perfectly respectable for drinking chocolate and kissing in. The top layer was very fine to be sure, but the combination of the two meant that not so much as a curve could be clearly seen. Stephen would not find her nightie embarrassing.

She had reached the door when he said suddenly, 'Hey, hang on a minute.'

'What?'

'Turn to face me a sec.'

She did so, glancing down at herself. Her striped shirt was almost long enough to hide her briefs, certainly it was decent by today's standards – so what did he mean?'

'What does that writing say?'

Sophie immediately tugged the shirt defensively lower, her face turning beet-red. Oh damn Penny and her clever ideas,

130

and damn the momentary lapse from good sense which had led her to buy the stupid things, and damn Stephen Bland for having such sharp eyesight, and damn . . .

'It's just silly, nothing really, I shan't be . . .'

She was almost through into the bathroom, almost safe, when he caught hold of her. He was laughing and he turned her to face him and then, before she could do more than gasp, he calmly lifted the front of her shirt and scrutinised the words printed so gaily and with such insouciance right across her . . . her *thingy*.

'Please do not squeeze me until I am yours,' Stephen read out. She saw his grin stretch almost from ear to ear before she dropped her eyes and began to tug furiously against his grip. Damn, damn, damn!

'It's a pretty feeble sort of joke really. I can't think why I bought them, only Penny dared me and I never dreamed . . . No one's meant to see them, I wash my undies and hang them over the bath, I never dreamed . . .'

Sophie could hear her voice gabbling on, high and defensive. Half of her wanted to laugh but half of her could have cried. Just because she now had a bottom small enough to fit into silly little briefs didn't mean she had to buy the things. And now look where it had led her – if only he didn't think to look at the back!

He did, of course. A ripe peach made him yelp with amusement before releasing her, with a pat on the peach.

'Marvellous! I knew I'd seen that slogan somewhere – it's what the barrow boys put on their soft fruit, isn't it? Sophie, you're a gem!'

The gem bolted into the bathroom, scarlet from the soles of her feet to the crown of her head, and locked the door, then leaned against it. Of all the foul luck – or was it? Slowly, it came to her that Stephen's laughter had been appreciative, affectionate laughter, the laughter of a friend who enjoyed the rudery written on a pair of frilly briefs. He had accepted it, had not found it funny that Sophie's bottom should bear the picture of a peach. He was laughing with her, not at her.

When she was washed and brushed, cool in her primrose nightie, she emerged a little shyly to find him lounging on her bed eating a chocolate biscuit and reading her copy of *A Dog Day*, and grinning. It gave her a little jump of pleasure to see

131

that he had rifled her weekend bag for the book. It was a sign of acceptance perhaps, that he felt no awkwardness in moving all those clothes.

'Right? You look very fetching, pet. Come and sit down here next to me and drink your chocolate.'

Sophie did so whilst Stephen lolled back on the bed and when she had finished her drink she lay back too, a little self-consciously, beside him.

'This is a comfy bed, but don't you go falling asleep on it, Stephen, or the hotel staff will think the worst.'

Stephen turned so that he could watch her face.

'Think? What do you think they think now? That you and I go calmly off to sleep in our own beds? Not likely. If they knew at the centre that you and I were in the same hotel they wouldn't even bother to think, they'd think they knew.'

'You mean they'd all think that you and I . . .?'

He nodded, his eyes still on her face.

'You bet your life.'

Sophie felt a slow smile spread across her countenance. She gave a snort of amusement.

'Gosh! I bet they look at me and wonder how on earth I did it!'

'Did what?'

She punched his shoulder.

'Don't be so conceited, you know very well what I mean.'

He leaned across her, looking down at her seriously, rather hungrily. 'I suppose you wouldn't like to give substance to their suspicions?'

'Stephen, you know how I feel! One day . . .'

Her words faded to silence beneath his mouth, were forgotten beneath his impatient hands, but soon, too soon for Stephen, she grew hot and embarrassed, almost as much by her own state of undress as by his seekings. Perhaps it had not been wise to wear such a – a short nightie!

'I think if you don't mind we really ought to . . . stop it, Stephen!' He stopped and lay back on the pillows again, pulling her head down so that it rested in the hollow of his shoulder. 'Now this is lovely, so nice and cosy and comfy. Without being . . .'

'. . . particularly interesting,' Stephen finished for her.

132

Darling, you've got to learn to accept physical contact one day.'

'Not as physical as that I haven't,' Sophie said firmly, though rather sleepily. She opened her eyes and tugged Stephen's arm in front of her eyes until she could see his wristwatch. It was either a quarter past twelve or three o'clock, she could not see which, but it was definitely late. She said as much in a drowsy mutter, but Stephen had suddenly become comforting, cuddly and not at all amorous. She turned her head and kissed the smooth skin at the side of his neck, reluctant to let him go, more reluctant to wake up.

'Shouldn't you go back to your own room now, Stephen?'

'I will in a moment.'

She closed her eyes again, just for that moment. By the time Stephen reached out and clicked the bedside light off, she was sound asleep.

In the circumstances perhaps it was not so strange that she should have dreamed.

She was walking along the Pantiles, glancing up admiringly at the hanging flower baskets above her head. There were not many people about but, as she walked, she could see what looked like a small crowd approaching, and presently they resolved themselves into a wedding party. Sophie quickened her pace. She loved looking at brides!

Halfway up the Pantiles, she glanced down at herself. She was naked.

Panic-stricken, she glanced wildly round. There must be something! But only the hanging baskets offered any sort of fig leaf, and they were above her head, which meant that she would have to stretch. She hesitated, but the wedding party continued to advance and there was a clergyman with them. This decided her. To be seen naked by a clergyman had to be worse than watching television in a bedroom. She leapt for the hanging basket, removing her hands from their strategic positions, and captured a goodly handful of flowers which she held, bouquet-like, before her.

There was little that she could do about her breasts, though she did her best with the hand that was not holding the flowers and then she began to walk once more towards the wedding party. If only she could get past them unremarked!

It was then that she recognised the bridegroom. It was Stephen, wearing the dinner jacket he had worn earlier and one of those awful green eyeshades that movie moguls are reputed to love. He was carrying a camera. And he was pointing it at her!

Sophie tried to sidle past, tried to pretend she knew no one in the wedding party, but they came to a stop directly before her, completely blocking the pathway. Stephen was turning his camera on different parts of Sophie and the bouquet looked as if it might fade and die at any moment. The clergyman, standing tall and forbidding by Stephen, spoke.

'Give the bouquet to the bride.'

Sophie looked at the bride, and it was the loathesome Tara, and then at the clergyman. She shook her head wildly, clutching the flowers tighter.

'No! I can't!'

'You must. It's the custom of the country, the bride must have the bouquet. Come along, my child, don't be shy, you're holding the procession up.'

'I can't.'

'You must.'

Tara settled it by snatching the bouquet out of Sophie's nerveless hand. Petals floated, soft as birds' feathers, on the mild air. And Sophie turned desperately to Stephen. The wedding party had noticed her nudity now and a hum of disgust and fury was beginning to make itself heard. She remembered, vaguely, that Stephen had once offered to lend her his jacket; he must help her, must hide her.

'I'll have the jacket, Stephen. Please, Stephen, let me have your jacket.'

The roar of disapproval was growing louder and Sophie knew that if she did not manage to make herself respectable, the crowd would tear her apart. She was crying, tugging at Stephen's jacket, repeating over and over, 'Please Stephen, please Stephen,' and the menace was getting closer, she could hear what they were saying now and it was terrifying. Someone was saying that there would be blood on the pavement for this, blood on the pavement, and her tears splashed, hot as blood, down onto her bare, shrinking flesh.

And then she woke.

It was dark, and she was still clutching someone, as she had clutched in the dream. Her nose was buried in a masculine shoulder and both her arms were round a masculine neck and the rest of her was as close as it could possibly get to a masculine form.

A *very* masculine form. She was still shaking and clutching, the dream only just below the horizon of reality, and she could not imagine how she came to be where she was, in bed with Stephen, and from what she could feel . . . a hand released Stephen's neck and travelled doubtfully down his arm and across his back . . . a naked Stephen!

As she had emerged from the dream she had heard her own voice. Small, shocked, pleading, she had still been repeating *Please Stephen, please Stephen*, as the dream faded into reality, so she could scarcely complain when Stephen had caught hold of her, rescuing her from being torn to bits by the angry crowd. Or was he? She felt two hard hands grip her buttocks and suspected that her saviour was about to grow horns and a tail. His mouth was on that part of her where neck and shoulder join and he was gripping her so tightly that she guessed there would be bruises tomorrow, yet far from escaping, her body seemed to be doing its best to co-operate. It curved sensuously close, shamelessly moving against his thighs and stomach. And things. She decided to be vague about just what it was that kept sliding across her lower abdomen in case she panicked herself into rushing, screaming and naked, from the room.

Naked?

Naked!

Yet she knew damned well that she had been wearing a perfectly respectable nightie when she lay down on this bed, on top of the covers and with Stephen also decently clad, hours and hours ago.

Naked?

She was waking up properly at last, becoming tinglingly aware of the whole length of her body as he manoeuvred it against him. She breathed his name and a half-hearted denial of what was happening and felt his mouth on her neck break into a smile. He could read her body's reactions better than she could, he knew she could not stop him now, would not stop him, did not even really want to stop him. Not for the world. When he turned her gently onto her back and began to kiss her

135

breasts, to mouth her newly supple and aroused flesh, she felt as if he was bringing her body awake after a long sleep, and rejoiced in the lively feelings which roared through her; rejoiced in the heat of desire which engulfed her; even rejoiced in the pain, when he entered her at last. She cried out sharply, and then her nails were clawing his back, her teeth fastened on his shoulder, and she was a surfer on the peak of a wave being carried further and further up the beach until she was cast high onto the shore. She lay beneath him, slippery with perspiration, bruised, her skin rosy with his kisses, knowing that for the first time in her life she belonged. He had been right to persuade her. Whatever else might happen, she had had this moment.

As he lifted his weight from her and began, peacefully, to caress her, she knew that she had been far luckier than she deserved. She did not just belong to the ordinary world, she belonged to Stephen. He might leave her tomorrow, might go off and marry horrible Tara as he had done in her dream, but nothing could ever steal from her this moment of acceptance. Right now she had her first lover and he was not just any man, not some Aubrey or Jeremy or Phil the haystack. He was Stephen Bland, who could have any woman he wanted and who had freely chosen her. And, having chosen her, had possessed her very sweetly.

Her thoughts began to blur together as sleep overtook her. Pleasure was there, because she had given and received pleasure, and warmth, and tenderness. It was good to give in, she told herself drowsily, both to Stephen's loving demands and to the sweet and subtle drag of sleep much needed.

Cradled in his arms, with his breath on her face, Sophie slept.

She awoke to the feel of his mouth on her cheek. He was kissing her with small, quick kisses and the room was fully of grey light. She moved and her body, which had begun to stir at his touch, woke up and protested that it was stiff, creaking, heavy with sleep and love. She opened her eyes as far as she could and smiled at him, her lids still slow with sleep.

'O-oh, Stephen, how I ache! I haven't felt like this since they made me do gymnastics for one whole afternoon as a punishment. Every bit of me hurts!'

He was smiling. She forgave him for the smugness of it.

'My fault. But there's no other way, there has to be a first time. I thought we might get up and go onto the common and watch the sunrise.'

Sophie sat up on one elbow and stared.

'Sunrise? What's the time?'

'Past five. And it's going to be a fine day.'

She lay back on the pillows again and stretched, luxuriously and slowly, shameless now, glad that he wanted to look at her, proud of her body. She could tell herself a great many things but not, any longer, that he had made love to her for any reasons of kindness or pity. He had made love to her because he wanted to so badly that he could not stop himself. She had not been the only one muttering love words, biting and groaning last night.

'Why do you want to watch the sunrise anyway, Stephen?'

'Because it's a sight worth seeing; it would make this weekend memorable for you.' He paused, his eyes drifting contentedly over her. 'Though if you're still tired . . . you're very beautiful, my love.'

Sophie chuckled as he took her in his arms.

'I'm all right from certain angles if you like your women cuddly, but I've got a bum like an elephant's.'

He laughed too and hugged her, then stroked down her flanks and across her buttocks, making her shiver.

'You don't resemble an elephant in any respect, though you're broad where a broad should be broad.' He slapped her bottom and then, apparently enjoying the sensation, slapped it again, harder. 'Come on, if we don't get up and go and watch the sunrise my urges will get the better of me, and you're stiff enough without that, poor darling.'

'I like being stiff, and I like your urges, they seem to coincide with mine,' Sophie said frankly. 'Sod the sunrise!'

Stephen tipped her chin so that he could look into her face. His mouth looked heavy, his lids half-hid his dark and gleaming eyes. He said nothing, but brought his mouth down over hers slowly, so slowly that Sophie moaned her impatience even as she curved her body hard against his, urging his urges to get a move on. They were both impatient now, desire smouldering beneath the thinnest pretext of restraint, two twentieth-century people with primitive appetites to which they fully intended giving rein.

Ten brief, crackling minutes later they lay back, glanced at each other, simultaneously whistled, then laughed.

'That was really something,' Sophie said, and saw him nod.

'It was. I've never had a woman like you.' He ran a finger down the side of her face. 'You make me feel like Adam when he made Eve out of his own rib.'

'I've never had a man, full stop.' She sat up. 'I don't want to miss a single second of this day – let's go chase that sunrise!'

'Right. If I've got the strength left to climb the hill.' Stephen sat up and loped across the room, got his own clothes and threw Sophie's over to her. 'Chuck something on, but not those jeans, for pity's sake. There's a pretty pink dress thing in there, I saw it last night.'

'I shan't be long,' Sophie said, standing up and pulling the pink dress down over her head. Refinements such as bra or slip seemed unnecessary when they were going to be the only people around. 'I say, have you seen my knickers?'

Wordless but smiling, Stephen pointed to a small, crumpled heap near the bed. Most of the slogan was hidden, but three words were plainly visible.

I am yours.

Sophie stared, then smiled and kissed Stephen exuberantly on the side of his face.

'How appropriate.'

Chapter Nine

Anya tapped lightly on Sophie's door, then opened it and poked her head into her room. Sophie was sitting at the typewriter, but she did not appear to be working and the moment she saw her friend a broad smile broke out.

'Hello, Anya, have you come to lunch? I can only offer you Stephen's coffee, but there's plenty of that. Oh, and a yoghurt, if you're in the mood for one.'

Anya came fully into the room and revealed that she was carrying a packet of sandwiches and a string bag with some fruit in it. She dumped the bag on Sophie's desk and sat down on the visitor's chair.

'I've brought my own lunch, thanks, but I could do with some coffee. I wanted to ask how your weekend went.'

'The Tunbridge Wells one?' The girls had not met for a week, since Anya's boss had been filming in the provinces and had taken his secretary with him. 'I had a lovely time, thanks. How did your week go?'

'Not bad. Penny said you came back from the weekend all aglow, though – Stephen propose?'

'What, marriage?' Sophie laughed. 'No, not exactly. We enjoyed ourselves no end. On Sunday morning we got up at five to see the sunrise, and that was wonderful, with mist in the hollows and every cobweb diamonded with dew. I've seen a summer sunrise before, of course, when we filmed it that time, but nothing could be as magical as last weekend's. The sun edged up and the light was so pure and clean, nothing could be cleaner, and the shadows were flat and blue and the wrong way round, and the air was as fresh as morning air when you're very little, and staying on a farm.'

'It sounds quite an experience.'

'It was. It was like when you believe in magic, you know how that haloes things? Well, if a woman with stars in her hair had formed in the mist, or if Aslan had come gliding out of the sun's core, I wouldn't have turned a hair.'

Anya, watching her, nodded.

'I know the feeling. Did Stephen make love to you?'

Sophie went scarlet and hung her head, started to deny it and then, sheepishly, nodded.

'Was it that, then? Was that what made the sunrise magical? If so, then love really *is* a many-splendoured thing!'

'I don't know, but Soph, why I popped in . . . it's a bit sordid, love, but when Penny sort of hinted . . . Did you take precautions?'

Sophie shook her head.

'No. How could I? I didn't know what was going to happen. But Stephen did. Take precautions, I mean. And he's told me how to get hold of the pill. I have to take if for a month before it's effective, he says, but until the month's up, he's going to take care of us, which I think means he'll buy those things, you know, the things they get at the chemist's.'

Sophie got up from behind her typewriter and poured two cups of coffee, then sat down again after handing one of them to her friend. Anya sipped the delicous brew appreciatively, then began to take her sandwiches out of their cellophane wrapping.

'Right, that's all I wanted to know. I'm not being nosy, love, but you're not very old and you've not been around much.' She sighed and bit into the first sandwich. 'But who am I to talk? Only I wouldn't want to see you landed, like I am.'

'I wouldn't be,' Sophie said, beginning to spoon yoghurt. 'Stephen isn't likely to disappear, and he'd stand by me, I know he would. He's being marvellous, Anya,' she went on eagerly. 'Advising me about clothes, and what I should do and shouldn't do. I never would have dared to buy black stockings, but he wanted me to, and they do look rather good on my legs.'

'Stockings? Crumbs, that's going back to the dark ages, isn't it?'

Sophie blushed but held her ground.

'No, not really. Stephen thinks they're sexy, and . . .'

The door opening cut her off short. Stephen walked in, already in full flow.

'Soph, I want . . .' He broke off and smiled politely at Anya, 'Oh, hi, I didn't see you sitting there at first.' He turned back to

140

Sophie, and even with his profile half averted from her, Anya could see the look of loving ownership he turned on her friend. Even if Penny had not hinted and Sophie admitted, I should have known they were lovers, she thought. How good it is to see Stephen out of his mind over a decent kid like Sophie.

Later, returning to her own office, the thought crossed her mind that Sophie was not only a decent kid, she was becoming a very lovely girl. She was still well-rounded, but her curves were luscious rather than overlarge and her personality was beginning to make itself felt. She joked quite a lot, was no longer afraid of answering sharply if she felt so inclined, and could hold her own in the flat even when Penny was at her most awkward.

She worships Stephen, of course, Anya told herself, taking her place behind her desk. She had always admired him and enjoyed working for him but now she just plain worshipped him. Was it a good thing? She had no idea, but since Stephen, also, felt strongly about her friend, it could surely not be bad?

Anya reached over for her shorthand pad and, as she did so, something stirred in her stomach. I was an odd feeling, more a sensation than a feeling, if one could differentiate between the two. It was as if, somewhere deep within her, a tiny fish had fluttered a fin, paused, and then fluttered again.

Odd. Surely it could not be the baby? Her heart hurt for a moment, giving a little twinge of pain, but she dismissed the idea as ludicrous. How could a splodge of jelly, and unwanted jelly furthermore, make itself felt? No, it could not have been the baby, because the baby was just a nothing, and a nothing that she was about to have ejected from her body without a qualm of conscience. It must have been wind.

The buzzer on her desk sounded but Anya sat where she was, staring at the internal telephone. Her mind registered that it was Derek Eade buzzing her, that he would want her to take dictation or buy him some tickets or do some other small task. She would go through to his office and he might very likely smile absently at her, or pat her shoulder as he gave her the money for the tickets. Otherwise, nothing. He was a married man, in love with his wife, so what more should she expect?

Unless you counted the baby? Given in a moment of loneliness or boredom, or both, given perhaps from a desperate desire

141

to prove to himself that he was *not* a dull and settled married man, that he was still capable of stirring passion in a woman, of arousing a female sufficiently for her to throw discretion to the winds whilst he made love to her.

The buzzer buzzed again, contriving to sound as though its patience was running short, but still Anya made no attempt to touch the instrument. Now that she thought about it, he had never pretended to love her, had scarcely pretended to want her. They had been working late and they were alone and he had taken her almost without a word spoken.

Did she love him? No more and no less than she had loved him since she had started work for him two – no, three – years earlier. He was kind and good, marvellous to work for, a man both strong and sensitive, she would have said. Yet he could possess her, use her, and simply walk away. Never refer to the incident again by a word or a glance. Want no more of her, it seemed, than that one, ego-building experience. He had cared nothing for the fact that she had gone to him willingly, had clung and murmured love-words and let him catch a glimpse of that other Anya, not the cool, calm, efficient one who managed her office work and her social life with equal ease, but the lonely, misunderstood child of elderly parents who longed for a love that was warmer, easier, than the mild and stilted affection that had come her way.

She was still sitting behind her desk staring at the internal telephone when the communicating door shot open and Derek strode into her room.

'I've been buzzing you,' he said peevishly. 'Is that bloody thing on the blink again? Get it fixed, there's a good girl, and then find out who's using Studio 4 on Thursday afternoon.' He turned to leave the room again, then turned back, staring at her. 'You all right, Anya? You're looking a bit pale.'

It flashed through Anya's mind that she could tell him, could let him prove his humanity. She imagined his face if she was to say, '*I'm pregnant and you're the father*,' and knew she could not do so. Because there was so little he could do, apart from helping with the money angle. And if he were to cast doubts on who had fathered the child she would hate him for ever, which would be a poor way of spending the years ahead.

'I'm all right, Derek, thanks. But I'm looking forward to

having some time off next week, whilst you're away.'

He smiled and nodded, relieved to be taken off whatever hook he had imagined he was on. Anya was sure he had never considered for one moment that she might be pregnant, because he must have assumed she was on the pill, like everyone else. He might think she was having a bad time with her period, and that would embarrass Derek. She smiled dismissively at him and picked up her phone, dialled, then spoke into the receiver.

'Hello, Madge? I wonder if you could tell me . . .'

'Look, there's absolutely no point in snapping my head off since I've got the afternoon off,' Sophie said with unaccustomed firmness as she and Anya approached the huge, red-brick building which housed the clinic. 'You said you could use company and here I am, so for goodness sake stop carping! If the positions were reversed you'd do the same for me, and I'd be glad, I wouldn't moan about you going back to work.'

'I'm sorry, Sophie, I'm being a bitch. In fact I'm scared witless and so thankful you're here that I can't put it into words,' Anya said fervently. 'But I can't help thinking it's terribly unfair – you're younger than me and you're not involved in any way. I ought never to have told you.'

'Shut up. I'm twenty and involved, to a greater or lesser extent, in anything my friends do. No man is an island. Anyway, think what a moral lesson this is – every time I feel inclined to chuck my pills down the loo I'll think of you! Oh, that reminds me, didn't you ever think of the morning-after pill? That was what Stephen gave me, that first time.'

'The devil,' Anya said appreciatively. 'Does it occur to you, love, that your handsome boss must have had every intention of seducing you that weekend? No one carries round morning-after pills just in case.'

'It didn't at the time, but it has since,' Sophie admitted. 'Of course I'm glad of it now, because we're together; at the time I never really thought past the event itself, if you understand me.'

'I do. Well, here we go.' Anya, with a resolute squaring of the shoulders, pushed open the door of the clinic and then stood still for a moment, a hand going to her throat. 'Glory, I'm scared!

What must the staff think of people like me, who . . .'

Sophie guessed that the staff had cause to be grateful to people like Anya, but was spared the necessity of answering by the prompt appearance of a woman in a pink twinset who came briskly out of a nearby doorway and smiled at them.

'Good afternoon. Miss Evans? Would you and your friend wait here, please. There are a few forms to be filled in – just a formality.'

They had barely settled themselves in the small waiting room, though, when a nurse, in a uniform so white that it hurt the eyes, came in with the forms and, when they had been filled in, smiled dismissively at Sophie.

'Miss Evans will be going straight to theatre, Miss er . . . er, so if you'd like to come back in about four hours . . .'

'I want to be with her when she comes round,' Sophie said, scarlet-cheeked. 'Can't I wait here? Then you could send someone to fetch me as soon as she begins to regain consciousness.'

'I'm afraid you wouldn't be allowed in the recovery room,' the nurse said, her smile growing a trifle fixed. 'Anyway, this waiting area will be needed for other patients, so if you wouldn't mind . . .'

'Do go, Soph,' Anya said. She was so white that the two patches of blusher on her cheeks stood out like clown's make-up. 'I'll be all right.'

'I want to be in the recovery room,' Sophie said obstinately. 'Why not, for God's sake? It would save a member of the nursing staff hanging about.'

'I'm afraid it isn't allowed,' the nurse said. Her smile had become a travesty; Sophie could see that the rest of her face was frowning with annoyance, she had simply forgotten to remove the smile. 'However, if you'd like to come back in four hours and see a member of the medical staff, you could do that.'

'My friend is paying a great deal of money for this operation,' Sophie said, her own smile long gone. 'I intend to be with her when she regains consciousness. Please tell that to the rest of the medical staff.' She turned, winked at Anya and made for the door. 'Good afternoon!'

Someone, somewhere, was crying. Anya registered the fact whilst she was still so heavy with the anaesthetic that she could

144

not have lifted an eyelid, let alone a finger. It was a sad little sound, and it made her wish she could comfort the weeper. When she began to listen she could hear words mingling with the sobs, words that she knew had a meaning for her as well as for the poor girl who was crying.

'Gone,' the weeper mourned. 'Torn from me, taken, killed! No light for it, ever, no sunshine, no bright colours. It won't know sweetness, sourness, warmth, cold . . .'

Another voice, brisk, impersonal, cut across the weeping, telling the girl not to tire herself but to rest so that, presently, all would be well.

Vaguely, from her great distance, Anya found herself resenting the brisk-voiced one. It was all very well for her, she did not know what it felt like, to have that feeling of loss heavy in one's breast, to suffer the wound of having a part of you torn away, to know the weight of your own wickedness.

The sobbing quietened, faltered, stopped. And, gradually, Anya began to regain full consciousness.

It was only when she opened her eyelids at last and felt the tears wet on her cheeks that she knew the weeper had been herself.

'Hi, Sofa, anything nice for dinner?'

Penny entered the kitchen cheerfully, noisily, then stopped short as Sophie put a finger to her lips.

'Ssh, Penny, Anya's in bed, she isn't too well.'

'Oh? I thought she looked a bit off-colour this morning. Have you called the quack? Want me to give him a ring?'

'It's all right, she's seen a doctor. I'm cooking up some chicken broth for her and something a bit more substantial for us. Oh, and there's a rice pudd in the oven.' Sophie saw Penny's face change, saw the frown flit across her brow, and wished, devoutly, that Anya had not wanted to keep her friend in the dark. It would not be easy to hide the truth if Penny decided to find out what ailed Anya.

'Chicken broth? What . . .'

She whipped round on the words and hurried out of the kitchen. Sophie heard her heels tap-tappeting down the hall, heard Anya's bedroom door flung open and Penny start to speak, then the heels tap-tappeted back again. Penny came

145

back into the kitchen, shut the door and leaned against it, scowling at Sophie.

'She's asleep, and there's an odd smell in that room. What's going on?'

'Oh, she's been overdoing it, I dare say. Look, make her a cup of tea, could you, and perhaps by the time it's done she'll have woken up and be a bit more talkative.'

As Penny began, grudgingly, to make up a tray, Sophie thought of the journey back from the clinic. It had been dreadful, for she had barely got Anya right round before the staff were ushering them, kindly but very firmly, into a taxi.

'Bring her back in three days for a check-up,' the nurse said as she prepared to shut the taxi door on them. 'If you have any problems, contact Miss Evans' G.P.'

It had not helped to find Anya either unconscious or asleep when they reached Gloucester Terrace again, either. The driver, helping Sophie to carry her friend up to the flat, had been frank, obviously knowing full well what had taken Anya to the clinic.

'They treat them young gals like kippers, fillet 'em wiv no more care than they'd give a fish, an' chuck 'em out soon's the money's 'anded over,' he said contemptuously. 'I wouldn't see no gal of mine in there, I tell yer.'

It had done little to ease Sophie's fears and she had already resolved to get in touch with Anya's doctor if Anya continued to sleep as deeply as she had been doing.

But now Penny finished the tray and left the kitchen, to return barely a moment later with the tea patently untouched. She slammed the tray down on the kitchen table and grabbed Sophie's arm.

'Anya's been my closest friend for *years*, long before you turned up Sofa. Look, I can see you know what's been happening, so you either tell me right now or you get out of this flat and never come near it again!' Fear was fighting with suspicion on Penny's normally bland little face. 'Why should Anya tell you anything, and not me? Unless you've been filling her up with a lot of lies about me! We've shared everything, or we did until you came along.'

'I haven't told anyone any lies,' Sophie said as soothingly as she could. 'Look, let's not quarrel now, with Anya ill; she's going to need both of us. We'll sort it out . . .'

'We only let you come here because you were so fat and ugly
that we knew you wouldn't interfere with us,' Penny said wildly.
'*You* wouldn't try to make up threesomes or bring fellows back or
anything like that, otherwise we wouldn't have let you share. And
you went creeping round Anya, trying to make her feel sorry for
you, and now you've succeeded and she's ill and you're trying to
push me out. Me!' Penny's voice was at full throttle. 'She's my
friend and this is *my* flat. Clear out, Markham, you fat pig!'

'I will, as soon as Anya's better. Tomorrow, if you like,' Sophie
said. She knew that it was concern for their friend which made
Penny behave as she did. 'Do keep your voice down, Penny, she
needs sleep; it won't do her any good to get startled awake.'

'Right. Either you tell me what's wrong with her and what's
been happening or I'll go in there, wake her, and browbeat her till
I get the truth. I mean it, I'm getting to the bottom of this if it
kills me.'

'Or Anya, presumably. All right, I know Anya would rather
tell you herself, but here goes. She's had an abortion.'

Penny sat down as if her knees had suddenly ceased to function
and picked up one of the cups of tea. Sophie took the other, watching as Penny wrapped her hands around her cup as if for warmth.

'Anya? An abortion? I don't believe it, she wouldn't, not without . . . and besides, she hasn't . . .'

Her voice faded into silence as she thought back. At last she
raised her head and stared at Sophie.

'Where? Not some back-street place? Who's the father? Surely
not Freddy, she hasn't seen him for yonks. Did the chap stand by
her? And how in hell did you find out?'

Sophie was glad that Penny took it for granted that she herself
had found out, rather than that Anya had confided in her. It was
the truth, too.

'She went to a reputable clinic, so that should be all right, and I
don't know who the father was, it wasn't any of my business; but
she did say it was someone she met by chance and wouldn't meet
again. I found out when she fainted in the middle of a game of
tennis, but she wanted to keep it from you until the operation was
over.'

Pointless as well as cruel to tell Penny that Anya had hoped to
keep her in ignorance for ever.

147

'I see. I wish to God she'd told me, but that's Anya all over – hates people worrying about her.'

'That's right. Look, I'm a bit worried because she's slept ever since we – the taxi driver and me – got her back here, so do you think you could take her a cup of tea and sit down by the bed and try to wake her very, very gently? She's seen enough of my face for one day, so if you wouldn't mind, I'll get on with the cooking.'

Penny nodded ungraciously and got to her feet, her cup in one hand.

'Right. I won't take anything through, I'll wake her very gently and slowly and ask her what she'd like.' She was half-way to the door when she hesitated, then turned back, slopping tea from her cup onto the lino. 'I'm sorry I was so rude, Sofa. In Anya's shoes . . .' She hesitated.

'What?'

'Well, if I got myself into that sort of mess, I'd probably rather have you than me hanging around when I came out of the anaesthetic. I can be a bit unfeeling. Seeing you was probably best for Anya, as things were.'

'That's the nicest thing you've ever said to me,' Sophie said. She fished out a hanky and blew her nose. 'You aren't unfeeling, you just find it difficult . . .'

'Yes I am, and don't snivel, for God's sake,' Penny said sharply. 'If there's one thing fat girls should never do, it's snivel. You look all blubbery and whalelike. I'm off.'

Sophie shut the door behind Penny and returned to stirring the chicken broth. You had to smile at Penny, she seemed to make a point of being thoroughly unlikeable to her own sex. Or is it just me, Sophie wondered, walking over to the vegetable rack and beginning to peel an onion. With tear-filled eyes, she sliced the onion into the broth and concluded that Penny was all right really. It had been sweet of her to apologise, because Penny was no believer in saying you were sorry. If you said a thing you said it, was her philosophy.

Presently she went along to Anya's room to see if the patient was awake, opening the door so quietly that neither girl noticed. Anya lay quiet, her eyes still closed, and Penny sat on the edge of the bed, holding one of Anya's thin, blue-veined hands in her own.

148

Sophie backed out as quietly as she had entered and returned to the kitchen. She felt ashamed, as if she had deliberately spied on Penny in her moment of weakness.

For Penny had been crying.

Anya was really ill for three days, and ill enough to stay in bed without complaining for the whole week. Sophie and Penny took time off and Deidre was marvellous, bringing baby Graham down in his pram and parking it in their kitchen, where she could attend to Anya without feeling that she was neglecting her child.

During the second week Anya got up and moved about the flat all day, but she was not herself. Quiet, pale, abstracted, she seemed curiously indifferent to her wonderful job and her wonderful boss, subjects which had obsessed her before the abortion. Now, she mooned round the place, playing with Graham whenever Deidre appeared with him, knitting an object which she said was a shawl, except that Graham would not be needing a shawl much longer, and occasionally watching the Flowers' television.

Sophie tried to explain to Stephen what was wrong, but with little success. She usually went out with him three or four times a week and they slept together once a week, though he had never suggested that she spend the night there, and this, though Sophie did not realise it, kept their relationship on a far more romantic and emotional basis than it would have enjoyed had they moved in together. But it did make honest discussion more difficult, since when they were together Sophie spent quite a lot of time longing to go to bed and trying to be blasé about the fact that Stephen, so much more sophisticated and experienced, plainly did not need sex as much as she did.

She would have been surprised and indignant had she known that Stephen felt much the same, and that he was holding back from a simple feeling that good things, such as himself, should be handed out in very small doses. Perhaps fortunately, since he did not tell her and she did not guess, Sophie merely looked forward all week to their love-making and when in his company waited eagerly for a sign that it was about to begin. So, asking his advice about Anya was really quite a sacrifice, since it meant that he would talk instead of acting.

She chose to ask him, as it happened, when they were at his flat, having eaten a good meal and seen an amusing play. Stephen, sprawled on the couch with an idle hand resting on the curve of Sophie's hip, had just decided to break with tradition and persuade Sophie into bed for the second time in a week, when she spoke.

'Stephen, Anya said she wanted the abortion, and she's ever so much better physically, so why should she be so odd and dreamy and uncaring? She cries, too, whilst we're at work. I can tell because her eyes are different when she's been crying, they go bloodshot. And before, she told me that work meant more to her than anything, yet she doesn't even ask about it any more, and she hasn't said a word about going back next Monday.'

'She's been through an exhausting experience mentally and physically,' Stephen said rather impatiently. 'Do you expect her to sing and dance around the flat within three weeks of something like that? She'll be all right if she's given time and plenty of sympathy.'

'But we do sympathise, and the doctor says . . .'

'If the doctor thinks she's all right then she is. For God's sake, darling, let the medical profession know best!' His impatient fingers played with the back of her bra strap. 'Why do you wear a bra when you know I think its unnecessary?'

'Well, we were going to the theatre and . . . Stop it, Stephen, how can I concentrate when you're doing that?' Secure in the knowledge that she had had her weekly nooky, as the irreverent Penny would say, she brushed impatiently at his hand. He seemed to have no notion how it churned her up to be stroked and played with, and then patted on the bottom and sent off home! 'You say do what the doctor says, but it isn't as easy as that; he wants her to go home. He thinks she needs to get right away from the scene of her crime . . . no, he didn't say that exactly, but that was what he meant.'

'Then tell her to go home,' Stephen said impatiently. He had wrestled her bra undone without any co-operation whatsoever, and now he was trying to undo some extraordinarily awkward little buttons so that he could get at the delectable, gently moving mounds which, freed from the restrictions of her bra, were simply begging to be touched, stroked, kissed! 'Just tell her to go home.'

'She won't go, though,' Sophie said miserably, trying to tell all her glands, pulses and nerve-endings that they had got it wrong again and might as well calm down, because this was just Stephen's idea of a more intimate goodnight kiss. She wished fervently that she could make the first move, tell or show him that she wanted him. But she could not do so. She knew, instinctively, that he liked to be the one to say what they would do and when, and she still shrank from the thought of being refused. Yet, well though she knew him, sexual taboos were still too strong to allow her to so much as suggest that it was not fair to work her up into a state of high excitement, to put it no stronger, and then to send her home.

'Then if she won't go, she'll have to stay,' Stephen muttered. He lifted a breast in his hand, supporting it up to his mouth, and pushed Sophie backwards onto the soft couch cushions. What a girl she was for talking – yet he had never noticed it before. He began to kiss, to caress, to fondle, to undress.

Sophie realised, suddenly, that she had been wrong and that Stephen actually intended making love, but her loyalty to her friend was strong. Just as she was about to go under for the third time, diving joyously into love-making, she remembered Anya and what she had been going to ask Stephen.

'Well, I . . . Oh, Stephen . . . I do have a way to . . . *Oooh*, Stephen . . . a way to make her go.'

'Then use it,' Stephen said, against the soft and sweet-smelling skin of her. 'Use it!'

When he took her back to the flat, Sophie asked Stephen in for coffee and he accepted, since it was not yet eleven o'clock. Anya had, it seemed, gone to bed long since with a book which she would not read. Penny, however, was in and obligingly made coffee for three and got out the shortbread. Then, everyone's attention being freed from customary obsessions, they discussed Anya in a far more practical way than had been possible earlier.

'She says she'll go back to work next week, but you can see she couldn't care less,' Penny confided. 'I said right, because I thought once she was back there things might improve, and then I suggested she take her leave – she's still got two weeks – and go home. But she just said she didn't think she'd .

151

bother, and the doctor did say he thought she needed to get right away for a bit.'

'Well, Stephen and I may have solved that bit,' Sophie said, giving Stephen an adoring look across the table. 'I told him that I'd got a sort of blackmail hold over Anya which I'd not used yet, and he said to go ahead, because it was for her good.'

'Oh?' Penny smiled at Stephen. 'Men can be pretty ruthless when they see it's for someone's good.' She turned to Sophie. 'What will you do, Soph?'

'It isn't all that much, really,' Sophie said. 'But you know how Anya's nagged *me* to go home? Says it isn't fair that I'm not prepared to let my parents see how I've changed and so on? She really does want me to go back, she's not just talking, and I'm pretty sure that if I promise to go home if she does, she'll do it. And Stephen is all for it, so that's what I'm going to do.'

'You've hit it!' Penny beamed with genuine pleasure. 'That'll do it, because Anya really has worried over your parents, Soph. Well, that's a turn-up for the books, and it's jolly generous of Stephen not to mind his woman leaving him high and dry for two whole weeks.' She smiled warmly at Stephen, who did his best to smile back.

Had Sophie actually said all that? If she had, even in his bemused state he was pretty sure he would have put a stop to it with some decisive words which would have left her in no doubt as to his feelings. The nerve of it, planning to go off and leave him for two whole weeks, when he was having a hard time of it with the latest play, as well! He would tell young Sophie a thing or two when he got her alone.

'Stephen is generous,' Sophie said gladly. 'I'll miss him horribly, but we both know we're doing the right thing, don't we, darling?'

With two bright young faces turned towards him, Stephen finally accepted defeat.

'Of course we do,' he said gloomily. 'Darling.'

Chapter Ten

In the end Stephen let her go without demur, however, just as if it had really been his own idea. This was not because he liked Anya, though he did, nor because he would not miss Sophie – he would miss her hellishly. It was because he was convinced that he had only to beckon and she would drop everything and fly to his side and, alongside this, was equally convinced that part of his power over her was his ability to manage very well without her. Or at least, he believed that Sophie thought him completely independent of her. So it followed, therefore, that in order to keep up the myth that he did not need her in the least, he was forced to let her leave him for a whole two weeks with what appeared to be a good grace.

So the parting on the station platform and then on the train was touching, tender even, but coloured by misunderstanding on both sides, for Sophie's conscience, which had slumbered for the best part of nineteen years virtually untouched by human hand, was awake now and making itself felt. Sophie had friends, and she would never have retracted a promise made to one of them, and Anya had made it clear that her own departure was subject to Sophie's.

However, Stephen did not know this, any more than Sophie realised that it was not just generosity and kindness which had persuaded Stephen to part with her, but a good deal of self-interest, so they were able to remain on the best possible terms, and to long, passionately, for their reunion at the end of two weeks.

Stephen had brought flowers to the station, too, for Devina, and a large bunch of grapes for his darling. He thought, without self-consciousness, that it had been a splendid gesture, and one which both women would appreciate. It would also ensure him a warm welcome should he ever decide to go home with Sophie. And vaguely, at the back of his mind, he knew that such a suggestion had been on the tip of his tongue right up to the moment that the train had begun to slide out of the station.

He adored Sophie – her curvy, creamy, althogether delicious body, perfectly shaped and fashioned for love and her gentle, tender personality. She was still unsure, needing to be led and protected, and her secret belief that she was neither pretty nor particularly desirable led her to regard him, he knew, as her saviour from the fate of a left-out fatty.

He was sure that she had slimmed for him and, now that she had reached his ideal of feminine womanhood, was equally sure that she must stop slimming, because he wanted her just as she was – not a penny more, not a penny less, he told himself humorously, making his way back to the car, which was illegally parked outside a greengrocer's shop on Eversholt Street. He reached the car and got out his key, then swung into the driver's street. Damn it, but he was going to miss her! He had neither wanted nor sought the company of other women since that weekend in Tunbridge Wells and he supposed, as he swung out into the traffic and got violently blared at by a passing taxi, that he had better start thinking seriously about marriage. He had had quite enough of casual affairs with casual women – actresses, flighty secretaries, girls of seeming softness hiding feelings which had been coated with hard gloss to give a brittle finish. He wanted cuddly, eager-to-please, vulnerable little Sophie.

Marriage, though? But he was in his mid-thirties and he wanted children, a real home, a wife who lived for him. He began to imagine Sophie's starry-eyed, stammering disbelief when he proposed to her and cut a corner unwisely, nearly amputating the nose of a traffic warden. It would have made a good after-dinner story, but Stephen drove on, oblivious. He would *enjoy* being married to Sophie!

Sophie turned at last from the window, when Stephen and the platform alike were no longer to be seen, and made her way back to her seat, hoping that everyone in the carriage realised that the incredibly handsome and dishy man who had been loping alongside the train as it slid out of the station was *her* man, that it had been *her* to whom all those kisses and waves had been addressed.

Reaching her seat, she stood by it whilst the elderly woman beside her rose to allow Sophie to squeeze past and then, on impulse, she handed the bunch of grapes to a couple of children, already squabbling in the aisle and bidding fair to be a darned nuisance by the time their destination was reached.

The children's mother thanked her, Sophie smiled and disclaimed, then sat down feeling smug. To be truthful, she had not been a bit grateful for the grapes which had make her feel like a gorilla at the zoo. Thank God it had not been bananas, but doubtless Stephen had been too aware of their calorific value. She smiled, opening the glossy magazine she had bought on the way here. Darling Stephen, he had got the grapes out of sheer kindness, she was an ungrateful cow – and that reminded her, she must dump those flowers before they reached Chester. She could just imagine Devina's face if she handed her the bouquet on the platform, telling her that they'd been sent by Stephen. She could see the embarrassment, the incredulity, the downright disbelief.

Having made up her mind that the flowers must be disposed of, it was an easy enough task. She left her seat once more, carrying the vast cone of cellophane as inconspicuously as possible, and went into the toilet. There, she tried to persuade the flowers down the loo but they were too wide, too enmeshed in satin ribbons and tissue, so in the end she poked them through the window one at a time and forced the wrapping through the loo hole with averted eyes and fastidious fingers. She left the small compartment as soon as the bouquet had disappeared, feeling a bit like an acid bath murderer, but no one challenged her and she quickly forgot it in increasing trepidation. What would it be like to see the family again? She still dreaded a reunion with Lavvy, for her sister had not so much as written a line during her absence. But still, worrying would not help.

The journey took over three hours and Sophie was grateful for it. She felt like an astronaut in an airlock, the train being neither one world nor another but an essential part of the two, and it gave her time to adjust to being a daughter again, who had so long been just a single girl.

The worst moment came when the train had stopped and she was on the platform. There they were, Devina, Dad, Poppy and Lavinia, and none of them recognised her; even when she called and went over to them, staggering beneath the weight of her suitcase, there was a moment's doubt before Devina began to coo and Dad to mumble greetings.

'Darling! Oh Sophie, my dearest child!' Sophie let Devina's kindly lie pass unchallenged and allowed herself to be fervently hugged. 'It's been so long . . . you look wonderful, darling, absolutely wonderful, and so slender . . . I scarcely knew you, my own dear little girl!'

'Yes , well, I'm doing my hair differently and . . .'

'Good to see you, luv. Come on, into t'car.'

Dad took her case, kissed her cheek, and then led the rush out to the car park but Devina took Sophie's arm, patting it, giving Lavinia, who was notably silent, a good old glare as she did so.

'Come along, darling, you and I will sit in the back and natter, Lavvy and Poppy can share the front seat. My, what a lovely time we'll have now you're back! A whole fortnight – I can't wait!'

The three days she actually spent at home were an almost unmitigated disaster. As soon as her mother could do so, she explained that Lavinia's unfriendliness was really nothing to do with her sister's return.

'She failed her first-year examinations and had to resit them, you see,' Devina explained. 'And she's been in trouble since, though I'm not sure exactly what she did wrong; some silliness, I expect. And then poor Poppy didn't get an end-of-term prize in June and last week we heard she'd failed her Grade IV. Only small disappointments, but it makes it all the nicer to hear how well you're doing.'

Over a homecoming dinner of home-made tomato soup, roast chicken and lemon surprise pudding, Sophie was regaled with more news, including the titbit which Devina plainly felt was almost unbearable. Janine's husband had left her.

As Devina and Lavinia chorused out the sad story, the deceptions, the lies, the extreme cruelty meted out to Janine after a mere four years of marriage, Sophie found herself feeling more and more remote, as if these happenings had taken place on some far-off planet, light-years away from her London life.

She refused the lemon surprise pudding and drank coffee, whilst the rest of the Markhams ate with undiminished appetite

156

and bewailed all over again poor Lavinia's ill-luck in failing her exams – though they were very sure that she must have passed her resits – Poppy's misfortune in not getting a prize or her Grade IV, and Janine's unhappy lot. And there sat Sophie, sipping coffee, murmuring what she hoped were appropriate remarks and trying not to notice how very small her home had grown, how shabby, how crowded. Far worse than the flat because there were more people here, and because outside there were the little streets full of people also obsessed with family matters, whereas outside the flat London flourished – wicked, vigorous, exciting.

After their meal they went into the living room to drink more coffee, to eat Devina's shortbread, which was every bit as delicious as Sophie remembered, and to talk. It was here that it occurred to Sophie that when she had left the family home, it had been like a Jonah quitting. Whilst she was there, all the troubles had swarmed round the head of the fat family Perdita, but once she left the troubles had not simply gone away, they had descended, a veritable swarm of locusts, on the rest of the family.

She might not have thought of it for herself, but she read it plainly enough in Lavinia's sly, sideways glances and even, to an extent, in her mother's voice as she related every one of the indignities poor Janine had suffered. No one actually said, *you left and did well for yourself and the rest of us paid the price*, but it was there, in Lavinia's attitude, in Devina's plaintive reiteration of Markham woes.

Lavvy really believes it, Sophie thought, half horrified, half unwillingly amused. She thinks that I should have stayed and kept all the bad luck and the failure for myself! Oh dear, oh dear, the girl's a worse idiot than Penny could ever be.

If it had stopped at that, all might yet have been well, for on the first full day home Lavinia took herself off out and Devina and Sophie settled down, first to strip the big old apple tree at the end of the garden of all the big, pale green fruit, and then to peel, core and slice it for the freezer.

'Now tell me about you, Sophie – are you going out with anyone? You did mention a Stephen something. I'm longing to hear your news.'

Devina was sincere, yet even so Sophie hesitated to say too

much. Her own good fortune and happiness would only highlight poor Janine's broken marriage, and she would be so embarrassed if Devina started telling her the facts of life, or giving her marital advice.

However, she could scarcely say nothing. She told her mother that Stephen was taking her out and was relieved when Devina murmured, in time-honoured motherly fashion, that she was glad and that she hoped Sophie would not be taken in, as Janine had been.

'I don't think so – he's my first fellow,' Sophie said, and heard the defensive, almost sulky note in her voice with impotent horror. What was happening to her? Devina had meant nothing but kindness and she had been on the verge of turning back into the old Sophie, the one who expected unkindness and so reacted to it, frequently before unkindness had been delivered.

'Oh darling, I didn't mean . . . It's just that poor Janine's landed with a home she doesn't want and a mortgage she can't repay, and yet she won't come home, let Daddy and I help her. She doesn't know any young men in Bedford, not many people at all really because Bill used to pretend he was working late so they couldn't go out, whilst all the time . . . So she doesn't know many people apart from the others in the solicitors' office, and they're all old and married. I've begged her to come home, but . . .'

'She'll be all right,' Sophie said, meaning it. 'She's only twenty-three and very pretty, she'll meet someone else and get married again, if she wants to, that is.'

'Of course she'll *want* to,' Devina said sharply. She was a married woman and could not imagine any female remaining single from choice. 'But she's lost that certain something . . . I mean, she's a married women, there are men . . .'

She lost herself in fumbling for an explanation which would not include the word 'virginity', and whilst Sophie was trying to find a way of helping her out, proceeded to put her foot firmly in it.

'Oh dear, you know what I mean, I've brought you all up right, I hope, so you know what happens to girls who are too generous with their favours and give away what can't be replaced idly, just because . . . Not that Janine did that of course, she was a married woman, but I can't help wondering whether any man . . .'

'Mother, you're being absolutely ridiculous and anachronistic,' Sophie said, giggling. 'Any moment now you'll be talking about damaged goods, and saying that Janine gave Bill the flower of her womanhood! For God's sake, Queen Anne's *dead*!'

'Does that mean what I think I means?' Devina was wearing the most sensible of her dresses this morning, because picking apples can be trying on delicate materials, but even so, clad in loops and whorls of blue-green shot silk, she looked more like a tragedy queen than a worried twentieth-century parent. 'Sophie, I hope you haven't let that Stephen take any liberties just because he's a television producer.'

Sophie had a delicious vision of Stephen's face, mouth curled into his most satyrlike smile, just in that moment before kissing. She could see his bare shoulder, almost feel his bare chest as he moved over her. But she answered precisely and truthfully.

'Have no fear, Mother, I wouldn't let anyone take liberties just because they were a television producer. And now I think we ought to take these apples indoors and start peeling them.'

'Yes, all right.'

As they carried the buckets of apples indoors, Sophie pondered on her mother's expression. Even now, she concluded, Devina did not quite believe in Stephen. So perhaps it wouldn't have have mattered much had she admitted she was his mistress; Devina would only have thought she was boasting.

The second day was complicated by the fact that Lavinia, who had been very quiet since Sophie's arrival, came back from a day's shopping in Chester with her arms full of bargains and with Peter Brewer by her side. They breezed into the kitchen where Sophie and Devina were making, part-cooking and then freezing large numbers of apple pies.

Peter, obviously warned in advance of Sophie's arrival, greeted her backview as she sat at the kitchen table, but when she stood up and turned to say hello, she wondered for a moment just what Lavinia had told him, since his glance of startled admiration was completely spontaneous.

'Nice to see you again, Sophie – I say, you're fearfully glamorous, even in your pinny!' He kissed her cheek. 'I claim a kiss because I'm the nearest thing to a brother you've got in this

159

kitchen – Lavinia and I have an understanding, you know.' He stood back, head tilted, one eye brow rising. 'Well, well, well! Who'd have thought it?'

You patronising little pipsqueak, Sophie thought, smiling noncommitally as she turned back to her work. He was so young, so callow – had she really once thought him wonderful?

'I said she'd lost some weight,' Lavinia said. She jerked Peter's arm. 'Come on, they're busy in here, come into the front room and I'll give you a mannequin parade of all the stuff I've bought.'

'I'll wait here, then we call all enjoy the mannequin parade,' Peter said. Sophie and Devina had made tea and he picked up the pot and poured a cup for himself, then sat down at the table. 'Go on, sweetie, off with you, big sister can amuse me with tales of London life.'

Lavinia left with an ill grace and came back in a pink dress with a slit skirt which did almost nothing for her, and her oft repeated rejoicings in its cheapness faded into sulks when Devina pointed out that the skirt was too tight and so badly cut that it would be impossible to alter, and Sophie, forgetting to be tactful in her interest, asked her sister if it had been available in other colours.

Lavinia, her voice rising, asked whether Sophie was criticising her choice and before Devina could do more than begin, nervously, to suggest that Lavvy show off the rest of her bargains, her younger daughter was in full voice, shrieking that if losing a bit of weight meant Sophie thought herself an authority on dress then she wished her sister was still a ton, or whatever it was she had weighed last year.

Sophie felt the colour wash over her face and neck and knew that if she spoke it would be in a yell as forceful as Lavinia's, so she very sensibly got up and left the room, hearing Lavinia screaming after her in a way which really tempted her to go back and give Lavvy a good slapping.

It blew over, of course. Devina came up and persuaded Sophie to go down again so that Lavinia could apologise, explaining all the while that Lavvy was only taking it out on Sophie because she was dreading the resit results and that she really loved her sister dearly. Sophie, wanting peace, listened and accepted Lavinia's grudging, sulky apology, and knew instinctively that worse was to come.

Worse came. On the evening of the second day, Peter Brewer made a pass that was so heavy and so uncongenial that Sophie was forced to slap his face hard, just as Lavinia walked into the kitchen. She promptly started screaming and weeping, accusing Peter of two-timing her and Sophie of coming home just to get Peter back. Devina, who knew nothing of Sophie's original friendship, if such it could be called, with Peter, started, open-mouthed, but Sophie assured her sister crisply that far from wanting Peter she had no intention of getting involved with someone who still needed nappy training. This, not surprisingly, put Peter's back up too and he assured her, nastily, that he shared her feelings.

'You think you're so bloody special, with all that London gloss and those nice clothes,' he sneered. 'Well, you aren't special to me – I wouldn't touch you with a bargepole when you tried to throw yourself at my head last year, and I feel just the same now.'

'Children, children,' Devina said weakly. 'Don't quarrel, what's it all about, anyway?'

Sophie, speechless, was fighting tears, but Lavinia had recovered. She crossed the kitchen and slapped Peter's face even more ringingly than Sophie had.

'You're despicable, Peter! You were making a nuisance of yourself but you haven't even got the decency to admit it. Just you apologise to Sophie, or I'll never speak to you again.'

'Huh! That's one of those promises you won't keep,' Peter sneered. 'Anyway, there are plenty more fish in the sea.'

'You bastard! How dare you . . .'

'Just watch your language, my girl, or . . .'

'Forget it, it's over,' Sophie interjected. 'Please, you two . . .'

'Mind your own business,' Lavinia shrieked and rounded on Peter again whilst Sophie, catching Devina's eye, tactfully left her mother to finish the apple pies whilst she watched the news on television.

Yet, despite the shouts, slams and shrieks, when Devina and Sophie were alone in the kitchen making late night drinks it transpired that Peter and Lavinia had made it up.

161

'They do quarrel,' Devina confided. 'Peter's a dear boy but he does like girls and Lavvy gets terribly jealous. I'm sure they're in love but it's such a strain, not being able to get married for at least three years, so they fall out.'

'Are they sleeping together?' Sophie asked thoughtlessly and was immediately horrified at herself as her mother, eyes saucering, assured her that they were not even *engaged*, so there could be no question of 'anything like that'.

'They're apart during term time, except for social events at each other's colleges and they always sleep in their hall's guest room,' Devina explained. 'And at home, Lavvy has to be in by eleven on weekdays and midnight at weekends. So there's no opportunity for any hanky-panky.'

Sophie did not feel she could tell her mother that what could be done after midnight could equally well be done at three in the afternoon, if her sister and Peter Brewer felt so inclined, and, anyway, it was none of her business, but she found herself wishing fervently that she was back in London, far from whatever mischief was brewing. She wondered if she could pretend she'd had a phone call from the Centre, but if she did she would be cheating on Anya and making things difficult for Penny, who had asked a cousin to stay in their absence and would also have her mother at the flat for a few days.

On the third day Peter Brewer came round with a box of chocolates for Devina and some roses for Lavinia. He was noticeably cool to Sophie and noticeably loving to Lavinia, and whilst they were all desperately trying to be natural the doorbell rang.

It was Janine, home for a few days. She had lost weight and her arms were like sticks of celery, and she had had her hair frizzed and bleached to the consistency of yellow wire wool. She was accompanied by a young-old man called Truman who had a completely bald pate, a boyish face with a tiny, goldfish mouth, and rimless glasses. Truman, it transpired, worked in television, for the Beeb.

As soon as Truman found that Sophie, too, worked in television, he tried to buttonhole her to talk shop, and it became clear that Janine bitterly resented Truman so much as looking at another woman. Sophie, who had seen at a glance that her sister's friend was not only a creep but was also at least partially homosexual, tried very hard to be polite but cool towards Truman whilst, at the same time, reassuring Janine that she had acquired a charming friend. This, not surprisingly, proved impossible and Sophie found herself most uncomfortably placed. Peter Brewer scarcely spoke to her, Lavinia was coldly sarcastic whenever she did speak and Truman oozed Sophie into corners at every available opportunity so that he could breathe bad breath into her face and try to pass on various titbits of probably apocryphal gossip.

That night Sophie went into her parents' bedroom when everyone else had gone to bed. Devina and her father were sitting up still and reading, but there was enough tautness in their attitudes to tell Sophie that they, too, were feeling the strain.

'Sorry to interrupt,' Sophie said. 'But I'm afraid I'll have to be moving on. You need my bed now that Janine and Truman are here, and though it's been lovely seeing you all again, it's been a bit of a strain, too. I'll come back for Christmas.'

Devina removed her reading glasses and dabbed her eyes.

'You can't go, darling, you said a fortnight; everyone knows you're home for a fortnight, what do you think they'll say? God knows I've tried to make you feel welcome, you mustn't take against Lavvy just because she's been a bit difficult, and then there's . . .'

All the time she was justifying herself and moaning about the shame of having Sophie leave after a mere three days, Sophie's father sat there, with his glasses on the end of his nose and his stomach protruding through the front of his ill-buttoned pyjamas, and watched her with eyes that said *this is my child and, though I don't understand her, I'm proud of her and I love her*, and Sophie's heart bled because she had never even tried to like him, not really. She had taken his love for Lavinia for granted and had never looked to see if she, fatty, had a corner of his heart. So that now when he found a solution to the problem she was hardly surprised at all.

'She's right, Dev,' he said mildly. 'Pack your stuff, Sophie luv, and I'll tek you down to the 'van. No need to say owt besides the girl needed peace and quiet which wasn't to be had here, with Janine and her fellow home. What do you say?'

The caravan! At that moment, it was like remembering

heaven to consider it. The Markhams owned a static caravan on a site in Anglesey to which the entire family repaired at holidaytimes, or at any rate they had done so when the girls had been younger. Sophie would not have claimed to have had a happy childhood, but the happiest times she had known had been spent at the 'van. It had meant being alone without being lonely, wandering along a rock-girt shore or up country lanes heavy with the scents of summer. It had meant a closeness with nature, seabirds swooping within ten feet of one's windows, rabbits feeding on the short-cropped grass as the sun sank, to say nothing of the pools with their sea-anemones, shrimps, tiny, penny-sized flatfish.

Even company of a sort had been available, for though children might not want to play with 'the fat one', there were dogs, owned by other people on the site and eager for rambles, and being with a child, be she never so fat and lonely, lent respectability in farmerly eyes to the most ragged and unkempt of canines.

'I say, Dad!'

Sophie knew it was the ideal solution from everyone's point of view. Devina, she could see, was already planning how she would tell people that Sophie, worn out by the exertions of London life, had gone down to the 'van for a few days' much needed relaxation. Everyone would accept that, even her sisters, because they loved Anglesey too and knew how happy Sophie had been there, how she had shed tears of sheer misery on departure day.

'Right, then that's settled, luv,' Sophie's father leaned back against his pillows and opened his book once more. 'Mother will pack you a box of food and you can get fresh milk from the farm. It won't be crowded, the site I mean, but there'll be others down, I dare say. They'll get you bread and such and give you the odd lift into Valley.'

'I'd walk,' Sophie said fervently, and then, remembering the seven miles, amended it to: 'or ring for a taxi.' She smiled at Devina, who still looked a trifle undecided. 'Don't worry, Mother, I'd rather be at the 'van than anywhere. I'll go and pack.'

Sophie and her father reached the site at eight in the evening and he had to turn round and leave again at once since he was working next day, so they said brief goodbyes, checked the gas and the level of the jacks, and then Sophie walked with him as far as the well and waved him off before filling her water carrier and returning to the van.

As she pottered about, charging the chemical loo, boiling the kettle, turning on the gas fire just to air the place through, she reflected that her departure had been worth it, if only for the new closeness which now existed between herself and her father.

He had not said much on the journey down, neither of them had. But, forced into the proximity of a three hour car journey – for the car was old and slow – they had exchanged some idle chat and, encouraged by the fact that he did not ask questions, Sophie told him a bit about her life in London, considerably more than she had managed to bring herself to tell Devina.

She appreciated the fact that he had listened, laughed once or twice, and then capped her story with one of his own about a chap at work; never, for one moment, did he give her the impression that he doubted what she told him, thought her actions foolish or, in fact, wished her in any way different. It was curiously relaxing to find herself to totally accepted.

Now, in the last grey and gold glow of evening, she made herself a large cheese and tomato sandwich and sat with it and a cup of coffee in the window, to watch the lights of Holyhead appear across the harbour as dusk deepened. The tide was right in, but for once it was a still, windless evening and the lights lay on the sea perfectly reflected, with even the moon's path ruled across the watered silk of the bay without so much as a ripple to break its perfection.

Only out to sea was there movement. Lights flashed rhythmically, shipping moved on the face of the waters and out of her view, beyond the ridge of rock which hid the beginnings of the long beach, the Skerries light would be flashing, its beam catching the quiet sea, the short turf of the site and the ruins which stood, stark, along the small cliffs. Romance personified, she had once thought. And I think it still, she realised now, smiling to herself. Sitting here with the window open so that the scent of shore and country drifted in, she knew that this was something altogether special, each incident unrepeatable, unforgettable.

She had not been here much since her sixteenth year. It had been too difficult and, besides, the older girls wanted to bring friends with them and they did not want Sophie. It meant two journeys for her father, too – one ferrying her, Devina and bedding, food and other paraphernalia, another taking the rest of the family. He had been prepared to do it whilst they were all young, but it had become too much of a chore once Sophie's size made it impossible for the family to travel down together. I made things so difficult, Sophie thought now, ashamed. It never occurred to me that I made things difficult – or perhaps it did and perhaps I thought it served them all right.

She thought, for the first time, of the day-trips out in the car which had come to an end round about the time Poppy had been born. Because Sophie overflowed the back seat. She had never consciously acknowledged the fact, but she acknowledged it now. What a selfish creature the Sophie Markham of two years ago had been, bemoaning her lot, miserably eating herself square and never allowing it to cross her mind that it was not only she who suffered for her size.

She realised that she was thinking of the former Sophie as though they were, in truth, two different people. The Sophie of now acknowledging for the first time that the Sophie of the past had been a coward who had never dared to look facts in the face. If she met that Sophie now, she would dislike her every bit as much as other people had disliked her – perhaps more. Understanding does not necessarily bring compassion.

She finished her sandwich, drained her coffee cup and told herself that she should move, light the gas, start getting ready for bed, yet she stayed just where she was. The view of the dark bay with its garlands of brilliant lights forbade her to steal its beauty, to rob the sky of its blue-black splendour and the moon of its peerless gold by turning on a silly little gas lamp.

She sat there for a long time, with the peace emptying her mind of any but gentle thoughts. The Sophie of long ago was forgotten, her peccadilloes forgiven, as the hushing of the sea and the tiny meadow night noises worked their magic on her.

She moved, in the end, because she was almost asleep, and knew just what she would feel like if she slept, fully-clothed and upright, after the sort of day she had had. She pulled the curtains, shutting out the hypnotic night, and padded barefoot up the length of the van to the bedroom at the end. There was a full-sized double bed in there and she had heard stories of its comforts from her sisters, though she had never taken a turn at sleeping in it. No one had fancied sharing even the fullest-sized bed with the old Sophie.

The bed had cool, pale blue sheets and a duvet with a flower pattern in pinks and purples, but now the moonlight had sucked all the colours to itself, leaving only stark black and white. Sophie dropped her clothes in a heap on the floor and climbed between the sheets. Bliss! She snuggled down, her cheek sinking gratefully into the softness of the pillow, and then remembered she had not drawn the curtains. Damn! She should, just in case someone came over early in the morning, before she was up, and spied on her through the glass. There were very few people on site, judging by the number of cars standing beside vans – she had seen two – but it was possible that others, like herself, were here in search of peace and quiet and had not brought transport. Reluctantly, she climbed out of bed and took the two small steps to the window, glancing out as she did so. There lay the caravans in the moonlight, the Ashleys', the Sullivans', the Barrass' vans, all curtained, carless, empty. And then, even as she went to draw the curtains and scuttle back to bed, a light appeared in the van to the rear and to the right of her. A small, flickering light like a will o' the wisp, which appeared briefly in the big, end room and then moved jerkily away.

Sophie watched until it went out, then drew her curtains and got back into bed. If she remembered correctly that was the Samuels' van, so either they were down here themselves or they had lent the 'van to friends. Unless it was a burglar, and that seemed unlikely. What was there to steal in a static caravan, where nearly everything was glued to the floor or taken home when the season was over? She snuggled down, speculating idly. She could not remember much about the Samuels though they had two sons whose names she could not recall. Two thin, dark boys, older than she, always out in a boat, fishing or putting down crab-pots or riding the long, low rollers on curved surf boards, or getting into the car with ropes and pitons and all the rest of the stuff they took on climbing expeditions to Snowdonia. Boys who regarded their holidays as one long out-door pursuit, a challenge to skill and muscle, who never lolled on the beach or helped Trevor with the haymaking or hung around the horses hoping for a canter. She had seen them, once, at South Stack, where the cliffs plunge three hundred feet sheer into the sea. A clever and resourceful climber can find a foothold in the tower where the cliff birds nest, and come up the echoing chimney from the wicked sea-surge in the caves and troughs below, up and up to the springy heather and the short, sheep-nibbled turf of the clifftop.

She had been proud, then, to know the Samuel boys, as holidaymakers had lined the steps and peered through the rock window from which you got the best view of the chimney, cheering the boys on. She could still remember the seeming casualness of their ascent, the quick, neat way they both climbed. And the way they had ignored their audience. But not their names. Their names had gone, into the mist of the years. They were just the Samuel boys.

One of them might be in the van now, or both. Though did boys come back? Were they like girls, in love with a place, relishing each moment there, or did they cut loose completely once they went? She had no idea. The thought made her remember other boys who had swum and chatted and flirted with the Markham sisters on those long-ago summers. Paul with the red hair, Aiden who liked to kill things, Barry and Chris who had vied for Lavinia's love all one long, hot summer. And Jeremy, who would not wear shorts though his parents devised every ploy imaginable to get him out of long trousers, and David, who wore glasses and had a dog called Flea because she was so small and who had befriended Sophie one year. That friendship had been very sweet, even though David was a good six inches smaller than she and had a pronounced stammer. But though she had longed for the holiday to come round again, by the following year David had outgrown fat Sophie. He'd lost his stammer for a start, and his parents had brought him a wet-suit with which he could go skin-diving far out, staying in the sea far longer than the others. He was keen on canoeing too, and the canoe which could comfortably take a Sophie-shape had not yet been invented. Not that she had not tried. Made brave by David's insistence that she at least have a go, she had wedged herself into his canoe and allowed his father to tow her out into deep water, since it was obligatory, it seemed, that she know what it felt like to drown before she was allowed to canoe alone (though David's father had not put it quite like that).

Once in deep water he had turned the canoe over, instructing Sophie to kick herself free of the craft, and when she had failed to reappear (for the simple reason that even the most panic – stricken of kicks could not free her from the canoe's loving embrace) he righted the canoe again, whereupon her weight had plucked it from his hands and turned it over once more, so that she had been forced to hang there, humiliatingly upside-down and desperately short of air, until father and son had manhandled the horrid craft right way up once more, holding it long enough for her to get out and be sick into the wretched thing.

Remembering, Sophie smiled. Bliss, to be able to smile over that stupid incident, to know that however silly she had been made to look, David's father had looked sillier. All that talk about safety and he could not even make the thing do an eskimo roll. And by the time the next holidays came round Sophie's proportions had made her safe from a repeat performance.

I could canoe now, if I wanted, Sophie reminded herself sleepily. And bathe, of course. Not that anything could have stopped Sophie swimming, only she had not used the long beach for years, but had taken herself off further along the coast, to small, unfrequented bays where she might wallow alone, bobbing in the surf like some exotic and over-inflated rubber doll.

Just before she slept, Sophie twitched the curtain aside an inch and gazed across to the Samuels' van. The roving light was out, the uneasy prowler sleeping. Sophie followed suit.

Chapter Eleven

Sophie woke, next day, when she heard the dull thump of a car door slamming, and before she could fully pull herself together, a voice hailed her through the window.

'Mornin', Sophie! One pint or two, dear?'

Out of season, milk was delivered by a plump and smiling lady who also cleaned the showers and the toilets and sold anyone who needed it cylinders of gas. She was in her mid-fifties and lived down in the village with a farm-worker husband and a number of cats. Sophie struggled up in bed and then climbed out and padded across to the back door. She dragged it open, and fumbled in her purse for the right money.

'Hello, Mrs Honeysuckle, lovely to see you again. I'd better have two pints, I think. How's your husband?'

'He's fine, dear.' Mrs Honeysuckle, named for her cottage to distinguish her from the hundreds of other Evanses or Joneses, put two cartons of milk down on the step. 'Would you like a shower, this morning? Only three or four of you on the site, see, so I've not switched the 'ot water on yet.'

'No, I don't think so, I'll be swimming later.' She laughed at Mrs Honeysuckle's expression; local people did not see the attraction of plunging into a cold sea just because it was there. 'So thanks, but no thanks. Who else is down? Are the Samuels? I thought I saw a light.'

'There's a car,' Mrs Honeysuckle admitted, 'But no answer, so I left no milk. Still, she can get some from the farm later, when she wakes. I'll be putting the 'eat on at six, if you change your mind. How's Mum and Dad, then? And the girls?'

'They're all well.' Sophie knew that Mrs Honeysuckle would dearly like to hear about Janine's broken marriage, Poppy's failure to get her form prize and Lavinia's resits, but she felt that the satisfying of the older woman's curiosity would have to wait at least until she had got some clothes on and a cup of tea inside her. 'I'll come into the village tomorrow, I expect, so I'll pop in, if I may, and tell you all the news.'

'Fine, dear. I'll put the kettle on, around eleven. I'll have finished up here by then.' She smiled and moved away, then turned back. 'Tell you what, you got no car, I'll give you a lift in my milk van if you like.'

'Mrs H, that would be marvellous,' Sophie said honestly, 'It's a date! See you.'

As she made her breakfast, she wondered what Mrs Honeysuckle had really thought, for though she was a friendly soul and had been very pally with Devina, she and Sophie had scarcely exchanged more than a few words on the price of milk and the state of the weather before this day. But she had the natural courtesy of all country people, and their hospitality, too.

Sophie was fully dressed and about to decapitate her boiled egg when there was another knock on the door. She sighed, but put down her spoon, and went across the kitchen part of the van, then opened the door and smiled enquiringly.

'Yes?'

A man stood there. He must be a holidaymaker, as she was, for he wore the standard holiday uniform of white T-shirt, blue jeans and plimsolls. He was very dark with almost black hair, a beaky nose and lines which ran from the corners of nose to the corners of his mouth. When he smiled, as he was doing now, you could see why. He was no one she knew, or at least she did not recognise him.

'Good morning. Has the milk been?'

'Yes, about half an hour ago. Mrs Honeysuckle did mention that she'd tried your van – you've come from the Samuels' van, I take it? – but couldn't get a reply, so of course she wouldn't leave the milk. I can lend you a spare pint, though, if you can let me have it back by lunchtime.'

'Bless you, that would be very kind.' He ran a hand through his dark hair. 'Are you here alone? You're very brave.'

Sophie got the milk out of the cool box and raised an eyebrow as she handed it over.

'Brave? Why? I'm not expecting to be nibbled to death by a rabbit or dragged under by a sea-anemone exactly!'

He grinned.

171

'No, of course not, but you've got no transport, and that can be rather restricting, don't you think? Do you drive? I saw Mr Markham bringing you down yesterday and quite thought he would be back.'

'No, I don't drive, but I'm not worried about being here without transport,' Sophie said. 'Some kind person will surely get me the odd loaf, or run me into the village, if I ask nicely.'

'Sure.' He paused, looking at her intently. 'You don't remember me, do you, Sophie?'

Sophie's heart gave a little hop of pleasure. He had recognised her, how nice it would be to return the compliment. But far too dangerous to pretend. Regretfully she shook her head.

'No, I'm afraid not, though if you *did* come from the Samuels' van, you must be one of the boys – I'm afraid I can't remember the names, though one of you was quite keen on a sister of mine, once.'

'That's right, I'm Roy Samuel. It was my brother, Matthew, who spooked your sister for a bit. Look, why don't you invite me in for breakfast? Then we could catch up on each other's news in comfort.'

Sophie, taken aback, blinked, then smiled and stood aside, waving him past her.

'I hereby invite you to breakfast, only you'll have to make do with a boiled egg, I don't have any bacon or tomatoes or anything. But since you've got a car, perhaps I'll get the chance to right such deficiencies.'

He grinned back at her over his shoulder. He was not a lot taller than she, no more than a couple of inches. Stephen, Sophie thought proudly, was huge in comparison, a good eight inches taller than both of them.

'The way to a lady's heart is via my MG, eh? Right, you're on – where are the boiled eggs?'

Over breakfast, for Sophie boiled herself another egg to keep him company, though she did not have a second slice of bread and butter, they took stock of each other. Sophie felt that he was familiar, in some way, though she could not imagine having met him before -- he was striking if not handsome, definitely not the sort of man you forgot. He grinned at her when he saw her puzzled look and shook his head.

'Can't quite remember, eh? Never mind. Tell me why you're

here all alone – I've been here two days and I was jolly glad to see you yesterday, I can tell you. I was getting a bit tired of my own company.'

'Were you? I don't think I could get tired of myself here, or at least, even if I got tired of me, I'd put up with it for the sake of being here. But actually I was supposed to be holidaying at home, only things got difficult, other guests arrived, and Dad had the bright idea of bringing me down here.'

It might not be the whole truth, but it would do very well, Sophie thought, eating her egg.

'I'm having a bit of a break before going off to the States,' Roy said, munching bread and butter. 'I don't know how long I'll be there, but I do know it will probably be hectic, so I thought I'd take a couple of weeks of complete peace. Odd, us both turning up here.'

'That's the second time you've been enigmatic,' Sophie said with spirit. 'Do stop it and tell me how I should know you – if I should.'

'Why should you? Unless you remember the Samuels clearly enough to recall that Roy was a year younger than Matthew. Any more coffee?'

'You've got a cheek, for a self-invited guest,' Sophie said, getting up. 'I'll have some too. Shall I put some toast on?'

He accepted the coffee but refused the toast, albeit regretfully.

'No, better not, otherwise the morning will have disappeared before we've finished clearing up.' He drank his coffee, sighed, then stood up.

'I'm going down to bathe later. Got anything planned? Why not come with me, then?'

The invitation was casual, yet it threw Sophie a tiny bit. She glanced out of the window at the inviting sunshine. She had a brand-new swimsuit in her case, it was pretty and it suited her, making the least of her curves and showing off her newly acquired waist. It would be fun to wear the costume and to go swimming with this dark young man. Of course she was Stephen's girl, but there could be no harm in swimming with someone else. And yet . . . well, she *was* Sophie Markham, not the sort of girl that men casually asked out. But he was watching her and she had to say something.

173

'Oh! Yes, I'd like to swim. When are you going down? It's a bit soon after breakfast yet, and I've got to wash up and clear away and so on.'

'True. Shall we say eleven o'clock? I'll call for you and we can walk down together. And then I'll take you to lunch to make up for eating your egg. How does that appeal to you?'

A thousand objections raised their ugly heads. Suppose he took her somewhere she could not get a salad? And she did not much want to leave the bay, she had only just arrived. What if conversation was difficult? She had meant to walk right along the curve of the bay today and make her way via Trefadog to Church Bay. Yet it would seem so churlish to refuse.

'I thought we'd bathe and then run round to Church Bay in the car,' he said, as though he had read her thoughts. 'There's a place there famous for its lobster salad and they do a very nice white wine. Come on, be a devil and accept. Don't force me into solitary drinking as well as solitary dining.'

'We-ell, I've never tasted lobster,' Sophie admitted. 'But isn't it awfully expensive?'

Across the caravan a pair of black brows rose in simulated surprise.

'Is it? Do you think I'm a pauper? Only my week's wages are good enough for you, fair lady.'

She laughed with him. Odd, that she should have come out with such a Markhamish remark, when she had grown used to Stephen's casual acceptance of being able to afford whatever one wanted.

'Sorry, it must be that down here we were always short of money. Five daughters are a lot of girls to feed and clothe, and it was always "Pie or chips, girls?", never both. But if you're sure your funds won't receive a crippling blow, I'd love to have lunch with you. Only . . . well, I'd much rather walk along the coast and then up over the cliffs. I like plenty of exercise whilst I'm here.'

For one awful, blushmaking moment she thought that he might have made some comment about this sudden desire for exercise, though it was perfectly true, she always walked a lot on the island, but he did no such thing. He just nodded, and made his way to the back door.

'Right, it's a date then.'

* * *

At eleven o'clock precisely Sophie left her van and saw Roy leaving his. She was wearing a brief yellow towelling top over her swimsuit and a pair of flip-flops and Roy was wearing a white towelling jacket, open over navy blue shorts. She went over to him and he held out a hand.

'The tide's on the way out, which should mean the water's warmer. Are you up to running down to the big beach?'

'Running!' Sophie took his hand without self-consciousness, then realised what she had done and promptly felt silly. 'Well, I don't mind running slowly, I suppose.'

They jogged, then walked, then jogged again. Down the lane with the sea marsh on one side and the empty camping field where the mushrooms grew on the other. The bulrushes were tall now, the irises had flowered long since, yet there was colour in the marsh, autumn colour of leaf and fruit, perhaps in its way even lovelier than the brilliance of spring and summer. Sophie felt that the bulrushes were watching her with some amazement – little Sophie Markham, running along the white and dusty lane, hand in hand with a man, they must be saying. Fancy!

They reached the beach in good order, as Roy remarked when they had got their breath back. He threw off his jacket, draping it across a convenient rock, and kicked off his old canvas shoes. He turned to Sophie and caught her staring. Never, she was thinking, have I seen or imagined a man so hairy! His chest was covered with thick, curly hair which rioted from the belt of his shorts right across his heavily muscled shoulders, to continue quite strongly on his back. He grinned at her obvious confusion.

'What do you think of the Samuel built-in pelt? I trust you aren't similarly equipped!'

He said that because Sophie was clinging to her robe, suddenly reluctant to take it off. Only Stephen had seen her in less, and it seemed wrong to be on a long, lonely beach with another man, clad in a costume which, in all probability, would show off all the wrong bits of her. But Roy's teasing tone had its effect and she wriggled out of her top, kicked off her flip-flops and pulled back her hair with one hand. She had a rubber-band on her wrist and looped her hair out of the way, then turned to face the sea. For a moment she forgot all about Roy and his hairiness

175

and the worry that she might be bulging over the swimsuit. That sea! Blue and white, the waves so gentle that they could scarcely count as surf, it enticed her with memories of other summer seas. It looks *warm*, she thought wonderingly, trotting across the hard, wet sand, eager as a child running to its mother. Oh, how she loved the sea, how she adored it!

It was not warm, it was freezing. She entered the water timidly, and then Roy rushed in beside her, running feet kicking up storms of spray, catching her hand as he passed her so that they could go in together. Sophie would have hung back because it was so icy but, as it was, shock and Roy gave her no choice. She was dragged, screaming if not kicking, right out until the water was waist deep and then Roy let go of her hand to dive through the next incoming wave and she overbalanced, tipping ignominiously into the sparkling, salty water, shrieking, gasping, and then launching into a fast crawl which helped to ease the breath-catching shock as the cold bit at her warm flesh.

Roy came up from his dive with his hair sleeked back so that he looked like a seal. He grinned at her.

'Isn't it great? Cold, but great! Come out a bit deeper, some-times you can find a warm patch if you do that.'

They swam for thirty minutes and then returned to the shore to flop, exhausted, onto their towels. Sophie patted herself briskly dry, then nudged Roy with her toe.

'It's none too warm, here. Shall we go up to the saucer?'

'Good idea.'

Side by side, they made their way to the saucer-shaped depression high up on a massive rocky outcrop. In high summer it would have been full of teenagers, loud with their voices, scented with their sun-oil and crisps and wet hair, but now it basked, empty, in the morning sun. The pair of them laid their towels out on the hot rock and collapsed, side by side on their backs. Sophie looked across at Roy and saw him relaxed, his face as peaceful as his sprawled body.

'We'd better not go to sleep, Roy, not if we want that lobster!'

He groaned and squinted at his waterproof wristwatch.

'Hell, you're right. Tell you what, we'll stay here for half an hour and then we'll drive round. I booked that table for one, I didn't think we'd have sun all morning. Suit you?'

'Yes, that's marvellous idea.' She smiled at him. 'And tomorrow, we can walk round to Church Bay and I'll treat *you* to lunch. Which means ham sandwiches and beer at the pub.'

He laughed but agreed and then they lay quiet, basking in the reflected warmth of the September sun.

After five days it was unthinkable to either of them that a moment of their holiday should be spent apart. As soon as they were up in the morning one or other came visiting – usually it was Roy, bouncing in to wake Sophie, telling her that, surprise surprise, he had come for breakfast and brought some bacon with him, all he needed was her to cook it.

It occurred to Sophie that they seemed to have bounded over all the usual preliminaries in a relationship, to settle for friendship at once. And it was such a good friendship, they had been easy with one another virtually from that first meeting, certainly from the first swim they had shared. It was odd and a little disquieting that she should feel so instantly at ease with a man she had known only vaguely, years ago, as a boy. Yet something about him made him easy to know. She remembered how awkward she had been with Stephen, ill at ease for a long time, stumbling rather than gliding into an understanding of him. Yet perhaps, in a way, her relationship with Stephen had been a sort of apprenticeship and as a result, because she had achieved understanding, then it would always come more easily in future. It seemed very unfair that Stephen should have had all the diffidence, the shyness, the hard work, but then Stephen had also had Sophie from new, so to speak. I was a bit like a car, Sophie thought. If you buy a brand-new model you have what they call teething troubles, and you have to run it in, driving it slowly for ages and taking it back to the garage for frequent checks. But if you buy a second-hand model, though you run a risk that it is not quite what it seems, you don't have to worry about speeds or services, you just enjoy the ride.

Sophie giggled. What a way to look at a loving relationship like hers and Stephen's! But it was true that she was a second-hand model now. She had been a virgin, and now she was not. So perhaps Stephen had not done so badly after all – depending, of course, on how highly he valued virginity. Modern men were supposed not to care, but she often felt that Stephen was an exception. The fact that he alone had possessed her gave her a special sort of rarity value to Stephen.

And Roy, of course, neither knew nor cared that she was a second-hand model, because their friendship was perfect, needing neither explanations nor apologies. They enjoyed each other's company to the full, without wanting anything but the occasional hand held to make them feel complete.

Or so she thought, on the fifth day of their holiday, as they sat on the cushioned seat in her caravan, overlooking the bay, taking it in turns to watch through the binoculars a Sealink ferry from Ireland docking in Holyhead harbour. They had spent the day on the beach and rocks, because the forecast threatened gales and already the wind was higher, so they had had a lovely, outdoor day, in case the weather forced them into indoor activities for a while. Now, after a chicken curry, which had been almost as good as Roy has thought it, they sat on the window seat and watched the ship dock, and felt full, and satisfied with their lot, and rather sleepy.

Or at least, Sophie did, and she had become used to assuming that she and Roy enjoyed the same things. He was watching the ship now, and she was watching him, wondering what was so satisfying about his beaky, rather aggressive profile, with the dark hair flopping across his brow and his mouth a little bit open, because he had screwed up his eyes to focus the glasses better.

'Is she docked? Those are good glasses, aren't they? When you think of the way we squabbled over them as kids it's a wonder they still work at all. What can you see now?' Sophie leaned back and closed her eyes. 'Go on, Roy, amuse me, tell me what you can see.'

He lay the glasses down on the cushions and leaned towards her. Sophie opened her eyes a slit. His face was very near.

'I see a beautiful woman. Her eyes are shut, but I know they're green, and her mouth is shut – for once – but I know it hides white and even teeth, and there isn't enough light to see her skin, but I known it's sun-kissed, with a sprinkling of golden freckles, and . . .'

'Shut up, you fool, I meant through the glasses, you know . . .'

His mouth cut her protest off short. Her eyes shot open and she saw his face, as close to her own as it was possible to be, his dark eyes half-veiled by the heavy lids, the prow of his nose blurred in her vision as her lids, too, began to droop, feeling his arms go round her, feeling her heart begin to hammer, her pulses to patter, her stomach to lurch with something that was neither surprise nor delight but a little bit of both.

He broke the kiss first. He was breathing quickly, but he took her face in his hands and his eyes were rather anxious.

'Sophie? Was that all right?'

'It was lovely,' Sophie said. She could not lie to Roy, nor did she want to do so. 'But I don't think it was very sensible, do you?'

He was grinning, plainly relieved by her reaction. He cuffed her gently, then picked up the glasses again.

'Perhaps not. But it was, as you say, lovely. Why don't you go and put the kettle on?'

She was half relieved and half disappointed by his prosaic reaction to what had been, for her, a tumultuous experience, but she told herself firmly that it was he who was sensible and well adjusted. She was just a mass of impulses, and what he had done, was to stir up all the feelings which Stephen stirred with such delicious thoroughness once or twice a week. Roy, of course, was like Stephen, and could keep his emotions where they belonged, so she would simply have to do the same. Besides, she did not in the least want Roy to make love to her, she wanted Stephen. Kissing was a harmless enough pastime, she supposed. After all, she knew that Lavinia had been kissing boys for years without apparently feeling anything but the mildest friendship. She must not make an issue out of what was, probably, a perfectly natural and normal salute between friends.

So she put the kettle on, and when they had drunk their hot chocolate and eaten their biscuits, she saw Roy off and locked up and went to bed, completely unaware that, with the embrace, her whole attitude to Roy had changed, as had his to her.

If Sophie had had time to consider, she might have wondered at the speed with which their relationship continued to change and deepen after that first kiss. But she was too busy, too happy and tired for much introspection. They got on so well and their

179

tastes were so similar. On the eighth day of the holiday, when the promised gales were at their height, they decided almost without discussion to go to Cemaes to visit the blowhole.

'It'll be really good, in this weather,' Roy said as they set off in his small car. 'The tide's in, what's more, so the sea will be roaring up the tunnel. I like it spectacular, don't you?'

'Mm hmm. I just hope we don't get blown off the cliffs though – this really must be a force eight gale, or whatever it is sailors talk about.'

Though they both laughed at the idea, when they reached the cliffs and began to climb they both thought it politic to cling tightly to one another, for the wind really was a force to reckon with, roaring off the Irish sea with enough strength to mean that it had to be battled against, fought with, as it dragged at their hair and tore at their clothing.

'I can lean on it,' Sophie shouted into the teeth of the gale, seeing Roy only as a shape, for the wind had almost closed her eyes and she was seeing life through tangled eyelashes. 'Oh, Roy, look!'

Perhaps it was something to do with the wild weather, but the sunset was fantastic, with flame-drenched clouds clutching a scarlet sun in their feathery depths. Open-mouthed, they attained the hill top and stared around them, incredulous that such beauty could exist, and watched, speechless, as the sun was gradually swallowed up by the dark silver line of the horizon.

When it had gone and only the afterglow dazzled, they began to walk across the cliff meadow and down to the place in the rocks that the Markhams always knew as the Amphitheatre, because that was what it reminded them of. Here the rocks were marble, veined and pale, and because of the bowl-like shape of it, rainwater and spray from wild winter seas had combined to make the place a strange mixture of fresh and seawater pools, with innocent country flowers and rushes blooming side by side with seaweeds and clumps of sea-holly and sea-pinks. The Amphitheatre was separated from the sea itself by a tall, marble, rock barrier, and thus the exciting tang of the deep sea bed and the scent of grass and earth mingled, making it mysteriously different from the rest of the island.

The blowhole was a chimney in the rock barrier, formed at

the end of a tunnel through that same barrier which led right out into the ocean, and tonight it was working well, making the odd, howling noise which had fascinated hundreds of children as the sea came crashing and roaring up the tunnel and forced its way through the narrow little passage into the biggest sea-pool, where it swirled furiously, making the seaweed whip far up the bare rocks.

Roy and Sophie, children once again for a moment, clambered up and sat above the blowhole, but it was dangerous there, with the force of the wind and the fact that, whenever a particularly big wave hurtled up the tunnel, some of it was forced up through the blowhole, to fountain six feet up into the air, soaking not only anyone near at hand but making the rocks themselves slippery and treacherous.

Roy bawled at Sophie to come down and cautiously they descended from the airy heights of the barrier down into the hollow. They collapsed, laughing, onto a flat piece of rock near the largest of the freshwater pools and Roy put an arm round Sophie, then two, and then began to kiss her.

Salt lips met salt lips, kissing gently, then more fiercely, and suddenly Sophie knew, as positively as she knew anything, that if she did not make a fairly drastic move they would make love right here and now, on the rock in the Amphitheatre, with the sea crashing so loudly that they could barely hear each other speak and their bodies buffeted by the gale. She also knew that, though her mind had not even considered the possibility of Roy making love to her, her body had been waiting for quite a while for this moment. And it wanted him. Wanted him with an urgency and lack of prudence which struck her as shocking even as she acknowledged the desire.

She had no intention of behaving in so unprincipled a fashion, however, so it went without saying that she must not let Roy take the first step, even though her body tingled with desire and her mind, too, wanted to have the confirmation of mutual need. She sat up, put her hands on his shoulders and pushed him away, then held out her hand. She was trembling, though not from the cold.

'We'd better be getting back, or it'll be too dark to see the path.'

He rose at once, his glance rueful, and Sophie knew that her recognition of that moment had been shared by Roy, knew, even, that he would not have drawn back but that he respected her right to do so.

They reached the car and climbed inside, into the calm after the storm. The warm atmosphere smelled faintly of leather, petrol, and of the perfumed talc that Sophie favoured. They settled themselves in their seats and Roy kissed Sophie lightly on the mouth.

'Dear Sophie! Shall we go straight home, or would you like to pop into the Douglas for a drink?'

Sophie thought it would be best to go straight back to the van, for she was as tightly strung as any bow-string and knew how impossible it would be for them to talk naturally in a crowded bar parlour. But as the car hurled itself against the wind, with the golden headlamps seeming to waver with the powerful gusts, they were both quiet. As they crossed the sea marsh the beams caught a rabbit unawares and, without having to say a word, Sophie knew that Roy would slow down and then stop, dousing his lights whilst the rabbit recovered its composure and scuttled off into the safety of the bulrushes. It occurred to her that, had she been sitting beside Stephen, she would have had to ask him to stop. Stephen was not a cruel man but he lacked the imagination to understand the rabbit's raw panic, and he could not read her mind with the accuracy that Roy had attained without, it seemed, even trying.

When they reached the caravan she unlocked the door and went to the cooker, fumbling for the matches so that she could light the gas lamp, but Roy's fingers closed over hers.

'No, leave it. Let's sit in the window and watch Holyhead light up.'

Was this foolish? But it was as if her denial in the Amphitheatre had used up her supply of firmness for the night. She complied, sitting close beside him. It might be foolish but she knew she was running no risk of Roy doing anything she did not want him to do. She was also sure that here, in the familiar surroundings she had known ever since she could remember, the wildness which had almost nudged her into surrendering out there on the cliffs would be unlikely to reappear. So they sat there, silent still, hearts beating, pulses ticking, blood cooling. And not only blood, Sophie thought guiltily. There was another part of me getting far too hot out at Cemaes and it wasn't my heart, either, it was a far more basic and prosaic part of my anatomy!

'Sophie, what's for breakfast?'

Sophie turned in his arms, for he had taken her into arms as he spoke, trying to gauge his expression in the faint starlight, but she could see very little through the darkness beside the gleam of eyes and teeth.

'Do you want to come over for breakfast? Well, I've got cereal and eggs, but if you want bacon you'll have to bring your own.'

His hand stole round the back of her neck, smoothing the soft skin, his fingers waking electric impulses which Sophie fought to kill.

'No, I don't want to come over for breakfast. I want to stay here. I want to go to bed with you, my love.'

Sophie heaved a great, tremulous sigh. A part of her, an ignoble part, wished that he had not made the choice hers by that remark. It would have been so much easier to have been taken by surprise, to have been kissed and cuddled and caressed into bed and into intimacy. But Roy played fair.

'I'm afraid we can't do that, Roy. You see, I've got a fellow. In London. He wouldn't like me to sleep around.'

His reaction, for once, surprised her totally. She expected him to be shocked that she had a boyfriend, or at least to object to the way she let an absent 'fellow' come between them. But he did none of those things. His caressing hand continued to caress, to tease at the soft nape of her neck and the little fronds of hair that grew there.

'You mean Stephen, I take it? But darling, he doesn't own you!'

She was so startled that she leapt away from him, heart pattering as if she had seen a ghost, but he was strong, even if he was not as tall as Stephen. He caught her and held her back against him, and the even thunder of his heart continued to keep time despite her struggles, though she knew that he would have let her go at once had he thought she really wanted to be released. He knew she had leapt from surprise and fright rather than from a wish to leave his arms.

'Roy, how on earth did you know about Stephen? I've never mentioned him, I know I haven't. I haven't said a word about

London, or scarcely a word.'

She knew he was smiling, though she could not see his face, held as she was against his chest, with both of them gazing out across the bay.

'I know all about you, Sophie mine! You're highly regarded at the Television Centre because you can keep your boss, Stephen Bland, in order, and because you're a very efficient young woman. But look, just because he's your boss . . .'

Sophie steeled herself. For the first time she knew regret for that night in Tunbridge Wells, because what you have once given cannot be taken back, and by the very fact of being the recipient of her gift, Stephen was linked to her in a way that Roy was not. And already she knew that she and Roy were good together -- not sexually, but as people. He was one half of a scallop shell, she the other. Whatever their faults, together they would transcend them. But it was no use, she could not lie to Roy.

'Stephen isn't just my boss. He's my lover. So you see, I can't . . .' Her voice quivered and tears stole down her cheeks. 'Oh Roy, I just can't.'

'I guessed he was, from his attitude.' His hand wiped her eyes for her, clearing the tears onto the heel of his palm. 'Is he your one true love?'

'I don't know,' Sophie said, anguish in every syllable. 'I thought he was, honestly I did, or I wouldn't have . . . you know, I wouldn't have . . .'

'I know what you mean, but did you think I believed a gorgeous girl like you would be a virgin? I should be so lucky!' He stood up, lifting her with him. 'Shall we go to bed, where we can discuss all this seriously?'

'I can't,' Sophie said flatly. 'If I could get in touch with Stephen, tell him that it's all off, then . . . well, that might be different. But I couldn't break it to him over the phone, I couldn't . . .

'But Sophie, my lovely idiot, you're not taking anything away from Stephen. He isn't here. Do be sensible and let me love you.'

Sophie wriggled out of his embrace and went over to the stove and lit the gas lamp. Then she turned to face Roy.

'That's just it, I would be doing Stephen dirt, really I would.

He puts a very high value on my – my niceness. I'm his, if you like, because he believes it. And that's my fault; I did give him reason to think it was true. Well, I thought it was true.'

'But it turns out not to be true, right? Then why shouldn't you and I love each other?'

Sophie heaved a sigh even gustier than the first one. Her eyes were filling with tears again, but it was no use, she still had to tell Roy how she felt.

'Because it would make me feel like the worst kind of cheat, that's why.'

For a moment they confronted one another, Roy standing very still, as if listening to unseen advice. Then his shoulders slumped.

'Then that's it. No more persuasion. Goodnight, my darling.'

Chapter Twelve

It says a good deal for their relationship that they were able to meet next morning, at breakfast, with affection and with a good deal of understanding, though, as she dished up bacon and eggs, Sophie was determined that they should talk about themselves and not merely sweep their disagreement under the carpet and continue with their holiday as if it had never happened. She was determined, in fact, to be firm with Roy.

As it happened, Roy was of the same opinion. As soon as they were both seated with the food in front of them and the coffee pot between them, he spoke of the matter closest to both their hearts at that moment.

'Well, Sophie, aren't you going to ask me just who I am and how I came to know about you and Stephen?'

'Yup.' Sophie spoke with her mouth rather full. 'Who are you, Roy Samuel – the Invisible Man in disguise?'

'Apparently. Did it keep you awake all night?'

'No.' Sophie looked up at him from beneath her lashes and gave him her most wicked smile. 'I didn't sleep for ages, but it wasn't that.'

Roy grinned.

'I can imagine, suffering as I was. Can you cast your mind back to late spring, when Stephen was doing a film with Sumatra Jones?'

'Yes, I remember it. He had a thing going with her; I always thought it ended when the film ended, almost as if one of them – or both, perhaps – had planned it that way.'

'Doesn't matter. But do you remember standing in for Sumatra, when some stills were taken?'

He had her attention now. She was staring at him, a little frown creasing her brow.

'Yes.' she said slowly. 'Where were you? I have the oddest feeling . . . I didn't see you, I'm sure I didn't, yet . . .'

'I took the stills. Including some shots of you. Since you never got in touch, I took it that you weren't keen on them. I wanted to give them to you myself, but . . .'

Light exploded in Sophie's brain. The photographs! The ones that Stephen had mentioned. Glory, how embrassing!

'Oh yes, them. I'm sorry, Roy, you'll think this is so stupid, but Stephen never actually showed them to me. You took them when I was still very self-conscious about my weight and Stephen just said perhaps I'd rather he destroyed them.' Since Roy did not speak but merely stared at her, Sophie added hastily: 'After all, they weren't of *me* really, were they? They were of the stars of the show, with my backview, that sort of thing. Weren't they?'

Roy laid down his knife and fork, wiped his mouth with the back of his hand, and got up. He left the caravan and Sophie, craning her neck, could see him crossing the grassy slope back towards his own van at a determined lope. Two minutes later he was back, throwing three large, glossy prints down onto the table between them. He sat down again and picked up his knife and fork, but did not attempt to eat. He was staring at the prints.

'Go ahead, judge for yourself. I brought them down in case your parents or one of your sisters were here, because I always had this stupid, mean feeling that Stephen . . . Go ahead, look at them, they won't bite you!'

Silently, shyly almost, Sophie picked up the prints. Roy was right when he said they would not bite, even in her sense of the words and not his. She had feared they would show her looking fat, clumsy, inelegant, climbing onto the podium, turning, showing her broad back view. They did not. Not one of the shots had been posed. In one she was talking earnestly to one of the cameramen, indicating something before them both, another was a close-up of her profile as she watched the stage, and the last was a full-length picture taken as she was descending the podium after the stills had been taken. They were all beautiful, easily the best photos of herself that she had ever seen, and though she looked rounded, perhaps even plump, she knew that it did not matter in the least. Roy had seen a pretty, eager girl and he had taken some pictures of her. Why on earth had Stephen seen fit to suppress them?

187

'They're wonderful pictures, Roy,' she said slowly at last, pushing them away from her. 'I can't understand Stephen! He did say he'd show them to me and then he didn't, and the next time I asked about them . . .' She paused, blushing as she remembered the circumstances,' . . . well, perhaps he just said that because he'd lost them. Or something.'

'It was because . . . oh to hell with it, forget it, you've seen them now, and you know how I know you. Satisfied?'

'No, not a bit.' Sophie finished her bacon and eggs and leaned her chin on her hands, gazing at Roy with shining eyes. 'Did you *know* it was me? Did you like me even then, a little bit?'

'What do you mean, did I *know* it was you? Dammit, girl, there's only one Sophie Markham. Oh I see, you mean did I recognise you. Yes, I did.'

Sophie beamed.

'*Did* you? Did you think "That fat one's done well", or did you think "hasn't she changed?" Go on, tell me everything.'

'No, I didn't think anything so puerile. I thought that's a very lovely girl -- my, my, it's Sophie Markham. I'll take a few shots and if they come out well I'll see if she'll come out with me. Only by the time I'd decided that you weren't ever going to get in touch with me about the pics, it was too late. You were, if you'll excuse the expression, up to your eyes in Stephen Bland. I doubt if you'd have noticed me if I'd fallen in a faint at your feet.'

'I would,' Sophie protested. 'You're very striking, you know you are. All that hair and everything. When we get back to London . . .'

'We've got three more days. Do we have to talk about going back?'

Sophie stared.

'But why not? Once we're back I can talk to Stephen and . . .'

'My dear dope, don't you remember why I'm here? I leave for the States the day after we reach town.'

Dismay robbed Sophie of speech. Of course, he had told her right at the beginning, before . . . But she had forgotten it, convinced herself that he would not go.

Seeing her distress, Roy leaned across the table and pinched her chin.

'It's not the end of the world, my love, it's only six months,

188

possibly not even as long as that. I have to go, it's the chance of a lifetime. I've been commissioned on about three different counts. And what's more, it will be better for us, too.'

'For us?'

'Yes, for us. Look, we'll talk about that a bit later, but I want to ask you a favour.'

'Ask away,' Sophie said rather forlornly. She was still struggling to accept the fact of his imminent departure.

'Will you pose for me? I've never used this place for my work, but now I'd like to do some studies of you. What do you say?'

'I'll try, but I take a terrible photo,' Sophie began, then laughed at his expression. 'All right, all right, I'm not subtly insulting you, I used to take a terrible photo. But I'd like to try, and see what sort of results you get.' She turned round in her seat to squint out of the window. 'It's a lovely, calm day, though it isn't particularly bright yet. Shall we bathe?'

In the end, however, they did not have their talk until the evening of the last day. They had spent the day in feverish activity and now, physically exhausted, they lay, as dusk gathered, on the cushioned seat which overlooked the bay and watched the lights shine out one by one. The photographs of Sophie had been developed, printed and then judicially enlarged and Roy was very pleased with them.

'I want you to take these to an address I'll give you,' Roy had said, after they had admired the photos. 'You've got the sort of face and figure that photographs extremely well. I think you could get modelling work on the strength of those pictures.'

'Oh, yeah?' Sophie scoffed. 'Who? Chocolate manufacturers?'

'It doesn't matter what they sell, it's whose face can best persuade the public to buy. You're different, you've got a very individual sort of style, not like the plastic ladies who abound on the modelling scene. You aren't conventionally beautiful perhaps ("thank you," murmured Sophie sarcastically) but people will end up thinking you are. And it will be good for you, my child.'

'Do you mean it will help the six months to pass more quickly? Roy, unless you're going to spend the drive explaining, hadn't you better do it now? Because I don't see why it will do me good to be without you for six months.'

'I don't suppose you do, and it's going to be a bit difficult to explain, but I'll do my best.' They had been lying facing one another with their toes almost touching, but now Roy swung his legs down and patted the cushions beside him. 'Snuggle up.'

Sophie came and leaned against him, her head cuddled into the hollow of his shoulder so that they could both look through the window at the lights.

'Right. Go on then, explain.'

'I'll try. Sophie, I know you're twenty, but you're still a babe in lots of ways. No, don't hit me, I'm not being unkind; I'm being truthful. You're a very young and naive twenty and it's my belief that you need some independence, some time when you can just be Sophie Markham, a single girl, who is learning all the things that she should know at twenty.'

'What should I need to know that I can learn more easily without you?' Sophie said hotly. 'To have you there would help!'

'No. I'd influence you, the same as . . .' He hesitated, then rested his chin on her hair; she could hear his voice both through her ears and, echoing, through the top of her skull. 'The same as Stephen has. I'd take a bet that everything you do with Stephen is his idea, that he tells you what to wear, what sort of make-up looks best on you, how to please him and how not to. Come on, isn't that true?'

'I haven't ever thought about it, but I suppose you're right. But Penny and Anya influence me, too. They tell me lots about clothes and make-up and so on.'

'Yes, I know what you mean. I'm putting this very badly, I'm afraid. You see, girls *should* influence you, because that's all a part of growing up, leaving the nest, whatever you like to call it. And I should say that your mother and sisters probably influenced you quite a lot, particularly your mother. And you've let them know best and tell you how to behave because you just didn't have the confidence in yourself to go your own way.'

'Isn't that what happens to all girls? Aren't you saying that I've just turned from my mother and sisters to my fellow? Is that what you mean? Well, it's what all girls do, or most of them – it's what my sisters have done.'

'Should we say you've taken longer than most, perhaps, to

crack the egg and struggle free from the shell, and now that you've done it, you find all that space and freedom a bit frightening, so you've accepted quite happily that a man should domineer over you in place of your mother.'

'Well . . . I don't see that it's so wrong, if other people do it.'

'It isn't wrong, but most girls, including your sisters, will have had a good bit of quite varied experience before they got married. Would it be fair to say that you've missed that sort of varied experience, because of the way you were?'

'If you spell that w-e-i-g-h, I suppose I know what you mean,' Sophie said ruefully. 'Don't be afraid to say it, Roy, nothing you could say would hurt me, because I know you understand. You mean that fatties don't have the range of experience that other girls do, right from quite early childhood; is that right?'

'That's it, more or less. And even now you're closing both your eyes and leaping in the dark from Stephen to me, because we're all you know. We're opposite ends of the spectrum as it happens; Stephen wants you in his life as a sweet, innocent girl who will hero-worship him for the rest of his days and never argue or disagree. I want you in my life too, but I want a . . . don't laugh . . . a well-rounded woman who thinks for herself and has discovered things for herself and chooses to marry me because that's the sort of life she prefers. I want you to go back to London, shake Stephen off a little, and do some living, for Sophie, not for anyone else. And that's why I said that six months apart would be good for us.'

'Gosh! Are you proposing?' Sophie asked. 'If so, yes!'

His arms tightened round her momentarily and she turned up her face to kiss his chin.

'No. I'm just asking you – begging you – to *use* this six months, to take it as a gift for your own good, not as a deprivation! If you'll try, my love, to meet other people, to mix a whole lot more, and to be truly independent, then I think you'll be capable of making a real decision about marrying. Damn it, you might easily decide that you want to be the type of wife Stephen's looking for, the stay-at-home, passive sort, with a couple of kids and plenty of money and a loving, dictatorial, rather selfish husband. Or you might decide you like being a career girl, because modelling is fun and it's lucrative, or so I believe. Will you do it? Fo me?'

'How do you know Stephen and I don't socialise nightly?' Sophie asked suspiciously. 'My life might be one mad whirl for all you know.'

'I know because I took pains, as they say, to find out. I even went to a lot of parties where you television people tend to turn up. Quite often I saw Stephen at functions, but not you, not once, not ever. And when I asked, I was told by people in the know that Stephen had a girl all right, and that he was keeping her to himself. A very quiet, lovely girl, they said. And I thought it wasn't right, keeping you under wraps so to speak.'

'You searched for me?' Sophie's beam was ear to ear. 'Well, I wish I'd known! Why did you search for me?'

'To give you the photos,' Roy said, disappointingly. Then, at Sophie's sigh, he relented. 'I fancied you, that's why. But you haven't answered my question. Will you give it a go, love? Will you hold back from Stephen for a bit and take those photos to the address I've given you? And just see how you enjoy life when you're going out a bit more? Try sailing your little boat single-handed for a bit, I think you'll be amazed how pleasant it is, and how many friends you make.'

'All right, if you really think I ought. But I'm not going to get promiscuous,' Sophie warned him. 'I've taken your point about going around with other men though, because to tell you the truth, Anya and Penny have both said more or less the same thing. They thought Stephen was wrong never to take me to parties, and though they like him very much they did say that I ought to know more people. Is that end of lecture?'

'Yes. I won't write for a week or two because I'll be moving around and in and out of hotel rooms, but as soon as I get any sort of permanent address I'll drop you a line, and I'll expect good, thick letters daily, telling me I was a fool to let you go, and announcing your wedding to the Duke of Devonshire.'

'I'll write,' Sophie said sleepily, cuddling round in his arms and rubbing her head against the side of his neck. 'I'll write screeds and screeds and you'll wish you'd never suggested it. Let's stay here all tonight, darling, so that even if we aren't lovers, we can say we've slept together.'

'Right. But we'd better get some sleep, I've got a helluva drive tomorrow.'

* * *

'Hi, Sofa, it's great to see you! Had a good time?'

Sophie and Roy had said their goodbyes in the privacy of his car and then Sophie had fled, dragging her case up the stairs with enough noise to wake the dead, because she was scared stiff of bursting into tears and giving the game away to the quick-witted Penny that she had met someone else. Penny had come onto the landing and now she grabbed the case and helped Sophie into the flat with it, then slammed the front door and dived into the kitchen.

'Hell, I left the kettle on. Hurry up and dump your case and I'll have a cup of tea ready for you.'

Sophie, still feeling dazed, went through into her room, dumped her case, threw her white cardigan onto the bed and then went into the kitchen. Penny, at four in the afternoon, was wearing a pale pink shortie nightie and high-heeled black mules. She looked unwashed, tired and faintly scruffy. Sophie, glancing round at the horrors of a kitchen which had known only Penny's cleaning for two weeks, shuddered.

'Penny, this place! What's happened, has the bomb gone off?'

Penny glanced round too, as if she had not noticed the state of the kitchen until it was pointed out to her. The draining-board was cluttered with dirty crockery and cutlery, the remains of what looked like several meals littered the table, there were cornflake packets on the floor and the milk had not yet attained the nirvana of the fridge but stood by the door like a supplicant pleading for admission. When Sophie opened the fridge a tomato, with a beard as long as the Ayatollah Khomeini's, fell out and burst on the tiles. An indescribable but foul smell floated up to Sophie's startled nose.

'It's got a bit untidy, I suppose,' Penny said placidly. 'My cousin went home early – detestable, self-righteous little ninny – and probably I've let things drift, rather. I say, pass me a pinta, would you?'

Sophie was just about to comply when something thumped on the floor, a door banged, and a man's voice exclaimed gruffly. Sophie looked enquiringly at Penny. That had been someone in the flat, or she was very much mistaken.

'Don't glare at me, Sofa, you and Anya weren't here and I was lonely after dear Suzanne left, so I asked a – a friend to stay for a few days. Don't worry, we've been careful not to draw attention to ourselves, so there won't be any complaints. He's just leaving, anyway.'

'What about Mrs Fletcher though? I've heard you grumbling that she can scent a man through the floorboards – don't say she thought Anya and I had been metamorphised somehow?'

Penny giggled. It occurred to Sophie that Penny might have asked the fellow to stay without worrying about Mrs Fletcher, but here she underestimated her friend.

'Oh, she'd have noticed like a shot, if she'd been here. But she was taken in to hospital to have her veins done. She was very apologetic but, as she said, she'd been on the waiting list for five years and she couldn't very well chuck her first chance when it came. And Deidre, bless her, said she'd keep an eye on things, so off old Fletcher went, and in came . . . my friend.'

'What about Dee? She must have thought you were being a bit mean, with us away and Mrs Fletcher in hospital.'

Penny raised a thin, perfectly shaped brow.

'Why on earth? All Dee's doing is making sure that the rent gets paid and the place is clean and no one vandalises it. She isn't in charge of our morals. Anyway, the kettle's boiled and the tea's made. Will you pour whilst I fetch my friend through?'

'If Dee saw this place and thought it clean . . .' Sophie began crossly, but she was speaking to a closed door. She went to the dresser to get cups for the tea, abandoned the idea and began to rinse some under the hot water tap. Plainly, it was useless to nag at Penny until the fellow had left, but once he had gone, Penny was jolly well going to help clean up before Anya got back.

'Here we are!' Penny ushered her young man into the kitchen, sat him down in a chair and picked up an empty cup. 'Hey, what's all this, girl, I thought you said you'd pour the tea? Honestly, Sofa, and I did all the hard work!'

'I had to wash up the cups,' Sophie said mildly. 'Do introduce us, Penny.'

The young man, standard Penny-issue, grunted a greeting and slumped forward onto the table, a stubby-fingered hand held out for his cup. He was fair and clean-shaven, if you could describe as clean-shaven his square, stubble-covered chin, and he was wearing nothing but a faded pair of canvases. He was

194

tanned to a gloriously even, deep brown, however, and his arms and chest were covered with tattoos. If I had to guess, I'd stake money on the fact that Penny grabbed this one from the nearest construction site, Sophie told herself.

'Evan, this is my flatmate, Sophie Markham. Sophie, Evan Jones.'

Sophie smiled and held out a hand which was gingerly shaken.

'Hello, Evan, are you as Welsh as you sound? I've just got back from two weeks on Anglesey, and you can't get much Welsher than that.'

'Aye, product of the Rhondda, I am.'

'Really? What are you doing in London?'

He chuckled hoarsely and reached for Penny's hand.

'Anyone I can get.' Penny, not appearing to appreciate this sally, jerked crossly at Evan's arm and he jerked back. 'Awright, gal, lemme finish my coffee, isn't it?'

Sophie finished her own coffee, and began to pile up the dirty dishes as Penny and her man disappeared in the direction of the bedroom. She ran water into the sink, then filled it with crocks, which she left to soak whilst she turned to the fridge. It had better be defrosted before they all got some horrible disease.

She was still at it twenty minutes later when unmistakable sounds of departure came to her ears. Penny and Evan had obviously finished whatever version of goodbye suited them best (Sophie tried not to let her thoughts return to that last quick, fumbling kiss as she struggled out of Roy's car), and a couple of minutes later Penny reappeared, with a lovebite a good two inches long on the base of her neck. Sophie's stomach turned. Oh dear, this must mean that the respectable if chinless Aubrey was no more.

'Well, you've changed in two little weeks, Sofa,' Penny said brightly, picking up a tea-towel. 'I waited for you to blush and stammer at Evan, or to go all cold on us, and you were quite human! Don't say you're glad to be back.'

'I am in a way.' Sophie closed the fridge, turned it on again, and made for the sink. 'I take it I'm washing up, since you've got the tea-towel.'

'Yes.' Penny said baldly, not bothering to dress up her demand as a request. 'I'm glad you're back, I'm absolutely bursting with gossip, and Anya's train doesn't deposit her in the Big City until tomorrow after lunch, so you're going to get it all.' She prodded Sophie in the back. 'Though I daresay you know the juiciest but – you've been in touch with Stephen whilst you were away, haven't you?'

'Nary a word,' Sophie said, clattering plates. 'I sent him some cards, but I didn't actually ring. We've both had two weeks without each other, if you see what I mean.'

'No! Honest? Then you don't know?' Sophie swung round to see Penny looking almost embarrassed. 'Oh hell, Soph, I wouldn't have said, only I was sure, really, that you'd know.'

'What has happened?' Sophie asked resignedly. Some tiny, inconsequential bit of talk was about to be revealed, obviously. 'Spit it out, Pen.'

'Stephen's been sacked.'

'Wha-at?' Sophie reeled against the sink. Surely Penny was joking? Stephen was too far up in the hierarchy to be *sacked*, like a little typist! 'Come on, Penny, pull the other one.'

'He's been . . . look, sit down a minute and I'll tell you the whole thing from the very beginning.'

Stephen, it appeared, had been having a difficult time of it with the new play. He did not like his leading lady and wanted a far freer hand than he had been given with the script and this, it seemed, had culminated a week ago in the most frightful row, with Stephen saying that his artistic integrity was being questioned.

'He called Elena a slag and Simon Waite a mindless joy-boy,' Penny reported with considerable glee. 'It was all round the Centre in half an hour, you can guess. And then when Mr Mattocks tried to calm everyone down, he told him a thing or two – Stephen did, I mean – and gave in his notice. Only Stephen had said so many rude things by then that Mr Mattocks shouted that he did *not* give in his notice, he was fired, and Stephen swept out and everyone waited for him to be reinstated.'

'And . . .' prompted Sophie, when Penny did not at once continue.

'And Stephen, the idiot, talked to the press about it. Not just a bit, but a lot. He told reporters from at least three daily papers and a Sunday that he had been sacked for telling the truth, and of course they splashed it all over the headlines next day, it being quietish for news, I suppose. They say at the Centre that he'll never work in television again.'

'I can't believe that,' Sophie said slowly. 'Why on earth did he go to the press, though?'

Penny shrugged.

'Don't know. He rang up twice, but he didn't have much to say except would I give him your mother's phone number the first time, and then the second time to tell you to ring him as soon as you go back. Which I'm doing,' she added belatedly. 'Look, leave that washing up and go down to the phone. At least with old Ma Fletcher in hospital you won't have to watch what you say.'

'I will, if you don't mind.' Sophie dried her hands, her thoughts in a turmoil. This was absolutely awful, the one thing she had not even considered when she had planned seeing Stephen again. It would not, she knew, have been easy telling him that she wanted to see less of him, but she had thought that, if Roy was right and this agent person whose name and address he had given her could get her modelling work, she might give up her job at the Centre and more or less ease herself out of Stephen's affections at the same time.

But the news that he no longer had a job as a producer changed everything. How could she, in cold blood, tell a man who had just lost the work that meant more to him than anything else that he had also lost his girlfriend? And anyway, she was still extremely confused by all Roy's advice. He had never actually told her to break it off with Stephen, he had just told her to see more of other people.

Sophie reached the telephone without having made up her mind what she would say when Stephen answered. But in the event, she had to say nothing, because Stephen did all the talking.

'Darling, you're home – thank God! Sling a coat on and come down to the corner, I'll be with you in fifteen minutes.'

He had not waited for her half-hearted protest, but had rung off, and Sophie, telling herself severely that it was a sign of his distress that he could be so dictatorial and not proof that Roy was right, rushed upstairs, told Penny that she was going out, and made her way to the corner.

Standing there, she thought how wonderful it would be if Roy came past; she could tell him everyting, explain about poor Stephen, and ask his advice. Then she chided herself. For one thing it would not happen and, for another, this was just the sort of situation that Roy wanted her to learn to deal with. He would not think much of her new-found self-confidence if she ran to him at the first sign of trouble.

She told herself, therefore, that she must concentrate for this evening on Stephen and on how best to extricate him from the spot he had landed himself in. She was going to think about Stephen, she would not let her mind dwell, even for an instant, on anyone but Stephen.

She was concentrating so hard on not watching for a red MG with a black-haired man driving it, that she completely missed the long silver car with Stephen's bronzy-gold head behind the steering wheel until he had hooted twice.

It was not an auspicious beginning to a reunion.

She spent the evening with Stephen and returned to the flat in the early hours of the morning, feeling more than a little depressed.

He had explained about the press; had he not talked to them, he told her impressively, no one would have known why he had been sacked. They might even had concluded that he had made a mess of the film he was working on. As it was, the press had spread the facts around.

Sophie refrained from reminding Stephen that, if he had not talked to the press, he might never have lost his job other than temporarily, because she could see that he was really suffering. He looked drained and ill, and though he kept reiterating that he would soon be in work again and working, furthermore, on a much more important and interesting project than wretched, second-rate plays, she could see that he was worried. Other producers, for other reasons, admittedly, had left the Centre to find more creative work, and most of them had returned to the fold, some sheepishly, others defiantly, but all glad enough of regular employment. Stephen, for all his talk, must know that such a backing-down was denied him by the furore which had surrounded his departure. He must also wonder whether any other television company was going to take a chance on him, never really knowing exactly why he had been sacked so ignominiously. Oh yes, he had talked to the press, but no doubt his bosses were even now telling people that young Bland had not been creatively oppressed or forced to work with his intellectual inferiors; he had been a troublemaker.

The best part of the evening, in retrospect, had come when she had told him that she, too, would probably be leaving the Centre.

'In the ordinary way I wouldn't have, of course,' she said rather mandaciously. 'But now . . . well, Penny says they've put Sebastian Chilvers in to produce the rest of your list, and I couldn't bear to work for him. I met a chap on holiday who took some snaps of me, and he gave me the name of an agent, Gillian Pound. He thinks I'd get quite a lot of work because I'm not too run-of-the-mill. I'm going to try.'

She was down-to-earth enough to know how he would have decried the idea had the status quo remained, but as things stood he was delighted to think that Sebastian would not have Sophie handed to him on a plate. He was so thrilled, in fact, that he hugged her, called her his darling, generous, loyal little Sophie, and suggested that she go to the Centre first thing on Monday morning and hand in her notice.

'You'll get a job easily, even if this modelling idea lets you down,' he said exultantly. 'What a slap in the eye for them – losing you as well as me!'

She had agreed unhesitatingly, glad to be able to back him up in this, yet to be following her own inclination and Roy's advice. Working away from him would help her to see more, clearly how she felt about him. And it would be easier to mix with other people, too, without having the feeling that Stephen's accusing and disapproving eyes were upon her if she became friendly with young men.

And now, back in the flat and getting ready for bed, she was thinking impersonally about Roy's advice and her life. He was right, she could see that, when he said she had known only Stephen and himself, and equally right when he had indicated that Devina had dominated the first nineteen years of her life. Not that he meant it quite the way it was – she had blamed Devina for her weight, her lack of friends, for everything that went wrong. No wonder Devina had been happy enough to let go the reins, when her daughter fled to London. Since then she had enjoyed a brief period of freedom which she had largely wasted in intending to diet, but not actually getting round to it, and lying to herself and the world at large about why she did not diet. Having at last faced reality and got herself into the state of mind to want to join the size fourteen world, she had then let Stephen walk decisively into her life, telling her what to think and how to act. He had not done it deliberately, she was sure, had not realised how he was influencing her, but he had picked up the reins which Devina had once held.

She had almost no idea how the mind and heart of the average young male worked, either. And having listened to Roy and absorbed most of what he had said, she had sufficient native wit to see further. She was entering, on tiptoe perhaps but nevertheless entering, the world of the modern, unattached girl. She would no longer be debarred from conversations about sexual mores because she had no point of reference, she would be able to discuss fashion, ethics and moral issues from the inside instead of the outsize. If she married anyone too quickly she would have skipped across and missed out on perhaps one of the most important and character forming parts of the modern woman's life, the years unshadowed by parents or husband. It was in the course of these years that a girl discovered her potential, if she had any. I might be potentially just a good wife and mother, but on the other hand I might be very much more, Sophie told herself, slipping her nightie over her head and jumping into bed. Now is my chance to find out.

Chapter Thirteen

As luck would have it, Sophie entered the modelling profession at a good time. Autumn collections were being shown and new faces were needed, Christmas advertising on television and in magazines was starting, and in addition to all this, on the day that Sophie walked into Gillian Pound's office, that lady was about to interview two girls for the job of secretary.

A slight confusion resulted, but Sophie took it so well, laughed so merrily, and admitted so frankly that she was probably far likelier secretarial than modelling material that she softened Miss Pound's very well-hidden heart. And then she produced the photographs and Miss Pound's head promptly got together with the aforementioned heart.

'Look Miss Markham, I think Samuel probably knew what he was talking about; you're a lucky girl, you photograph like a dream and on the strength of these pictures I'm sure I can get you work. But, as you say, you're a secretary, you've worked in television . . . Can you guess what I'm going to say?'

Sophie could, and took the job on happily, though she was destined to spend much less time behind the typewriter than either she or Miss Pound guessed. And that was because of the Slimmabix account.

'They want a girl who is curvy,' Miss Pound told her tactfully when the job first came up. 'Not a stick, because they say that a picture of a Twiggy doesn't convince the sceptical slimmer. I'd like you to go along, because even if they only use you once, it's experience and the money is very good.'

Slimmabix did not just use her once, they used her for a whole series of advertisements including three short films which they would show after Christmas. Inevitably, Sophie was not depicting a girl who had already lost countless stones, but one who had put on 'those few extra pounds' after a very jolly Christmas. But who was she to quibble? They paid her more than handsomely, they paid extravagantly, and after only one of the films had been shown she heard people murmur, 'It's the Slimmabix girl,' as she passed.

It was an amusing advertisement, too, with Sophie playing party games, wearing paper hats, reaching up to get a sugar mouse off a Christmas tree – and Sophie's fingers dipping into a bowl of nuts, Sophie's plate polished clean after a big turkey dinner, Sophie's eyes sparkling at the camera over the rim of a champagne glass.

And she had to look equally festive and pleased with herself, of course, as she reached for the Slimmabix – delicious! – and drank the Slimmajuice which the firm recommended, and ate salad liberally sprinkled with Slimma Salad Dressing.

'I've had enormous fun, which I didn't expect,' Sophie told Anya one day, as the two of them sat on opposite sides of the kitchen table, peeling pickling onions and streaming with tears. 'What's more, though you wouldn't think it, it's led to a lot more work being offered to me, so I'm earning hand over fist.'

Anya had come back from her own holiday with a whole new outlook on life, as she had confided in Sophie. She had sorted out her feelings and her priorities and intended to waste no more time over a man like Derek, who was not only not worth it, but married into the bargain. She had gone through the abortion only to realise that what she wanted more than anything else in the world was a husband and a baby, preferably but not necessarily in that order.

'I'm not going to make a fool of myself or throw myself into the arms of the first man who comes along, but I'm going to try really hard to find someone decent and honourable and loving, who'll make me a good husband and my children a good father,' she told Sophie. 'I thought I was a career woman, but I'm not.' She had eyed Sophie with lively curiosity. 'What about you, Soph? When we went off, you were all starry-eyed about Stephen and heading straight for marriage and endless domesticity. Now, I don't know, you're much more a person, much more determined. In a way you're happier, in a way you aren't. Tell!'

But Sophie would say nothing about Roy. She told Anya that she had not so much fallen out of love with Stephen as realised that she simply did not know what love was, nor how she might react to other men.

'I needed the experience of being a single girl without ties,' she said, quoting Roy. 'I'm enjoying that side of it enormously, as I've probably proved, but of course it's painful to see Stephen struggling the way he is.'

And now, over the onions, they discussed the first real job offer that Stephen had had; a chance to produce a film for Scotia Television. They were a small, new company working in the far north of Scotland, and Stephen hovered between thinking it insulting that anyone should invite him to go so far for so little and jubilation that he would be producing again, and with a free hand.

'He'd be gone a month or six weeks, and that would be good for us both,' Sophie admitted, throwing another onion into the big plastic bowl. She blew her nose and mopped more tears. 'Gracious, these bloody onions are killing me; how many are there left to do?'

Anya peered down at the string bag through her own watering eyes.

'A couple of pounds, I should think; trust Penny to agree to pickle onions for Christmas and then to disappear magically the moment they arrive. Now tell me about Stephen's flat and this job and everything.'

'Well, he's had an offer for his flat; a chap wants to buy it outright, but Stephen isn't sure. He'd rather sub-lease, or something, for three years, by which time he thinks he'll need it again. And the job is to produce a film about a clan, tracing its history from the first written evidence they've got right up to the present day. It would be a challenge, he says, and the script, if you can call it that, has already got him excited, though it means he'll be right away from London for a fairly lengthy period.'

'I see. And you think it would be better for you to have Stephen in Scotland for x number of weeks?'

'More or less. You see, though I'm meeting people and mixing with them, I still feel bound to spend a lot of time with Stephen, not because I need to any more but because I feel he needs me. And lately – I suppose it's because he's out of work – he's been awfully naggy.'

'He always told you what to do,' Anya reminded fairly. 'Then you liked it, now you call it nagging. Are you sure the difference isn't in you?'

'No, I'm not sure,' Sophie admitted. 'Another thing is that . . . well, I made a friend, rather a close one. He went to the States with all sorts of promises to keep in touch, but he never has, he hasn't even sent me a postcard. I've been edgy over that, so probably my change of heart over Stephen is six of one and half-a-dozen of the other. But that doesn't make it non-existent, unfortunately.'

'A friend,' Anya said slowly, peeling away. 'A friend. Hmm. Holiday friendship?'

'Perhaps. I didn't think so, but perhaps you're right. Anyway, it's no use wondering. I have high hopes of Christmas – surely he'll send me a card, even if he only regards me as a friend?'

Christmas came and went. Roy sent nothing – not a card, not a line. Sophie took to careering downstairs at breakneck speed the moment the telephone rang, but to no avail. He did not ring. Anya, always kind-hearted, pointed out that, since the telephone was in the name of Fletcher and Wintle-Smy, it was unlikely that her friend would even consider ringing, but Sophie could not help hoping against hope. Roy knew Gillian Pound, even if only vaguely; surely he could have contacted her, asked her for Sophie's number? Men, she knew, did not like writing letters, but she had been so sure that Roy would write.

Stephen took the job and disappeared from the London scene for eight weeks. Sophie found that she missed him. Her life was fun, a whirl of parties, theatres and photographic sessions, yet she missed Stephen. It confused her. *Did* she love him? Was Roy right when he said she might indeed find that she loved Stephen more than she had imagined? Was it a case of *out of sight, out of mind* where Roy was concerned? Perhaps, she told herself scornfully, you just miss your regular sessions in Stephen's bed. But she knew that this, at any rate, was not true. She had received plenty of offers and had not been tempted for one moment to allow any of her numerous escorts to do more than kiss her goodnight.

Anya said she was working too hard and not eating enough

and Sophie, proud of a suddenly tiny waist, pooh-poohed the idea and continued to lose weight. After all, the Slimmabix job would not last for ever and the slimmer she got the more likely she was to get the better paid jobs.

Then there was the big row. After Christmas, when everyone was feeling a bit flat and when heads were tender and stomachs still rumbling uneasily, Penny came slouching into the kitchen where Anya and Sophie were setting out their salad, quiche and yoghurt supper on the table.

'God, my poor head,' she exclaimed, pinching a slice of green pepper off the top of the salad and crunching it down. 'New Year next, eh? I'm popping out for a sec to post a letter to the late lamented Aubrey – want me to post yours, Sofa?'

'Mine?' Sophie said, not understanding. 'I posted one to my parents yesterday and I haven't written to Stephen yet because he phones me most evenings.'

'No, the one . . .' Penny broke off and then, apparently deciding that it would be fun to put the cat amongst the pigeons, concluded the sentence, '. . . the one I was reading in your room just now. I went in to borrow your new eye make-up and it was lying on the dressing-table, so . . .'

Sophie had never hit a girl who was unrelated to her by blood in her life before, but she hit Penny. A resounding clack round the ear was promptly returned and in two minutes a cat-fight was taking place all round the kitchen as Sophie, scarlet with shame and embarrassment, tried to wipe Penny, and her stolen knowledge, off the face of the earth.

Anya stopped the mayhem by emptying a full saucepan of ice-cold water over them both as they bit, kicked and clawed on the floor.

'Get up, you stupid cows,' she said breathlessly, grabbing a handful of Sophie's hair in one hand and Penny's in the other. 'How *dare* you behave like tho whores fighting over a sixpence in my kitchen? Penny, just you say you're sorry right now for reading a letter which was none of your business, and Sophie, it was you who hit first, you know.'

'I'll fucking well make her sorry,' Sophie squeaked, and got her hair jerked mercilessly by the furious Anya. 'Let go of me or I'll kill you both!'

Despite the pain of her pulled hair she turned to claw at

Penny once more and stopped short. Penny was giggling. Sitting on the floor, with her head strained back by Anya's hold, and giggling like a maniac. Sophie, reluctantly, smiled herself. What on earth had come over her to behave with such a total lack of decorum? It was because of the letter, of course. She wrote to Roy daily, long, loving letters full of all the funny little details of her life, but she could post none of them, lacking an address. She knew it was silly, yet she could not stop herself, and she knew that it was the happiest moment of each day when she settled down in front of the dressing-table, got out her pad and biro, and began 'talking' to Roy. And to have Penny read those artless, futile letters, those love-babblings of the heart . . . well, it had been more than she could bear.

'I'm very sorry, Sophie, that I read your letter,' Penny said now, between giggles. 'Only I didn't really read it, because your writing's so bloody awful. But I did see that it was a letter. Am I forgiven?'

'If you swear you'll never do such a thing again,' Sophie said, still smiling a bit. 'Anya, you can let go my hair now.'

Anya let go and helped the two girls to scramble up from the floor. They could now see that she, too, was laughing helplessly, though she had managed to contain her mirth whilst the fight was on.

'The pair of you were funny enough,' she said now, getting a cloth to mop the water up with. 'But when meek old Sophie started swearing and threatening to kill us both . . . it was enough to make a cat laugh.'

'You keep telling me how much I've changed, and now you know it,' Sophie said. She took the cloth from Anya. 'Here, let me do that, you should always make the children clear up their own mess.'

Oddly enough, this open warfare brought the three girls closer together. Anya had known of the tensions in Sophie, but Penny, seeing it for the first time, was more sympathetic than usual.

'You want a man,' she said bluntly a few days later, when Sophie had burst into tears on finding nothing for her in the second post. 'Why don't you take a few days off, go up to Scotland and visit Stephen?'

'Because I don't want to,' Sophie snapped. 'Anyway, he rang

last night and said he'd be back on 21st January, all being well, and that's quite soon enough.'

Penny shrugged, but she and Anya exchanged worried glances. They did not like to see Sophie's placidity and happy outlook so obviously ragged.

'You could go home for a bit of a break,' Anya suggested diffidently. 'Or if you feel the difficulties there are too tiring, you could go to the caravan for a bit.'

She had heard about the difficulties which Sophie had faced last time and sincerely sympathised, but now Sophie just stared at her for a moment, and then, with trembling lips, ran from the room.

Anya turned to Penny.

'What have I said now? I thought she'd had such a wonderful time at the caravan.'

'Yes, so did I, and perhaps that's why she won't go back,' Penny said slowly, with rare perception. 'Sometimes there's nothing worse than going back to a place where you've been happy.'

'Why? I love going back to places where I've been happy,' Anya objected. 'Especially childhood places.'

'Ah, yes, but suppose you know you'll never have happiness quite like that again?'

The two friends stared at each other, then Anya spoke.

'I see. Poor Sophie.'

Stephen returned as he said he would on 21st January, and Sophie was at the station to meet him. He had sold the long, silver car but the flat had only been leased for a huge sum whilst he was away. It had been empty for a fortnight and Sophie had been in that very morning, putting fresh flowers in a vase in the hall, turning on the electricity, the water, the gas, warming the place through, making it seem like home.

For a moment all they could do was hug, arms folding tight, feeling the familiar curves and planes of each other's body. And then Stephen held her back from him. He was smiling, but he looked faintly aggrieved.

'Sophie, darling, you've lost weight. My sweet, this won't do at all, I can't stand by and see you shrink to nothing. Have you missed me so much?'

207

The magic quality of meeting a dear friend soured a little; if she had lost weight that was *clever*, not something for Stephen to grumble about, and whether it was clever or not, it was certainly nothing to do with the fact that she and Stephen had been temporarily parted.

'I have missed you. I've been at the flat most of today, though, getting it straight for you, so I've not eaten. Shall we pick up a take-away at one of the Chinese restaurants?'

He had a big suitcase, but he put it on a trolley and then began to push it briskly towards the entrance one-handed. The other hand was tightly grasping Sophie's.

'They call them carry-out's in Scotland. No, let's not bother with food just yet; let me get home and dump my case and then I'll take you down the road and we'll have a curry, whilst I catch up with your news and you catch up with mine.'

'All right,' Sophie said. 'I've kept today free. When do they show the rushes of your latest film?'

'Soon. It's going to make a big splash, Soph! Everything went right, you know how it does, sometimes. The mist was there when we needed it and clear when we didn't, the colours blended, the shots all came off. Just you wait until they see it at the Centre; they'll probably buy it, the poor sods, and gnash their teeth because they let me go.'

They had let him go now, had they? The ignominious sacking was forgotten, or at least would not be referred to. But Stephen was very sweet, and it was lovely to hear him being very nearly his old self again.

Back at the flat they sat on the couch with their arms round each other, talking and talking and talking. For an hour or so the illusion that everything was all right now, that they were together in mental as well as physical harmony, persisted.

It shattered temporarily over Sophie's plans for the next day. Stephen was incredulous when she said she had to work. Why should she work, when he was home, and at a loose end? Patiently, she reiterated what she had learned from Gillian, that a model has a fairly short life in front of the camera and on top of the heap. She might last a year, or five, but work would probably never again come seeking her out the way it was doing now. Gillian and she liked and respected each other, what was more, and Gillian had arranged sessions for her, knowing she

208

was a reliable person and would turn up. Stephen laughed indulgently and said that he would have a word with Gillian – how could she book his girl up, and he back after so long away?

He did not know Gillian, that was the trouble, but by now Sophie did. Her agent would make very short work of a man who rang her up and tried to teach her business, and Sophie had no wish to see Stephen humiliated.

'Please don't do anything of the sort,' she said with some asperity. 'I dare say you'll find your day is pretty full, anyway, and I'll be round here at seven o'clock – we can have a nice, cosy evening together.'

Stephen stared at her.

'Oh, you will? How do you know I haven't got plans for my evening which don't include you?'

Sophie sighed, stood up, and patted his shoulder.

'Right, Stephen. If you'll give me a ring when you're free, I'll see if I can fit you in. 'Bye, now!'

She turned to leave the room, but Stephen was up before her, barring her way to the door, half laughing, half contrite.

'Darling, I'm sorry. I've had a hell of a day, I'm tired out, and remember I'm used to having you with me all day long. Forgive me?'

'Of course,' Sophie said steadily. 'But do remember, Stephen, that you aren't the only one who's changed. I'm in a very independent sort of job and I'm meeting lots and lots of people, and men simply don't speak to me in that dictatorial sort of way any more. Perhaps I've simply outgrown our friendship, and if that's the case you're probably better off without me.'

'Without you? Friendship? Darling, I want us to *marry*, not to be friends,' Stephen said, looking cut to the quick. Sophie thought that it was mainly the surprise of her answering him back; this was not the gentle, easy-going Sophie that he had been so fond of. 'Please, love, don't take any notice of me, I told you I was tired out.'

'It's all right, I'm sorry too,' Sophie said sincerely, patting his hand as it clutched hers. 'Only . . . *do* try to understand about my work, Stephen, because it's as important to me as yours is to you.'

'I'll do my best.' He kissed her on the tip of her nose, then

209

walked past her to hold the door open. 'I'll come down with you and see you into a taxi, and in a few days I'll be buying another car. If you can spare the time you can come with me to choose it.'

Sophie considered saying something really crushing and decided against it; better to take the remark literally.

'Lovely. Tell me when you're going and I'll try to keep a couple of hours free. Goodnight, darling Stephen, I'm glad you're home.'

Left to himself, Stephen prowled round the kitchen, made himself a cold chicken sandwich and an outsize mug of coffee, and returned to the now empty living room to think.

The truth was, he thought, he should never have gone away and left his darling girl to fend for herself. She had been hardened and spoiled by all the attention and admiration she probably got in her job. He would have to marry her quickly, get her out of the atmosphere of tension and high fashion which had changed her so disastrously, and then she would speedily become his own dear Sophie again. Mine was the fault, he told himself dramatically, taking a huge bite out of the sandwich. I should never have left her to go to Scotland, I should have taken her with me. She could have been quite useful, taking notes, running errands, that sort of thing. And up in Scotland he could have made sure that she ate properly. The fact was, she was well on the way to becoming scrawny, and that would never do; he loved her curves, he did not wish to find himself marrying a stick!

So what should he do? He thought about asking her to move into the flat, but some native caution prevented this. He had a feeling that his idea of marriage and Sophie's might prove to be rather different, for he wanted the sort of wife that stayed at home, baked bread, made fruit pies and reared a family. Not the sort that rushed off each morning to a studio, took off a good many clothes and smiled at cameramen. No fear, he'd seen enough of those sort of marriages to last him a lifetime! And the fact was that, if he simply suggested Sophie should move in, no one would expect him to want a family and so on. No, the answer was definitely marriage, yet he would have to approach the whole subject carefully. Sophie, bless her, was having a wonderful time by her present standards, and would see marriage in a far less glamorous light now. He wished sincerely that he had asked her to marry him before he had left for Scotland, but, fool that he was, he had not wanted to commit himself quite so definitely.

The problem was certainly a difficult one, but by the time he had finished his sandwich and coffee and poured himself a very small whisky to help him to sleep, Stephen felt he had solved it.

He would make a great fuss of her, give in to her, spoil her like anything, and then in a few weeks he would suggest that they name a day. By then, if he made sure that she spent whatever free time she had with him, she would see marriage to him as every bit an enticing a prospect as he believed it to be. And furthermore, she would realise that, if she turned him down, life would promptly cease to be as delightful. He just knew that the film on the clan would bring him the sort of publicity and popular acclaim that he most needed at the moment. A new, exciting and challenging career was about to open up before him, and Sophie could share it.

He slept well that night.

'You should have seen his face though, Anya!' Sophie, making her own night-time drink, grinned across the kitchen at her friend. 'He looked like a man who sprinkles food on a goldfish tank and finds his fingers have gone missing! The awful part is, though, that I felt angry with him, and sorry for him, and even a little bit in love with him throughout the whole performance.'

'It's love that counts,' Anya said wisely. 'If you love him then you'll put up with his never really thinking your work's terribly important, putting you down sometimes, cutting across the middle of your funny stories. If you don't, then leave him now, not later.'

'I don't think I love him enough to put up with any of that,' Sophie admitted. 'But though he mentioned marriage, I dare say it was just to keep me quiet and stop me kicking against the bricks. I don't mean to marry anyone, not for a long time.'

A month later, towards the end of February, Stephen proposed marriage formally. And Sophie refused him.

She had not had a good month. There had been no word from

Roy and all her efforts to find out what had happened to him had been in vain. People – a great number of people – knew and admired Roy, informed Sophie that she would love working with him, and told her that he was at present touring in the States. Equiries about his brother, his parents, his home, merely met with vagueness or downright indifference. Some said he came from Dorset, others from Lancashire, others still maintained that his parents lived in London. But nobody knew for certain, any more than they knew when he would be back. Six months, people said vaguely, usually these things last about six months.

Stephen's film of the clan was every bit as successful and sought after as he had expected it to be, and the result was immediate. He was offered a job producing a historical drama of unusual length and scope – it would follow one apocryphal family virtually from the dawn of history and would continue up to the present day. The scripts were sketchily written on purpose so that Stephen would have a free hand, and the very big company who were making the film were flatteringly generous, both with their money and with promises of future work. Stephen bought another car, longer, sleeker and more silvery, and threw a party in the flat to celebrate. He gave Sophie so much champagne that she spent the last hour of the evening flat out on his bed, and he told everyone who would listen that she was his future wife.

Her refusal of his formal proposal brought first incredulity, then annoyance, and finally sulks; he could not think why she treated him like this – she had known for a long time that he loved her and only her, that he could not wait to make her his wife. Sophie listened, nodded, sighed, and told him that she was still too busy becoming known in her own right to relish taking second place to a husband.

'You nag me because I'm so thin, you criticise my commercials, you tell me the dress I like most doesn't suit me, and then you expect me to fall at your feet and marry you,' Sophie said furiously, when he lost his temper with her and said she did not appreciate her good fortune. 'There are men who seem to like me as I am, not as I was!'

They quarrelled more than than they had ever done. and at times Sophie cried herself to sleep, as sad for Stephen as for herself. After all, he really was the innocent party in this whole imbroglio; it was she who had changed, not he. There were other times when she imagined meeting Roy and telling him just what he had done to her life. He had spoiled her for Stephen and just left her, abandoned her to loneliness.

Because, though the meetings with Roy were not real, the loneliness was. She had Anya and Penny, dozens of new friends and acquaintances made through work, and the practical, common-sense comradeship which Gillian offered. Above all, she had Stephen, a man to lean on, to confide in, to take her about. But nothing could make up for the depth of intimacy which she missed, having once experienced it, with Roy. Nothing could take away the rawness of the loss she experienced whenever she awoke from dreaming of him, or came down to earth after reliving some small episode of their time together.

Anya was startled and more than a little worried when she found out that Sophie really had refused Stephen's proposal, and about a week later she cornered Sophie one Saturday morning and took her out for coffee in one of the big stores on Kensington High Street.

'Look, Sophie, I'll come clean at once, because I know you'll prefer it. Stephen rang me. Don't start glaring, he's honestly concerned about you and he's not the only one. You know how heartily I've approved of your more independent attitude, but I don't approve of the continuing weight loss. No one who's fond of you could, and Stephen is frantic. He loves you very deeply, no matter how often you may fall out, and he thinks you're becoming anorexic.'

Sophie snorted and bit into the cake she had chosen to compliment her coffee.

'Anorexic my foot! I'm simply not hungry. I trained myself out of living to eat and into eating to live and now, when I practise it, you all jump to the conclusion that I'm ill.'

'But Sophie, love, you're getting positively gaunt. And one of the reasons why you and Stephen have quarrelled so much lately is because you're tense, tired . . . and undernourished. Stephen wants you to see a doctor.'

'A psychiatrist, no doubt, because anyone who fails to leap at a proposal of marriage from Stephen Bland has to be off her head? Well, Stephen can want; I'm perfectly all right, I don't want to see a doctor, and I'm not marrying anyone!' Sophie's voice had risen to something perilously akin to a yell. 'Understand?'

'No,' Anya said blankly. 'Where's your sense of humour gone, if there's nothing wrong with you? Why don't you get fun out of the silly things that happen any more? Why are you quarrelling with me? You never used to quarrel with anyone.'

Sophie started to speak, choked, and put her hands over her face. From behind them she muttered something. Anya leaned closer.

'What was that, love?'

'I wish I was dead.'

Anya glanced round the large, airy restaurant with its green tables and its yellow cloths; at all the middle-aged, middle-class housewives sitting around, drinking coffee and, it must be admitted, eyeing herself and Sophie with placid curiosity. She leaned forward and pulled Sophie's hands down from her eyes.

'We'll go back to the flat and you can talk. Poor love, you are in a miserable state. Tell Auntie Anya though, and you'll find a trouble shared is a trouble halved, besides which two heads are better than one, and any other cliché which fits. Honestly, it does help to tell someone. I can still remember the enormous feeling of relief which came over me when I told you I was preggers. Come on, let's leave.'

'I didn't think I'd ever tell anyone,' Sophie said ruefully, when they were settled, with the inevitable teapot between them, at the table in the flat's kitchen. They were safe from interruption, since Penny had gone home for the weekend. 'I still feel that it's unfair to Stephen, but since he's showing such concern . . .'

'Just tell me, stop beating yourself over the head with whatever it is and tell me,' Anya advised. 'I won't pretend I'm not bursting with curiosity, because I am, but I won't think any the worse of either of you, or I'll try not to.'

'Right. Well, after Stephen came home I tried very hard to make him see that I was still fond of him but I didn't want to be domineered over. He thought, I suppose, that it was just the result of having an interesting job and that, like a disease, it would pass. And in a way he was right. I don't mind his bossiness most of the time, because it's his way of saying that he loves me and wants me to need him. And I *do* need him. Only I couldn't bring myself to burn my boats and agree to marry him.' She sighed, then looked straight into Anya's eyes. 'Damn it, I thought I was in love with someone else – I *was* in love with someone else! But he never got in touch the way he promised, never sent a forwarding address or anything. It's taken me a long time to accept that he just isn't interested, but I'd begun to accept it, to begin, very slowly, to turn to Stephen. And then, last week, something happened which made me question whether I would be right to consider marrying Stephen. He behaved in a way I hated, and he made me think that perhaps I don't know him after all, perhaps you can't know anyone until you've been married to them for ages, I don't know.'

'What did he do?'

'Well, I'd gone round to his flat to make dinner, after spending hours outside the Houses of Parliament doing a fashion session in coloured capes with umbrellas. I was tired out and freezing when I arrived, and Stephen was sweet . . .'

She could remember the whole evening with painful clarity. Her arrival, the big fire that Stephen had lit and tended, the fact that he had cooked her a meal to save her the trouble of cooking for them both. They ate by the fire, with a tray each on their knees, and Sophie felt tired and content, seeing Stephen now as the ideal companion, for he chatted about his new show, poured her wine, fussed round her, without once complaining that she was working much too hard or looking much too thin. She was grateful for this and as a result became easier with him than she had been for some time.

He had got some stills of the episodes of his new film and was showing them to her, both cuddled up on the big couch before the fire, when tiredness, which had receded under the influence of food and warmth, came rolling back. She managed to mutter to Stephen that she was worn out, and he slid his arms round her, kissed the side of her neck, and called her his poor darling.

Then he had started cuddling, undressing, patting, stroking, pinching. And Sophie, drowning in sleep, had felt extremely cross.

'Stop it, Stephen, I'm not in the mood!' she had said.

215

It was the first time she had ever refused his love-making, and she felt still, as she had felt then, that he should have understood and let her alone. But he had not and did not.

'You're not in the mood? What rubbish, girl.' She had opened sleep-heavy eyelids to find that he was looming over her as she lay on the couch, an elbow planted each side of her so that she was trapped by his body. In the faint light from the fire she had seen his eyes, gleaming with determination, his mouth heavy with lust, his nostrils flared. 'Anyway, it's my job to put you in the mood!'

What followed had been a nightmare of struggling, denial and attempts to reason with him, whilst Stephen laughed at her increasingly frantic efforts to escape. He had, in the end, exerted his full strength against her, indifferent to her weeping, until at last he possessed her.

He had added insult to injury then. Triumphantly, he had exclaimed over her bruised and battered body: 'There, all you needed was a bit of persuasion. You enjoyed that just as much as I did!'

She had remained on the couch, saying nothing whilst hot tears coursed down her cheeks and soaked the cushions. And when he failed to get some response from her by teasing, tenderness, kisses, Stephen had turned nasty.

'I'll ring for a taxi, if you're going to sulk,' he said abruptly. 'Get a coat on.'

She would have got a coat on, had he not come back into the room, looked at her for a moment, and then informed her that he had changed his mind.

'You're not well. I've put a hot bottle in the spare bed.'

She still had not spoken when she climbed stiffly into the spare bed, falling asleep with the abruptness of total exhaustion.

She awoke in someone's arms. For a moment, because she was being cuddled so tenderly, she thought that Roy had come to rescue her. Then she knew it was Stephen. She was in the big double bed that they shared and he was loving her gently, tenderly, as though she were infinitely precious, infinitely fragile.

She opened her eyes to find his face near her own, his eyes full of compassion. He kissed her bruised breast, then, very gently, her chin, her cheeks, her eyelids.

'My poor darling, my poor baby,' he crooned. 'I didn't mean to hurt you, I ought to be kicked.'

He did not attempt to do anything other than cuddle her and presently he got up and brought her breakfast in bed, and during the course of the day they became easier with each other. But though he had been gentle and kind he had never actually apologised for the incident.

Since then she had tried to rationalise his actions. He had done it in frustration, since he had believed her to be entirely submissive and happy to be dominated. The fact that she had never pretended to be in favour of rape – for it was rape, she realised that, even if he did not – was beside the point. She had, by her behaviour, she supposed, led him to believe that he had only to indicate that he wanted her for her to fall eagerly into his arms, therefore perhaps she had no right to act like an outraged nun because he had insisted on what he obviously thought of as a right.

But there was another side of her mind which refused to see it like that. He had used his strength to dominate her against her will. What he had done once he might do again, and this, in a way, was another side to the male dominance idea. She would, if she married him, have to do as Stephen said. It would work both ways – they would have sex when he wanted it, never when she did – because Stephen saw her in a purely submissive role. She would be his woman, his lie-beside. Until that night she would have sworn that, whatever his faults, Stephen was a considerate lover. Now, she realised she could not know what sort of a husband he would be until they had been married for a while. In a way, she blamed it on the odd way he ran his – their – sex lives. To allow her to stay in the flat with him once or twice a week was wrong, and not only in the biblical sense. It put strains on them both which neither were capable of withstanding. She believed to meet, as they had met, solely to have sex was reducing her to a sex object and him to a stud. Horrible words which conjured up horrible pictures, but they were true enough. They should cement their relationship by either marrying or living together, or they should part.

And there, of course, was the rub. Had she never met Roy last September there would have been no question of her leaving Stephen, any more than she would have dreamed of telling him she was 'not in the mood'. Roy had forced her to open her eyes all right, but to what purpose? It seemed as though he had done

217

so merely to make her independent, a reluctant career girl.

But the story was told at last and she had to face Anya. Her friend looked terribly worried.

'I'd never have thought Stephen would . . . but Sophie, darling, you've made it clear enough that you don't entirely blame him. It was awful, of course it was, but the strains you've both been under . . . That wretched photographer, if only he hadn't turned up on the island . . . don't cry, you silly dope – surely you don't still hold out hopes that he'll appear?'

'Not really,' Sophie said with a watery smile. 'I'm not even sure that I ever did love him, except that sometimes I can see his face so clearly. I didn't think that a man's face stayed in your memory once he'd gone, not like that. I mean, I couldn't tell you what Peter Brewer looked like if my life depended on it, but every line and hair and ugly bit of Roy's face is there, inside my head.'

'He isn't handsome, then? Not like Stephen.'

Even in her unhappiness, Sophie chuckled.

'No, not a bit. He's very dark, thin-faced; he needs to shave twice a day if he's going out in the evening; he's covered with hair, I've never seen a hairier man – and he's a bare two or three inches taller than me. But we were a pair, or I thought we were. Now, I just don't know.'

'I see.' Anya tipped the teapot and a thin stream of tepid, ominously black tea trickled into her cup. She grimaced. 'We need a fresh pot here. Well, from what you've told me the worst part of it all is not knowing whether to take Stephen or leave him, because, love, Roy . . . you did say that was his name? . . . Roy doesn't enter into it. How long's he been gone?'

'Five months.'

'And not a word? But he'll be back in England in a month, from what you said. How about telling Stephen that you'll give him his answer then? After all, it won't hurt him to wait a bit.'

'I'd sooner say no, and get it over with,' Sophie said listlessly. 'We're wrong for each other in so many ways, why prolong the agony?'

'Because even if Stephen's wrong for you, which I by no means agree to be the case, Stephen patently thinks that you're very right to him. Look, Sophie, was it just Stephen forcing you that time which put you off him? Because, if so, the sooner you

218

confront him with it and clear it up the better.'

'I don't know. Yes . . . no, I'm not sure. I suppose the truth is that I need someone, and Stephen was very nearly ideal. Only I didn't want to get married, and then that pouncing made me see how marriage could be. I'm being a fool over Roy, I quite see that, but on the other hand wouldn't it be very wrong of me to marry Stephen whilst I'm still half Roy's?'

'Wait a month; Stephen will understand. And speak to him about the other business, or let me, if you feel shy about it. Surely you'll know by then?'

'I don't see that I'm ever going to *know*, exactly,' Sophie said impatiently. 'Marriage is a gamble, I've heard you say so frequently. All I can do is talk to Stephen.'

Stephen was making himself an omelette, taking time and trouble over it, but dreaming as he did so, nevertheless. He was feeling smug. The new production was turning out to be an even bigger thing than he had supposed, the script lacked imagination, so he was doing a lot of rewriting, and the girl who starred in the first three episodes was turning out to be a first-rate little actress with almost no temperament. Work, then, was satisfactory.

And his love life was about to become satisfactory, too. He and Sophie had had a long, sometimes embarrassing, but nevertheless useful talk. In his heart he had been rather proud of having raped her, because it seemed such a manly thing to do. He, Stephen Bland, would not have his appetite denied by a mere woman. Anyway, he had always believed rape to be impossible, yet he had achieved it, which made him feel, if he was honest, one hell of a fellow. Mixed with that, of course, had been regret that he had hurt and humiliated her, made her weep. Shame had not been far behind the masculine swagger. So getting it all out in the open had done nothing but good. It had given him the opportunity of explaining what had happened, of telling her how very sorry he was, and of promising how he would never, under any circumstances, attempt to force her again, against her will. And he had seen for himself how her eyes had shone with the old, sweet generosity, how she had become for a moment his beloved little apple dumpling once more.

In her turn, she had tried to explain her own changed attitude, though he had not really taken it all in. Something about a man – no, they had not been lovers – who had given her advice, made her look at herself and her life. A lot about her career, how much it meant to her to be successful instead of just fat. He understood that part, in a way, but he regretted that she no longer gave him the credit for her slimming. And anyway she had overdone it, he wanted her to get her squeezable, well-rounded bottom back, and those generous breasts. He could see for himself that she did not eat nearly enough, but had little doubt that, once they were married, he could feed her up like a Strasbourg goose. She would be stuffed in every sense of the word, he thought complacently, and grinned at his own pun. it would be marvellous to be married to Sophie, for he had no doubt whatsoever that a mere week of marriage to him would bring Sophie back to her old self, the one who never questioned his decisions but merely agreed eagerly with everything he said.

Stephen smiled to himself, stirred his omelette gently with a fork, and then tossed a handful of prepared mushrooms and tiny pieces of pepper into the thickening goo. He did not, of course, intend to see her continue her career once they were married, no matter what she might think. He neither liked nor approved of career women, and he was earning so much money in his own right that it would be downright selfish of them both to earn. Besides, he wanted babies and fully intended to spend many enjoyable nights getting Sophie pregnant. She might think her pills would prevent such a lamentable happening, but he could soon deal with *that*: a few harmless aspirin mixed in with the others and she would be clinging to him, starry-eyed, telling him that she hoped he didn't mind but . . .

He decided to be magnanimous about it and forgive her, and chuckled at his own kindly deceit, for it was a kindness to get Sophie out of this rat race, which had changed her from comfortable sweetness into the prickly and suspicious girl who examined his every word, it seemed, for some hidden meaning. She would love children, too. And he had never heard of an anorexic mother-to-be, so that would stop that.

Stephen flipped his omelette over, conveyed it carefully onto a warmed plate from the oven, and garnished it with a sprig of parsley. He enjoyed fancy cooking sometimes. He had already prepared a dish of new potatoes in sour cream, white wine and onions with grated cheese on top, and now he got the small baking dish out of the oven, sniffed approvingly, and set it down on his tray. Good, everything was done to a turn, and his film was about to start on the telly. A perfect evening stretched before him.

He carried his tray through to the couch before the fire, kicked off his slippers and put his feet up, then clicked the remote control switch through the channels until he found the one he wanted. There was another five minutes of a comedy programme, then the commercials, then his film. Whilst he was waiting it occurred to him that today was the day Sophie was supposed to give him her official answer to his proposal, not that he doubted for one moment what it would be. But she was busy, of course, having been whisked off down to Kew to lounge amongst the daffodils whilst photographers stalked her. She had said she would ring though, and she knew he would not be best pleased if she left it until his film had started.

The telephone rang during the commercials. Good girl, he thought approvingly, reaching for the receiver, she knows me so well!

'Hello, darling? God, I haven't stirred from the phone all evening. Well? Don't keep me in suspense, dammit; this has been the longest month of my life!'

Her voice was so quiet that he had to ask her to repeat what she had said, but then he was jubilant, throwing down his knife and fork, begging her to come straight round – no, he would call for her if she just gave him five minutes to finish his meal.

'No, it's all right, your film's on in a few minutes and I'm terribly tired.' Her voice was small, strained. 'I'll come round tomorrow evening, shall I? I could cook you a meal.'

'Darling, that would be wonderful. I've got a full day tomorrow, so if you could pick up some steak, you'll find mushrooms in the fridge and potatoes in the vegetable rack. I'll manage the rest – we'll need champagne, of course! Oh darling, darling Sophie, are you as happy as I am?'

Presently, replacing the receiver, he turned the set up to full volume again, feeling a tiny bit impatient with his Sophie.

Of course he was delighted, if not surprised, that she was going to marry him; but did she have to sound quite so stunned and lethargic about it? If he had not known better, he would have thought that she was crying.

Chapter Fourteen

The wedding date was fixed and the preparations went ahead so smoothly that it seemed as though God and all His angels wanted to see Stephen and Sophie joined in holy matrimony. Lavinia and Poppy were to be bridesmaids and would come down to London with Devina and Ben three whole days before the wedding, so that they could be present at the rehearsal. Sophie had written asking her sisters if they would like to be bridesmaids and both had replied in the affirmative, but only in Poppy's letter could Sophie detect enthusiasm; Lavinia was taking part, it seemed, under protest. But both girls loved their dresses, which Devina had described in such detail and so many times that Sophie felt she had as good as chosen them, and both looked forward to their first visit to the city.

It was to be society wedding, rather to Sophie's distress. A successful model was marrying an up-and-coming television producer and one, moreover, who had been sacked, ostracised and had then fought his way back to success against all the odds; rumour was already giving Stephen's serial top ratings. The guest list was formidable and every day, it seemed, someone would rush in crying: 'Darling, surely you haven't forgotten to invite so-and-so? You must send off a quickie at once or feelings will be lacerated!' Sophie would have lacerated feelings without compunction had her parents been paying for the reception, but Stephen's mother and father had quietly insisted and Stephen, she knew, was putting up a lot of the money, so if they wanted to make a splash, who was she to refuse them?

Sophie's wedding dress was a model gown, white, shimmering, low-cut. She thought the bodice too immodest for a bride, but Stephen laughed her to scorn, kissed her, and told her that if she blushed like that on The Day then everyone would love her as much as he did. So she smiled, agreed to the dress, and tried not to let it matter that she thought the gown too low and the reception too large.

They were to be married in a fashionable church and the reception was to be held in an even more fashionable West End hotel. Afterwards, the newly-weds would go by taxi to Heathrow and from there would fly to Corfu, for a fortnight of spring sunshine. Everyone envied her; other girls who were on Gillian Pound's books went out of their way to be extra specially nice to her, and Sophie herself went round in a daze.

Sometimes she realised that she did not really expect the wedding to happen, that it was just a dream, not an unpleasant one but a dream from which she would presently awaken. It was that which kept her quiet and biddable beneath the mountain of work, the preparations for the wedding and the sudden rush of firms wanting her to appear in advertisements.

Sometimes she reminded herself that the wedding would not be happening had she not visited the Mirror Room at the Handley, one lunch hour when she had been filming in nearby Dorset Square. She had gone in hurriedly, bought a double-filled salad roll and a coffee, and carried her tray over to the nearest empty table. Sitting down, she had started on the roll and then, out of all that crowded room, one movement had caught her eye. The roll had dropped, unregarded, into the coffee whilst she stared at the figure before her.

It was Roy! How often had she seen him and been wrong, but on this occasion there could be no doubt; he was reflected too many times, in too many mirrors. His back was towards her, but through the glass she could see side views, front views, three-quarter views.

She had jumped to her feet, about to scream, to wave, anything to attract his attention, when he leaned across and put a hand round the neck of the girl with him, pulling her towards him. He was smiling. So was the girl. He kissed her mouth.

There had been sufficient tenderness in that kiss to bring Sophie out of the Mirror Room and halfway down Baker Street before she had shaken off the horror of it. Roy *loved* that girl! She knew he had no sisters but she might have kidded herself that he had a cousin, or a dear friend, and she not been watching his face when he kissed. No cousinly, dear friendly kiss, that one. It had been the kiss of an ardent lover, who kisses lightly to conceal from the world the depth of his passion whilst revealing it totally to the one kissed.

She had not returned to work that afternoon. She had walked, instead. Miles of London paving had passed, unseen and unregarded, beneath her feet, whilst she tried to come to terms with what she had seen. For the first time since she had started working for Gillian she had missed appointments and ignored the clock. She just went on walking and thinking.

Afterwards, she realised that she had walked without pausing for a rest for seven solid hours, but at the end of that time she had made up her mind. She would marry Stephen and she would make him a good wife, be the sort of woman he wanted, and that would show Roy! Him and his stupid ideas! He had to go and make her fall in love with him, didn't he, and then he had to go off, ignore her very existence, never write . . . and return, to fall in love himself with that red haired-chit he had been kissing in the Mirror room.

She had telephoned Stephen at once, burning her boats, and ever since had forced herself to continue to view life through her own particular form of tunnel vision. She *would* marry Stephen, it was what they both wanted, even if she had not always been sure. And she would make him happy, what was more, and be happy herself.

Odd, then, that for all her determination, her dreams should so often let her down. Over and over, she was the Pearl White of an ancient movie. Tied to the tracks, she saw the express thundering towards her, and knew that she would be saved at the eleventh hour.

But the dreams were only dreams and the days continued to pass with relentless speed. Bouquets were ordered, the choir agreed to sing a couple of special hymns, the cars for the bridal party were booked. Sophie worked and worked and never even wanted to rest, because if she was working then she had less time to think. She began to look pale and dark-eyed and was forced to use blusher for the first time in her life. Anya was worried, and Stephen begged her to cancel her remaining bookings. But in the end it was Penny who prevailed.

'You're going to look a hag on your wedding day if you don't ease up,' she said dispassionately, after a particularly gruelling photographic session. 'What are you trying to prove? I know you think you're making a mistake in marrying Stephen, but do you want everyone else to guess? And other models say you're working like a dog, because you're scared they'll take your place whilst you're in Greece.'

Sophie looked in the little mirror which hung lopsidedly by the sink and pulled a face at her reflection.

'Yes, you're right, but I don't want to let Gillian down. Besides, I'd be bored to tears by myself.'

'I've got a few days leave owing,' Penny said, with the abruptness she always effected when she was being kind. 'Gio's away and I've got nothing much to do at the office. Why don't I take time off too? I'll speak to Gillian for you, explain it all, and we can loll around and relax a bit.'

Sophie agreed, largely because she knew Penny was right, but also because Penny had a streak of ruthlessness that she herself lacked. Penny would tell Gillian Pound just where to go if Gill rang and said she had booked Sophie for a job. And again, Penny would insist on Sophie going out with her, leaving the flat, window-shopping, sightseeing. Left to myself all I should do would be to watch the phone, listen for the doorbell and imagine things, Sophie told herself.

Even with Penny's company, of course, she could not help listening and watching, but no one called or rang. Or rather, a thousand people rang and called, but none of them were Roy. And Sophie, who had seen the red-haired girl, knew that he would not come, not even out of friendship, and that it was better that he did not. When the first prize has been won, go for the second, she told herself firmly, unthinkingly insulting poor Stephen, who had always considered himself very much a first prize. No use, Sophie Markham, to cry for the moon – take the lantern which is nearer to hand and easier to grasp; it won't just disappear when morning comes.

Excellent sentiments, perhaps, but difficult to believe when you are not yet twenty-one. And time continued its relentless march and very soon it was five days to the wedding, four, three.

Devina, Poppy and Lavinia arrived for the rehearsal, with Benjamin bringing up the rear. Everyone was delighted with the bridesmaids' dresses and congratulated Devina on her taste and skill, and Sophie felt proud of her sisters. They were both pretty girls – Poppy was charming with her clustering dark curls and budding figure and Lavinia, so slim and blonde,

226

would have been worth a second glance even if she had been dressed in rags instead of the rose-pink organza dress.

Sophie found a cure for indifference, and that was fury. Be angry with Roy, furious because of what he had done to her little life with his high-falutin ideas. Tell yourself that if he turned up at this moment that would be just fine, because you could give him a piece of your mind.

'Huh! Damn your eyes! Get the hell out of it! I ha . . . I ha . . . Oh, dear God, I *must* hate you!'

But he did not come and Sophie soldiered on, picking at her food, crying herself to sleep, telling Anya and her mother that it was pre-wedding nerves and that once she was married she would be all right. And she believed her own propaganda because she thought of marriage as a closing door which, once it slammed shut, would put Roy out of her reach for ever, even beyond her dreams.

Sophie knew that she worried Anya a lot, Devina a bit and Stephen not at all. Stephen loved her very much, but he believed implicitly that all she wanted was a good dose of marriage to make her happy and fat. Or if not fat, at least fatter. And she did think he was probably right. Once she knew there was really no hope, she might just as well eat as not!

For she knew that Roy had not bothered to return because she had been so fat; that went without saying. At first she had striven to lose weight so that when he came home he would see her beautifully slim and come back to her. She had dreamed of his appearing at the studio, on the doorstep at the flat, even in the street. It had not happened, hope had fled, but so had her appetite. No amount of urging could now make her eat except like a bird, pecking at salads, sipping at coffee, pushing hot food round and round on her plate until she had altered the shape and substance if not the content.

And quite suddenly there was only one more day to go. Her dress hung on the picture rail in her room, a slender white ghost, the bouquets were made up and ready, no doubt kept on ice by the florist, the church was decorated. The choir were prepared, the guests pleasantly anticipatory. In thirty-six hours or so Sophie, on her father's arm, would float down the aisle. Devina would be sitting in one of the front pews wearing the cobwebby black and gold suit which accentuated her tiny waist. She reminded her daughter irresistibly of a wasp.

Everyone, Sophie reminded herself, would be in their best clothes and on their best behaviour. Elsa had chosen a pale green linen suit and would look statuesque; her two spoilt brats would probably scream during the service and be sick at the reception. Janine would wear a lemon-coloured, hand-knitted suit and would be possessively clutching the arm of the latest ghastly young man. Poppy would be thrilled and more than a little nervous; Lavinia would pretend boredom to hide envy.

Sophie knew they would all cry, though for different reasons. Climbing into bed for her last but one single night's sleep, she thought she would probably cry herself, longer and more bitterly than they. But not out loud, not in public view. She would cry inside, where the worst tears are always shed.

She thought she would never sleep, but as soon as she did she dreamed. She was walking into the kitchen at Clydon Grove and Devina was at the table, icing a cake. Sophie sniffed the good smell of baking and went over to her mother.

The cake was large, shaped like a doll, and exquisitely iced in pink and white icing. Devina was regarding it proudly, with a most loving smile.

'Darling, it's your wedding cake; do you like it?'

Sophie looked more closely at the cake, and it was not a doll but a replica of herself. It was perfect, right down to a tiny gold ring on the third finger of the left hand. Devina stepped back the better to view her creation.

'Isn't it lovely? Stephen's going to be so pleased with it!'

Sophie was about to explain to her mother that the cake should not have been made solely with Stephen in mind when, in the manner of dreams, she was transported. This time she was in Stephen's flat and he was working at his kitchen table, just as Devina had been at hers. He seemed to be cutting out a garment of some description.

'What are you making?' Sophie asked. She went and perched beside him on the edge of the table.

'It's a model gown; for you, of course.' Stephen gestured to a corner of the room where a wax model stood. It was naked and featureless and rather formless, too; it had breasts but no nipples, a stomach but no belly-button, feet but no toes. Stephen smiled at her.

'I knew this dress would suit you, but it's easier to try it on the model, which is exactly your size.'

He took the pieces of material off the table, waved his hands, and the dress was complete, though it was still open down the front. Sophie watched, fascinated, as Stephen went over to the wax model, slipped the dress on it, and waved his hands again, conjuring the dress closed, perfect. He picked up a lipstick which lay nearby and drew a smiling mouth on the model's otherwise empty face, and it smiled at him and for him with Sophie's own warm, ingenuous smile.

'See? I knew it would fit and that you'd love it.'

She wanted to tell him he was wrong, she could not love it because it was his choice, not hers. Everyone has the right of choice, she wanted to say; but then the scene changed again. She was back on the island, or rather, just off it. She and Roy were in a little boat and the sun shone across the sea, which rocked in a gentle breeze. Waves slapped the hull and Sophie was sitting in the stern with a hand on the rudder whilst Roy adjusted the sail, glancing up at it as he did so. Sophie followed his gaze and saw that the sail was purple, not white, and that it was blindingly beautiful against the blue of the sky.

Roy said nothing, but he smiled at her. His smile seemed to convey much more joy than other people's smiles could. His face was very tanned and his hair longer than she remembered, but the faded jeans and tatty shirt were the ones he had worn when first she saw him.

Presently he began to sing, quite softly, so that she had to strain to catch the words:

> *The purple sail above me catches all the strength of summer,*
> *Fishes stop and ask me where I am bound,*
> *I smile and shake my head and say my little ship is sinking,*
> *But I kinda like the sea that I'm on and I don't care if I am drown'd.*

Sophie glanced into the sea and she could see the fishes, swimming in the translucent water. They were smiling and there was music playing faintly somewhere. She thought of the song Roy had sung, and saw that there was water washing about in the scuppers of the boat. She glanced across at Roy; had he chosen to sing that particular song because this little ship was sinking?

Roy finished adjusting the sail, lashed the rope he was holding, and came over to her.

'I'm afraid you'll have to swim for it, my dear love. This little boat is too small for two, but you can swim, you'll reach the shore. You've got to swim strongly, my darling, or you're no good to either of us.'

He came over to her and she did not resist when he lifted her over the side and dropped her into the milk-warm water, though as she started to swim towards the land she began to weep. Tears ran down her nose and dropped into the sea, crystallising into diamond drops which she watched as they fell, fathoms deep, into the dark water below.

Sophie swam on but could not resist a quick glance after the boat. Roy was sitting where she had sat, a hand on the rudder, holding the rope that would bring the sail up to the breeze. He was sailing away from her and she must swim on, reach the distant shore, because when she reached that far-off strand Roy would acknowledge her feat. He would know that she could make it alone, that she was an independent girl at last.

But her arms were growing terribly tired. A heaviness crept over her and clouds hid the sun. It was no longer a dream sea in which she swam but a nightmare one, with the water heaving itself up into huge, white-crested waves. She sensed evil forces beneath her, sharks, sea-monsters, rip tides, but she knew she must swim on, for she would find safety on the length of pale sand that she could now see clearly. If she could just continue to swim strongly she would be there in no time at all.

But she could not resist glancing back, at Roy's little boat. It was a long way away now, the sail bellying out as the breeze freshened, and she knew that very soon it would be out of sight, not even a speck on the far horizon.

She glanced at the beach, wonderfully near, so near that she could hear the sigh and drag of the shingle as the waves advanced and retreated, and then she was turning, swimming strongly out to sea again. She forged onwards, forcing her tired arms to hurry, and above her the sun came out again and fishes swam beside her, singing, whilst gulls swooped, mewing and calling, and Roy's broad back was turned on her because he did not think she would be such a fool as to return to his little, sinking boat.

She reached it and clutched the gunwale, calling his name, and he turned, his expression lightening into incredulity for a moment before he came quickly towards her. She flinched, believing that he would thrust her back into the water for her own sake, perhaps, but then his hands were strong and warm around her and he was heaving her out of the water, laughing, calling her love-names. She tumbled onto the bottom boards, exhausted, half-drowned, but with her heart singing more loudly than the fishes. She had been right – Roy would not let her drown, not even for her own good!

She awoke to find herself falling from the gold of the dream into the chilly uncertainty of morning. She lay still for a moment, getting her everyday body and her dream-self sorted out. Cripes, what a weird sort of dream! I've dreamed an allegory, she thought with awe, how on earth could my subconscious mind be so clever? It was all there, if you cared to look. Devina had made a Sophie to suit her, and because she loved cooking, her Sophie had looked like a cake. She had wanted to give that cake to Stephen. In holy matrimony, no doubt! With this cake, I thee wed, with my currants, I thee worship . . .

Stephen had made and dressed a wax model because he worked with people, telling them what to do and how to do it. He wanted a Sophie just like that wax model, a girl who would let him dress her, tell her what to do, what to think. A girl who would smile just for him.

And Roy wanted her to be independent, yet the dream had not quite said that. It seemed to say that he wanted her to be independent, but not to the extent of leaving him completely. Or did it have some other, deeper meaning? Did he want them to drown together, in the little, sinking boat with its purple sail?

As she lay, realisation dawned. Morning had come. This was her last day as a single girl. Pearl White, securely lashed to the rails, was losing some of her starry-eyed optimism. Tomorrow was the Day of the Train.

Or was it? Could a dream be sufficient cause to call a wedding

231

off? She could tell everyone she had had a prophetic dream which warned of dreadful consequences if she married Stephen. But she did not think she could do it. Devina's iced-cake Sophie would not have wanted to, let alone dared, nor Stephen's wax-model Sophie. But Roy's girl? Ah, she would do it without any qualms, but that part of life, and the dream, had never happened. She was not Roy's Sophie and never would be, so the sooner she stopped dreaming about him and got on with her real life the better.

She was crying, because it seemed that even her dreams would not long be left to her, when the door opened and Anya, bearing a tray of tea, appeared.

'Morning, Soph, only one more day of freedom!' She set the tray down on the bedside table. 'Anything special planned for this morning? Oh, love, what's the matter?' She had noticed Sophie's wan and tear-stained appearance.

'Anya, I don't think I can go through with it. I had this dream . . .'

'Dreams are only dreams, sweetie. Drink your tea.'

'Oh I know, I don't usually worry about dreams, but this one . . .' She told Anya about the dream, leaving out nothing, but Anya only smiled very kindly at her and poured herself out a cup of tea.

'Typical bridal, cold feet type dream,' she said firmly. 'I remember my cousin Patty telling me she nearly fled the country on the day before. Your mother's arrived, incidentally. She's cooking a huge breakfast which we'll all be too excited to eat, so get ready to be very deceitful with bacon, eggs and fried tomatoes.'

'Oh. Where are Dad and the girls?' The Markham family were staying at a small hotel nearby.

'Your mother left them to have a lie-in to recruit their strength for the party tonight.' Anya settled herself on the edge of the bed. 'How many people have you asked, incidentally? I feel it only fair to tell you that Penny has cordially invited half the staff at the Centre -- the female half of course, since this is a hen-party. I think she felt that since it was our wedding pressy to you she was entitled to include her personal friends. You know Penny!'

Sophie, sipping her tea, shrugged.

'I don't suppose it matters and I didn't formally invite any-one, really, I just kept telling people to pop round if they had a moment on Wednesday evening and they could see some of the presents and so on. So we might get five people or fifty.'

'You should have told them it was a wedding shower, that's what Penny and I did,' Anya said reproachfully. Then they feel bound to bring tea-towels and toast racks and things. At least it pays for their drinks.'

'I didn't think. Anyway, we've got heaps of stuff for the house, what with Stephen's place being already fully equipped and all the presents that have already arrived. We could equip several homes, in fact.'

'Penny and I will be getting wed one of these days,' Anya said practically. 'Not to each other, mind! No, but seriously, when we do you can turn round and give us all your unwanted gifts. We're not proud, we shan't mind.'

'You can have anything they bring tonight,' Sophie said, throwing back the bedclothes and swinging her feet onto the floor. 'I'm going to have a bath and then I suppose I'll have to help with the cooking. I just hope we'll have enough food for them all.'

'We aren't providing food, just drinks and a few cocktail snacks.' Anya got up and made her way to the door. 'The way we've planned it people will pop in for half an hour, have a quickie, hand over their pressies and then, please God, go again. All very informal and fun and it'll stop you succumbing to pre-wedding nerves. Shall I run you a bath?'

'No, I'll do it.' Sophie slung her shabby old blue woolly dressing-gown round her shoulders in deference to her mother's presence and followed Anya out of the room. She went along to the kitchen, exchanged good mornings with Devina and with a Penny who glowered at the world from beneath a thick canopy of rollers, and then shut herself in the bathroom.

After this bath, I bet there'll be no more peace until I climb into bed tonight, she told herself gloomily, beginning to run the bath. And after tomorrow, no peace any more, not ever.

The last thought came unbidden, dismaying her. Of course she would have peace, how stupid she was being! The honey-moon in Corfu might be a bit hectic but after that, when they returned to London, she would be as peaceful – or as busy – as she wanted to be. But she knew what her subconscious had been getting at when it had sprung that thought on her. After tomorrow she would no longer belong to herself. She would be Stephen's Sophie, for better or worse, for richer or poorer, in sickness and in health.

Sighing, she turned off the tap, tested the water, and climbed into the tub. She admired her ribs, which showed when she took a deep breath. Nice, to be thin. She was well down in the water and beginning, dreamily, to soap herself, when she heard the voice echoing through the door.

'Darling? I've cooked you a good, hot breakfast, so don't be long in there.'

Sophie sighed again but splashed upright. Duty was duty.

'Just coming. Mother. I shan't be two ticks.'

It would appear that peace was an even rarer commodity, the day before a wedding, than she had thought.

She had assumed that the day would creep by on leaden feet, but in fact it flew. At five o'clock Stephen came round; he kissed her passionately, Devina fondly, and her sisters teasingly. He was elated, easy with everyone, just wanting, he said, to be sure that her case was packed, her passport easy to find, her Greek money to hand. He shook hands with Benjamin and managed to dispel the worried frown from her father's forehead, and Sophie saw all over again how good Stephen was with people. He could joke with shy men, brash men, stupid men, until they were comfortable in whatever company they kept, and even fat, middle-aged postmen who felt ill at ease in London became more natural in his presence.

Her mother adored him, her sisters thought he was wonderful, her friends envied her. Yet he still has no magic for me, she remembered guiltily. He comes into a room determined to please and he shines with a warm, clear light which envelopes everyone. Except me.

But though she might not succumb to his charm, she was proud of him. She appreciated his good looks, his good manners, and the air of quiet command which sat so easily on his broad, well-tailored shoulders. He was handsome in a shaggy sweater and jeans; incredibly handsome in a dark suit and a white shirt. Love him truly, she begged herself. Love him! It

234

will make things much easier if only you give in, let yourself fall in love.

But love will not come for the asking, any more than hatred will. At six she accompanied him to the door of the flat, kissed him, clung for a moment, and then returned to the living room. She saw her mother's eyes moisten sentimentally, saw Lavinia's brighten and sharpen with envy.

Then the phone rang.

Poppy thundered down the stairs to answer it, then hollered up them.

'Sophie! It's for yo-oo.'

Sophie was struggling into a chocolate-coloured dress with gloriously full sleeves and a skirt so tight that she could only take teeny weeny steps. Cursing, she slipped on the dangerously high heels which matched the dress and took teeny weeny steps down the stairs, using a wicked word when her ankle turned on the last one, all but pitching her onto her face. Damn whoever was so stupid as to ring just as she was preparing to meet her guests! She grabbed the receiver and held it to her ear.

'Yes?'

She knew, as soon as he spoke, that it was Roy. She had not heard his voice for seven months, had never heard it on the phone, but she recognised it immediately.

'Sophie? It's me. Why didn't you answer my letters?'

'You never wrote, and I didn't have an address for you.'

'I wrote dozens. I even sent some to the Centre. As soon as I got back today I went round there and they said you'd not worked there for months and that Stephen Bland had been collecting what post there was.' There was a pause. 'They said you were getting married. You and Stephen.'

'Yes. I thought you . . . Did you say you only got back *today*?'

'That's right. About an hour ago. I tried to phone you from the States, I phoned every Markham in the London directory, but they weren't you.'

'We're under Wintle-Smy. Penny's father had the phone put in, you see. Did you say you only got back today?'

'Yes, Can I come round?'

'Oh, please, but it'll have to be later. There's a party going on, just for women. It's for people who can't get to the wedding to see the presents and the dress and that.'

'It's all fixed, then? You really are marrying him?'

'Yes. Tomorrow. At eleven o'clock.'

'I see.' There was a pause, then Roy said briskly, 'It'll be better if I don't come round, then. You've made up your mind? You know what you're doing?'

'No, I don't! Roy, please, you must come round. I have to see you.'

'Right. I'll come at ten. I won't ring, but I'll tap on the door at ten precisely. We can have a quick chat on the steps. Will that do?'

'Yes, fine. On the steps at ten. I'll be there. Or . . .'

She knew, all at once, that if she was to marry Stephen in the morning then she should not go out and meet Roy tonight. It would be wrong, totally inexcusable. She hesitated, not sure what to say, but it seemed that Roy could even read her silence. When he spoke his voice was gentle.

'If you aren't there, I'll understand. Have fun at your party.'

'Roy? Roy, of course . . .'

There was a click, then the buzz of an empty line. Sophie replaced the receiver very slowly and carefully and walked up the stairs again. She took teeny weeny steps.

They must have thought her strange, her guests. Smiling, polite, but incredibly remote, her mind was a thousand miles away. Firstly, it could not have been Roy in the Mirror Room, it must have been someone else. Who did not matter, it only mattered that it was not Roy. Secondly, Stephen had taken mail addressed to her and had withheld it. Why, for God's sake? Roy would never have written a love-letter to her at the Centre, she was as sure of that as she was of anything. He must know as well as she did that the chance of it being opened in error before being passed to her was too great.

She remembered the photographs which had never reached her, and supposed that Stephen had had some sort of sixth sense about the letters. If it was true, then it was just another of the tricky, cruel faces of love and she would be the last person to blame him. Right now, bathed in the golden glow of having spoken to Roy, she could not bring herself to blame anyone who loved.

Yet she was supposed to be marrying Stephen, tomorrow.

Her mother was in seventh heaven because her plain daughter was making a good marriage, her father was glad because he believed she would be happy as a wife and, eventually, a mother. Her sisters were really proud of her, even Lavinia was getting mileage out of the fact that her brother-in-law to be was a television producer. And she was sincerely fond of Stephen and he was so happy. He loved her and trusted her. He expected her to float down the aisle tomorrow so that they could sing hymns, exchange rings, make vows. And then fly off to Corfu, to live happily ever after. She would be the envy of all her friends, and she had fully intended to be a good wife to Stephen.

But now? Knowing that Roy was here, not in love with that red-haired girl? She knew that he was in love with her, the only strange thing was that she could ever have doubted it. Could she marry for duty, for honour, because she had said she would? That would be masochism, a mad act!

Yet . . . to let them down, when it was all arranged? The whole paraphernalia of a society wedding was lined up and ready to go. Bell ringers, choir, cars, bouquets, corsages. And the reception. Even her dress, and those of her sisters. They would all be bitterly disappointed, particularly her family. Could she bear to disappoint the people she loved most?

Ah, but Roy would be disappointed if she lived a lie, went and married Stephen. And then, without consciously bringing it to mind, she remembered the dream. She had learned to swim for the shore, she had the strength to do it if necessary, to battle on alone. But it was not necessary, not now. Even in her dream Roy had been glad when she turned back. He had never meant to cast her off for good, he had just wanted her to discover her own abilities.

The question would not be solved, she knew, until she could coolly and calmly make her choice, and that moment was not yet, with guests milling round the flat, admiring the dress and their presents, drinking, eating the delectable food that Devina had spent the afternoon preparing. At ten to ten, however, she managed to catch her mother's eye.

'I'm just going down to ring Stephen,' she murmured, and saw Devina nod approvingly. She slipped out of the flat and pulled the front door closed behind her. She went down the stairs gingerly, with teeny weeny steps.

The phone rang several times before Stephen answered it, and then he was breathless, impatient, only thawing when he realised who it was.

'Darling! Sorry I snapped, but I decided to repack my case, take a bigger one. We'll want to bring stuff back, souvenirs, presents and so on, so I'm taking the big case after all. Having fun?'

'Stephen. I'm going to cry off.'

He laughed. It was a tender, teasing laugh but it rubbed at her nerves, already raw with apprehension over the hurt she was about to inflict.

'You're tired out, pet. Go back to the flat, make yourself a hot drink, and then go to bed. When you've slept on it you'll see things differently, I promise you. Will you do that for me?'

'No. I mean it, Stephen, I've changed my mind. I shan't be in church tomorrow morning.'

'Sweetheart, you're under too much stress to talk sense tonight. Go to bed, take a couple of aspirin if you can't go to sleep at once, and then ring me first thing in the morning. Honestly, I know just what you're going through, it's a nerve-racking business, marriage, but be brave and remember that after eleven o'clock tomorrow I'll always be there to hold your hand.'

Sophie sighed. She said in a small voice. 'I've tried to explain. All right, I'll go to bed when everyone leaves.'

She replaced the receiver and then, having second thoughts, lifted it up again and laid it gently down on the telephone shelf. He might ring back and she had no wish for anyone to come running down from the flat in the next ten minutes or so.

Sophie glanced at her watch, and was unprepared for the flood of bright anticipation which she felt when she saw that the hands stood at ten o'clock exactly. She glanced hopefully at the glass panels of the front door. It was whirly, coloured glass, not very good for seeing through, but she would know his shadow, could probably get to the door before he had a chance to knock. Her mouth was quite dry and by five past ten there was a painful ache in her throat. But anyone could be a few minutes late, he would not let her down.

At ten past ten she turned back to return to the party. Her disappointment was so heavy on her that it was like a physical

238

weight. She wondered whether she would ever manage to get up all those stairs with her high, high heels, narrow hobble skirt, and the disappointment, like Pilgrim's burden, bearing her down.

But it would do no good to stand here, staring at the empty glass panels of the front door.

Wearily, she began to climb.

She was half-way up when someone rapped hard on the glass panels. She found herself at the bottom of the flight and rushing across to the door without any clear idea of how she had got there. She must have dragged her skirt above her knees and just risked life and limb, she supposed. wrestling with the yale lock.

The door shot open. Roy stood on the doorstep. He was panting, breathless, almost unable to speak, and he had a beard. It was a settled, established beard, not the sort of thing he could have grown in a few days. And he was very tanned. She knew for sure now that it could not have been him she had seen in the Mirror Room, though she had never doubted it from the moment he spoke on the phone. His chest was heaving, but he was smiling, too. He grabbed her hands.

'I went to No. 17, I thought that was where you lived. She kept me waiting ages, the old brute, before she came grumbling out and told me I was at the wrong house.'

Sophie, dizzy with happiness, held onto his hands as a drowning man grasps a rope.

'I see – no wonder I didn't get your letters, if you sent them there! Miss Marshall lives at No. 17 and hates us all like poison. I dare say she burnt them.'

'Marshall, Markham, what a bloody fool I've been!' He released her hand for a moment to clutch at his head. 'And Stephen never gave you the photos, so of course he wouldn't pass letters on, no matter how innocuous.'

'No, he never did.' Sophie tried to look sad, but her heart was singing too loudly and her mouth would keep curving into a smile. 'You're so brown! You look terribly fit.'

'I am.' He looked at her searchingly in the fitful light of the sixty watt bulb which illuminated only parts of the hall. 'You don't look as radiant as you should. Are you well?'

Wild happiness was bubbling up inside her, singing through

her veins, as heady and sweet as champagne, because it had all been a stupid misunderstanding, because he loved her, she could tell that from the strained look in his eyes. He had suffered, as she had.

'I'm well now. You're back.'

Their hands met once more and locked and then Roy leaned forward and kissed her lips, very gently, very lightly, and weird sensations churned in Sophie's stomach. Love is gut-curdling, Sophie thought wonderingly, the poets have got it all wrong.

Quiet now, they stood face to face, needing no words, only closeness.

'Anya dear, could you run downstairs and tell Sophie she's been talking to Stephen quite long enough?' Devina called across the crowded living room as Anya entered with a trolley laden with coffee. She hoped that this mild hint might cause some of their guests to decide it was time for the party to end. 'She went down a good twenty minutes ago, and though I have every sympathy with lovebirds, I do think she should come upstairs again now and say goodbye to Auntie Lil and Stephen's mother; they have to go, the car will be waiting.'

'Oh, is that where she is? I thought she'd probably decided to change out of that dress into something a bit comfier,' Anya remarked, wheeling the trolley into the middle of the room. 'Lavinia, would you be a dear and dispense coffee whilst I fetch your runaway sister? I shan't be a sec.'

Anya hurried downstairs, but there was no sign of Sophie in the hall, so she retraced her steps and went into Sophie's bedroom. It was empty. She tried the bathroom and, though Sophie was not there, the toilet door was locked and the light was on. Good, thought Anya, she's in there. She hoped that Sophie was using the toilet for the usual purpose and not as somewhere to be sick, but it was possible. Her friend had been pale and distraught all day.

However, when the door opened it revealed only Penny, a little the worse for drink, coming out still adjusting her dress as the saying goes. She grinned at Anya.

'Dying for a pee? Be my guest. I've just unloaded about three bottles of white wine and a jug of black coffee.' She wandered into the bathroom to wash her hands, addressing Anya over her shoulder as she splashed water into the basin. 'God, I'll have a head in the morning! Still, there'll be champers at the reception, won't there, and there's nothing like a hair of the dog that bit you for a hangover. Although it won't be a hair of the dog exactly since white wine is white wine, no matter how expensive and sparkly. Where's Soph?'

'I don't know, I was just going to ask you if you'd seen her,' Anya said hopefully. 'Her mother wants her; apparently someone called Auntie Lil and Stephen's mother are leaving.'

'Jolly condescending of them to come at all, I think,' Penny said, not bothering to lower her voice. 'How many times has she been married? The first Mrs Bland, I mean.'

'Shut up, Pen, it's not polite to . . .'

'I did see Soph going downstairs, come to think of it,' Penny remarked suddenly, turning from the basin and dragging a towel off the rail to dry her hands on. 'She just about *fell* down the last few steps, I've never seen anything like it. There was someone at the door. That must have been after she telephoned Stephen.'

'Someone at the door? But no one new's come up. Oh, glory, don't say Sophie's lame-ducking someone! I bet that's what it is, I bet someone came to the door asking directions or wanting change and Soph's out there now, trying to remember which is her right and which is her left. I'd better go down and have a look outside the front door. All I did really just now was peer over the banisters.'

'I'll come with you,' Penny said gallantly. 'Fresh air might do me good. My head's a bit thick, to tell you the truth.'

Anya giggled.

'You never said a truer word. Right, let's find her before Stephen's mother begins to feel neglected.'

They went into the hall. It was empty, of course, and so was the roadway outside. There was no sign of Sophie. The two girls glanced at each other and then, just as they were about to return to the flat, Penny noticed something.

'Hey, the phone's off the hook. Do you think that she and Stephen quarrelled?'

'I don't know. I don't know what's happened. Look, we'd better get rid of all those people and then search for her. Darn the girl, I'm beginning to get really worried.'

She was not the only one. Very soon Devina, Lavinia and Poppy, to say nothing of Benjamin, and everyone in the flats, were searching the surrounding streets, knocking on doors, desperately ringing friends.

As Penny put it, where the hell was Sophie?

Chapter Fifteen

It was three o'clock the following morning before they reached the farmyard, slowing down as they approached. Roy dimmed his lights and beside him Sophie demolished a family-sized steak and kidney pie in huge, starved bites.

Outside the car, the stars blazed in a clear black sky and in the golden beam of the headlights they could see the white and frosted grass, the tall, sugar-dusted reeds and the puddles, iron-hard, glittering as the light found them out. Inside, they were snug, with Sophie now clad in a shaggy sweater of Roy's and a pair of his old jeans, with his tie round her waist to keep them from ignominiously descending.

They had stopped in Maidenhead, because the brown dress and the high-heeled shoes were neither warm nor comfortable for a long journey, and Sophie had changed into Roy's spare clothing, huddled down below eye level, she hoped, in a large, deserted car park. Then they had rooted around and found a sheet of paper and a pen, and Sophie had written a brief, apologetic note to Devina. Lacking an envelope she had just folded it, addressed it, and even managed to find a stamp machine so that she could send it first class.

'I wouldn't like her to think I'd just run off,' she explained to Roy as the letter plopped into the box. 'I'm afraid tomorrow is going to be awfully flat for them.'

'That's true,' Roy said, with a quick, astonished glance at her. 'Sophie, you are mistress of the understatement. Don't you think you ought to ring them, perhaps, let them know you're not dead or kidnapped?'

'Should I? Surely they won't jump to conclusions when they find that I told Stephen I wasn't going through with it?' She caught his eye and sighed. 'Must I?'

'Ring Anya,' Roy said, relenting a bit. 'Just to let them know you're safe.'

'Oh dear, I suppose I ought.' They were back in the car now and Sophie sighed again. 'I'm *not* unfeeling, I know how dreadfully badly I've behaved, but remorse doesn't grow on trees. And if it did, I wouldn't be searching for it when I'm so terribly happy.'

He squeezed her hand, kissed her, and then led her firmly into the nearest phone box.

Fortunately, Sophie realised afterwards, the line was bad. She spoke to Anya, scarcely needing to say anything other than that Roy was back and she was with him, and then the howling of static took over and probably even her quick, conscience-stricken goodbye had not been heard.

Now, bumping over the rutted track which led to the caravans, happiness was so strong that it was almost tangible. When they turned left over the cattle grid Roy's hand reached out and he grasped the back of her neck lightly, his fingers caressing.

'Still happy?'

'You know I am.'

The car purred to a halt outside the Markham's caravan and Roy turned off the engine and leaned back in his seat, his hand still on the nape of Sophie's neck.

'Well, here we are! Open up the door and I'll go and fetch some water so we can have a cup of something before . . .' He stopped as Sophie exclaimed sharply. 'What's the matter?'

'No keys. Have you got yours? We could . . .'

He groaned, though there was laughter hovering.

'What a pair of fools! No, I haven't got my keys either. I lent them to my brother so that he and his woman could go down and tidy things up for the winter. Trevor's got spares, of course, but I'm not going to knock him up at 3 a.m! I'm afraid it's a night in the car for us, love.'

'Your brother! Does his woman have red hair?'

'She does. Have you met Elaine? She's very sweet, according to Matthew. They met whilst I was in the States and since I only got back this morning – Christ, it seems a year ago – I've not met her yet.'

'You came straight to find me!' Sophie's gratification showed in her voice, though in the dark he could scarcely see her smiling. He laughed.

'Of course. That is, I went to the Centre and they gave me your phone number.' He pulled her into his arms. 'Well, love, a sports car isn't an ideal love-nest but it's all we've got. I bet no one will credit it when you tell them how you spent the early hours of your wedding day.'

'The car's fine. Do you realise that we've got the rest of our lives to . . . to sleep in double beds together? To *be* together?'

'It has crossed my mind. I wonder if these seats would recline a bit more if I jerked around with this lever thing?'

The seats refused to co-operate and, what with the gear lever and the steering wheel, Roy's attempts to get Sophie cuddled up on his lap were totally unsuccessful. Finally he settled for hugging her and turning her face up to his.

'I'm sorry about all this, but we're stuck here until about seven, I suppose. What do you want to do until then, play I Spy?'

'We could talk,' Sophie began, as his face got nearer and nearer. His lids drooped closed and their mouths met. Roy made a soft, contented sound against her lips and Sophie, unknowing, echoed it.

They began, giddily, to kiss.

Someone Special

Katie Flynn
Writing as Judith Saxton

On 21st April 1926, three baby girls are born.

In North Wales, Hester Coburn, a farm labourer's wife, gives birth to Nell, whilst in Norwich, in an exclusive nursing home, Anna is born to rich and pampered Constance Radwell. And in London, Elizabeth, Duchess of York, has her first child, Princess Elizabeth Alexandra Mary.

The future looks straightforward for all three girls, yet before Nell is eight, she and Hester are forced to leave home, finding work with a travelling fair. Anna's happy security is threatened by her father's infidelities and her mother's jealousy, and the Princess's life is irrevocably altered by her uncle's abdication.

Set in the hills of Wales and the rolling Norfolk countryside, the story follows Nell and Anna through their wartime adolescence into young womanhood as they struggle to overcome their problems, whilst watching 'their' Princess move towards her great destiny. Only when they finally meet do the two girls understand that each of them is 'someone special'.

arrow books

You are my Sunshine

Katie Flynn
Writing as Judith Saxton

Kay Duffield's fiancé is about to leave the country, and her own duty with the WAAF is imminent when she becomes a bride. The precious few days she spends with her new husband are quickly forgotten once she starts work as a balloon operator, trained for the heavy work in order to release more men to fight.

There she makes friends with shy Emily Bevan, who has left her parents' hill farm in Wales for the first time; down-to-earth Biddy Bachelor, fresh from the horrors of the Liverpool bombing, and spirited Jo Stewart, the rebel among them, whose disregard for authority looks set to land them all in trouble.

arrow books

First Love, Last Love

Katie Flynn
Writing as Judith Saxton

A powerful story of two sisters, and the love that changed their lives.

It wasn't a privileged childhood, but it was a happy one. Sybil and Lizzie Cream, brought up in a fisherman's cottage on the edge of the cold North Sea were content to leave privilege where it belonged: with their friends the Wintertons. Christina Winterton was the same age as Sybil and the two girls were inseparable, but it was Lizzie whom Ralph Winterton, three years older, found irresistible.

Then war came to East Anglia, and so did Manchester-born Fenn Kitzmann now of the American Army Air Force. At their first meeting he is attracted by Sybil's subtle charm, but before he sees her again her own personal tragedy has struck, and he finds her changed almost out of recognition...

arrow books